* Special thanks to my Mom & Christina for a great job of proof-reading and editing*

THANKS FOR YOUR SUPPORT!
FOR MORE INFO
OR TO COMMENT PLEASE SEE:
folliesofalazywriter.com
ALSO: folliesofalazywriter ON facebook

ENJOY!
☺

ONE

White clouds in an otherwise clear blue sky drifted over a canopy of big deciduous trees, and it was the beautiful day in the park Janet had been hoping for. Well, "hoping" might not be entirely accurate because, in truth, her presence there was a little more spontaneous than that. She had just needed to get away from her television that had somehow, almost accidentally, been taking up way too much of her time; and she knew there were more creative things she could be doing, more creative things she should be doing. She could feel that damn tv almost literally sucking her brains out through every sensory orifice in her head, and it slowly became apparent there were better ways she could be spending her day. In fact, anything would have been better than continuing to let the evil black box do all of her thinking for her, and going outside for a walk proved to be the best immediate solution. It was a big sigh of relief just to step out the front door.

The park which was only a few blocks away seemed like a logical direction to go. It was almost subconscious, really, but the park had always been a good place for her to clear her head. Its wide dirt paths criss-crossing the nearly twenty-seven acres were peaceful and quiet, a good place to get back to nature if you will. The fact that it was near the outskirts meant the surrounding wilderness often blended into the town, and several deer including a small fawn cautiously didn't mind her presence that day. They noticed and kept their distance, but all parties involved seemed to passively agree not to bother each other. To each

1

his own, and she appreciated their provisional company. The park was big enough for everybody. A squirrel gathered nuts and a few birds sang in agreement as well...

It was good to be there as she slowly let her mind drift in and out of the present moment. The breeze and the trees and the rabbits and the bees were all easy enough to appreciate, and the intermittent bursts of creative thought weren't unwelcome either. She let her mind drift wherever it wanted, which in most cases wasn't a bad thing. Creativity had to come from somewhere and, if a park could serve as a muse, so be it. Natural beauty had always had a way of doing that....

As a writer, Janet needed this little walk on this particular day. Given that it had been nearly a year since her last work had gone off to the publisher, eventually something would have to give. She was going to have to get back to work at some point. Nobody can live well doing nothing, although for her it wasn't necessarily for monetary reasons. In fact, money was practically flowing from a tap as the result of a series of successful travel books she'd written in previous years; so financially she was pretty well set. Fortunately the urge to write was just that- it was pure. She simply wanted to get back to doing her thing. She wanted to express something, although she had absolutely no idea what that might mean yet....

It wasn't stressful in any way though. These kinds of things had to flow naturally, and taking some time to think about it was just a necessary first step. Allowing herself some time in the park was, in a way, honoring the process; and her inadvertent arrival there was proving beneficial already. Wandering around and kicking a few rocks was a good opportunity to consider the limitless possibilities of a new project. It was great knowing she could do absolutely anything she wanted, like the feeling a painter gets when looking at a fresh blank canvas. It's exciting. It's the unknown in its best form, because the reality is there's no downside. Even if things went horribly wrong, (and that would purely be a matter of perspective) writing a new book would have to be a good experience on some level. How could it not be? And any thought of things going wrong was just the universal neurotic impulse that most people have a hard time avoiding occasionally- including her. Although, speaking generally, she'd always been pretty good at evading these kinds of negative thoughts....

Eventually, a lush sunlit patch of grass seemed to invite her to lie down, and she willingly obliged. She smiled and closed her eyes, very happy to be where she was. There was nothing not to like about how her afternoon was unfolding, and she continued being pleased with herself for getting away from the mindless indulgence of television. Lying in the sun taking a little time for introspection seemed like a much better option...

A new project was coming. She could feel it. So it was easy to just relax with that notion. She let her mind continue to roam freely without the cumbrance of any self-imposed restrictions. It was all right to think about anything she wanted and, very naturally, she drifted into thoughts of some of her previous work. She'd been involved in some fantastic projects that had taken up huge portions of her life. Some of her best works had taken years to complete....

As a travel writer, she'd been everywhere- almost literally. And she'd never been afraid to take her time when she got there, wherever it happened to be... She had visited all seven continents, including Antarctica. She reminisced about sitting, watching, and relating to a large gathering of penguins for hours on one particular day. She remembered the amazement she felt at their unique existence. Here were living breathing creatures thriving in an environment that wouldn't take long to kill any of us, and it was a great lesson in the huge diversity of life on our amazing planet...

She'd had plenty of mind-opening experiences that had all been helpful in reinforcing how incredible it was to simply be alive. Compared to your average person on the street, her perspective was enormous. She'd spent time immersed in a huge variety of different cultures and witnessed the human condition from numerous angles. First world, third world, eastern, western, tribal, agricultural, communist, socialist, dictatorships, and democracies were all societal situations she had first hand knowledge of; and it all left her feeling very confident in her ability to write something interesting. After all, she was an interesting person..... and gifted, too....

As a talented writer, she had written about her travels in a unique way that had been well received by fellow travelers, who had always been her target audience. In practical terms, she saw her books as travel guides. They described things such as the easiest ways to get around, where the best places to stay and eat in any particular region of any particular country were, what the "must sees" were- and in a very entertaining way. She seemed to have a unique ability for traveling well and a writing style to succinctly, although with delightfully descriptive prose, describe how anyone else could do the same. In short, her books were extremely useful and yet fun to read at the same time. It was a combination that had proven to be extremely successful, and the financial rewards from all of this were now giving her the freedom to explore some other possibilities.....

Not that her previous works hadn't been fun- and she knew that another great adventure was probably somewhere on the distant horizon- but, for the first time, she was starting to think about another kind of writing too... She thought about what it might be like to write fiction, if for no other reason than she'd never done it before. It might be entertaining to try to create something from nothing, just completely invent a story from beginning to end. How could that not be interesting? It would mean tapping into some universal creative well that all good fiction writers must certainly know something about. She considered some of the quotes she'd heard from creative people throughout the years, about how it was possible to come to a place in which creativity just seemed to flow through you. It could be a artist working on a great painting, a sculptor working on a masterpiece, a composer working on some brilliant new piece of music, or a novelist writing what might turn out to be the great American novel- and, in the end, they were all tapping into the same great flow. Wow! Wouldn't it be awesome to feel that, whatever "that" was...?

Still lying in the grass with her eyes closed, she smiled just thinking of the endless possibilities.....

TWO

It's not good to be thrown from a moving vehicle onto the rain-soaked shoulder of a road, only to go tumbling down a steep embankment and find yourself lying in the mud next to a flooding stream. It happened so fast that there wasn't enough time to even think about it, but it was obvious there was nothing about the situation to like..... and then the pain hit.

What the hell just happened? John struggled to lift his head out of the puddle before realizing the cool water almost felt good. Maybe he could just stay where he was for a few more seconds? So he did. But he knew that his situation needed to be assessed. Was he alright? Was anything broken? He definitely knew he hurt, but it was still questionable whether or not he could actually function.... and it would be important to find out.

After prying himself up to his knees, he rolled over into a seated position and took a few deep breaths. He leaned over and spit up some blood, realizing a couple of his front teeth were missing. His elbows, hips, and both knees had abrasions. His hands were a little skinned up and burning. Basically his entire body ached. But, as he started to stretch and move around a little, it seemed possible that no life-threatening damage had been done...

Not long after, he discovered that he could indeed stand up; and, for the first time, the thought crossed his mind that things could have been much worse. Considering what had just happened, he was lucky to be alive. He shuttered- coming to terms with the fact that the car he was in only a few short moments earlier must have been going at least sixty miles an hour when he'd so unwillingly departed.... Holy Shit! That was intense!... For a few minutes, he even chuckled at his ridiculous situation. It was raining. He was in a lot of pain. But, all things considered, he found the fact that he'd actually survived strangely amusing.

Minutes later he was over it, though, and he started thinking about what needed to be done to get himself out of this mess. Slowly and painfully, he started scrambling his way back up to the road. It took a while, but he eventually made it. Once there, it took another few minutes for him to catch his breath. He laughed again and moaned in pain at the same time. His salty sweat was making his various bloody wounds burn even worse, and the new stitch in his side wasn't helping either. Maybe I've got a few cracked ribs too?... Damn....

The thought passed as he surveyed his surroundings. This was a beautiful place. Clouds and mist were rolling into and caressing the densely forested hills and mountains. It was the heart of Appalachia on a remote back road somewhere between Knoxville, Tennessee, and Asheville, North Carolina. There was no traffic, and the stillness was almost eerie. The only sound was the lightly falling rain hitting and dripping from the leaves of a nearby oak tree. Under much different circumstances, the solitude of the situation might even have had some pleasant qualities. But this was just too bizarre and difficult for him to get his mind around. His head raced- wondering about possible

5

explanations for why this was happening. Before being thrown from the moving car, he thought his fellow passengers were his friends- an obvious fallacy. Something had gone wrong somewhere. He didn't know what, but things had definitely taken a turn for the worse.

The day had started out well enough. He had awakened early, in the arms of his girlfriend Janet Freemore. They were at her place, a beautiful ranch-style house on a gorgeous sprawling property only several short steps inside the city limits of Knoxville…. What a pleasant thought, considering where he was now.

He and Janet had originally known each other as students at the University of Tennessee years earlier and had been friends ever since. Although, it had often been very easy for them to cross the line into something more than just friendship. In truth, they were probably in love with each other, but neither of them had ever wanted to be that committal about it- which was fine. They were both fairly content with this assessment. Their lives sometimes kept them apart for years at a time anyway. A real monogamous relationship just wouldn't have been practical, and they both understood this. Neither of them ever tried to make it into something it wasn't. Nevertheless, it was always good when they were both available and could get together, which had been the case for the previous several weeks.

They'd been having a great time getting reacquainted. She really didn't have any pressing commitments, although she knew she wanted to get back to writing something at some point. And he was enjoying taking some time to relax after having spent the previous seven months in South America working on his latest project, a documentary film on how cocaine production affects the surrounding cultures. It had been extremely exciting, although understandably very stressful at times too. Visiting Janet was a great way to decompress from all of this, and she was of course very happy to see him too. It was definitely mutual. Things had been going great, in fact. And these were the thoughts now scrambled together in the mind of John Myles as he stood at the side of the road wondering how the rest of his day would play itself out.

Unfortunately his cell phone was still on the seat of the car he'd been so comfortably riding in. Although, as he looked around, he wasn't sure he could have gotten a signal anyway. The only real solution was to hope for some kind stranger to come along and give him a ride…. Somebody will come by soon….? After thirty minutes or so he noticed a pick-up truck coming down the road. As it approached, he smiled the best he could as he put out his thumb. The guy driving noticed, looked at him rather annoyingly, and then didn't even bother to slow down. A nice wave of road spray landed on his already soaked shoes…. Hmmm, that was disappointing…. It was starting to get cold and, on top of that, it would be dark soon. To further punctuate his misery, a drop of blood fell from his chin and landed on his hand. He kicked a can… This is great…just great!!

Pacing suddenly seemed like a good option. Even if it were painful, he had a lot of nervous energy that needed to be expressed somehow; and talking to himself about the absurdity of the situation seemed to help a little too… This went on for a good twenty minutes or so before it finally dawned on him that he may as well start moving down the road. If he were going to be moving anyway, it seemed like a good idea to at least try to make some forward progress. After all, all roads had to lead somewhere- right? It wasn't easy, and he wouldn't be getting anywhere fast, but it felt good to at least have made a decision . He would be making an effort to help himself, which made him feel a little better…. Everything will be fine. Sure it isn't pleasant, but I'm bound to get out of this somehow. It isn't the end of the world. Things could definitely be worse…. Little affirmations like this were helping too.

Eventually darkness fell; and, when it did, it fell hard. It was so dark that he could barely see the road. With the cloud cover, there were no stars and no moon. It was basically the middle of nowhere, so there were no street lights. There weren't even any house lights in his immediate view. The only place that could possibly have been darker would have been deep inside a cave somewhere; and after an hour or so, the darkness started playing tricks on his mind. Every sound was enhanced, and he started wondering what kind of animals were out there with him. Were there bears in the area? Do big wild cats of any kind live around here? Occasionally he could hear branches cracking in the forest…. He started feeling a little vulnerable, and, if anything at all was changing, his situation seemed to be getting worse. It was getting colder and a slight wind had started to blow. His strange day was only getting stranger, and he really started to think about where he was in the world. Geographically he had a rough idea. He knew where he was within, say, a hundred miles for sure. But at the present moment that didn't seem like enough information to be even remotely helpful….. What the hell?… And he found himself laughing again. It was all just too ridiculous. Maybe he should have asked some more questions- not that they would have been answered honestly. He had definitely been naively trusting, and this obvious hindsight now seemed to be laughing at him. He hadn't known these people at all. They had seemed nice enough, and friendly enough. But the truth was they were really only

7

friends of friends, and probably even more accurately, business acquaintances of business acquaintances. But there'd been no overt reason not to trust them. It had appeared that their relationships would be mutually beneficial, and there were no red flags or gut feelings suggesting he shouldn't have been involved with them. Granted, there had been a lot of shady characters surrounding the topic of the film he'd been working on. But, given that fact, he had had even more faith in his intuitive abilities concerning the people around him. He was used to the idea of being cautious regarding the people he was dealing with. So how could he have missed this? Maybe in these last few weeks of lounging, and relaxing, and just generally goofing off, he'd let his guard down a little. Plus there was the feeling that he'd left all the shadiness of the topic far behind on a continent far, far away. He was back in America now, and it was ok to relax. It made sense to trust people who came with good references. When they said they were taking the back roads just because it was a beautiful drive and there was no hurry anyway, that made sense too. The fact that their objective was to deliver some unedited film wasn't even the least bit troubling. Sure, the content of that film could have been very incriminating for certain individuals. But again, those individuals were in some remote rainforest in South America, not in the south eastern United States...... Hmmm, he wondered how his supposed new friends must have been involved. He would have been very worried about the film, too, if he hadn't had other copies, that is. So whatever they thought they'd do with theirs didn't seem to matter...

He kept walking, slowly. It was just good to be moving. It was helping him keep warm, and he continued to comfort himself with the thought that this couldn't last forever. It had surely been hours since his ordeal began, and he figured it had to be getting close to midnight. He knew Janet would be expecting to hear from him at some point. But she wasn't the type to worry, and probably wouldn't be too terribly distracted if she didn't hear from him for a couple of days. Things had kind of been left up in the air. She knew he had friends in Ashville and could easily end up spending some time there. At most, she might be irritated that he wasn't answering his phone; but it could be a while before she'd actually put any effort into looking for him, and she was probably the first person who would ever start looking...

Ok, now he was getting carried away. Someone was bound to come along; and, if not, he'd eventually come to farm house. He might even accidentally stumble into a town. But, whatever the case, somebody somewhere would help him. He'd make a phone call and this would all be over- which was good, because he was getting very tired. He was hungry and thirsty, too, and more than ready to be finished with all of this.

Another couple of hours passed without any apparent progress. He couldn't believe it. It was getting ridiculous, and the simple need for sleep was slowly becoming a bigger and bigger priority. The paved road on which he had started long ago turned to gravel, and he questioned his original decision about which direction to go. If nothing else, he seemed to be getting further away from civilization..... but at least it had stopped raining. There were even some big open patches in the sky which was strangely comforting. He stopped for a minute just to look up and around.... Well...What now? I'm cold and I'm tired, and I really just need some sleep... He had, for the most part, gotten over being nervous about his odd surroundings. After all, he had recently spent months in the jungle. He was hurt, but not badly- and he reminded himself that the situation was bound to resolve itself eventually. It just might take a little longer than he'd originally hoped; and, with that thought, he surrendered to the idea of finding a comfortable place to get some much needed rest. The ground was still wet, so he didn't want to lie down; but a close tree to lean on would serve nicely. He took off his torn jacket to use as a blanket and sat down, grateful for the opportunity to close his eyes.

Within a few minutes an approaching light appeared in the distance. It was so far away it would be several more minutes before he even noticed- not that he was asleep yet, but close, and he was enjoying the peace. The light was getting brighter, though, and eventually it would come to his attention. It would have taken longer; but in a brief moment it took to change positions, he blinked and it caught his eye....

There was nothing terribly impressive about it yet, but it was definitely a point of interest in the sky. It was like an extremely bright star that was slowly moving towards him. It looked like a satellite except for the fact that it seemed to be getting brighter - brighter because it was getting closer.... What the hell is it?

It was mesmerizing! And he sat and stared, like a person might stare at a campfire. He couldn't take his eyes off of it, and it kept getting brighter and brighter, and closer and closer. It was incredible! What was this thing? He rubbed his eyes and squinted hoping to get a better focus, hoping to get a firmer grip on what he was seeing. It was baffling. No matter how hard he tried, he couldn't make sense of it. But it was beautiful.... It was so incredible, it was almost as if he were having some sort of strange and unsolicited spiritual experience. It was

9

spectacular! An unexplainable tear came to his eye, one that welled so deep it actually ran down his cheek. A strange sense of joy was slowly falling over him like a warm blanket, like this odd experience was somehow an extremely rare privilege. Everything he'd been through throughout the day, all of his supposed troubles, suddenly seemed meaningless. None of it was even coming to mind.....

Never taking his eyes off of it, he eventually stood up and slowly walked away from his tree out into the adjacent open field. He was practically in a daze as he gradually moved towards the light as it was approaching him. His eyes were wide open, and he expressed nothing but a stunned grin on his face. Whatever this thing was, it was getting really close now. He could even hear it, barely, but it was definitely making a sound- like a vibrant fiery crackling. It was amazing! It was getting closer and closer and louder and brighter. It was even beginning to light up the surrounding area, like the light of a dozen full moons. Now it was really close, and getting very loud. Yet, strangely, he wasn't the least bit frightened by any of this. He just stood and stared. He was having one of the best, most awe-inspiring, experiences of his entire life. His heart was pounding and he was sweating a little, but it was never out of fear. He was experiencing an intense emotion of some sort for sure, but it was never fright.... Amazement would be a better word to describe what was pulsing though his body at that moment......... And then it was over.

John never knew what hit him, quite literally. Because, depending on how you look at it, he was either in the wrong place at the wrong time, or maybe, just maybe, he was in the right place at the right time. But whatever the case, the odds of what happened to our friend that night happening to any of us are very slim. In fact, we'd probably be more likely to win the lottery three times. So none of us should spend much time either worrying about it or even hoping for it, because it's just not going to happen....

John's highly unlikely fate that night began billions of years ago as our solar system was being formed. As bits of debris were slowly gathering to form the planets, there would inevitably be some left over, some that never fell anywhere, but still had the potential to someday.... They were called asteroids; and one very dense one about the size of a small car somehow got tugged out of its normal orbit and into the earth's gravity. From there, its destiny was to finally, at long last, become a part of the earth forever.... and John was there to witness its arrival. It hit him going thousands of miles an hour, and he is now forever a part of it at the bottom of a huge crater in the rural Appalachian mountains.....

Wow! What a unique way to go?... Who could have seen that coming...?

THREE

Half an hour or so later Janet, still smiling, slowly opened her eyes as she yawned and stretched. It felt good. She hadn't exactly been sleeping, just relaxing into an interesting little daydream. She sat up and looked around, although she really wasn't thinking about where she was looking. At the moment, she still hadn't completely left John in the field at the bottom of his smoldering crater. She chucked to herself about what she'd decided to do to him....

The truth was that his story would just be too difficult to tell. Right from the beginning it was too complicated. Sure, throwing him out of a fast moving car was fun; but, at the time, she had absolutely no idea what it meant. Why was he being thrown out of the car? It was like watching the beginning of a movie. It was exciting, but as of yet there was no real context. She was simply trying to think of a thrilling way to start a story, and that was the first thing that came to mind- poor John tumbling out of a car at sixty miles an hour.....

She didn't want to kill him, just scrape him up a little. After all, if he was going be an interesting character, he'd have to live. Why was he even there? He must have been up to something? He must have been involved with some unscrupulous people. Nice people don't throw people out of cars. But she didn't necessarily want him to be one of the bad guys. The possibilities were of course endless, so she needed to start narrowing things down a little....

She thought about herself and how this newly developing character might relate to something she knew about.

Travel.....Writing......Story telling...... and, slowly, a back story started to form.... Maybe he could be placed in some exotic land, telling some exciting and exotic tale? The South American rainforest might do. There had to be plenty of stories there to tell. But she didn't necessarily want to make him a writer. That would've been too close. She needed to change things up a little bit. So she decided to make him a filmmaker instead. He would still be telling a story, just in a slightly different way than she was used to. But she'd still be able to relate and hopefully write about it somewhat convincingly. Wow, what fun!... It seemed a completely fabricated story was actually starting to take shape, and she was happy about the fact that John was basically ok lying down there by the muddy river. He was still conscious and breathing; but, obviously, she wasn't going to let the day be easy for him....

Standing on the road pondering how to get himself out of this strange predicament, he started wondering about how his day had suddenly gone so terribly wrong when it had started out so well. And, strangely, this is where the story first started showing some of its inherent problems. She had decided to write herself in as his girlfriend, and it didn't take long to realize how uncomfortable this might be- but it wasn't a deal breaker quite yet....

She continued on..... John was left standing there unable to get a ride and having to fend for himself. She figured stumbling down the empty pavement would be a good place for him (her) to ponder why he was there in the first place.... (a back story was still slowly forming).... He started thinking about everything he'd been involved in and was starting to put some of the puzzle pieces together, or at least he had the beginnings of some viable theories. He figured that somehow it had to be related to the film he'd been working on. It was just too volatile a subject for it not to be. There's nothing about cocaine production (hmmm, cocaine production?) that doesn't involve a lot of potential trouble. First and foremost, it's highly illegal under almost any government. And secondly, and it's not exactly a distant second, there's a hell of a lot of money involved. Trouble seemed inevitable, like a very heavy boulder hanging from a thick burning rope with a conveyor belt full of people running under it... The rock is eventually going to fall on somebody. Maybe the rock had almost fallen on him? Or maybe he was very lucky, and it had just grazed him? (a bigger rock would come later). But, whatever the case, the fact that he was in a car full of strangers delivering film of this crazy business had to be why he was staggering beaten and bloody on the road that day....

Eventually, it dawned on her what this story would inevitably involve if she were to truly write an entire book based on this crazy character and his problems.... In order to follow through, she would want to make a hero of the guy somehow- but that was getting way ahead of herself. It could take a long time for the story to develop, and in the meantime she would have to do a substantial amount of homework. She would need to systematically investigate everything that's involved in real-life cocaine production so she could write about it intelligently. It would require researching South American organized crime, drug lords, attempted law enforcement, and drug smuggling- and it might even require getting a little too close for comfort herself. Who knew whom she might offend by writing about such an explosive topic? But there was more to it than that too. The truth.... she was simply losing enthusiasm for the project altogether. Thinking about all the work involved in addition to the actual writing was slowly changing her mind about the whole thing. She would have to reveal just a little too much about herself too. ...

And making herself John's girlfriend was just way too complicated; but instead of simply writing herself out, she decided to kill the whole story instead.....

However, she didn't want to just let it drop..... Keeping in mind not one word of this had actually made its way to a page, there was still room for a creative conclusion. After all, lying in the park had simply invited all of this in a daydream, so she was perfectly content to keep going with it long enough to at least give John an interesting departure. And when you stop to really think about it, if he was going to die anyway, she did him a great favor. I mean, Wow! The flaming meteor must have been spectacular as it came screaming in to crush him. You almost wanted to be there with him.... although it might have been best to see it from a distance.... In the end, there were no regrets about how the story worked itself out; it was all just a creative thought anyway....

Slowly returning to the present, she leaned back and propped herself up on her elbows.... She noticed a nearby dandelion, picked it, and briefly held it up to her nose. It was easy to keep smiling as she put the stem in her mouth continuing to look around. What a beautiful afternoon. It was almost hot in fact, so she decided make a move into the shade. She stood up and stretched a little more. There were plenty of big shade trees to choose from; but, on second thought, it felt good to be moving again. Not that she wanted to leave the park yet, it was a great place to be. She just didn't want to sit anymore and a little stroll felt like a better option. By now plenty of other smiling people were out appreciating the park too. They were walking, walking their dogs, kicking and throwing balls, basically entertaining themselves anyway they wanted. It was all great, and there was certainly no good reason to go anywhere else ....

She continued thinking about possible book ideas, but didn't feel guilty about drifting either..... She laughed at the last story again for a second, wondering why she had bothered to change her last name. Without hesitation, she'd invented a name for herself and given imaginary John her real last name. What the hell was that all about? Did she think she might marry this make-believe character someday or what? It was funny.

She'd always enjoyed being single, and yet it was much too easy to get carried away with a completely fictitious significant other. Maybe on some subconscious level she was hoping the perfect person would come along?... Wait a minute, everyone knows nobody's perfect, so maybe her love of the single life was truly genuine?... On the other hand, maybe it was natural to want someone to share your life with? But then again, on another other hand, maybe she was completely over analyzing this goofy little story she'd made up in her head? She knew she was happy and content most of the time, which is all anyone should really ask for in life. In fact, she wished everyone else in the world could say the same. She was, however, cognizant of the reality that unfortunately far too many people claimed to be miserable in their lives, and for no apparent good reason. And many of them were married.... and she briefly pondered that reality.

Hmmm, maybe this was a possibility?.... Maybe she could write a fictitious book about a couple trying to understand why they were both miserable. That might be fun, and again the possibilities were endless.

Couples claimed to be unhappy for all kinds of reasons, and she smiled at some of the visuals that instantly came to mind. Plates and cups and vases flew against the wall as some crazy old couple flung them at each other. They were so old they barely had the strength to do the throwing, but they were giving it a hell of an effort anyway. And who knew what might be possible with enough hateful energy? They were in a dingy old house in a dingy old kitchen. As she was imaging all of this, she could almost smell the musty old-people smell. The appliances were all fifty years old. The floor was stained and cracked yellow linoleum. The table and chairs were in a similar condition and appeared to be leftovers from the fifties, too. The curtains were ancient and torn. No wonder these people were miserable. The place was depressing. If they had put some of the energy they were using to hate

14

each other into fixing up their place, maybe they'd both be a little happier?... Maybe working together on the project really could make things better? But judging from what was currently happening between these two crazy imaginary people, that was probably too much to ask. Based on this crazy dish- throwing episode, their resentments must have run deep- and some new curtains probably wouldn't be enough to help... But why did they hate each other to begin with? Maybe they had both always claimed the other was the reason their kids were stupid; but, whatever the case, Janet had fun laughing at them for a minute. Should she name them? Were these characters worth exploring further? She supposed they might be? With enough thought, they could probably be fascinating.....? But....... no, that was enough of them. They'd been a very entertaining mental image, but that's as much life as they would get. The crazy old couple existed in thought for only a few brief minutes, and then they were gone as quickly as they had appeared...

However, she was not entirely ready to give up on the idea of writing about "a couple." There were interesting, actually captivating, possibilities within the dynamic of the relationship of "a couple"- whether "functional" or "dysfunctional." Because even in a seemingly perfect scenario, things don't run smoothly all the time. She had talked to some great couples who'd been together for many years, and they'd told her so. In fact, they were more than happy to tell her it wasn't always easy. But if they truly were a great couple, they were also quick to add that the hardships were worth the effort....

This was good.... In real life, she considered this to be encouraging for society in general- if only because it seemed best for kids to grow up with two parents. Although, and she backtracked a little, she knew there were a lot of single parents out there doing their best to do a good job. She just figured it couldn't be easy and therefore probably wasn't optimal, that's all.... She paused and laughed at herself again for a second, for wanting to be so politically correct even in her own personal thoughts. It was funny....and a little ridiculous....

Hmmm, a couple?.....not necessarily a family........just an interesting married couple?

FOUR

The Smiths? No, that didn't seem right. Hadn't a movie recently been made with the same name, Mr. And Mrs. Smith? Maybe "The Jones's"? No, that didn't feel right either. It was too generic, plus she didn't like the awkward double "esses" at the end. Then she thought about how silly it was to be trying to come up with a title first anyway. Probably the easiest part, a title could just happen anytime during the process- unless of course the name of the couple was somehow a clever word play that tied directly into the story. She tried to think of some examples off the top of her head, like maybe Mr. And Mrs. Toller who happened to own and operate a toll bridge. It could be a small toll bridge......on a remote two-lane road in the middle of nowhere... But she didn't think that was the direction she wanted to go either.... She caught herself laughing as another funny thought crossed her mind: maybe she could call Mr. and Mrs. Mouse "The Mice." It was stupid, but funny.....

Finally, she decided to name her couple the Parks, Mr. and Mrs. Park. It was simple and unpretentious. She didn't have to commit to this as the title of the book; she just needed a name so she would have something to call them. That is, of course, if whatever story she was about to try to tell ever even became one? "The Parks" could be the title, but that certainly didn't need to be declared at this point....

At 5:43 pm, she decided to name him Jim. Jim Park pulled into his driveway, put his car in park (no pun intended), and turned off the engine. But he didn't get out immediately. Instead, he just sat and thought for a while, because the truth was he didn't want to go inside and have to face his wife just yet.... she decided to call her Joyce.... He'd had a long day already and knew dealing with the situation inside would just make it longer. There wasn't a fight waiting for him. No, whatever it was, it was more passive than that, which almost made it worse. It might have been better if there were going to be a fight. At least then there would have been a remote possibility of something actually getting resolved. But he knew he didn't have the fortitude to actually instigate a confrontation, and history suggested that neither would she. By now it seemed things were too far gone to even care. They'd been married for nearly eleven years; and throughout the last half of that, they'd both fallen into a pattern of neglecting their relationship.... finally, it had collapsed. They had separate unrelated careers and, because of a simple lack of talking to each other, they barely knew anything about each other's lives anymore.

She was a nurse, and he was a math professor at a local community college. They'd both been practicing their chosen careers since before they even met nearly fourteen years earlier. They'd been introduced by mutual friends who had invited them over one Thanksgiving Day when neither one of them had any other place to go. It wasn't exactly love at first sight, but almost. They'd definitely been attracted to each other. Conversation had come fairly easily and he'd asked her out for a drink the following Saturday.... They had a great time. Over a couple of beers, they talked for hours as the time just seemed to fly by. It was nearly 2:00 in the morning before they knew it, and neither of them wanted the date to be over. So, very naturally, they ended up back at his place... and the rest was, as they say, history. Several months later they were living together, and three years after that they were married.... and it was very good for a long time.

When they first met, she'd been living in a comfortable one-bedroom apartment, but he had a nice house in the middle of town; so, if they were going to live together, it was only logical for her to be the one to move. There was a fenced-in backyard that was great for their dogs. His boxer, Corky, and her border-collie mix, Trixy, had gotten along well right from the start. Jim and Joyce shared the view that, if you have dogs, they should be allowed to be a part of the family; and it's difficult to get that feeling if they have to stay outside all the time. But Trixy had a tendency to shed, so there was always dog hair all over everything. It didn't bother Jim for a long time; but later, as things slowly started to unravel, it was just one more in a long list of annoyances......

For quite a few years they had been extremely attracted to each other and genuinely found one another to be interesting and fun. They knew almost everything about each other because they'd made a habit of asking pertinent questions, resulting in ease of conversation and expression- whether a good day or a lousy one. It was awesome. They were both completely comfortable just being themselves in the relationship, and it seemed they had the perfect situation...... So what had happened? Where had they gone so terribly wrong?

Jim thought about all of this as he continued to sit in his car.... It was depressing. At this point, it didn't seem possible for things to ever be that good again. It had been months, if not years, since they'd had a genuine conversation, and the idea of trying to start one now seemed completely overwhelming. He just didn't want to make himself that vulnerable. Recently, communication (if you could call it that) between them had consisted only of pointed snide little jabs at each other. If he could bring himself to say something sincerely nice now, and got rejected, what would he do then? He would just be left there, hanging in the breeze... It didn't seem worth the risk.

Finally he forced himself out of the car. He grabbed his briefcase from the passenger seat, closed the door, and slowly made his way toward the front steps. At least a cold beer, the evening newspaper, and a seat in front of the television were waiting for him. If he kept busy thinking about something else, he obviously wouldn't have to think about her and their tension-filled relationship..... However, what was actually waiting for him that day was far from expected....

As he opened the door, he found Joyce on the couch crying. What was this? He knew she wasn't happy either, but she wasn't normally so open about it. She'd known he would be home soon. Why was she letting him see her like this? What was going on? Something out of the ordinary must have happened? He just didn't know what, and he wasn't sure how to go about finding out. At first he just stood there with a stupid dumbfounded look on his face, like someone had yanked his pants down to his knees. He was embarrassed that he didn't know what to do, how to immediately react. It was an odd feeling. He almost wondered if it was a trap before suddenly giving himself the mental slap he needed.... Get over yourself Jim!! Go find out what's wrong..... And with that, he snapped out of it and went over and sat down beside her. He looked at her and his eyes asked the question before his mouth eventually got around to it..... What happened Joyce? Do you want to tell me about it? She sniffled and continued to cry as she looked up long enough to briefly catch his eye. She didn't say anything for a couple of minutes..... They both just sat there. It was a strange moment for sure. Whatever was going on with her allowed Jim to let his guard down and he was completely and genuinely right there with her. It was ok if she didn't want to talk about it right away. In fact it was ok if she didn't want to talk about it at all. He just knew that, for whatever reason, she genuinely wanted him there with her, and he was completely willing to oblige. She was obviously vulnerable...... he put his hand on her shoulder.

Finally she attempted to chuckle, trying to make light of her obvious distress.... This has been a bizarre day Jim.... I'm not even sure where to begin.... She knew the truth would most likely be very difficult for her estranged husband to understand. She wasn't even sure she fully understood it herself and was now feeling a little embarrassed and second guessing her decision to be so open with her emotions. Although, as she looked at her husband, she was impressed with how well he seemed to be doing so far. He wasn't saying anything, yet he was very present and supportive. As little as they'd talked lately, she honestly didn't know what to expect; but, as she continued to look at him, she could glimpse the guy she'd once known, and it was comforting. Maybe she'd continue and give him a chance?

Joyce was an ER nurse, so she was accustomed to being in the middle of some pretty grizzly scenes. As far as just general blood and gore were concerned, she had a very strong stomach. It was all in a day's work. So what she had experienced that day really had nothing to do with that aspect of it. Although, the devastation that had come through their doors that morning would have tested anyone's ability to keep a clear head, no matter how seasoned. When she'd said it was a bizarre day, she wasn't kidding, and it was true on several levels. No question, it would be hard to explain, but she was willing to give it a try.

It was crazy, Jim…crazy…… I'd never seen anything like it. Sometime before noon a gentleman in his mid-forties was brought in by his entire family- his wife, a couple of sons, both in their late teens or early twenties, and a young daughter who was probably around nine or ten. They had transported him in the back of a borrowed van. His condition was not only bleak, but one of the strangest I've ever seen. Apparently the car they'd been riding in had stalled on some railroad tracks, and the man and his boys had been trying to push it off. But there must have been a problem. Maybe it was stuck in gear or something, not that it's even important what the circumstances were? But, somehow, while struggling with his car problems, the man got run over by a train and was literally cut in half. As he was finally getting the car to move he must have slipped under at the last second, and nobody seems to know exactly why he didn't just get the hell out of the way. There must have been something really special about that car……. Again she falsely chuckled, as often people will in trying to relieve the horror of a particular situation….. She continued…. His sons carried him in, each had one of his arms, and they were both frantic. There were tears rolling down their faces as they were yelling for someone to help them, and people did help. Practically the entire staff rushed in and took over. They put the man on a gurney and wheeled him to where they could put IV's in his arms and hook him up to whatever else was necessary. But the strangest thing about all of this

19

was that the man himself was completely conscious and aware of what was going on. He knew what had happened to him, and yet he seemed remarkably calm. His family, on the other hand, was understandably not very calm at all. It was more than obvious to them that the situation was bad, very bad. One of his sons had even bothered to bring in his lower half, as though he thought they might be able to do something with it. Of course there was no hope of that. Without a blood supply, the rest of his body was dead already…

All we could do was try to get him stabilized as best as possible and let the people who loved him gather around. It was only a matter of time before he would shut down. Too much of him was gone for there to be any hope of him actually surviving. He was eventually going to die right there where he was; and everybody knew it, including him. The only thing that even might have been fortunate about his situation was that he didn't seem to be in any pain. His body had been sealed up like the bottom of a tube of toothpaste by the weight of the train and he wasn't even bleeding. He was just lying there on the propped up bed, remarkably composed. A resolute serenity seemed to envelope him. If he was going to go, he was going to go with a sense of peace and dignity. And as everyone else mellowed enough to realize this, it slowly translated around the room. Everyone was at least trying to maintain a sense of composure. I think, in a way, they were trying to honor him by following his lead, and it set up an environment unlike anything I've ever seen. I've seen a lot of death in the ER, but nothing like the way this played out…and it took nearly five hours, time used more wisely than I've ever seen before….

As things slowly calmed down, each family member got a chance to say what he or she needed to say, and everyone closest to him was there. Watching these people take the opportunity to express their love and devotion was very moving. There was a lot of crying, of course, but occasionally they'd all laugh as they recalled a common funny moment. They were a close family, and this was obviously extremely difficult. But at the same time it gave all of them the chance to reaffirm just how close they actually were. The love in that room was so thick you could feel it, you could practically smell it and taste it. It was incredible. At times they were all just quiet and reflective; and, at other times, someone would bring up a poignant memory that felt good to relive in the moment. At some point, each of the family members took some individual time at his side to say goodbye and personally express his or her love and affection. Probably the saddest and most moving moment was when the little girl was saying goodbye, if only because you knew she didn't fully understand what was happening. She sat up beside him and told him she loved him. She knew the situation wasn't good, but it was hard to tell if she really knew this was the last chance she would have to talk to him. That was the hardest to watch. This was the end, this was the last time they'd all have together, and it didn't seem appropriate to try and explain this to a little girl as it was happening...

At one point his wife took a few minutes alone with him to say her goodbyes. Everybody knows that no marriage is perfect, but you could tell whatever differences they may have had in the past were far from their minds now. They had a very heartfelt deathbed discussion and parted under the best terms anyone could possibly hope for. Granted, they both wished they could have had another forty years together; but in those few short hours they both seemed to make peace with the idea of that not being possible. It was amazing to watch a family evolve to such a point in such a short amount of time.

Shortly after 4:00pm the man slipped into unconsciousness.... and not long after, he died. One minute he was there, and the next he was gone. They all stayed in the room for a while though. They just weren't ready to leave yet.... as if they wanted to stay with him long enough to make sure he got a good start on his journey into the next reality. I'm sure that must have meant something a little different to each of them....

Jim felt a strange sense of irony that his wife had been so moved by such an experience on a day when he'd been feeling particularly melancholy about their own circumstances. He found himself feeling especially willing to sort of re-negotiate their situation, if you will. He had largely surrendered himself to a somewhat more indifferent position; but on this particular day, he'd spent an unusual amount of time thinking about his own broken relationship. Maybe it was because there'd been some little reminders? For one thing, Valentines Day was approaching, and he'd overheard some of his students talking about their enviable plans. Then a colleague had announced his new engagement and casually invited him to the wedding..... It was all adding up, and he wondered where and why his once-great relationship with Joyce had gone so terribly wrong. Was there any hope of things ever being any better? Was it hopeless, or did they still have chance? He didn't know. When he had first gotten home, he hadn't even wanted to go inside, and yet the day had taken an unexpected turn..... It was strange that a man had had to die in such a grizzly fashion for Jim and his wife to suddenly have some common ground.

Joyce, having witnessed such a strange event, was also moved toward making some type of reconciliation with Jim. Watching this man die so gracefully, surrounded by his loved ones, had worked wonders to reinforce the idea that it is not wise to live with petty bitterness. To be cliché, "life's too short.".….. and she began to think about her husband and what a wonderful relationship they'd once had. She, too, thought about the strange possibility of things being good again. That evening, they found themselves on the sofa in the seemingly unlikely position of both being open to a new negotiation…. Or, more specifically, just being open to each other….. for the first time in years. It was an interesting moment, one that Jim and Joyce Park both enjoyed taking advantage of…..

Janet laughed at herself again. By now she'd been walking in the park for a long time and was finally starting to head for home. The story she'd been creating in her mind was very funny in a way. She smiled and kicked a fist-sized rock off the path. She'd started with the idea of writing about a couple and their difficulties and ended up cutting a guy in half with a train in order to get them back together. She wondered,… Is there something wrong with me? Am I a violently morbid person or what? I mean, so far today I've let myself drift pretty deeply into two different stories. And in the first one I had a guy thrown out of a moving car only to later be killed by a meteor; and, secondly. I severed a good family man into two pieces with a train in what was supposed to be a story about two people trying to navigate the often treacherous road of marital relationships. Should I be worried about myself?…

The thoughts were all in good fun… The truth was, she liked the fact that her mind seemed to wander into some pretty strange places…. What fun would it be to try to restrain it anyway?

She knew she was a good person….. She laughed some more….. What about Steven King? I'm sure he's a good guy, and look at what he does to some of the characters in his stories…..? Everything's fine…

22

It was almost dark by the time she finally got home. There was still a little light above the western horizon, but it would soon be gone. She stood on her front steps and watched for a minute.... Then, sighing contentedly that she'd spent the day well, she went inside with thoughts of cooking herself some dinner. It dawned on her it had been hours since she'd eaten, and she was hungry....

After turning on a few lights and rattling through the pots and pans to find what she needed, a blinking light on the answering machine caught her attention. Very purposefully, she hadn't had her cell phone with her, but by now she was a little curious about who might have wanted to be in touch...

The first message was from her sister Carey who, she could tell, probably didn't want anything important. Then there was a recorded message about mortgages from some extremely annoying telemarketing firm; and, last but not least, there was a call she must have just missed. It was from her friend, editor, and agent Mark Delancy, obviously her closest liaison to her publisher. He was an important person in her life on both a personal and professional level; and, based on his voice on the machine, she couldn't tell which relationship the call involved. But because it had been a while since she had published anything, she assumed that it was most likely both. He probably wanted to know how she was doing and what the hell she was doing work-wise too. She wasn't sure what she would tell him either, so it wasn't a priority to call him back right away....

The truth was, all these thoughts of writing fiction went back considerably farther than just this afternoon's walk in the park. In fact, she'd been thinking about it fairly seriously for the last several weeks, and the idea had even been discussed with Mark, who was of course very supportive, as she'd known he would be....possibly even too supportive. Because it didn't take long for him to, almost inadvertently, mention it to some of the people in the publishing house who'd practically started to salivate at the idea... What? Janet's going to write a novel? That's awesome!........ It was awesome, just because it was nice to be so wanted, but it was putting some pressure on her that she could have done without. What she had in mind was relaxing and simply letting a book happen. She didn't want to feel like she was being rushed or forced into doing anything......

Pasta was always a good "go to" food group for something quick and easy. The water came to a boil as she poured in some over-sized macaroni noodles. She'd never been a very fancy cook. Cooking just wasn't her thing. She'd simply never given it much thought. Her view was basically that eating was something that served a purpose and not necessarily an event, especially when she was only cooking for herself....

As she stirred, she decided to call her sister back. It was mostly just a way of putting off calling Mark, but she was curious what Carey was up to, which as she suspected was basically nothing, or nothing out of the ordinary anyway. She had just wanted to talk, that's all. It wasn't about anything special, and it was always nice talking with her sister.

She strained the pasta, stirred in some red sauce and seasoning, and started eating it right out of the pot. After pouring herself a big glass of ice water, she turned on a few lights and plopped down on her big over-stuffed couch to watch a little news on the big TV. Catching a lap of CNN was always a good way to get a sense of what was going on in the world. If anything big and interesting had happened, they'd definitely let you know, but apparently it had been a fairly uneventful day. Of course there were stories about the various wars going on the around the planet, wars we were involved in and otherwise, and today didn't seem to be any different? She thought about calling Mark back......

Hey! How's it going? I saw that you called earlier.... Yeah I did, thanks for getting back to me.... She told him about her day, and he did the same. It was a good conversation. The subject on both of their minds was basically swept under the rug for a while. For whatever reasons, it seemed they were both trying to avoid it. Mark probably just didn't want to hear what he already assumed to be the truth- that she'd been thinking about the book but as of yet didn't have any brilliant ideas. He didn't want to seem like he was pressuring her, knowing that approach could go either way. It could either be helpful and motivating or extremely irritating and therefore counterproductive. It was a fine line, and he was hoping she would bring it up first so he wouldn't have to...

He was grateful when she eventually did..... You know I told you I spent the better part of the day in the park. Well, you'll be happy to hear I spent most of that time at least thinking about writing. It was interesting for sure, but the bad news is I still don't have any idea what I'm actually going to do yet. I've been having all sorts of fun random thoughts about it but nothing I'm ready or want to commit to..... That's alright, and I am glad you're thinking about it... I probably don't need to tell you, but a lot of the people at work have been asking what you might be doing. People are definitely looking forward to whatever it might be. Not that I want to sound like I'm cracking the whip here, but is there any chance you can give me a rough idea when I might be able to tell them something?...... Mark, believe me, I understand where you're coming from, but the truth is, NO! I'm not ready to commit to anything at this point, and I really have no idea when I will be. I'm sorry if you feel that puts you in a bad spot... She laughed... You shouldn't have opened your big mouth, should you?... He laughed too, a little discouraged by the conversation, but he knew she was right. He also knew she would eventually come up with something great, but in the meantime he shouldn't have mentioned it around the office... Damn it!... They both hung up smiling though..... Don't worry Mark, when I actually do get started, you'll be the first to know....

The truth was, he wasn't worried. Janet's previous books had all been excellent, not to mention bestsellers, and he knew that somewhere down the road there were most likely more true-adventure stories coming. That's what people really liked about her books. There were always good stories. After all, there were tons of guide books on the market, but hers were actually entertaining. Which made the thought of her venturing into an entirely new genre very intriguing, and everyone who knew her professionally basically felt the same way... that whatever she came up with could be some extremely fun reading.

A hot shower felt good. Then a few cold veggies to snack on and a big glass of red wine hit the spot as she sank back into the couch to do a little channel surfing. Satellite TV was both a blessing and a curse. At first all the choices had been a little overwhelming, but after a little time, she'd narrowed the couple of hundred channels down to a select few she liked. They were mostly documentary channels of one kind or another, including PBS and a couple of different brands of news. Politically, she considered herself a moderate, so she understood there was a difference between Fox News and CNN, but she was very comfortable watching either perspective. Although, interestingly enough, she enjoyed listening to conservative talk radio, mostly for the sheer entertainment value. She found it amusingly ironic that for the most part it was all about complaining about the other guy's news, almost as if they were against free speech and freedom of the press. Listening to how grouchy most of these people were always made her laugh.... Maybe it was all just a show, and they simply knew who their audience was?

The wine was going down nicely as a show about the history of the space program caught her attention. Specifically, they were talking about the Apollo missions and our race with the Russians to the moon. It was fascinating. Not that she didn't know a little about the subject already, as most reasonably educated Americans do, but watching all the old footage was still exciting. Everything from the initial liftoff of the enormous rockets to the landing module eventually and ever so gently touching down on the lunar surface was amazing. They described how it was basically a trip made on sheer willpower, how today's modern laptops have more computing power than those entire missions had, both in space and in the control center. The fact that we made it at all was astonishing, given the level of technology of the day. If the federal government had continued throwing money at the space program at the same rate after we beat the Russians to the moon, we could have easily had settlements on Mars by now....

Some might say it was unfortunate that it took the cold war and fear-based motivation to advance civilization in such a profound way.... Pictures taken of the earth from the surface of the moon had changed the way we thought about ourselves forever.... Then she thought about the wars again, on a previous channel, and wondered how fun it might be to spend some of that money on the space program... We obviously have the money it would take for such amazing and exciting things... But then she came back down to earth herself a little bit, realizing even if that vast amount of money weren't being spent on unfortunate military operations, most of it could probably be better spent on things here on earth, things like healthcare and education. Although, wouldn't it be fun to spend some of it trying to get to Mars? After all, it's human nature to explore and think "big." We're bound to go someday anyway, so why not start sooner rather than later? Hmmm...

All of these thoughts were keeping her from completely focusing on the show, and she didn't mind. If the television inspired other thoughts, that seemed like a good thing. It was simply serving as a muse. Compared to what was happening earlier in the day, this was a marked improvement. She'd just been just lying there with a glazed look in her eyes, not accomplishing anything. Now, it seemed she was capable of thinking about fun things even with the TV on. Maybe she wouldn't have to destroy it with a big sledge hammer after all......? With that thought, she turned it off...

Reading seemed like a better idea. She'd been into an interesting and well-written book on the mechanisms of evolution. Now seemed like a good time to pick it up again. She went into her huge master bedroom, stacked some pillows against the headboard, and climbed into her king-sized bed. The book was waiting on the nightstand where there was a beautifully sculpted stainless steel lamp, perfect for reading.

She opened it to a chapter about the giant asteroid that had landed in or near the Caribbean sea some 65 million years ago, the one that most likely caused the demise of the dinosaurs. It was much much larger than the one that hit John in the middle of the field that night......... She laughed......

The main point was how massive global catastrophes can immensely affect the history of biological development. As the giant reptiles slowly suffocated and starved to death, the few mammals that remained (mostly small rodents) survived by going underground and basically "waiting out" the devastating global winter. There were enough resources underground, like insects and roots, to live on until things ever so slowly improved. And ultimately the critters emerged to find all the big predators were gone. The small mammals seemed to have the run of the place, and they flourished. An eventual point being that periods of mass extinction, in the end, lead to a diversity of species. The mammals thrived and spread all over the planet, specializing for different climates and environments as they went. Out of this, primates eventually emerged, and somewhere way down the road, eventually, us..... Wow! This was great stuff!... She smiled, snuggled into her covers, and kept reading. She'd vaguely known about all of this from different college classes she'd taken years earlier, but it was fun getting back into the details of it all.... There was never any shortage of amazing things to think about....

About an hour and a half and quite a few pages later, she finally turned out the light to surrender to sleep. She awoke with the birds a little before 6:00, just as a little twilight was beginning to show itself. It would have been easy to just go back to sleep, but she didn't want to waste a single minute of what was sure to be a good day...

A fresh pot of coffee was always a great way start to any day, so getting that going was an obvious first step. It only took a few minutes, and in the meantime she put on some clothes and brushed her teeth, pausing briefly in the mirror to check in with herself.... It's going to be a great day. I'm going to make it so.... After pouring a hot cup and grabbing a muffin and a banana out of the pantry, she went out on her huge deck through the living room door... You could get to it from the master suite too....

27

She sat down at the table under the big umbrella and slowly ate breakfast, sipping her coffee. A few minutes later she stood up, walked over to the wooden handrail, and set the cup back down. The sun would be rising soon and it was nice looking out at the brand new day. It was beautiful. The house was on somewhat of a highpoint and she could see the fog that had settled into some of the lower valleys. Just then a deer wandered into her yard, as they sometimes did. She took a deep breath and appreciated the moment. She loved where she lived, her house, her enormous yard, the surrounding area, the people. Life was good.......she continued to stand there for a while...

She refreshed her cup and sat back down, unfolding yesterday's paper as an ad from a local sporting goods store fell on her lap. She didn't mind. Maybe she would stop by later and look around? She'd been thinking of buying some new rock-climbing shoes anyway.....
She had never considered herself a great climber, but it was always fun to do a little of what she liked to call "social climbing" with friends. Luckily there were some great places to go in the area- peaks and valleys and gorges with ancient hard rock hundreds of millions of years old.... The Appalachian Mountains were remnants of a once gigantic mountain range.....

Continuing......she read an article about pollution in one of the local rivers, another about an upcoming arts festival, and yet another about some enrollment issues at the University of Tennessee, her alma mater. Glancing over the classifieds was next, just to see what was there. The newspaper was a fun little diversion, but there was nothing earth-shattering to think about... She set it on the table and leaned back in her chair taking another sip of coffee...

Hmmm, what's today going bring? Maybe actually typing some words would be a good idea?... She loved her laptop and decided to go get it. She checked her email and deleted most of them before googling a few random things just to see what might come up- guitars, archery, racing bikes. It occurred to her that perhaps all she was really doing was putting off the inevitable. The truth was, as hard as she had tried not to, she was feeling some pressure- pressure not only from Mark and the publisher, but even more importantly, self-imposed pressure. She wanted to get started on something and wished she had a concrete idea to actually dive into. She wanted to "put pen to paper" as they say, but as of yet her thoughts about it had all been extremely random and not well thought out. Maybe she should start writing anyway, just to see what might happen?

With that, she pulled up a word processing program and at the top center wrote the words, CHAPTER ONE.........

Then she called Mark and left a message... I started writing again, but don't tell anyone else yet.

SIX

Feet on the ground, rubber to the road, pen to the paper, c'mon let's get something going here...enough screwing around..... She stretched a little, touched her toes, and sat back down putting her hands on the keyboard....

Hurtling through space at tens of thousands of miles an hour was remarkably peaceful, as he'd expected it would be; but the actual experience of being there seemed somewhat more peculiar than he would have anticipated. There was no sensation of the speed at all. It was a silky smooth ride. But, even after several weeks, the tiny space capsule was still a bizarre place to wake up from a long "night's" sleep. Of course the concept of night lost any real meaning in the vast void between earth and Mars, but suddenly becoming aware of where he was after pleasant dreams of earth-bound things was always strange. It almost seemed it should have been the other way around. Dreaming of flying through space and then waking up at home in bed had always been a far more likely scenario. In fact, Scott Williams had been dreaming of this his entire life. Ever since he was a little boy, he'd imagined what it would be like to be an astronaut. So, while some probably would have found his circumstances a little disturbing, he was loving every minute of it. There was no place in the universe he would rather have been.....

Whew! What the hell? That was exciting!.......As she reread what she'd just written, she thought maybe it wasn't half bad. But, even more importantly, she'd actually done something. It wasn't just hypothetical anymore. Granted, it was only a first paragraph; but it was a start. Maybe even a real start....? Just the night before she'd been thinking about the inevitable trip to Mars looming on the human horizon. And, based on the book she was reading, she was obviously a fan of science in general.

So......why not write plausible science fiction, something that hasn't actually happened yet, but probably will, or at least could someday! This was good..... it seemed she might actually have something.....

Julie Bowman, Larry Parsons, and Joann Luzern were all Scott's teammates on this incredible adventure, and they all shared his same passion for what they were doing. They had to, or they wouldn't have been there in the first place. This was no job for undedicated people; and, although they all had great fun-loving spirits, this was obviously something that had to be taken very seriously. For one thing, everything about it was extremely dangerous. There were certainly no guarantees they'd even survive. The long trip had never been made by humans before, and nobody was sure what to expect every step along the way. Everything had been gone over and thought through and then gone over again by some of the most brilliant scientists and engineers the world had ever seen, but this was a new frontier. There was no way to know what all the variables might even be. It was exciting for sure, but it took some unique individuals to put themselves in such overtly vulnerable positions. Additionally, they had to be willing to sacrifice years of their lives for the cause, not only in the incredibly thorough training, but in the mission itself. At an absolute minimum, they would be gone for at least three years, and it could very easily be longer than that....

In 2017 a concrete plan had finally been laid out describing how this would all be accomplished. Due to the remarkable success of a long series of robotic missions, it was decided that these helpful, friendly machines should be assigned a task other than just pure research. It seemed entirely plausible that they could set up a base camp of sorts for the humans that would eventually follow, which is exactly what they'd done.

Over the course of nearly twelve years, our hardworking mechanical counterparts had constructed what was, given the incredible obstacles, an amazing and welcoming facility. It consisted of ten big transparent inflatable domes, 2000 square feet each, that were configured in groups of two, and all within a very few miles of each other... There were several different reasons for this. First and foremost was the consideration of safety. The groups of two were for safety in redundancy. If something happened to one, the inhabitants could retreat to the other, and part of the reason for the way they were spread out was for similar reasons. If something slightly more catastrophic happened, say a meteor hit a couple of the domes, there would still be places to retreat. It seemed they really had tried to think of everything, but there were even more reasons for all of the enclosures. Three of the five camps were setup in a valley where subterranean water was known to be, and one was on a nearby highpoint. Last, but not necessarily least, one was placed at a site deemed important for its mineral content. The one on the highpoint was strictly for the view, offering an immense panoramic perspective on the surrounding geography. A person could see for miles and miles, and who knew how many ways that might come in handy? There were obvious reasons for the ones near the water. Water was life, both immediately, and for agricultural purposes. And the mineral site was simply interesting for scientific purposes. For one thing, it was the place where the ancient single celled fossils had been discovered early in the 2020's, the life that finally let us know the earth wasn't unique in the universe. It was perhaps the most important discovery in all of human history. It let us know we probably weren't alone. If life had gotten a start on such a close neighbor, it opened up limitless possibilities for what else must be out there. It let us know life in the cosmos must be common. In short, it changed everything....... Mars was indeed a fascinating place....

The preparations took place over five very extensively planned missions, each with its own similar set of goals. Almost miraculously, they'd all gone flawlessly, in practical terms anyway. A couple of times there were minor glitches, but nothing that couldn't be fairly easily managed. Given the nature of the task, that was flawless. There was systematic planning for contingencies and the unexpected. There were preparations for everything imaginable that could possibly go wrong, and how to prevent it- and perhaps even more importantly, how a situation could be dealt with if and when it did occur. There were multiple redundancies built into practically every system, especially in the software. The software was the "brains" of the mission. It allowed the craft and the robots to essentially think for themselves. If there was a problem along the way, the technology would, in most cases, be capable of fixing itself.

Huge rockets were commandeered for the initial launch of the missions, which might sound a little primitive given the recent talk of other possible propulsion systems. Things like theoretical atomic, magnetic, or even such unrealized ideas as anti-matter engines could someday be used for such purposes. But, as of yet, they were still only future possibilities. For now, the huge fuel-burning rockets would have to do; and, all things considered, they worked very well. For one thing they were extremely powerful, which was very important, given the enormous size of the payloads. They'd have to push many thousands of pounds of equipment up and out of the earth's atmosphere to speeds great enough to be freed from the earth's gravity. Once there, after dropping some of the payload, a second stage would be fired to reach an even greater speed. No small task, and the big rockets were the only practical way to go. Plus, based on decades of previous experience, they knew the technology worked and the reliable work horses of the day could still be counted on.

Each mission contained everything needed for an individual encampment. The two big inflatable enclosures, two robotic rovers to set them up, and all the equipment needed within were all onboard. The trips themselves took an average of six months before the capsules finally fell into a steady and predictable orbit around Mars. Then, when the timing was right, the booster rockets were fired to direct the mission down into the thin Martian atmosphere. Not that the entire project wasn't extremely difficult, but this was always one of the most crucial and delicate aspects. If they didn't get it right, the thing could land miles, if not hundreds or even thousands of miles, from where they wanted it, leaving it for all practical purposes useless. The tight grouping of the five missions was crucial because, in many many ways, they were all dependent on each other.

The biggest variable in the successful landing of each craft was the behavior of the atmosphere below at the moment of entry. In simpler terms, what the weather was like? Timing was everything, and there was no need to rush the process. All sorts of sensitive instruments and cameras were used to carefully analyze the situation beforehand. And on more than one occasion it took several weeks for everything to be deemed satisfactory. There was no such thing as perfect. "Perfect" would have meant a dead calm, and there was no way to expect that would ever be possible. "Calm enough" was the best anyone could hope for; and, once the descent began, minor adjustments would have to be made along the way. Small booster rockets would fire on cue, slowing things down, speeding things up, moving a little to the right, a little to the left, until the giant parachutes opened and the real fine-tuning began. The same rockets would then continue to fire for all the same reasons, until finally, at long last, a nice soft landing on the surface was achieved. ....Whew..... There was a huge sigh of relief every time it happened...... Perhaps the most incredible thing about all of this was that most of it was accomplished by the onboard technology itself. The computers were analyzing all the data and making all the necessary adjustments. The control room on earth was of course monitoring it all very carefully but with a fairly long delay. Meanwhile, the craft itself was making decisions in real time..... Pretty amazing to think about.....

Once safely on the ground, the work started almost immediately. First, work in the form of preparation for work. It took a while for things to simply unfold, literally. Packing to best utilize virtually every cubic inch was absolutely necessary, and it all had to be undone slowly and in the right order to make sure nothing was damaged in the process. Watching, perhaps a blooming flower would have come to mind. A panel opened here, a panel opened there, and the whole thing slowly began to expand. At a certain point, individual packages rolled away. The two enclosures, a bundle of tools, another bundle of equipment, were all packed as spheres. Then other smaller spheres were packed around those, things like dehydrated food, seeds, and medical supplies, so when the craft initially opened they would all simply roll away to uncover the central rovers. The basic force of Martian gravity would do most of the initial unpacking.

Once the landing craft opened, its interior walls, now flat on the ground, began to activate as solar panels to keep spare batteries charged. The rovers started to come to life as their camera lenses began to open. They were opening their eyes to have a first look around, assessing the situation, so to speak. As their own solar panels were opening, they were slowly preparing themselves to become mobile. They were stretching, as if awakening from a long deep sleep, ready to do their jobs.

They were setting up camp, and the first objective was to find a flat spot free of big rocks. Then, one of the packaged enclosures was rolled into place. A cord, not unlike the one on an airline lifejacket, was pulled and a compressed oxygen container began the initial inflation process. Once the bottle and about 1/3 of the total process were complete, a small compressor kicked in that took advantage of the existing, predominantly carbon dioxide atmosphere to complete the process. Getting both up and at least "looking" ready only took a matter of the first few days. Things were of course far from actually "being" ready, but this was always a good start.

The missions generally overlapped a little in one way or another. Often as the general public was watching and monitoring the set-up phases on Mars itself, the scientific community making it all possible had much more to think about here on earth. Not only were they paying close attention to what was happening up there, but more than had their hands full here as well. There were always continuing preparations for what was happening next. Another launch of another mission was always just around the corner and it was a constant juggling act to make sure everything went well and in the right order. Just making sure one mission didn't land on another was always one of the most stressful little details. For obvious reasons, nobody wanted the missions to ever literally overlap.

Eventually, everything was as ready as it was ever going to be, and on April 12th 2029 the moment of truth finally arrived. Scott, Julie, Larry, and Joann took the long elevator ride to the top of their enormous launch vehicle ready to have their lives changed forever. They'd all been preparing themselves for this in one way or another their entire lives, and this was it! They were about to change the course of human history. We would now forever be a species who had moved out into our own solar system. It would be the biggest scientific accomplishment since landing on the moon, and yet this was so much bigger. It was so much farther away, but there was no turning back now. Once they were all strapped in, the countdown refused to relent. 10...9....8.........3....2....1......LIFTOFF! The mission of the century was off and running.

Taking her fingers off the keyboard, Janet stretched and cracked her knuckles. Over six hours had passed since she'd sat down and written her first words, yet she'd barely noticed the time passing... Wow, that was awesome! I can't believe how much fun that was.... She'd completely drifted into the story and, most importantly, she'd actually been writing it down as she went. She had finally started working again and wasn't just letting the fun random thoughts bounce around in her head anymore. They were being put to use and her imagination was finally working for her instead of simply seeming frivolous. It was a great feeling...... but she was really needing to stand up and move around a little bit.....big yawn... big stretch.... oooohh that feels good.

She paced and looked around her deck for a few minutes before going inside to get something to drink. Peering into the fridge, a sandwich suddenly seemed like a good idea too. A few minutes later the ample kitchen island was covered in food preparation, and a late light lunch was hitting the spot.... A little exercise seemed like a good idea too.

A phone call to Sara, her friend and neighbor down the street, resulted in a late afternoon mountain bike ride. Only a couple of miles away there was access to some great single-track trails that she hit fairly regularly. It was always fun and a great workout when she had some pent-up energy that needed expressing.... About forty minutes after the call, Sara showed up ready to go.

In the meantime, she'd called Mark again to tell him about her day to that point. It was a good conversation, and of course he was very happy to hear about all the productivity. However, she wouldn't give him the first inkling of a clue as to what she was actually writing about. It was too soon. She just wanted him to know that she'd started working, that's all. He was curious, of course, but figured he'd find out soon enough what it was all about and didn't let it get the best of him....

In the same conversation, he let her know that he'd soon be in the neighborhood. He spent a lot of his time in New York and had an apartment there, but he owned a house in Knoxville as well. It was Tuesday and he'd be getting in Friday night...... They agreed it would be good to see each other.....

SEVEN

Sara was a good friend.... She was divorced and had done well in the settlement but made a good living on her own, too. She sold educational software of some kind, which was about as much detail as Janet wanted to try to understand. She and Sara were financial equals, in that they each had enough money not to have to worry much about it. And they both had fairly flexible schedules when they were in town, so they made good playmates.

Janet put on her biking gear (shoes, shorts, helmet), filled a water bottle, and joined her friend who hadn't even gotten off her bike. Several minutes later they were at the trailhead where diving off into the lush forest was a great thing to be doing. The first half mile or so was a fun, fast, somewhat technical downhill with a few rocks and roots in the way to keep things interesting... As the trail leveled out, it followed a little creek for a few miles, crossing back and forth across it several times. It was a great way to be getting dirty and sweaty, and they were both loving every second of it......and they were getting a fantastic workout....

After several more miles, a fairly significant uphill led into a big open field of tall swaying grass. The sun was still an hour or so above the horizon, so they decided to stop and take a break for a few minutes. It was roughly seventy-five degrees; and, by all rational accounts, a beautiful afternoon. They were both thirsty, so they had a good excuse to stop, catch their breaths, and appreciate where they were...

Naturally, they started talking. Sara was well aware of the issues Janet had been having starting a new project and was happy to hear there may have been a breakthrough. It was easy to see she was excited about writing again. It had been a while.... What are you writing about?... Janet started to tell her, but suddenly felt a little unexpectedly shy about the subject. As she was about to actually say it for the first time, it somehow sounded silly even in her own head..... In a somewhat self-deprecating laugh, she said.... It's about the first human mission to Mars.... Sara laughed too..... Mars? What do you know about Mars?... It was the obvious response given the way the news had been delivered.... Well, to be honest, that seems like a fair enough question, because the truth is, not a whole lot. I mean it's not like I'm an actual scientist or anything. I just think it's an interesting subject, that's all, and that should be a good enough reason. Plus it's not like I don't know anything. I read! You know I like reading about stuff like that; and, if there's a good documentary about anything related, I usually try to watch it. Beyond that, I'm figuring I can just kind of wing it. I'm a creative person, and I'm pretty sure I can at least make it sound good. That's all that counts..... Ok, good...it sounds like you feel good about it. If that's really true, then you should go with it.... Yeah, I guess I do feel good about it.... Having to defend her position made her feel somewhat better about it again already.... After another big drink of water, they took off riding again.

The trail made a big swooping curve through the field and eventually dipped back down into the trees where it crossed the creek again. As the sun was getting lower, the forest was getting darker..... It had a kind of eerie, almost fairytale-like quality that Janet liked. She chuckled to herself....... Wouldn't it be fun if some elves or maybe a talking bear made its way onto the trail?.... On that thought, a couple of deer crossed the path about fifty feet in front of her, almost as if she'd willed something out of the woods.... There was a dead calm, and the only thing she could hear was the sound of her own breathing and her bike pounding down the trail. Then, suddenly, just as she was trying to make a tricky move down a particularly steep and rocky pitch, a giant owl swooped down from nowhere just over her head... Oh Shit!... Instinctively, she hit her front break and the wheel instantly locked up sending her flying over the handlebars... Ooooohh, this isn't good!.... Now there were sounds, the sounds of tumbling down the hill tangled in her bike... This Sucks!.... The whole thing probably only took a few seconds but seemed to happen in slow motion. Luckily, she hadn't been going all that fast. And, by the time she finally stopped and was able to stand up, it was obvious that things could have been worse. She was definitely glad she'd been wearing a helmet; but she'd had this kind of fall before, and it wasn't the end of the world. As she looked at her skinned knee, hands, and elbows, she started laughing. Meanwhile, Sara had stopped behind her. At first she looked shocked; but then, seeing the situation for what it was, she started laughing too..... Did you see that owl! That was awesome!...... Duh! It scared me right off my bike.....Damn!......So, you're alright, right?......Yea, I'm fine.....Both laughing now, they knew they'd be back to the road fairly soon anyway, way before it got too dark to ride. The trail they were on was basically making a big loop that came out less than a quarter mile from where they'd started. It made a great twelve-mile ride that they both did often, together or otherwise, but it was always fun when they could do it together.

By the time they were out of the woods the sun had gone down, and Janet invited Sara over for dinner. Sara accepted, and soon they were pulling their bikes into the garage. For both, a big glass of cold water was a first priority, followed quickly by popping the caps off a couple of cold beers. Janet suggested they throw a couple of steaks on the grill, and who wouldn't agree to that? She also suggested they take the time to get cleaned up a little. She wanted to take a shower and wash her battle wounds, which seemed reasonable enough. Sara only lived a few houses away and appreciated the opportunity too. Some thirty or so minutes later, they were together again cracking open another couple of beers. Janet started steaming some veggies on the stove and, before long, a nice two-course meal was on its way…. Sara basically knew what to expect when she accepted….

….So, Janet, how are you feeling? You took a pretty good tumble there….. Yea, I'm fine. I'll probably be a little sore tomorrow, but whatever? It was funny anyway…. It sounds like you're excited about starting on your new book idea…. That's good…. I know you've been itching to get started on something; although, when you first said you were writing about spaceships and whatnot, I was a little surprised. I mean I know you're interested in a lot of things, but writing about space flight and science fiction- I can honestly tell you I never would have guessed it….. Really, well what would you have guessed……? I don't know, but I mean look at your life. Look at some of the amazing places you've been, some of the amazing things you've done. I figured that, if you were going to write fiction, it might be some action-packed thriller about things a little more down to earth, in a manner of speaking…. You of all people should know our own little planet is exciting enough…… Yea, you're right. I know, and believe me I've had thoughts along those lines….. She told Sara all about John the filmmaker, how she'd killed him with a meteor late one night in the middle of an open field. She told her about cutting the guy in half with a train and a few of the other crazy ideas she'd briefly considered….. They both had a good laugh……The thing is, I really like this Mars idea. I mean, for one thing, the potential for where I can go with it is limitless. Anything is possible, and I love that, especially considering I'm not sure exactly where I'm going. As of right now, the plan is to sort of let the story carry me, just to see where it might lead; and to me that's very exciting. So for now I'm going to keep going with it….. although I'll be curious to see what Mark has to say….. She smiled……By the way, he'll be in town this weekend. We should all get together…..

It was a nice night, and eventually they made their way out to the deck. Before the evening was over, they'd both consumed several more of those cold beers that were going down so smoothly. They enjoyed each other's company and hashed through whatever needed hashing through. Solving the world's problems as they saw them was always a good time. They talked about politics, government, religion, and whatever other big unsolvable questions came to mind. It was partly serious, but mostly it was just laughable…

By the time Sara left on her bike it was close to midnight. She called a few minutes later to say she was still alive and safely home again. The time had flown by, and Janet realized just how tired she actually was. When she finally stopped to think about it, she'd had a really long day. It had been a great day, productive and otherwise....

She stopped for a minute and thought about how glad she was that she'd told Sara what she was working on. Having to stand up and defend it a little bit made her feel even stronger about the idea. Maybe she was on the right track? In fact she thought about picking it up again right then... but, on second thought, she was too exhausted. Bed was a better way to go. As she got ready, she caught a look at herself in the big full length mirror on the wall. She was definitely a little skinned up and probably going hurt in the morning. Laughing at herself, she thought maybe this was revenge for throwing John out of that car the other day....? See, I do have a good imagination....

The next morning she slept in a little, just because she could; but, finally, at about 9:15 she crawled out of bed, put on a pot of coffee, and got dressed. Then it was out to the deck with a muffin, a hot cup, and most importantly, her computer......

EIGHT

At 51, Scott Williams was the oldest one on the mission; and, perhaps somewhat ironically, he was also the only one who'd never actually been in space.... He'd wanted to go. He'd wanted to his entire life and had always been a great candidate, but for one reason or another it simply hadn't happened until now. There was always something that kept him from being atop the next scheduled launch. Sometimes it was personal. But, but more often than not, it was because of the typically political nature of the space program. It wasn't always easy to understand why one person got to go and another didn't. Whatever happened along the way though, he was never bitter. He had a thorough understanding of how the game was played, and his patience was finally paying off. It was a great honor to be one of the first humans headed for Mars. However, going back a very long way, he'd been earning his ticket with much more than just patience… The vehicle in which he and his friends would be making this journey of millions of miles was largely his concept.

He knew a large environment would be needed if this was to be done with even the slightest amount of comfort; and, given the amount of time they were talking about, comfort wasn't just a luxury- it was vital, both physically and psychologically. There needed to be enough room to move around, exercise, and allow a certain amount of privacy. So, as an integral part of the team that designed and executed the five big preparatory missions, he had come up with a way for big pieces of the travel module to be dropped off in earth's orbit, close to the international space station, before the second stage continued on its way to Mars. This way, the astronauts aboard the space station could be doing various space walks to put the thing together in the meantime….

Scott had an impressive engineering background going all the way back to his childhood, making him well-suited for these planning aspects of the project… As a gifted kid growing up in the rural midwest, he'd had to come up with creative ways to entertain himself, which was never a problem. Designing interesting games and gadgets from whatever he could find in the garage came naturally. He knew he was unusual; and, for the most part, he liked that about himself, except when it occasionally got him in trouble. Being smarter than most of those around him, it was easy to sometimes get a little carried away. Although the advantages of his intelligence would definitely come in handy, it wasn't always practical in terms of day-to-day life to be smarter than his teachers. "Smart ass" was what he was often more likely called. Making the figures of authority look stupid may not have been wise at times, because it usually led to some unpleasant consequences. But he just couldn't seem to help it. It was too easy and too much fun, and he did have a good sense of humor. Plus there were some benefits, the best being his classmates thought he was hilarious, which made him popular…. Of course the fact that he was fairly good in sports never hurt either. He was never a superstar, but he was a decent athlete who played every sport he could possibly fit into his schedule all the way through high school.

Following that, it was off to an Ivy League college on an academic scholarship where three years later he'd earned his first engineering degree. After several more years, he had a PhD in engineering from MIT, and a couple of years after that, yet another in physics. Scott was no dummy; and he took it all in stride, too- meaning he was always well liked. Although he had a very confident air, he had learned not to come across as arrogant or condescending. Luckily, he largely outgrew his adolescent need to occasionally cause trouble in order to get attention. By now, he was getting enough attention just by being the interesting guy he was.... and after a while it wasn't about that anyway. He had more important and, for that matter, more fun things to think about than how entertaining he was to other people. His education and life experiences were showing him a much bigger picture, and he was realizing more and more what an interesting time it was to simply be alive. Mankind was on the brink of amazing things that he wanted to be a part of, and he worked very hard to that end.

After finishing the second of his two graduate degrees, he decided to stay in the world of academia for another couple years to teach and continue his research. As a physicist, he was studying advanced string theory and enjoyed being around people who were as fascinated by the possibilities as he was. The idea of our everyday reality consisting of many more than the knowable three dimensions (four, if you count time) was way too much fun to just let it drop. Although, it didn't take long to realize that, in practical terms, any real world applications for this knowledge were probably decades, if not centuries, away. So eventually he went to work for NASA, which he'd known he would ultimately do anyway.

His first post was as an engineer at the Jet Propulsion Laboratory in Pasadena, California, where he started working on the robotic rovers that paved the way for the ones that would eventually set up a base camp for humans. The ones he first dealt with were designed strictly for exploration and research; but, as things progressed, his work also led to designs that would begin doing the active preparatory work. So, from very early on, he was an integral part of the entire manned Mars mission project. He was laying a foundation that would make him a prime candidate to be one of the astronauts actually on board. He was grooming himself for the inevitable first trip, and it was exciting. He would later realize, however, that no plan is without its possible faults, especially when planning for something of this magnitude.

In the meantime, the three other people who would eventually make the cut were already in the space program as actual astronauts, or at least astronauts in training.

41

Julie Bowman came from a shining military background as a Naval aviator; but, even before then, she too was showing signs of being an exceptional individual. Throughout high school, her education had almost been too easy for her even in the advanced classes. In fact, the "gifted program" hadn't even seemed like a choice; however, it was the only thing the school system knew to do with her. But it was never a serious challenge. It was a strange life having such an extremely high IQ, and she wisely knew not to flaunt it. She had always been a sweet girl; and, perhaps unlike Scott at that age, she'd never wanted to use her intellect to make anybody feel uncomfortable, including her teachers. In fact, her kind sensitive nature may even have kept her from showing her full abilities. And it probably wasn't until Annapolis that she finally learned false modesty would not be an advantage in life.

Other things came naturally too, things she couldn't have hidden if she wanted to. An adventurous and inherently curious spirit meant she was into all kinds of things- things like swimming, fishing, and simply running through the forest just to see what was out there. She was into archery and, at the age of eleven, won the national gold medal for accuracy in her age division. At age sixteen, she'd already done all the necessary preparation to earn a private pilot's license, which she received on her birthday as the best sweet-sixteen present she could have hoped for.

Luckily her parents had enough money to support such activities and were supportive and encouraging of her diversity of interests. As an avid reader, she devoured books of all kinds, especially books on a variety of scientific fields. To her, the world had always been an endlessly fascinating place, and she was usually too busy to even notice anyone else who didn't feel the same. She loved biology, marine biology in particular, and knew everything there was to know about SCUBA diving way before she was old enough to be "legally" certified- but fortunately her father taught her anyway. Safety was a big priority, and they always dove cautiously. But he knew she was capable and always took her along whenever possible. Living in northern Florida they had the opportunity to go often, frequently making the long drive down to the Keys and sometimes even flying over to the Bahamas. She loved it and knew by name virtually every living creature they saw, and probably more than just its name. In most cases she could have told you details about its lifecycle and lifestyle, what it ate, when it mated, etc....... She had a great childhood and always greatly appreciated her parents for providing it....

At first, the naval academy was a rude awakening from all of this. The regimented discipline was intense, but it didn't take long for her to fall into the ranks. She'd had a rough idea of what she was getting into anyway. They tell you it's not going to be easy before you ever get in, and that's part of the attraction. It's for people looking for a challenge, a chance to prove to themselves they're capable of anything- and she was. As life in the military progressed, she did very well, impressing pretty much everyone around her. Not everybody gets the opportunity to fly the most technologically advanced planes the world has ever seen, and she, even as a relatively petite woman, was at the top of the list of those who qualified. She passed every test they could throw at her, physical, mental, psychological. It didn't seem to matter. If ever there was a person cut out for the job, she seemed to be that person- and she loved every minute of it. Having been an aviator since she was basically a kid, this was fantasy coming true. Most pilots in the world could only dream of flying these amazing planes. She loved the incredible acceleration, the speed, the tight maneuvers, just the feeling of raw power at her fingertips. The sensations of flying at hundreds of miles an hour at treetop level only to point the aircraft straight up and accelerate through MACH 1 were indescribable- and she couldn't get enough... Then there were the aircraft carrier maneuvers. Landing a fighter jet on a ship in high seas wasn't exactly dull either. It took extreme concentration, and she later recalled that the first time she ever had to do it was probably the most nerve-racking moment of her life, but she smiled when she said it....

She loved her military career, staying in as part of the reserves; but, after eight years, she decided to move on to other things..... Having also earned a biology degree while in the service, it dawned on her that she wanted to go to medical school, and she was easily accepted to Harvard where she also excelled. She was fascinated with the human anatomy; but, more than that, she had a genuine desire to help people. It seemed like a good way to give back to a world that was being so good to her, and, right on schedule, she graduated at the top of her class. But that wasn't it. She wanted to continue her education, specializing in cardiology. In short, she wanted to be a heart surgeon. She was on track to do pioneering work, developing new techniques, and shortening recovery periods when the headhunters from NASA came calling... Some might even say it was unfortunate timing, but she never saw it that way.....

Continuing down the list, Larry Parsons wasn't exactly an

43

uninteresting person either. In fact, everyone on the mission was an extraordinary individual who'd been very carefully handpicked. Each had his or her own particular set of skills that complemented those of their teammates. The idea being that they would function as one, and as a unit they would be capable of dealing with nearly any situation. They had overlapping skills; but, if one person had to be named the pilot, it was Larry.

From childhood he'd had the most natural tendencies toward thrill seeking, and growing up in southern California had played into that well. His mother started teaching him to surf practically before he could walk. Unfortunately his father had died in a car accident when he was three, but his mom did everything possible to make up for the loss. She had friends and dated some nice guys who loved to surf, and they all liked Larry. He was a fun energetic kid who took to the water like a seal. By the time he was thirteen, his mom had remarried a great guy named Simon who lived and breathed surfing. He owned a surf shop and, as a younger man, had even been a great competitor, competing in and winning surf competitions all over the world. However, by the time he'd come into Larry's life, he had mellowed considerably. Although he still loved waves, he was happy to settle into a slightly more conventional lifestyle, everything of course being relative. In other words, it wasn't unusual for him to take Larry and his mother on exotic "vacations" specifically in search of those waves. Since Larry was such a capable surfer, he and his mom and Simon sometimes even went in search of big waves- which had the potential to get Larry into trouble.... In fact there was an incident one winter in Hawaii that almost got him killed.....

He was seventeen at the time, and they had gone with the intension of riding one of the most notorious breaks in the world, JAWS, a long way out off the north shore of Maui. Everyone in the surfing community worldwide knew it existed, although very few had the necessary skills and confidence to actually try to catch it. In fact, it was so big no one could catch it without the help of machine. It was just too big and too fast to ever be able to paddle fast enough.... But one day a bunch of, some would say crazy, Hawaiian surf natives figured out that with the help of a jet ski they could be towed into the ride of their precariously balanced lives. The waves reached fifty or even sixty feet tall at times. A person had to be at the absolute pinnacle of his ability to even think about what these guys were doing- and this is what Larry and his stepdad, with the very reluctant permission of Mom, were out to try to do.

44

It was awesome! Larry was having the most incredible afternoon of his young life. Before anything went wrong, he'd been pulled into several monstrous rides. He recalled the feeling of the first time he realized he was actually on one of these things. As the wave stood up, it was like looking down the vertical face of a five-story building, or snowboarding down an incredibly steep mountain face, the biggest difference being that the mountain itself was chasing you, trying it's best to devour you. The moment was brilliantly alive with adrenaline-soaked excitement. Nothing else existed. "Now" was critically important. In short, it was more fun than one person should ever be allowed to have, but it would catch up with him, literally. On his fourth wave, something went wrong in the timing, and the mountain did catch him. Thousands of tons of seething chaotic energy came crashing down on his head knocking him unconscious, which in a way, was probably good. It meant he couldn't actually feel the beating he was taking for at least a minute. When he did come to, his lungs were full of water and he was still being tumbled like a rag doll. He couldn't even tell which direction the surface was. It was terrifying, but then he got a break. Miraculously he surfaced with no effort of his own and started coughing and vomiting up water just as one of the feverishly looking skis was less than twenty feet away. They scooped him up and got him the hell out of the way of the next oncoming wave. He was broken and badly shaken, but he was still alive.

The reality was that his brush with death only resulted in a few bruised and broken ribs, a lost surfboard, and a hell of a good story. In fact, the following year he even returned with a couple of his surfing buddies from California in hopes of trying it again. Unfortunately, they thought at the time, the big break never came and he was denied the opportunity, perhaps forever. The following year he was in the Air Force Academy, and to date, he's never ridden the mighty JAWS again.....

As a naturally gifted student he'd always gotten good grades. Without even trying, he'd graduated from high school at the top of his class. Not that he was lazy by any means, but he'd just found many things other than school to be more interesting. Military school would change that however. Even with his intelligence, he would have to work hard to stand out, but he adapted quickly. He wanted to stand out, because he wanted to be a pilot, and he knew they didn't let just anybody fly multimillion dollar airplanes. And he didn't want to just fly any airplanes either. His goal from the start was to become a test pilot, flying the most cutting-edge experimental technology of the day.

To his family and friends, the military had at first seemed like an odd choice. Going from such a free-spirited lifestyle to the discipline of the Air Force didn't seem natural, but they were supportive. Actually, it was a logical step. He'd always been the type to be out on the edge, and joining the military was the only practical way to pursue such lofty ambitions. It was the only institution with the financial resources to pursue the technology. So that's where he ended up, and he did well. Within several years he was indeed a test pilot.

It turned out he was more gifted than anyone would have first imagined, a prodigy if you will. He was a natural, and although he had a little trouble keeping his ego in check at times, he got along very well in the Air Force and was well respected for his abilities. In fact, when he was recruited at the age of twenty-three, he was the youngest astronaut NASA had ever accepted into the program.

Last, but certainly not least, Joann Luzern rounded out the list. She, much like Scott, came from a more academically deep background. She too had a couple of different advanced degrees, including PhD's in both mechanical and environmental engineering, and had taught at some of the top schools in her field. From this experience, she went on to work for the space program as an engineer at JPL where she first met Scott. As professional colleagues, they had always gotten along well. Although it was unusual for them to be working on the same projects, they did cross paths. They liked and respected each other; and, before Joann went off to the astronaut program first, they even dated a little bit.

She was the only one on the mission who was not a native born American, but it wasn't obvious- unless she was so inclined to tell you. Having spent her childhood on Vancouver Island, she was originally a Canadian and proud of the fact, often taking the opportunity to tell people who usually jokingly gave her a hard time about it. She didn't care. She'd loved the island. It was spectacularly beautiful, with streams, lakes, waterfalls, and lush moist forest of tall coniferous trees. There were rocky beaches and the beautiful surrounding Pacific Ocean. It was a great place for any kid to grow up, and she took full advantage of the limitless opportunities to play outside, often running through the woods with her friends. Obviously she, like her other fellow astronauts, was unusually intelligent, observing things most people miss. Even as a kid, she was thinking about the "how" and "why" in everything she saw. While she was happy just to be outside playing with her friends, the truth was she was experiencing her environment on many more levels than they were. As an avid reader with an amazing talent for finding things on the internet quickly, she would later go home and find facts about anything (everything) that peaked her curiosity- just for the fun of it.

On top of that, she slowly discovered she actually enjoyed the "running part" of running through the forest and was the endurance athlete of the group. She realized she could run for hours and was the best runner on her track team throughout high school in any event, but she generally left the sprints for someone else. She even started running marathons at an early age and, at fifteen, ran her first in just under two hours and forty minutes. For anyone who doesn't know, that's an incredible achievement all by itself, for anybody. In fact, it's a very rare natural talent, despite the fact that she worked very hard too.

Later, she took this talent and went to Yale on an athletic scholarship, although she most likely could have done the same based on her academic achievements. After graduating in just under three years, she went on to her various graduate programs. Then it was on to teaching and, later, JPL where she moved into the astronaut program faster than Scott realized he probably could have too...

And that was it..... This was the group chosen for the trip of the century, and all were passionate about it...... No doubt, the MARS team was an interesting group of individuals....

NINE

The technology was incredible. Scott and his cronies had done well in designing the mission around the needs of its human passengers. Unlike the original spaceships that had carried people like Neil Armstrong to the moon, this capsule was designed to meet more than just the astronaut's most basic biological needs. The Apollo missions had been carried out in cramped tiny spaces, barely big enough to stretch out. The priority was the moon itself, not the comfort of the individuals involved. Getting them there and back alive was the only thing that mattered and, given the knowledge and technology of the day, they'd done an amazing job. But we had made a lot of progress since then. Today, each astronaut's personal notebook had way more computing power than those entire missions had; and, as far as room was concerned, the Mars vehicle was enormous by comparison.

Shaped like a large cylinder, it had a magnetic wall going down the middle that essentially divided it in half, and they wore special metallic boots so they could be anchored to a floor as they moved around either side. The idea wasn't to simulate gravity necessarily, because it obviously wasn't. In fact it was a strange thing to get used to at first. But the reasoning was that it would give a sense of stability and orientation familiar to the brain, so things would be easier psychologically..... Sure it was great fun to go flying around for a while whenever they wanted, but it was really nice having a floor to come down to when they were finished....

Of course, everyone still had to do a considerable amount of exercise to make up for the fact that there was no gravity, to keep from losing muscle mass. A minimum of five hours a day was required from everyone, and that was yet another ingenious part of the plan. Every piece of equipment designed to serve this purpose also served to charge batteries as it moved. So this, combined with the solar panels, meant they had more than enough power for anything they wanted. They could brew coffee, microwave food, power personal computers and video monitors, light with personal lamps. It was great and did wonders to curtail the inevitable feelings of being cut off from the rest of humanity. They could even have video conversations with friends and family back home anytime they wanted..... Granted, the further away they got, the more challenging this became because of the delay; but they gradually figured it out and worked around it.... The basic key was to say everything they wanted to say and then wait for the person on the other end to do the same. It was far better than nothing, but as things slowly progressed, they weren't exactly real-time conversations....

Considering both sides of the middle wall, they had just over 2000 square feet of living space. So, in that regard, it was comparable to an average American home. Each crew member even had his or her own room.... There was about a ten-foot square hole in the middle of the floor for easy access to either side and at one end of both sides another wall that divided off more space. Those spaces were then divided in half again constituting each person's individual room. They were cozy, roughly a hundred and fifty square feet each, but easily enough room to serve their purpose. It was a place to escape if need be, to read, listen to music, meditate, or probably most importantly, just sleep..... His little room is where Scott was waking up every day briefly wondering where he was in the world, so to speak.......

Scott often used the time to think about everything that had previously transpired in his life to get him to this point, just to recognize and be humbly grateful for who he was. He and his friends were participating in the most exciting event in human history, and yet they all remembered numerous reporters asking beforehand how they would fight the inevitable boredom of such a long trip. None of them ever really knew how to deal with the question. They were all such inherently interesting and, perhaps more importantly, "interested" people that it never made sense. What do you mean boredom? They'd always do their best to answer politely.... Well, the truth is, there will be plenty to do...... explaining that they had work to do and exercise would be very important, but none of them ever wanted to spend much time on it simply because it seemed like such a silly line of inquiry...

They did have plenty to do. They had to very diligently monitor everything about the mission, constantly checking to make sure all the systems were up and functioning properly. They had to keep an eye on the ball at all times and not lose focus, because the truth also was that there was a very repetitive routine involved. So they did need to engage in other things to keep their minds sharp throughout this trip of many months.... They had digital access to just about everything ever written, so they had literally endless amounts of reading material. Plus they all spent a substantial amount of time writing, too, chronicling everything about what they were feeling and doing on a day-to-day basis. It was a good exercise for them as individuals, but each had the definite sense that it was also serving a greater purpose. People would be curious about their mission for generations to come. They were all living history and felt a very real sense of social responsibility.

While privacy was critically important, the big common areas were where the majority of time was spent, and where most of the exercising took place. The equipment was fairly simple in concept, consisting of straps and pulleys to effectively move and work virtually every muscle in the body depending on the configuration. It was possible to hook into the system from an individual's room, but most of the time no one felt the need. Working out was fun and felt social, and the system itself was entertaining. A person could see from digital readouts everything from heart rate and calories burned, to how much electricity they were producing. They could listen to music either privately through headphones, or publicly if everyone agreed. Sometimes it even turned into a rhythmic competition to see who could generate the most power if they were all working out at the same time.

It was good when the team was interacting. Putting effort into strengthening their personal bonds was important not only to them as individuals but to the mission as a whole. By now, they all knew each other and got along well. And, given the nature of what they were doing, it was important to make a conscious effort to insure that things stayed that way. Festering personal differences had the potential to make things miserable for everybody, so they simply weren't allowed. If a conflict arose, it was mandatory to resolve it and figure out a way to move forward on genuinely good terms. Everyone understood how important this was. Any smoldering resentments between crew members could be catastrophic.

A crew of two men and two women was chosen very purposefully, and sexual compatibility was encouraged way before the mission ever started. In fact, it was an open factor in whether or not a person was even chosen. Everybody knew that this assignment would last for years, so the possibility for companionship on multiple levels was a serious consideration. Sleeping together beforehand was certainly not mandatory, but everyone had to at least be open to the ultimate possibility..... It was for their own sakes and for experimental purposes too, to see how different types of personal relationships might develop under such extreme circumstances. Needless to say, nobody was allowed to be married and leaving a family behind. It wouldn't make sense. Being single was one of the first of many important prerequisites, with consideration of many aspects.........

Scott was the commander, which at first may have seemed like an odd decision since he was the only one who'd never logged any actual "space time." The rest of the crew had spent time orbiting in the international space station; so, in practical terms, it seemed they all knew more about it than he did. But he won the title anyway. Both his calm laid-back nature that everybody appreciated, combined with his overwhelming technical knowledge of every aspect of the mission, had earned him the position. Nobody disputed that he would make a great leader.... Joann was named 1st officer for similar reasons- she was well liked and respected for her thorough understanding of the mission. Julie was first medical officer for obvious reasons. And, as we already know, Larry was named the pilot because of his natural abilities and calm sensitive touch at the controls of anything that flew.

A few weeks in, the mission was off to a perfect start. They had launched atop their enormous rocket as two out of every three people worldwide was watching. And, a couple of days later, they rendezvoused with the actual Mars vehicle attached to the space station. Roughly forty-eight hours were spent there, getting some rest, and having some fun with the crew who'd been anxiously preparing for their arrival. These were the last people they would see before heading out into the long dark void.

Leaving was a heavy moment and the final goodbyes emotional.... They boarded, detached, and actually waved goodbye out of one of the three big windows...The engines were ignited; and, not long after, they were moving at a rate of sixty thousand miles an hour, quietly and peacefully through the immense vacuum of space......

The common area was comfortable and very versatile. It could be used as anything from a living room, to a gymnasium, to a surgical suite if need be. Four flexible magnetic chairs could be set up wherever in the room people wanted them. It seemed strange, but they would actually Velcro themselves in.... again, it gave a sense of familiar stability and orientation. The chairs could be used at various work stations, or sometimes they'd all face the one big monitor so that the crew could watch and participate in briefings from the control center. It was fun having meetings with home but, again, the interactive delay got longer and longer the further away they got.... Or occasionally they'd just pop some popcorn and all watch a movie together or maybe a downloaded episode of a favorite television show..... The Simpson's never seemed to get old.....

As things progressed, everybody got used to the idea of their journey taking a while. There was plenty of time to appreciate and reflect on what they were doing. Hours were spent simply looking out the big windows. The stars were incredible, billions of them everywhere... Just the darkness itself was amazing, reinforcing the idea that, of all that exists, most is empty space. It was easy to get philosophical.... Maybe the Buddha was right? Maybe god exists within this seemingly empty space....

Everyone on the mission had a spiritual side which was openly acknowledged, although no one was particularly religious. As members of western culture, they had all been exposed to Christianity in one way or another growing up, and Scott probably came the closest to actually retaining it in that he still claimed the title of Christian. But even he acknowledged there must be more than one path to spiritual fulfillment. So, very boringly, they all pretty much agreed that spirituality was meant to be an individual pursuit and not something that should be prescribed by someone else. It was a view that left little room for debate…

The conversations that were the most fun and most volatile usually revolved around different scientific theories, but most of this discussion was so complex your average Joe wouldn't have understood a word of it. They'd talked about their previous lives and everything that had led them to this point. They all had a lot of funny stories they eventually got around to sharing. A good sense of humor was another, although difficult to pin down, prerequisite. Scott often laughed at himself for taking so long to get into the astronaut's program. He knew everyone else had been on a faster track, and they couldn't help but occasionally give him a hard time about it. It was all in good fun though. They knew that in many respects he was the most qualified one there. After all, he'd been a key engineer in designing the entire mission, and they respected his leadership and command….

The training had started more than three years before the scheduled launch, and it had been intense. Everyone but Scott had already ridden a shuttle to the space station at least once; and Julie had gone five times. Larry followed with four previous missions, and Joann had been once before the training began. They had tried to get Scott on a mission, but scheduling conflicts always came up. In the end, it wouldn't matter anyway. They could simulate virtually anything they could think of that might happen. Granted there was nothing like actually being in space- but as far as the actual knowledge was concerned, it would be there. And when they finally did launch, Scott was like a little kid getting to ride a big roller coaster for the first time. He was so excited he could barely maintain his professionalism, but he managed…. the emotional side of leaving for so long combined with the total weight of the mission in general kept everybody in check…

Weeks into the journey, it was still exciting, but the reality of the long trip also started to set in. It really would be at least six months before the next phase…. time that would actually have to be spent.

In training, Scott and Joann enjoyed getting reacquainted from having known each other at JPL. She was only a few years younger than he; and although all the crew members had a lot in common, these two had the most obvious connection. They were good friends and would eventually have a tendency to take the relationship a step further, too, although not pushing it. Realizing they were both at the top of a very short list for the Mars mission, it just didn't seem prudent to be openly pursuing a romantic relationship with a co-worker, even when the management was practically encouraging it. The problem was it had just been too culturally engrained not to. Everybody knew how much potential trouble was involved in sleeping with a close colleague. Granted, this was a much different situation than most; but it still seemed wise to keep things very low key.... They did spend time together outside of work, but just agreed not to talk about it....

By the time the mission began, they still weren't talking about it, and they even managed to stay out of each other's rooms for a while. But, before long, they were sneaking around like they were trying to hide something. And then Julie caught Scott coming out of Joann's room at a time when he thought she and Larry were both sleeping. As far as Julie was concerned, it was a funny, although somewhat awkward, moment. Scott was obviously embarrassed, like a kid caught with his hand in the cookie jar, and she laughed.......Uh, well uh, ...I was just uh......... Finally, after way too long, he started laughing too, realizing he was only making himself look guiltier..... It was funny... And it wasn't like Julie was all that surprised anyway. Apparently they'd been far more transparent than either of them had realized.... and now it was out in the open....

Interestingly enough, it seemed Larry and Julie had been keeping a little secret of their own. There had always been a very positive energy between them, too. Although, they'd possibly been a little better at keeping it under wraps than their friends. Hmmm...... but now that Scott and Joann had been exposed, it only made sense to come clean themselves. So, in one big open meeting soon after, Larry and Julie admitted to Scott and Joann that they'd been sneaking an occasional quickie ever since the third day past the space station. It was a fun and funny moment for everybody.... they even opened a bottle of wine to all toast each other. It seemed the four people assigned to the mission were already two couples.....

53

TEN

Late Saturday morning Mark arrived on Janet's front steps banging very loudly on the door, just to be funny. She'd known he was coming and he didn't have to be making so much noise. He would have come over the night before but got in much later than expected. Instead of knocking some more, he let himself in right as Janet was about to open the door. They both had big smiles as they gave each other big hugs.... So what's this I hear about a new book...? Yea, I'm excited.... I've actually written the rough drafts of three chapters already... But let's not talk about that yet..... How have you been? I haven't seen you in weeks... Actually I think it's been a couple of months now, but who's counting....?

They'd known each other for a long time, practically their entire lives. They'd grown up together. Living only a block and a half apart as kids, they'd gone to the same grade school and were even in the same grade. Even their birthdays were only a few days apart. His was April 12th and hers the15th....

Had they been close friends? Yeah, most of the time, but sometimes petty childhood differences did get in the way. As a kid Mark had been a real brat at times, even mean. Once, when they were about eight, Janet and one of her girlfriends were playing dolls outside. They'd spent hours very carefully cutting up cardboard boxes to make doll houses out on her front lawn. By the time Mark came along, they'd made an entire village. Maybe he'd had a bad day or something, but, whatever the case, he proceeded to kick their little town apart, laughing as he did it...... This is stupid..... Don't you have anything better to do?..... Janet and her friend ran in the house crying.... It really was a horrible thing to do, and Mark felt bad about it for years afterwards too... He honestly didn't understand himself what had gotten into him that day....

Janet didn't forgive him for years; and Mark, not knowing how to react, acted like he didn't like her either. They called each other names and made faces at each other in class. The tension lasted all the way through junior high; but, when high school came around, they fell into a common group of friends and their differences slowly faded away. Maybe they were growing up a little bit? For one thing, it started dawning on Mark that Janet was a girl, maybe even an attractive girl. It was funny. He went from being an obnoxious brat to almost being too shy to talk to her. It seemed he may have had a crush and, perhaps unfortunately for him, a crush was all it ever was. While she'd gotten over hating him, she never thought of him as someone she wanted to date. And, as they slowly became friends again, Mark never had the nerve to tell her he felt any differently anyway.

Eventually it didn't matter. They started dating other people; and, without the pressure of any possible romance, they could become really good friends... and they did. With similar interests, good conversations eventually came easily.

They were good students, but both had a wild side as well, often going to the latest and greatest keg party together along with other friends. There was a time when they both smoked, and neither of them had ever been afraid to smoke a little of the green either. It was the same rambunctious misspent youth a lot of people can claim, and neither of them ever saw any harm in it...... No harm, no foul, was basically their view...?

Later, after graduating, Janet stayed local and went to the University of Tennessee to save money on housing. She'd gotten a partial academic scholarship and was trying to avoid going into debt by living with her parents for the first two years. They were easy to get along with and gave her all the freedom she wanted anyway, so it just made sense. Mark, on the other hand, moved to Boulder Colorado. He also had a scholarship but was more than willing to spend some of his parents money too. Plus he'd been itching to get out of town and see the world for himself. But he and Janet talked on the phone every month or so just to see how the other was doing. Their freshman years were going well for them both. It was almost ironic that Mark had gotten out of town first considering the great world traveler Janet would later become.....

Mark decided to go to graduate school in New York where he got a Masters Degree in literature and, soon thereafter, started on a great career in publishing. Meanwhile, Janet had already started her travels, spending a couple of summers in Europe before she'd even graduated. She'd spent the first summer in France working in a vineyard... It was a decision that ignited a spark. For the first time, it dawned on her that she was not only an American but a global citizen as well, and she wanted to see it all, literally. She developed a passion for travel unlike she'd ever known before. She loved it and couldn't get enough. She would raise money along the way by doing odd jobs or even have fund raisers at home. But, whatever the case, she always found creative ways to finance her expeditions. It was incredible, like she was born to travel....... like doing it well and on a limited budget was a natural gift. She saw it as an art form; and, from very early on, she started journaling every detail of what she was doing, just for her own sake. It took quite a while to realize the information she was gathering might be marketable to an eager traveling audience, if done correctly that is. And that's where Mark would later come back into her life in a very meaningful way.

When their tenth class reunion rolled around, they hadn't seen each other in several years but had managed to stay somewhat in touch through occasional postcards and phone calls.... When the time came, they had a great night. It was a good party, and all their old crew was more than willing to turn it on again like they'd done back in their day....

Nursing some pretty serious hangovers, a bunch of them got together the next day for lunch; and this is where Mark first mentioned that she should consider publishing some of her work... Publishing some of my work, what work?.... Didn't you tell me just last night that you'd been keeping detailed notes about everything you've been doing with yourself over the last decade....? Well, if you took the time and put it together in the right way, that's some pretty exciting stuff. They could even be guide books of a sort, inspiring people into thinking they could have the same life you've been having. You should think about it?... Hmmm, maybe I will think about it, but this afternoon I think I'm just going to take a nap.... And with that, the conversation was dropped.

The next day Mark had to get back to New York. He'd recently gotten engaged and needed to get back to his new wife-to-be. Unfortunately she hadn't been able to come because of some previous commitments to her job, and it seemed reasonable to her that Mark shouldn't be gone too long either.... a precursor? Several years later when he was divorced, he complained that she'd been incredibly demanding and hard to live with.... Live and learn......?

Less than a week after the reunion, Mark contacted Janet again, reminding her of their brief discussion at lunch; and this time she was in a better position to be receptive..... Well Mark, the truth is I have been thinking about it, and it's not a bad idea...... Hell no, it's not a bad idea and, and with my help and my connections, we might really be able to do something with it......Ok, I'm listening. So let's say I agree... What would the first step be? What would I need to be doing?... Well, I've been thinking about it, and I'm way ahead of you. What I would suggest is you pick a country, or even a continent, and start working on putting something together in book form. I know you spent a good part of last year in Australia, for example. So start telling the story in your own words and at the same time throw in all the details of how, when, where, and why you did everything as you went. You might even have to do some additional research. I don't know, but do you see what I'm getting at? If you've got a creative bone in your body, and I know you do, you can make this work if only because you've got such great material. You've been living an inspiring and exciting life that people will be interested in......Wow, Mark, talk about inspiring, you must be good at what you do too. Ok, I'm convinced. I'll think about it and try to get started on something......Whew, good! See, I knew I was right. This is going to be great!....... And it was great; they were off and running. Some two and a half years later Janet was already a best-selling travel writer, and they were both reaping the rewards....

Now, a decade or so later again, they were reaping a lot of mutual success. Since that first effort, Janet had written seven successful books; and Mark was, very fairly, getting a nice piece of those too. So, now that she was writing another book, it was good to get the opportunity to see her again. First, it was obviously good to see her again as a friend. They really were close and greatly enjoyed each other's company. But, a new book in a completely new genre was exciting, and he could hardly contain himself wanting to know more about it. So far she'd been really tight-lipped about the whole thing, and he didn't have a clue what she was working on....

.....I'm fine Janet, and I know you're fine too.... So tell me about the damn book already....... Ok Ok, calm down... Come in and make yourself comfortable... I was thinking about making myself a Bloody Mary. Do you want one.....? Sure, why not.....a little disappointed that this might take a while.... It's a nice day. Maybe we should go out on the deck?.....

It was a nice day, about eighty degrees with sunshine. Although, some big dark storm clouds had started to form out on the horizon, but that was alright too. Who doesn't like a good thunderstorm? And they sat out there and watched it build for a while, chatting. She knew she was making him suffer a little and enjoyed it..... So why did you get in so late last night......? Oh, I got tied up at work and missed my flight. It was no big deal. There was a later one anyway..... When are you going back? How long are you going to be here......? Tentatively, I'm going back on Wednesday, but nothing's written in stone. I guess I'm just playing it by ear. I'll be here for a few days though…..

About half an hour and a lot more small talk later, a big gust of wind blew up just as big drops of rain started to fall. They went inside to watch from a dryer and more comfortable position, behind the big glass doors and windows. It was an awesome storm with big loud booming thunder and lightning bolts. At one point some pea-sized hail even fell with the heavy rain. It was great but only lasted about twenty minutes at full blast, and in less than an hour the sun was out again….. Hmmm, that was interesting…..

So what do you want to do today? I'm wide open……Well, first of all, I want you to tell me about your book. You've been toying with me long enough….Ok, you're right….. The big brunch drinks had gone down well and she was finally feeling ready….. Great!…..So,…..what is it?…..It's about the first human mission to the red planet, Mars……What? You mean like science fiction…..? What the hell? Are you serious?….. Yes, I'm serious, and I want you to sound a little more enthusiastic about it…….Ok, I'll try. It's just not what I would have expected you to say at all….. Really, hmmm… You know, I was talking to Sara about it the other night and she said the same thing….. I'm not sure why this is striking everybody as so odd….. I mean it is fiction, and I told you I was thinking about writing fiction. If you ask me, that's a pretty wide-open category. So why are people having such preconceived notions about what I should be doing…..? Yea, but Mars? Are you sure that's really what you want to do…..? Yes, I already told you I've written three chapters….. Yea, but that doesn't mean you're committed, just delete it and start over on something else….. He laughed as he said it….. He was just giving her a hard time, but there was some truth to it too. Wasn't there an old saying "many a truth is said in jest?" Without even waiting to hear more about it, he was already making judgments in his mind, and they weren't necessarily good….. Look Mark, I'm excited about this, and I want you to have a better attitude….. She walked over and literally kicked him in the ass…… I'm going to print off what I've already written, and I want you to read it when you get home. But, until then, I don't want you to think any more about it…… For now, let's just move on… Damn it!…. Let's do something… Let's go get some lunch somewhere and do something else..…..Damn it again!…

It was frustrating, but she got over it. They went to nice little restaurant and then milled around town for a while. She bought some climbing shoes at the sporting goods store she'd seen advertised in the newspaper a few days earlier. There was an area in a park just outside of town with some short top-rope climbs, and they decided she should go play with her new toys for a while. The rest of her stuff was already in her truck, but Mark needed to stop by his place to pick up gear. And they called Sara and Janet's sister Carey to include them too… It was a fun afternoon. The new shoes did what they were supposed to do, and Mark was having a great time climbing with three cute women…. That night they all went out for a few beers…… It was a good day.

The following night, they all agreed to have a little get together at Janet's place. They even invited both Mark's and Janet's parents who'd also known each other for years. Steve, Carey's husband, brought their three children. Carey and Janet were the only siblings, and Carey's kids were probably as close as Janet would ever come to having kids of her own. They were all a close and supportive family. Buying a house so she could continue to call Knoxville home had been a good decision……… Ribs on the grill, everything else you could eat or drink, neighbors and friends stopping by, all made for another great evening…

A week or so later she got a call from New York….. First of all, it was great to see you as always, and I finally got around to reading the beginning of your book…. He chuckled and she could tell he was smiling…. I hate to admit it, but it might have some potential…. See, I told you….. Yea, but to be completely honest I'm still not bowled over by the idea… I mean is this really who you are? You've never been one of those weird science fiction nuts, wearing your Spock ears to the Trecky conventions…. I guess I just don't understand where you're coming from…. And, on top of that, although I know this stuff is only a rough draft, there are already some inherent problems…. Don't get me wrong. It's not all bad. You've definitely got some interesting characters starting to develop here, but aren't you going to have to work way too hard on something you know very little about to make this work…. Plus, on top of that again, you've already got the main characters sleeping together. Where's the drama in that? I mean it's not like you're talking about a fun little one night stand here. These characters lives are closely interwoven on multiple levels, and to simply throw them all in bed together already might be killing some of the tension, tension that would be a lot more fun to build slowly…. I don't know…. You know I've always been frank with you about your work, and I don't want to stop now…That's just some of what's been on my mind, that's all……. I don't know either Mark…. I mean I was excited about this….and still am. So far when someone has questioned

59

the idea I've fairly staunchly stood up for it, but they weren't you.... You know I respect your opinion.... If you're serious, maybe I should think about it.... By the way, I haven't even written anymore anyway... I've spent the last few days backpacking on the AT (Appalachian Trail). I did about forty miles just to get out in the forest for a while... It was great!..... Cool, that sounds awesome..... I love that about you Janet, how spontaneous you can be... In fact, I think that must be a big part of why your books are so successful. They inspire spontaneity in other people. That's how I know your next "real book" will be good. Whenever that happens?.... He just couldn't help giving her a little more grief.... Speaking of being spontaneous, why don't you come to New York for a few days..... I'll even line up a book signing for you if you want... Your fans will love it, and you can sell another couple thousand books..... She chuckled. What makes you think I'd even want to come see you? You're not even a nice person.... There was a brief pause as they both stood smiling.... Actually it's not a bad idea...Sure why not........... I'll catch a flight out tomorrow.... Or no, on second thought, I think I'll drive. It'll be a fun little road trip.... But sure, that's a great idea in fact. I'll give you a call and let you know when I'll be in, but you can probably expect me sometime in the next few days....

ELEVEN

Janet loved her truck. It had an extended cab and a topper on the back. It was comfortable and had a nice stereo. She could carry anything, anywhere, and have a good place to sleep. The thought of driving it to New York was fun, especially since Mark would have a place for her to park it. Not everybody in Manhattan was so fortunate...

She took three days to do it. It easily could have been done in one long one, but it seemed spending a couple of nights camping along the way was a better option- and, why not? It felt like a good idea, and there was no good reason to deny the impulse....

She arrived in the middle of the afternoon knowing it would be several hours before Mark got home. It didn't matter. The building he lived in had a valet, and the doorman who knew she was coming gave her the key. She let herself in, took a shower to scrape off a couple days worth of campfire grime, and made herself comfortable.

Mark had a great place. No question, he was doing well for himself. The apartment he owned was well over three thousand square feet, enormous by most New York standards. It was on the twenty-seventh floor, had a great view the city, and even overlooked Central Park a couple of blocks away. If a person were so inclined to live in New York, this was definitely the way to do it, in style. And, although Janet's visits were fairly seldom, she didn't have a hint of reservation in taking full advantage of Mark's fortunate situation. After all, she'd contributed to all of this. Granted, she was far from being his only successful client, but she'd definitely pulled her weight...

He finally showed up around 7:30. It was early summer, so it was still light, and would be for a while..... Hey, glad you could make it.... Let's get out of here and get something to eat. You're in the city now. You don't want to spend all night hanging out in this stuffy place.... For all his wealth, he was still very down to earth.

They took a short cab ride to one of his favorite restaurants, a nice unpretentious place with a full bar and great food. Impressively, as far as Janet was concerned, he seemed to know everyone there...... Wow, you're popular..... Sarcastically, Ahhh shucks.... He honestly wasn't trying to show off. Janet knew him too well for that anyway... This was just a place he and his friends liked to hang out, so here he was popular. Plus, he was just a fun friendly guy that people naturally liked, and they were having a good time as he introduced her around.... A few of his friends she'd met before under other random circumstances....

They had a good meal and a few drinks before leaving again several hours later. After another short cab ride, they were in the SoHo arts district where it was always fun to mill around and maybe do a little bar hopping. Walking the streets of New York was never boring. The contrast between this and where she'd been a couple of days earlier was very entertaining.... The social energy was palpable, it was vibrating in the air....

Finally, after a long enjoyable evening, they made their way home just after 2:00 a.m. and soon retired to their rooms. Or, perhaps more accurately, Janet retired to a guest suite- a big room with its own deluxe bathroom, deluxe bed, and even a couch and big screen TV. She opened the curtains that were drawn over the big wall-length windows and looked out over the city for a few minutes before turning out the lights and climbing into bed....Wow, I understand why Mark likes living here so much..... Not bad....

The next morning when she woke up, he was in the middle of making them both a nice breakfast. There were bacon, eggs, pancakes and, most importantly, a ready pot of hot coffee..... So, did you sleep well?.... Yes, thank you very much. I'd almost forgotten how nice your little guest room is there... You really do have an awesome place here Mark..... Well thank you, you know you're welcome anytime... So I was thinking about our day. I figured since you don't make to the city all that often maybe we should do some of the typical New York stuff? We could go to the Met and maybe another museum or two. And then tonight I thought we might catch a Broadway show if you'd like? I have a friend who can probably get us tickets to see anything...... Sure, that sounds great, thank you. Show me the New York you love....

The Met has one of the most incredible art collections in the country. A true art lover could spend days there, but a few hours was fun too. They both appreciated art, and it was fun seeing works by all the big names, paintings by Picasso and Kandinsky, sculptures by Brancusi and David Smith...

At one point, Janet spent a considerable amount of time just standing and staring at one of Smith's large stainless steel pieces of randomly attached geometric shapes. The first thought that came to her mind was how much fun it must have been to work on.... He must have had a great time building this thing... Then she thought about one of Picasso's cubist paintings she'd seen only a few moments earlier and wondered how consciously he must have been influenced by it...... It seemed there was an obvious and relevant connection..... Hmmm, didn't these people always think about their work in the context of what others were doing just previously? It was an interesting observation, and, with that thought, they moved on. One of them suggested a cup of coffee, and they both agreed the café sounded good.....

.... You know, Janet, it's getting kind of late in the afternoon. I was thinking that, instead of killing ourselves trying to squeeze in whatever else, maybe we should just relax and go for a walk in the park. It's just right across the street.... You know you're welcome to stay as long as want. Maybe you can go exploring around the city later, when I'm working...... Sure, whatever, that sounds good to me. I'm in no big hurry to do anything. As far as I'm concerned, we're having a great day. I'm perfectly happy to keep following your lead, Mark....

The weather was beautiful and Central Park was a great place to be.... For a moment, she found it amusingly ironic that most New Yorkers thought the park was the best place in the city too... Here were all these millions of people claiming they loved the fast-paced city life, and yet they couldn't wait for some free time to get out into this huge open expanse of beautiful trees.... But then she thought about it a little more, and maybe it did make sense after all..... It gave people the opportunity to think they were getting the best of both worlds..... To each his own....

.....I'm really glad you suggested this little trip Mark. This is fun.... So, anyway, I've been thinking about what you said about my book and trying to figure out where you were coming from.... Maybe you were right? Maybe I should at least give it some more thought.... Although I've been thinking about something else too.... What if I wrote a book of short stories and the Mars thing was only one of several or more...? Sure, Janet, whatever, but you know I was just giving you what immediately came to mind, and that's what you want from me. That's just the plain and simple of our professional relationship....which isn't saying that this "space" thing isn't what you should go with if that's really what you want to do.... I was simply trying to make the point that it wouldn't necessarily be easy, and it would be very hard to tell if something like that would be well received by your fan base.... It would be really foreign to them... Essentially you'd be trying to push into a completely different market, and science fiction is a very long way from anything you've ever done before.... It would catch people off guard for sure, but maybe that's one of those big risks you're legitimately willing to take?..... I'm a numbers guy to a large degree, Janet. You've always been the more adventurous risk-taking type......but I will be supportive both personally and professionally of whatever you decide to do...... Thanks, Mark...I appreciate all that. It's good food for thought.... She laughed.... Now I'm more confused than ever, but that's ok.... Yes, it is Ok, but in the meantime we should start thinking about tonight. I've got us tickets to something. I can't even remember what the name of it is, but I'm sure it'll be fun. It's Broadway! It's always exciting just being there... And of course it was...

After another long great day, they were back at Mark's place by the wee hours of the morning, tired and ready to get some sleep. Janet went to her room and took a long hot shower under the massaging shower head reminiscing about the day. She couldn't help thinking about the conversations on her writing. She really did appreciate Mark's frankness. The fact that he didn't mince words was a good thing.... Hmmm, what to do?...More and more, she was liking the idea of a book of short stories.... That might be more fun anyway, and besides, it would spread out the weight. The book's success wouldn't be riding on the shoulders of a single idea....

The shower itself felt amazing. It was so relaxing she almost fell asleep standing up; and, not long after, the big bed and deep covers were like jumping onto a cloud..... She left the curtains open to get one last glimpse of the city before the deep sleep that quickly followed.... It felt incredibly good to be exactly where she was...... although, sometime later, she abruptly woke up for no apparent reason....

Glancing at the clock on the nightstand, a little over an hour had passed since she'd first lay down.... Hmmm, that's strange. Suddenly and unexplainably she was wide awake, and there was something strange in the air, something very present but impossible to define.... Wow, this is kind of bizarre?.... She sat up and looked around the room... Everything was in its proper place. The city skyline was lit up and twinkling, but at the same instant, still and silent. Not knowing what to do, she didn't do anything for a few minutes.... Everything was almost too still, contradicting the unexplainable energy permeating everything around her. It was very eerie. She couldn't see it or hear it, and she could barely feel it, but there it was nonetheless.....it and seemed to be traveling in waves.... It was very odd, and a little unnerving.... As the sensations grew stronger, the hair on the back of her neck stood up and a chill ran down her spine. She decided to stand up. Taking a few tentative steps, she slowly moved toward the center of the room... What the hell's going on?... She just stood there for a second before suddenly noticing herself in the big mirror above the dresser. She made some slight and subtle movements, slowly turning her head one way, then the other. Something wasn't quite right. Her reflection was ever so slightly out of sync with her actual movements, or was it just her imagination.....? She stood there longer, slowly lifting her arms and lowering them again. She couldn't tell, maybe it was just a case of an overactive mind. She'd had plenty to think about that day..... Maybe she was getting carried away....? Ok, calm down.....

After a moment, she figured she'd take the opportunity to use the restroom. Turning a light on seemed to help. A few minutes later when she came back out, it seemed possible everything was back to normal..... Hmmm, interesting....? Twenty minutes later she was sound asleep again...

At breakfast, she felt a little silly trying to explain all of this to Mark, but the fact that she mentioned it at all was a testimony to how close their friendship was. It would have been very easy never to say a word about it..... However, his response was a strangely pleasant surprise, because he wasn't surprised at all..... Oh, it sounds like you may have had a little run-in with Billy.... Mark was smiling...... Don't worry, he's harmless...... Billy, who the hell is Billy?..... Apparently he's our resident ghost....William Winters..... When this building was being built back in the forties, there was a fatal accident. Apparently William fell from this floor, although nobody is completely sure about that little detail, because there are stories about him from all over the building...... REALLY? What do you mean? What kind of stories?...... Well, a lot of stories like the one you just told, a strange energy or presence. Some people have claimed to hear him talking as he moved though a room when nobody else was there. A few have even claimed they've seen him just walk by only to disappear into a wall..... Oh yea..... people have been talking about this guy for years. It sounds like he may have even paid you a little visit last night, but I wouldn't worry about it. He's never caused any trouble..... Wow! Well that's kind of fun. I was visited by the resident ghost..... Have you ever had any experiences with him....? I'm not sure, maybe, nothing too overt though. But I have gotten the strange feeling I wasn't the only one in the room at times. I guess I've just assumed it was him.... I've even said hello.... Hey Billy, how ya doin'? I've never spent much time thinking about it though...

....So anyway, I have to go in and get a little work done today. I was thinking that, if you want, I can make a couple of calls and get you into a book signing tomorrow.... You don't have to, of course, but I thought you might have fun mingling with some of your people.... Hmmm, sure, I would like to do that.... Ok great.... You know how it works. I'll call one of my favorite busy bookstores downtown and set it up. Then I'll call a couple of local radio stations and get some talk show guys to mention it on the air. Before you know it, there'll be a line of people out the door....He smiled... I love hooking up my writers, everybody wins.... In the meantime, you should get out and goof off in the city today.... You know as well as anybody there are endless ways to keep yourself entertained here….. Yes I do know, and I will. That all sounds great, and thanks again for everything… Ah shucks, ain't nothin'…. Whatever you decide to do, have an awesome day!

As Mark left, she sat down in one of two big leather living-room chairs facing the wall- sized window that overlooked the park. It truly was an incredible view. Briefly she wondered how much his apartment must be worth, millions for sure. She got another cup of coffee and sat down again…. This is awesome!… There was no reason to rush into anything; and, on top of that, she was curious. Maybe Billy would make another appearance? Now that she knew he was around, she at least wanted to give him another chance…. But after an enjoyable and relaxing hour or so, he hadn't taken the opportunity…. Ok, so maybe I should get up and do something…?

Walking at a brisk pace, it was nice to be outside moving through such a great American city. She could almost taste the incredible opportunity all around her. It was amazing. People from all over the world were happy to be taking advantage of our free and capitalist society. Many were smiling and doing their best to fulfill their own American dreams. Occasionally, it was good to simply appreciate how lucky she was to live in such a great country.

She had no idea where she was going and it didn't seem to matter. It was just fun to be there, and a destination didn't seem important. Strolling by the park again seemed natural, and a squirrel briefly approached. It came within a few feet, stood up on its hind legs, and made eye contact as if asking for a bite to eat. She didn't have anything, and wished she did, but it was a fun little moment anyway… She kept moving…. There were people walking and talking and running, people selling things to eat and drink from handy little carts. There were cars and taxis passing by….. New York was not exactly a quiet place to be…

Hailing a cab, she decided Time Square seemed like a good destination. After all, as a tourist in New York, wasn't a person almost obligated? The driver, whose country of origin she couldn't quite determine, was friendly, and soon she was there. It was a very busy place, with thousands of people, most of whom seemed to have some very important place they needed to be. It was a little crazy, but exciting, as she ducked into a crowded little restaurant to get a bite to eat. Sitting at a lunch counter, she ordered a sandwich and was impressed with how good it was. The guy sitting next to her started a pleasant conversation. She told him about who she was and why she was there, and he turned out to be a fan. They talked for a while before parting ways, and she thought, wow, that never gets old! It's so much fun to be appreciated just for being you, which led to thinking about the next day's book signing. She called Mark to see if he had any details yet, but he didn't pick up. Oh, well, she'd find out soon enough.

Several entertaining hours later, she decided to take the subway back towards his building; and, by late afternoon, she was home again. Mark wasn't there yet, which she'd assumed would be the case. The thought of having his huge luxurious apartment all to herself was nice. The cold beer that was easy enough to find in the refrigerator made it even nicer as one of the big brown chairs by the window also welcomed her back. Looking out over the tremendous energy of the city from this cushy hideaway in the sky was a great place to be, and she toasted Billy sitting in the chair opposite. She laughed... She didn't actually see him of course. But, strangely, he did seem to be there; and now that she knew who he was, she liked the idea. Although, several minutes later when she heard the refrigerator door open and bottles of beer rattling on the door, she wasn't so sure.... Holy Crap! Did I really just hear that? She laughed again, this time with considerable more trepidation.... Very tentatively, she got up to have a look.... Sure enough, the door was open by a few inches.... Hmmm.... Billy?.....Billy?.... Are you there?.... I guess if I were going to toast you, I should have at least offered you a beer first, huh?..... Chuckling, she grabbed herself another one and shut the door... Wow, that was weird.... As she sat back down, she realized the feeling of the whole day had changed. For a few minutes, all she could think about was the possible presence of Billy the ghost... Was there really the spirit of a dead construction worker in the room?.... It was fun, in a tense and scary kind of way.... Then Mark walked in the door, and it was all released as he asked about her day..... Hey Mark, yea I had a great day, and on top of that, I'm pretty sure I was just having a little chat with your neighborhood ghost. He might have even opened your refrigerator. Either that, or I was imagining things and I accidentally left it open myself, which is entirely possible... Anyway, how was your day?.... It was great!.... And tomorrow you're going to have a great day too..... He was so excited to tell her about the next day's signing that the ghost conversation was completely dropped...

It turned out he was right to be excited. The signing was great! Just like he said he would, he had lined up on very short notice what turned out to be a great event. It was very impressive, both on his part, and on hers. His ability to rally a little press so quickly and her ability to draw fans were a good combination…When she arrived at the bookstore there was a life-size cardboard cutout of her with a list of all her books, which was always a strange thing to see. It was just some generic promotional material that had been printed up months earlier for such occasions. Nevertheless, it always felt odd to be presented with herself in such a unique fashion.

A group of people had already gathered in anticipation of her arrival, books in hand, looking forward to getting an autograph. Plus they were just happy to see her and lit up when she walked in. There was nothing not to like about that. It felt good to be appreciated. Typically, she could go walking down any street in any town in America and not be recognized. So, on the occasions when she and her fans were united for one reason or another, it truly was a mutual appreciation. She was happy to talk to people, answer their questions, and even listen to lengthy stories about their own lives and travels. In fact, she could easily get carried away, and employees at the store sometimes had to butt-in to make sure the line kept moving. For the most part, people understood and appreciated the brief time they did get. At the end of the scheduled five-hour signing, she stuck around for a while anyway, just to chat and sign a few more books. It was a great day for everyone involved, and she'd made a few bucks in the process. Janet Myles had satisfied a number of her fans and herself in the process. That was what counted….

A couple of days later, after having spent another fun day hanging out with Mark, she found herself back at her own beloved home in Knoxville. The trip to the big city had been great fun, but it felt good to be home……. mostly because she was inspired to start writing again. The thought of writing short stories was intriguing; and, strangely, she was feeling somewhat stimulated by her knowledge and experience of Billy the ghost. Not that she necessarily wanted to write about him specifically, but he'd simply given her a pause to think about the subject. It was interesting. Maybe she'd pick up the Mars' story again later?…. But on this beautiful morning out on her deck, she started working on something else….

Hmmm, a first person ghost story of sorts…. That might be fun?

TWELVE

As she opened her computer and turned it on, she contemplated her own death and how it might lead into this little story. There were, of course, a limitless number of ways to die, so there was definitely some room to get creative. However, it was also true that the method of her death really wasn't all that important given the direction she was headed, but it was fun to think about it for a few minutes nonetheless….. She thought about the possibility of a big meteor hitting her in the middle of an open field somewhere late at night… That would be funny… Then again, maybe she could be hit by a fast-moving train, or, on the other hand, it didn't even matter if it was moving fast. A slow moving train could cut her in half just as easily. Either way, that would be funny too….. Then, after considering it a little further, she decided maybe it wasn't supposed to be funny. And, again, since it wasn't that important to the story anyway, she decided to give herself a massive heart attack in the middle of the night while sleeping comfortably in her bed…. It was a perfect and peaceful way to go… And, with that, she put her fingers on the keyboard.

My bedroom suddenly became very vividly alive, as if I could literally feel the energy in every atom of every piece of furniture, every object, even in the molecules in the air. It was incredible, and it took a moment for the thought "why?" to even make itself known. Why was this happening? Or, perhaps an even better question, "what" was in fact happening? I was having the most incredible experience and feelings I could ever remember. And then, finally, it dawned on me to wonder- wonder about a possible explanation. I wasn't dreaming? In fact, if anything, I was more conscious than I had ever been in my entire life. What was going on?….. Whatever it was, it was awesome! It was the most unexplainably joyous feeling…… Maybe it was ok to just relax and enjoy it for a second, just stop and appreciate the moment?…. Ok, everything seems fine…. Then, slowly, things started becoming clear….

The first clue was that, as I was standing in the center of the room, I began to realize my eye line was slightly higher than I was tall- as if I were standing on a stack of books or a small stool. I looked down. Sure enough, there I was, dressed in my pajamas just the way I'd been when I went to bed. And then, as I noticed my feet on the floor, I realized my line of sight had suddenly dropped to where it normally was… Hmmm, that's strange… and I slowly started to turn around. Still feeling the most vibrantly alive I'd ever felt, I noticed myself lying on the bed. I was standing at the foot of my bed looking at myself in the bed sleeping…. And then it hit me…. How can I be standing here looking at myself over there? Maybe myself on the bed wasn't sleeping at all? It was a stunning realization! Then, as I looked down again at the body I thought I was standing in, nothing was there for a few seconds. I was conscious in empty space; and, as I realized this, my body suddenly reappeared, almost as if it made it easier to imagine it was there for the time being. It was funny. I wasn't scared at all, just amazed. In fact, I was overwhelmed with a sense of fun whimsical power, as if suddenly anything was possible. I jumped off the floor and simply stayed there, hovering. Wow! This is incredible! I decided to move around the room, floating over here, over there. I went up to a corner of the ceiling and just looked around, the endless potential of this new circumstance slowly coming into focus.

Briefly, I pondered my body on the bed that I was now sure was dead; and, for the first time, it dawned on me that I could never go back. My existence and reality as Janet Myles was now over; and it was briefly sad, difficult to let go for a second. For a brief moment, I worried about my friends and family who would have to grieve my passing, but then, a much deeper understanding began to well up inside me. I suddenly became aware of what might be described as a large pool of universal wisdom and knowledge that was now mine to drink from- for everyone to drink from….. Amazingly, it had always been there, just much more difficult to tap into as a living human form; but it was always there just beneath the surface of everyone's day-to-day reality….. Now, without the restrictions of a human body, I suddenly had full access. I realized that ultimately the people I knew would have access, too; and my physical death was only a brief setback from which they were meant to learn something about the wonderful, fleeting, transient nature of everything….. and they'd all be joining me in this experience soon enough. Everything was fine, and my lingering attachment to myself didn't seem to last long…

I wanted to start finding out what this was truly all about. I wanted to start exploring the limitless freedom I now knew was at my disposal. I floated up through the ceiling, through the attic and roof, and hovered above my house. I looked down at it, down at my beautiful yard and neighborhood that I had loved so much. I floated higher and looked out over the entire city. It was incredible; and then, understanding that I was a part of something so much bigger yet, I flew straight up to an altitude of hundreds of miles above the earth. The view was spectacular! Knowing that all I had to do was conceive of wanting to go anywhere to make it so, I sped off in orbit around our beautiful blue planet. Laughing to myself, I thought, wow! I feel like a super hero. This is amazing!…. Then I dove back down through the atmosphere, deciding to slow things down a little again.

Gently floating a few thousand feet above the South American rain forest, I decided to descend to a big rock on the bank of the remote upper Amazon. It was a beautiful sunlit morning, and the roar of the river pouring though a rapid was casting out mist that was casting up rainbows. Just for the fun of it, I imagined I was in my body again; and it appeared. Now, I was sitting on the rock with my legs crossed, looking at my extraordinary surroundings and smiling. I could see my body again, and it was interesting and comfortable. I realized I could have imagined myself in any form, but since this was the one I'd most recently known, it simply felt easy and natural. So there I was, Janet, able to instantly transport myself anywhere, loving my rocky perch in the Amazon.

The environment was beautiful in its own transient form, and I was keenly aware of everything about it- the resonance of the water, the sounds of the birds and numerous other creatures. But I was now capable of feeling it on a much deeper level as well. Again, I realized I was aware of things more profoundly than I'd ever been capable of as Janet. Right down to the atomic level and below, I could feel the pulsing vibrant energy that made up literally everything. I was a part of that energy, capable of interacting with it in ways I couldn't have imagined, ways that would have been impossible to believe until suddenly knowing it to be true….. I decided to melt into the rock on which I was sitting and visually watched it happen, laughing like a giddy school girl as it did. Suddenly I was the rock and could feel its presence from the inside out. I could feel and understand that I'd been there for millions of years- but even in this form, I was transient in nature. I was ever so slowly eroding away, becoming grains of sand to perhaps become part of a beautiful beach someday. It was awesome! And with that thought, I rose out of the rock again and slowly started making my way downstream.

Floating only a few feet above the water, I glided out of the spectacular mountains that were the river's source, and it slowly started to mellow. As the geography flattened, the sounds of life in the jungle surrounding became more keenly apparent. There were thousands of species of flora and fauna all closely interwoven in this mystical web of life. Each was dependent on all the others in ways impossible for any individual to understand in its present form. But now, as pure conscious spirit, I could sense the underlying oneness. I could literally feel that one universal source. It was much more than just a conceptual understanding. It was at once plainly simple and universally complex, and it was just so. Stated simply, it was wonderful! And I started spinning through the air, becoming the air, before diving beneath the surface of the water to become part of the awe-inspiring Amazon.

There, I was surrounded by a grayish-brown hue. The silt that was a natural part of the river due to the never-ending erosion process made it opaque, forcing the creatures therein to use and adapt senses far beyond sight. I could feel this, too, and I understood. There were tiny vibrations of sound and movement that, if felt sensitively enough, created an image of the surrounding area much like a visual. And of course the river was teeming with life, everything from millions of microscopic species, to a huge variety of fish, reptiles, amphibians, and even mammals. It was a thriving ecosystem for sure; but, from the perspective of an individual in this environment, it was a potentially very dangerous place to be. Existence here for any life form was precarious. I was closely witnessing this as creatures were constantly devouring each other all around all the time. It was the great circle of life. I could even briefly feel the spiritual nature of a fish as it instantly lost its life to another. Its energy would escape into the environment before quickly blending into other life forms around it; and I understood this eat-or-be-eaten existence not as something sad or frightening, but rather as a humming harmonious chord of life energy. It was all functioning like a well-oiled machine, if the crude analogy can be excused.....

The power of the river itself was enormous. As I became a part of it, its remarkable energy spun and pulsated as it created eddies and whirlpools. As a whole, it was of course moving downstream. But strangely and simultaneously, it was also moving in any and every other direction as well. I could feel that the river itself was alive, a life force that seemed to have a playful personality of its own…. As a living person, I'd always been attracted to water, moving streams and rivers, as most people are, but this was giving me a new understanding of why. I think in many cases the rivers liked us, too, or were at least relating to us in ways we never fully understood. As human forms we're mostly made of water ourselves and, therefore, related to the life force of a moving body of water. It even makes sense conceptually.

However, everything I was experiencing about all of this was far more than conceptual.

It was exhilarating being in the river, of the river, as I noticed a large anaconda swimming nearby. It must have been over twenty feet long and moved very gracefully through the water. As I watched it, I became increasingly curious about its motive. So I stayed with it for a while. I got in front of it as it moved and looked into its eyes, wondering about its obvious mission. My curiosity increasing, it suddenly dawned on me that I could simply become the snake, not in an intrusive way, but just go inside its head and observe its thoughts as it moved. So I did. I got behind its eyes… I quieted my own thoughts so I could become more acutely aware of his, and it was fascinating. I was swimming through the Amazon as a giant anaconda in search of its next meal. As I let my own consciousness slowly dissolve into his, nothing but prey mattered. It was an extremely focused way to be in the world. My entire existence consisted of perceiving my surroundings in search of clues. I moved with extreme intension, flicking my tongue out into the water to taste, feel, and smell every movement around me. I had a deep, almost subconscious feeling of extreme purpose in life. My purpose was life itself- simply to survive was my only responsibility, and I was good at it. I was fine-tuned to fulfill this purpose, feeling the millions of years of evolution that had led me to my current perfection…. Suddenly there was harsh splashing, a vibration I could feel from well over a hundred feet away. With incredible speed, I moved in that direction… A small monkey had fallen out of a tree and was scrambling toward the shore trying to get himself out of the water, but he would never make it. Without even thinking about it, without even having time to think about it, I grabbed his tail in my mouth and instantly wrapped myself around his comparably frail little body and started squeezing. I could feel the giant muscle that was my body tense up as it crushed him. I could feel his tiny little bones crunching as he exhaled for the last time, his life force slowly surrendering to its fate. It was incredible! I felt nothing but gratification, much like the satisfaction you experience when the waiter shows up at your table with your order. There was no remorse of any kind in what I was doing. It was simply the natural way of things. And, as I slowly exited the situation, I now had a more keen, firsthand, understanding of this. I even sensed the monkey's energy and knew he somehow understood too. There was no bitterness towards the snake. The monkey simply moved on as well….

Slowly floating upward, I continued to contemplate my endless options… What should I do now, next?…. The possibilities were exciting, yet there was no hurry to do anything. I could feel eternity in both directions, both past and future, but with no sense of urgency... It was very strange, but I felt completely calm and yet extremely excited all at the same time. Then, gradually, my next move came to me...

Realizing it was midwinter in the southern hemisphere, I decided to head south towards Antarctica. I thought it would be fun to see the South Pole in its most harsh state, and the next thing I knew, I was there. In an instant, I had willed it to be. In many ways, the pole was the bizarre environment I'd expected. First and foremost, it was of course extremely cold- well over a hundred degrees below zero. I could feel it, too, but in a very neutral way. It wasn't uncomfortable, just interesting being in the deep freeze, where every direction was north. It was dark around the clock but the "always night" sky was the clearest I'd ever seen. There were more stars shining more brightly than I'd ever contemplated. It was easy to simply look up and around absorbing it all, and then I noticed something I'd nearly forgotten. Amidst all this remote tranquility, there was a large manmade structure- the research station. Wow, what a cool place for these people to be? (pun almost intended) I remembered that, as Janet, I'd always wanted to go but had never gotten the opportunity. I had been on the continent but had never made it all the way to the pole. Now, recalling all of this, I was even more excited and decided to drift inside. There was only a handful of people there during this roughest part of the year, and they all happened to be sitting down for a meal. It was ham and rice and canned vegetables (not bad considering where they were), and they all seemed to be enjoying it well enough. Observing, I slowly drifted around the room, curious about their mutual circumstances. They were all scientists of course, studying things like climate, climate change, and simply what it was like to inhabit such a place. No doubt, they must have all been very interesting people in their own right.... Then I considered myself again.... and became aware of others new to this spiritual realm who'd also been curiously drawn to this place....

For the first time, it became overtly apparent that others were sharing in this same experience. It seems obvious but, until this moment, it had all been so joyfully overwhelming that I hadn't taken the time to think about it. Of course there would be others. It turns out that, as spiritual beings, we're all very naturally curious. And, strangely, many of us are curious about the poles soon after our own physical demise, like we want to see for ourselves what the most remote and harsh places on this beautiful planet are like. And, since it's so easy to do, we briefly congregate at the places that would first come to mind. The poles are naturally at the top of that list, along with locations such as the summit of Mt Everest, inside the great pyramids, and the deepest ocean trenches. So there I was, for the first time fully aware of others like myself, newly departed from the physical realm. It was fun, but oddly not social the way we would normally think of being social with those we've never met. There were no false masks, no awkward moments of shyness or social tension. In a way, it was like we'd all always known each other, and there was no need to even discuss it. It felt good just to be in each other's presence, completely exposed for everything we were- and it didn't matter. It felt extremely good. In this new reality, it really was reality, and there was no need for pretense of any kind...

Again I wondered about the human inhabitants of this place. I wondered if they had any inkling we were there. They must have felt something? This place was so full of spiritual energy that they had to be aware of us on some level. How were they aware of us? What, if any, was their understanding of what was happening here...? It was amusing to think about actually. There must have been "ghost stories" of some kind. Hopefully they were fun ghost stories. The energy here was definitely benevolent. It was peaceful, even joyful. There was certainly nothing harmful in any of it. So, if there were ghost stories, I sincerely hoped they were pleasant and entertaining and not frightening in any way. And then, for the first time, I wondered how, if at all, we could interact with the physical world. Were ghost stories actually true? Was it somehow possible to make our presence known to living breathing people? It was a good question... and I just stood still and observed for a while. Those like myself were coming and going from all over the world; but, from what I could tell, the people who actually lived here were completely oblivious. I wondered if they'd want to know? Were there any subtle hints that we were there with them? Maybe there were those who were more sensitive to it than others? If there were clues, what were they exactly?

I started to experiment.... I moved through the people sitting around the table, trying to see if they could somehow sense that I was there. They didn't seem to.... Then, I thought about some of the surrounding objects. There was a mustard bottle on the kitchen counter, and I hovered around it trying to figure out if there was some way to manipulate it. I pictured myself in my body again. I looked at my hand and tried to grip the bottle, but nothing happened. My hand became the bottle and mustard rather than having any external effect on it. I tried again, only this time with more of a slapping motion, as if I were trying to knock it down. Again, nothing.... Hmmm, interesting....? It seemed that, if there were a way to make yourself known, it might take a while to understand..... And then something occurred to me..........

Having spent the better part of my own life in the southeastern United States, I recalled there had always been hundreds of ghost stories from all of the old Civil War battle grounds. Maybe that would be a good place to look for my own clues? So, I left- intent on finding some answers.....

Upon arriving, I went to a site well known for such occurrences; and, sure enough, the place was rippling with spiritual activity. There were many like myself who were just curious about the location. But others were there for different reasons. There were the kind we'd always heard about as living people, and it turned out to be exactly true. It seemed there were certain individuals who were more aware of the spiritual reality than others, those who were capable of conveying a universal truth that had been passed down through the ages through mythology. In other words, some ghost stories actually were true, and the people who propagated these stories were, for all practical purposes, correct about how they came to be. Some who cross the boundary between the physical and the spiritual realm do so reluctantly. Perhaps their physical death had come in a way that felt unjust, untimely, or maybe they simply weren't ready to go yet and strongly resisted it? For them, this was very unfortunate, because it meant they were unable to surrender to the beauty of the next reality- a reality that was ready to welcome and embrace them if they could simply understand that it was there for their choosing. It was much the same as when some people have unpleasant things happen to them in the physical world and then spend the rest of their lives defending the choice to be miserable because of it. For whatever reason, they decide that being unhappy and making those around them unhappy is a reasonable thing to do, and this same circumstance can occur in death. Ghosts are beings who resist the reality of their situation and, therefore, cannot seem to move past it. They continue to relive the circumstances of their death instead of just accepting it and moving forward. Being a ghost is being spiritually neurotic, if you will; and, here on the battle grounds of the Civil War, I was witnessing it for myself. There were soldiers who had died under gruesome circumstances, fighting for a cause they deeply believed in, and they'd somehow gotten trapped in this reality, unable to let it go. It was fascinating; but, if the word "sad" applied to anything I'd witnessed so far since my own death, this was it. But I assumed that even this was a transient reality, and they would eventually figure it out. So I just watched and tried to reason for myself exactly what was happening. Could I interact with these individuals who seemed to be caught somewhere in the middle? I decided to attempt to make my presence known.... But then something very interesting happened. At the exact same moment I tried to reach across, I first noticed the **LIGHT**.... It was amazing.... and a further enlightenment to my own situation. This circumstance, like all others, also had a duality.... There were polar opposites.... I knew immediately what the light meant and what it represented. And yet, on my other side, there were those still caught in the misery of death itself....

It was wonderful to realize that I still had so much to learn.....

THIRTEEN

She sat back in her chair, feeling good about herself. Taking occasional breaks along the way, nearly twelve hours had passed since she first sat down; and now, a fun chapter later, she wondered where it had even come from. Whatever had just happened, it was pretty intense, and she'd loved every minute of it. She'd written and written and written- and, somewhat oddly, it had even seemed to come fairly easily. It was the most fun she'd had writing in a long time. She thought, WOW! That's exactly what I knew writing fiction could be like. It was very strange- it almost seemed as if the story had come from somewhere beyond her..... Hmmm?

The sun was just falling below the horizon, and it was a beautiful clear summer evening. Just for the fun of it, she printed the chapter so she could more easily kick back in one of the deck loungers to have a look at it.

As she went carefully over the pages, they were as exciting as when she'd written them, which seemed like a good sign. This was good stuff, and she wondered, even hoped, that there may have even been some truth to it. This was the most reasonable explanation of a death experience she'd ever heard, and it had come from her. It was fascinating actually because, before today, she'd never really taken the time to think about it all that seriously. Sure, it had crossed her mind; and, in the past, she'd read about different religious perspectives on the subject out of curiosity. But this was different. It was exciting! While she'd never actually feared death, this almost made it sound like fun…… Not that she wanted to die anytime soon of course. Like most people, she hoped to live a long and fulfilling life and, up to this point, she'd been doing exactly that. But nonetheless, the story of being a giant snake in the Amazon was very entertaining, even thought provoking. Could we really have the opportunity to choose such experiences someday….?

As with any first draft, she noticed a few issues with grammar, spelling, and the occasional missing word. She'd always found it amusing that her brain could be thinking a word that never actually made it to the page as she was writing the sentence…. What was going on there? But, these were all little issues that could easily be dealt with later… She chuckled to herself….. It was always funny to think about how long it took to write what takes such a short amount of time read… She hoped readers everywhere appreciated their writers, whatever that meant…?

As it got dark, she finally went inside, made a little dinner, and sat down in front of the television. A tall glass of ice water, an egg sandwich, and a few baby carrots hit the spot as she sank into the couch with the remote. She caught a little news and watched a show about a guy who filmed himself supposedly "surviving" in the wilderness. It was entertaining but seemed a bit suspicious. A catering truck was probably within a few hundred yards….

The next morning, she climbed out of bed knowing most of this day would be spent at her computer. She was on a roll and certainly didn't want to stop now. After grabbing a piece of fruit and the obvious cup of hot coffee, she went out to the deck and sat down under the big umbrella. The first hour or so was spent doing a fairly thorough first edit of the chapter she'd written the day before, and it seemed the sensible thing was to continue the story. It was a good one for sure, one that obviously wasn't finished yet, so she knew she would be coming back to it at some point. It would be fun seeing where it eventually led. But for now, something else seemed to be tugging at her.

There were no immediate examples in her life, and it wasn't something she had ever thought much about. But maybe she really was on a role? Maybe now, she was suddenly being used to relate thoughts that had been on a lot of people's minds collectively? Maybe she was somehow serving as a vessel of sorts? Wow, what a heavy thought. But maybe it was true, maybe it was always true of creative thought, and she was simply doing a better job of channeling it now out of a simple willingness to do so? And, although it had no immediate relevance to her personally, there was a story that almost seemed it "wanted" to be written... It was interesting.... As she surrendered to it, she wrote the first words at the top of the page in the form of a question... The Amiable Divorce?...

Kathy and Brian Buckler had been married for twenty-one years, and most of it had been quite good. They had three kids: Todd, 19, and two girls, Kimberly, 18, and Carla, 15. They were all well-behaved, well-rounded young people, and their parents were proud of them all. The fact that they had such good kids was evidence they were good parents, which in turn seemed to prove that, for the most part, they must have had a good marriage too...

They had a nice house in the suburbs, and both were successful in their chosen careers as sales people. Brian sold real-estate and Kathy high-end cars. Between the two of them they made a very nice living, so money wasn't a problem. Whatever the issue was, it had nothing to do with the surface things people usually blame for their divorces. In fact, they really didn't even dislike each other and had a deep and mutual respect for one another. They were both intelligent interesting human beings who could hold a good conversation. Both had a strong sense of moral responsibility to the world in which they lived and had done well in relating that to their children. They were good people who knew bringing a positive energy to the world was an important thing to do in life. Certainly neither of them had a mean or cruel bone and would never do anything to intentionally hurt anybody..... So what was it then? Why now, after such a long good run, were they both willing to walk away from their marriage? Don't good people always stay together no matter what? According to society, isn't that always the "right" thing to do?....

Perhaps that wasn't always true? In fact, for the first time in either of their lives, it seemed entirely plausible that it wasn't even natural... Maybe nature hadn't set it up that way at all, and those who did manage to stay happily together for a lifetime were the true exceptions that made the rule.... HAPPILY obviously being the key and catch word in such a concept, because everyone has known couples who for one reason or another stayed together miserably.... However, Brian and Kathy were both mentally balanced enough to not want any part of that type of situation. They were very lucky in that they both realized at basically the same time their relationship had run its course and it might be time to part ways. The way they understood it, it was a very enlightened position, but one of them would have to bring it up first....

One evening when they were alone, Kathy mentioned to Brian what she was sure he already knew.... You know, Brian, things aren't exactly the way they used to be between us..... Yes, of course I know, and I'm so glad one of us finally had the nerve to say something.... Wow, what a great response.... and it was the beginning of one the most honest and real conversations they'd had in a long time... They discussed how much fun they'd had together in the past and what a good job they'd both done raising their kids, giving each other the credit they each fairly deserved. They even talked about how they still loved each other in the truest sense of the word, meaning they definitely wished each other the best in life. Each genuinely wanted the other to truly be happy. The problem was, if there indeed was a problem, they just didn't feel the need to be married anymore. Both just felt that their lives could be lived in more fulfilling ways under different circumstances. Their marriage had in many ways been a great experience for both of them; but now, a good many years since the beginning, it seemed it was probably time to switch gears. They both knew this to be true, and they smiled and cried and hugged each other as they discussed it... Wow, they were really going to get a divorce..... Now, the next big step would be telling their kids...

Several days later they managed to get the whole family together for a meeting, both acknowledging how potentially stressful this could be if not handled very delicately. As they gathered in the living room, it was obvious something was up, but the kids had absolutely no idea what it was all about. Brian started, as the tension in the room rose......Your mother and I have some interesting news, and neither of us wants you to be alarmed.... The thing is, we've been doing some talking lately, and it seems there are going to be some changes in our family. But, first and foremost, we both want you to know we love you all very much..... In a way, it was a fairly cliché speech to begin with, the only possible difference being, it was entirely genuine..... Kathy chimed in..... The thing is your father and I have had a lot of good years together, but it seems our relationship is entering another phase.... We still love and respect each other very much, but we're both feeling the need to move on, that's all. We'd both be happier if we could simply move in our own separate directions, and so that's what we're planning to do.... Brian interjected...... The bottom line is we don't want to beat around the bush about this. Your mother and I are getting a divorce.....

Of course this came as quite a shock.... None of the kids had any idea it was coming. For all they knew, they could have been announcing that they were about to adopt a kid from some third world country, or maybe planning a great family vacation.....? A divorce was the last thing they expected. As far as they were concerned, their parents had always had a great marriage. For them, this seemed to come completely out of the blue. What the hell's going on? Can this be true? No question, it was hard news to digest. Of course it was- kids don't want to hear that their parents are getting divorced. However, as it slowly started sinking in, they at least tried to understand....

They had a lot of questions..... How long have you guys been thinking about this? Are you sure this is what you really want to do......? They were emotional questions at first, an attempt to understand if it was really happening..... It was happening, and their parents went on to explain that this didn't have to be a negative event for any of them. It was simply a matter of perspective that needed to be hashed through. They explained that society, through religious and other social institutions, had often put a false emphasis on lifelong monogamy that simply didn't make sense for everybody. Continuing, they expressed that morality had often gotten falsely intertwined with those concepts leading people to feel uncomfortable with something that was, in truth, perfectly natural.... Lifelong monogamy simply wasn't for everyone, and it had nothing to do with what kind of people they were. There were plenty of very good people, people who were a very positive influence on the world around them, who simply didn't feel the need to conform to those so called "societal norms"... Your mother and I are simply realizing that we're a part of that group. We don't mean anybody any harm in this decision, and especially not you guys. Maybe, if looked at it the right way, we could even be setting a good example of how to be true to yourselves in your own lives?...... Sometimes it happens that people put so much pressure, and create so much stress over the idea that their relationship "should" last forever, that they lose the wonderful state of their relationship in the present. We see it all the time, people holding on so tightly that they crush something beautiful. Obviously that's never a wise way to live. It's far more important to appreciate what you have as you have it, and when you feel it evolving and changing into something else, recognize that too, and deal with it appropriately.

Now we don't want you to get the wrong idea of course. We're certainly in no way condemning couples who do make it work for a lifetime. In fact, it's a beautiful thing to witness a relationship that's that deeply successful. We're certainly not trying to make the point that all couples should split because of an occasional case of boredom. And we certainly don't want to condemn the choices of others as long as they are not consciously trying to negatively impact other lives. We're just trying to make you understand where we're coming from, and that there is nothing wrong with our choice either. We've simply decided to move on, because that's what is best for us. And it could be what's best for all of you too. The two of us will in many ways be living separate lives for the first time in many years, but we'll always be connected through you guys. If we all put a little effort into it, we should be able to strike a balance that gives us more opportunities in life than we might have had otherwise. It may take a while to realize what that might look like exactly; but, if you think about it, it's easy enough to see the potential. Obviously it will double your parental life experiences, because your lives will always be so closely intertwined with us as individuals instead of as a single unit…... Brian, in an effort to lighten the moment…. It'll be double the fun!

Obviously there was nothing about any of this to be taken lightly. What Brian and Kathy were talking about was of course a very big deal, and neither of them was making this decision without first giving it a considerable amount of thought. They hoped that their children would eventually see this too. They truly believed that this could be a very positive move for their entire family. After all, as a society we'd come a long way since the colonial days of religious oppression when individual freedom had been so falsely and hypocritically restricted. We had evolved and become more keenly aware of what true morality actually meant. Granted, divorce could be a very immoral act, and it was obvious when that was the case too. We've all been aware of people who use and damage their children in an effort to hurt the spouse when a marriage comes flying apart in a neurotic and dramatic fashion…. each feeling his or her own need to be right to far outweigh the health and stability of their innocent children, which is of course extremely immoral….. These acts of complete selfishness despite who gets hurt in the process are obviously not a positive way to live, and that negative energy will no doubt follow the offenders. But what Brian and Kathy were trying to do was nothing like any of this. They were simply facing the fact that monogamy forever wasn't how billions of years of evolution had set things up. The obvious truth was, it wasn't natural.

Romantic love was natural. It was something that served the species. Designed to last for several years, it was for the good of the offspring. It was in many ways highly functional, two parents protecting and providing for essentially helpless little children were obviously better than one. It was practical and served a survival purpose, but beyond that, modern humans had tried to make it something it was never naturally intended to be… That had not necessarily been a bad thing…. In fact, in many ways, it was probably even a very good thing, pushing our level of consciousness forward. After all, couples who've been happily married for fifty years must have something to teach us all. They know on a level far beyond the rest of us what's possible in human connectivity. They know everything about their partners- the good, the bad, and the ugly. They accept, appreciate, and love everything about them despite this intensely intimate knowledge. There has to be a lesson in there somewhere for everybody….

As Brian and Kathy separated, there were obviously a lot of little details that needed to be worked out. Kathy decided to let Brian keep the house, and together they looked for another house fairly nearby for her. Because they had kids, they didn't want to be separated by any great distance in order to both be equally involved in their lives. They were doing everything possible to make this dramatic change go as smoothly and stress-free as possible. When they found a suitable place, it didn't take long for the physical separation to take place. As far as they both saw it, there was no good reason to drag things out…. It was the same theory as pulling a bandage off fast. Something healthy, yet potentially painful, should be gotten out of the way as quickly as possible.

In the weeks that followed, some stress was an inevitable part of the deal. How could it not be? But more important was how everyone was dealing with it? It was a personal choice for all of them, and all Brian and Kathy could do was maintain a positive supportive attitude to fall back on….. and in doing so, they created an atmosphere that was highly conducive for success, and for the most part it worked. Sure it was emotional for the kids, but as things slowly settled into this new situation, they realized their parents were probably right. This didn't have to be seen as a negative thing for any of them. Maybe it really would provide new opportunities they wouldn't have had otherwise?

Slowly, as the weeks turned into months and years, everything was fine. They were all as happy and well-rounded as they'd ever been. The children realized that their parents did still love them, and the fact that their lives were evolving into something completely right for them did set a great example. It set an example of open-mindedness, making them far less likely to be judgmental of the life decisions of others. If done correctly and morally, most any life decision or lifestyle can have a positive impact on the surrounding society- "positive" meaning being true to yourself, and in doing so, allowing others to do the same....

....To each his own, and live a good life....

FOURTEEN

Walking in the park, it was fun telling Sara and Carey what she'd been up to. The morning after writing the "divorce story," she'd called them both in hopes of organizing their little get together. It was a Saturday, so she knew Carey would probably be available and want to bring the kids, and she was pretty sure Sara was in town too..... It was a nice day, hot and sticky, but nice...

The kids were having fun running around like crazy people. They were chasing their big brown dog Bongo, who was in turn chasing them, as well as a few squirrels and birds. You could tell from all the laughing that they were enjoying themselves, and it was fun to watch them play.

Janet was a good listener and enjoyed hearing about Carey's life,

84

which in most cases meant the lives of her nieces and nephews. The three kids were pretty much the center of Carey's attention and, for the most part, she loved it. Carey was a good mom doing a good job raising good kids. Justin was nine; and he liked soccer, running through creeks, playing in the mud, and whatever else most little boys liked to do. Sally was seven and a bit more reserved but probably very intelligent. She was very curious and already showed potential playing the tiny little violin she practiced every day. Jessica was four and absolutely adorable. Almost accidentally, she was spoiled rotten and pretty much ran the family, but nobody seemed to mind….. It was good being cute……

Janet thoroughly enjoyed being an aunt to them all. They'd had a lot of fun together already, but she looked forward to days ahead when she'd have the opportunity to start showing them the world. They were still a little young, but there would eventually be a time when she'd have the opportunity to start sharing her love of travel. Being perfectly content with probably never having kids of her own, it was fun sharing in the lives of her sister's. Carey was glad she was a part of their lives, too. Janet was a good aunt….

Sara wasn't shy about joining the conversation, as all three were good friends. Her job had taken her to the west coast the week before, Los Angeles to be more specific, and she'd had a good time. She'd spent the first night in a West Hollywood hotel, which meant easy access to the world famous Sunset Strip where she'd gone out and enjoyed the comedy clubs and bars. Then, the next night she moved to a nice hotel on the beach in Santa Monica where she wisely spent the rest of her stay. The entire area was great fun and, when she wasn't busy selling thousands of dollars worth of software, she took full advantage. She played in the sand and the surf and spent an afternoon flying a giant stunt kite with a new friend…. Just looking out over the endless Pacific Ocean was enjoyable…. Janet appreciated all of this, having spent time in the area herself.

The conversation was lively and animated by all three. However, on this particular day, Janet's latest writing efforts seemed to attract most of the attention. Carey and Sara were genuinely very curious, so it was ok with them if she monopolized the conversation for a while. She started by telling them how "less than thrilled" Mark had been about the Mars idea. His reaction had been a little disappointing at first for sure; but, as it slowly sank in, it seemed his hesitance may have proved helpful. She was beginning to see his point, about how it was a far cry from anything she'd done before…. But, she'd come up with a great ending and wanted to let the story play itself out.

Mark had a talent for saying just the right thing at the just right time to steer his authors in the right direction. When his comments sometimes sounded negative, there was almost always a point. It was instructive constructive criticism that frequently gave the writer pause to rethink his or her own ideas, often providing opportunity for evolution of thought. And that's what had happened for her....

Carey asked the most obvious question first..... So, what else are you going to write about? Have you thought about that?........Well, yes, as a matter of fact I have. I've got quite a few ideas actually, a couple I've even started working on. Just yesterday I spent pretty much the entire day out on my deck writing a story about a couple getting a divorce, and I'm not even completely sure why...... It was the strangest thing. For whatever reason, I felt the need to do it. The thing is, it wasn't so much about divorce as it was a commentary on contemporary morality. I took it as an opportunity to showcase an example of how any life decision can be positive, and nothing should just be thoughtlessly condemned by people who know nothing of the specific situation or individuals involved...... It was fun to write.... But perhaps even more interesting is what I spent the previous day doing, and it's far from even being finished.... Smiling, she paused, staring out into space for a few seconds.... Well.... What was it already....? Oh yea, well the first thing that happened was I killed myself.... As she continued to smile, Carey and Sara had the expected look of horror...... Simultaneously, WHAT!...... Don't worry, it's not exactly the way it sounds.... I don't actually kill myself... I die naturally in my bed. I think it was a massive heart attack, but that part is almost irrelevant..... You both know I went to New York last week to hang out with Mark for a few days, right?.... Well, it was a great time of course, but something a little strange happened while I was there. It seems Mark's building might have a ghost and, more importantly, I think I may have had a run in with it.... She went on to explain the night in her bedroom with the strange energy and the next day when she thought a ghost had possibly opened the refrigerator...... They both anxiously wanted more details, but she shrugged it off...... I don't know... It might have just been my imagination; but, whatever the case, it got me thinking about the story I'm trying to tell you.... I thought about the possibility of writing a story from the perspective of the so-called ghost, and that's why I was dead in my bed. That's where the story starts, and it was the most fun I can ever remember having writing..... Well, recently anyway...... It left the door wide open to do whatever I wanted, and it was awesome. I did everything from orbit the planet to swim as a snake in the Amazon River. It made death sound like the most fun thing that will happen to any of us. It felt so good, and I couldn't even tell where it was coming from. And it's not even finished yet. I love the idea that I'll eventually have to get back to it...... However, when I first sit down again, I think I'll write another chapter of the Mars story. It's been a while, and I don't want to completely lose that train of thought either. It's nice having a couple of different things that'll be great to get back to.... In a way, it's kind of like reading a good book that you can't wait to get back to.... Only this way, you're strangely the one creating the story.... It's pretty incredible actually. Even if this project is never successful in any financial sense of the word, it still will have been incredibly worthwhile just because it's so much fun.... She smiled... The thing is, I really have no idea what the end result will even look like, but I'm starting to get a really good feeling about it regardless....

There was a natural lull in the conversation for a few minutes. Then Sara broke the silence with a question.... What does Mark think about all this, you writing fiction......? Oh he's great. It's kind of funny because he's definitely not afraid to speak his mind. In fact, he really didn't like the Mars idea at all. But, behind all that brutal honesty, you always know his intentions are pure. And, in the end, you're free to make your own decisions anyway, knowing he will be genuinely supportive. I'm sure he looks forward to the day I hand him another travel/adventure manuscript, because, with good reason, he has faith it'll be financially successful. But, deep down, he's supportive no matter what... He really is a great guy. I'm lucky to have him...... So have you actually talked to him about this short story idea?...... Yes, but until I actually get some things going on paper, I don't like to give him many details. That's funny, too, because I can tell it drives him crazy.......

Somewhat reluctantly, Carey suddenly asked another seemingly obvious question. Although, as far as anybody could recall, nobody had ever had the nerve to bring it up before. It was personal, and everybody knew Janet had a habit of playing things like this fairly close to her chest ...... Have you and Mark ever thought about getting together?.... I mean you're single, he's single? You obviously like and care about each other. I'm just curious if it ever crosses your mind to take it a step farther? You know what I mean?..... She laughed and tried not to blush but could feel her face turning red anyway.....What? No, Mark and I are just friends and have been for a long time.... Just because it was fun, Sara decided to jump in and push a little, too….. Yea, but don't you think he's cute? If you ask me, he's never been ugly and seems to get better looking with age. And, not that you need the money, but the fact that he's rich doesn't hurt either….. They tried some more, but she continued to laugh it off…… No, Mark and I get along great, and I don't think either of us ever thinks that way. Even if we did, it could end up ruining a great thing…. Her answers were fairly convincing, but not completely. The conversation didn't get much further, though, just because she wouldn't let it. But they had a good time poking at her with their pointed little questions nonetheless….

The thing about Janet was that she'd never been big on long-lasting relationships. Therefore, she really wasn't all that comfortable talking about herself in relation to relationships in general. She knew her lifestyle wasn't exactly the norm, and a lot of people had a hard time relating to it. She was somewhat aloof and didn't necessarily think she needed the emotional support of a significant other. She didn't seem to value the notion like most people and was, for the most part, perfectly content living alone. She was very genuinely comfortable with herself. She liked herself and was her own best friend… She knew she was an interesting person; and, probably even more importantly, she knew the world was an interesting place, and just being alive was a fulfilling experience in and of itself. She was genuinely happy for those who found great fulfillment in their intimate personal relationships, but she didn't necessarily place a great importance on it in her own life.

However, it might also be important to note that she hadn't exactly been celibate either. Guys had always wandered into and through her life, and she enjoyed that fact. She wasn't overly promiscuous; but, when a genuine connection occurred, she went with it. She could go with it simply because she wasn't beholden to anybody else. No one was going to get hurt. She never wanted to use sex to hurt anybody and had a greater understanding than most of how sexual conduct had often gotten entangled with people's concepts of morality. It was because sexual conduct did have the potential to be cruel, so it did have the potential to be immoral. But it was also easy enough to understand that two consenting adults enjoying each other physically could be a great time… and very natural. It had absolutely nothing to do with whether or not a leader from any given religious sect had given them permission. In fact, she thought trying to make people feel guilty about their natural sexuality was the real immorality. It was oppressive, and oppression was always the real evil. It was a tricky area, actually, because she also saw how easy it was for less-than-completely-intelligent-fully-functioning people to get confused by all of this, which is largely why it made her uncomfortable to openly talk about it…. Her life was her own, and she was very happy about it. But that didn't mean she wanted to push her views on anyone else…

However, given that, she wasn't completely closed to the idea of a serious relationship either. She saw the potential value in having someone in her life with whom she could be completely comfortable sharing her whole self, someone who could completely love and appreciate her for who she was. But she knew that, if that person did in fact exist, he would have to be a pretty unique individual, too- someone who could truly understand how important her independence was to her and, indeed, appreciate his own independence. Such a relationship could be nice…..

Later that night, long after the walk in the park, she chuckled at the thought of Carey and Sara giving her such a hard time…. Were other people thinking the same thing? Did other people think she and Mark would make an interesting couple? They did seem to be ganging up on her about it. Was there a conspiracy going on that people weren't talking about….? No, that couldn't be true- now she was getting carried away?…. She smiled as she climbed into bed and turned out the lights….. Hmmm, maybe they did have an interesting point though…..?

….The next day, she enjoyed a very consciously lazy morning. She made herself a good substantial breakfast and sat down with a hot cup of coffee to read the paper. There was no need to rush into anything, and she kicked back fully aware that she was taking her time…. But eventually, a little before noon, she picked up her computer and started writing again….

FIFTEEN

Some twenty-three weeks after the initial launch, the Mars vehicle, with its anxious crew stirring inside, finally approached its destination.

Staying away from the windows was difficult as they continued to get closer. There was a lot to see as they were slowly being drawn in both physically and, perhaps even more so, emotionally. Up close and personal, the red planet was spectacularly beautiful. There was incredible detail of texture and brilliant variation of color that almost made it seem like a living being, a being that seemed to welcome them out of the long dark lonely void. After countless long hours, days, and weeks of traveling, it was slowly becoming apparent just how incredibly worthwhile it had all been.

The red planet truly was red. Its rusted iron-rich surface made it so, but there were infinite subtleties too. Endless variation of darks and lights, oranges and reds, gave the surface a simultaneously complex, yet simple, subtle beauty all its own. This was Mars. It was its own unique world. As a planet, it was an individual with its own personal charms. Its ancient rivers had carved beautifully sculptured lines into its surface that resembled the veins of a changing autumn leaf. There were mountains, valleys, craters, and vast expansive plains. While some features seemed random, others appeared to attempt patterns. But, regardless of what was happening at any specific geographical location, as a whole, it was absolute serene perfection….

As they completed the first full revolution, the crew was awestruck. In many ways, it was completely mind-blowing to fully realize and appreciate where they were. Theirs were the first human eyes to ever witness such a perspective of a planet other than earth. It was a very heavy thought. Everything they were seeing was so incredible that it might even have been tempting to stay in orbit for a while, just to soak it all up…. But it wasn't a temptation that would present a problem. For one thing, they were going to have some time. In fact, it would take at least several days of orbiting just to make sure everything was lined up correctly for the inevitable descent. So, by the time they actually were ready, they could hardly stand the wait another minute. Sure it was fun and provocative to view the planet from above, but, when it finally came time to move toward the surface, they were all more than ready to go.

Booster rockets were fired for the first time in months; and, as testimony to the preparedness of the mission, they responded right on cue to start slowing things down. Their speed needed to be reduced before dropping into the thin Martian atmosphere, for control purposes and to reduce friction. As the process began, everything looked great. They were right on the money and exactly where they needed to be. All the careful preparations and calculations were now paying off. The crew was confident everything would go smoothly. All that was left to do now was to go through the motions and trust the technology. They'd spent endless weeks and months anticipating this moment, the moment of truth. It was incredibly exciting and a little nerve racking.... but the nerves were to be expected. Not only were their individual lives on the line, but in many ways the hopes and dreams of all humanity... It was intense....

Larry anchored himself into the pilot's seat, meaning he'd be in control of the descent if anything didn't look right with the automated guidance systems. If something went wrong, he could switch to manual and land the thing himself- but nobody anticipated that would be necessary. After all, all the robotic missions had made it just fine without a pilot. Nevertheless, it made everybody feel better to know someone like Larry was ready to take over if need be... Scott anchored his command chair near the center of the vehicle to have the best possible view out of all three windows; and, last but not least, the two women each selected windows and anchored themselves in their seats directly in front of them... Whatever was about to happen, they didn't want to miss a thing....

Ever so slowly, they started feeling the vibrations as the enveloping atmosphere grew thicker. They were all securely strapped into their seats, but they instinctively held on so tightly their knuckles turned white.... It was scary. They all knew that, if something in the mission were to go wrong, this was a prime time. They were in the midst of one of the most crucial and delicate maneuvers of the entire trip. The vibrations were growing stronger and stronger, and they could hear it. There was a fierce deadly wind pummeling their craft, and they were all too aware that only a few well-crafted inches of material separated them from certain and immediate death. Finally, it was more like a violent shaking; and, as the Martian surface moved toward them, it was obvious they were no longer in orbit- they were falling....

After several long minutes, the exterior cameras revealed that the first small parachute had been deployed in an effort to begin slowing the huge ship down, which would be done in several phases. If the largest parachute was released first, the stress of the sudden jolt would be far too great on everything involved, the passengers, the ship, and even the chute itself that would most likely just blow apart. After several more minutes, they felt the slight jolt of the second slightly larger parachute being successfully deployed. It was obvious they were slowing down now- for one thing, everything was suddenly much quieter. On the central monitor they could see the canopy overhead, and it was yet another beautiful sight. Now they were just waiting for the third and final parachute to deploy….

….Waiting…..Waiting…..Waiting….. Still waiting……Several minutes later, still waiting……..Hmmm, shouldn't it have opened by now….? What's going on? Was everything alright? The optimal window of time for deployment was quickly closing. And then the alarm started to sound, warning that there was a problem….. Not long after, a system analysis report came up on the big monitor detailing the situation. For whatever reason, the small explosive devises that were supposed to release the main parachute had failed to go off; and, as critical minutes passed, they continued to fail. There was a redundancy device that was supposed kick in if the original failed, and nothing was happening with it either. Then a second alarm started going off, which seemed odd in an annoying sort of way because it was basically announcing the same problem of the nonfunctioning parachute. Scott shut off both the alarms. They weren't helping anything and were so loud a person couldn't think straight.

Unfortunately, there wasn't a backup parachute, and that had been a conscious part of the plan all along. None of the previous preparatory missions had had backup chutes either. So much thought and thorough engineering had gone into the primary chute that a secondary had been deemed unnecessary. All the studies showed it had 99.999 percent reliability and, as far as everybody was concerned, that was good enough. Adding a secondary of the same caliber would have added so much cost due to the extra weight, they decided they could simply go without it. It was thought that redundancy in the deployment system would keep the risk to enough of a minimum. The chances of anything going wrong were very slim…..

However, none of that seemed to matter as the capsule was plummeting toward the hard rocky surface of a planet millions of miles from home at a speed of well over a hundred miles an hour. If they couldn't find a solution to this immediate and very desperate problem, they were all about to die, not to mention the death of a trillion dollar mission. Somebody needed to think of something fast…. Given it was Scott's job not only as the commander but as one of the chief engineers, he knew what their last option was. The time had come and gone for waiting to see if the automated system would eventually work, and action had to be taken...

There was a panel on the inside of the capsule, behind which was the tightly packed parachute. Scott scrambled by the shaking and forces of gravity that were now exerting themselves on everybody, made his way over and opened it. Behind the panel, there was another thick wall; and, directly on the other side of it, was the explosive device and then the parachute itself. In the center of it, there was a mark that resembled the butt end of a center-fire riffle bullet, and next to it, there was a mechanical spring-loaded hammer that could be cocked by hand and then released.... As he was busy doing all of this, his teammates continued looking out the windows at a situation that was very obviously getting more dire by the second. The ground was rising quickly; and, if this didn't work, it would all be over in a matter of a very few short minutes. They were all encouraging him in a very frantic matter...... C'mon Scott!.......C'mon Scott!...... Hurry up Man!.... You can do it!..... C'MON.....!!!

Sure enough, he pulled the trigger and due to the removal of the sound padded panel, there was a very loud BANG!.... It worked! As they all watched on the monitor, the large packaged parachute shot out the top of the vehicle; and, in a matter of a few long seconds,   it opened....... WHEW!.... Collectively, it was a Holy Shit moment for sure. It seemed they were going to live, at least for the moment.....

However, they still had to land, and it would happen soon whether they liked it or not. Obviously it was good they weren't going to burn in, but their troubles were far from over. First of all, the long delay of the main chute opening had them way off course, rendering the guidance system essentially useless. In other words, it had no idea where they were. It had lost all points of reference, and they'd be on the ground before it had time to figure it out. Pretty much immediately, Larry switched the controls to manual and took over. He was amazingly calm, too. His pilot's instincts kicked in and, suddenly, he was all business. First he tested the control rockets just make sure they were working. A short burst and they seemed to be working fine... From there, he had total control of the descent. The monitors were showing him camera views of the ground below, as well as sonar relief images.... and the news wasn't good. They were descending into a Martian mountain range, which was problematic in and of itself. But it also meant secondary problems. If they survived the landing, they would obviously be miles from the facilities that were supposed to welcome them so comfortably…..... But, first things first…. As they got closer and closer, Larry continued pulling the control trigger on the rockets- a little shot here, a little shot there, moving back and forth, trying with everything he had to find the flattest spot possible to set them all down. His years of training were boiling down to this moment…. In a matter of seconds, humans would be landing on Mars for the first time….

It was noisy….. It sounded like a car accident and seemed to happen in slow motion. But, as everything actually did stop, it seemed the vehicle was still intact. For what seemed like an eternity, they all sat silently and looked at each other. The looks were saying "are you ok?…… and asking themselves the same question, "am I ok?" But mostly they were just looks of confusion, the obvious confusion of…… What now?

In a matter of minutes, the plan had changed drastically. Essentially, there was no plan. From here on out, they would be improvising a new plan. They'd all known from the first day of training, years ago now, that the mission on which they were embarking was extremely dangerous. It wasn't going to be easy, and they'd spent days upon days training for every imaginable contingency. But from the minute they touched down, they knew this would test them to their limits. In fact, it was fairly obvious to everybody that their very survival was now keenly in the balance… If it weren't for all that intensive training, it could have been a very somber mood; but, after a few minutes of reflection, a new discussion began….

As commander, Scott kicked into gear first….. Ok everybody, obviously this is far from the scheduled plan, so from this minute forward consider it thrown out the window. We're starting from scratch. We're making a new plan….. First of all, is everybody alright?….. Everyone seemed to be….. Ok, second, let's try to figure out where we are in relation to the base camp. Joann, that will be your job. Julie, you start relaying the situation as best you can back to the NASA control center. We'll need as much help as they can give us. Larry, you'll start running and analyzing all the system status programs. We need to know exactly what kind of condition our little space ship is in here. Meanwhile, I'm going to get ready to go out. I want to see the ship from the outside, plus, I just want to have a look around in general. We need to start getting an idea what all aspects of our situation truly are….

Within a few minutes, Scott was in his spacesuit, and minutes later he'd sealed himself into to the small closet-like airlock that would let him exit. As he opened the door to the outside world for the first time, he could hear the air pressure being released. This was indeed a much thinner atmosphere than earth's...... and then, unceremoniously, it happened.... without much thought about the weight of the moment, without any grand "One small step for man"..... he put the first human footprint on Mars.....

However, walking away from the ship to get a look at the situation as a whole, he paused just before turning around. Looking out across the vast landscape, suddenly it hit him, and it nearly took his breath away......WOW! This is absolutely incredible.... I'm standing on the surface of Mars.... It was beyond beautiful- and, for a moment, he completely forgot about the downside of his true circumstances. He was looking out into an enormous reddish plain that seemed to go on forever. The horizon could easily have been more than a hundred miles away, and the kid in him just wanted to run out towards it. It was a joyous moment as the reality and privilege of where he was fully sank in. He could have stood there much longer just pondering it all..... However, there was another serious reality.... and, after another few minutes, he snapped out of it and finally looked back.....

The first thing he noticed was how lucky they had been. The ledge in the otherwise incredibly steep terrain where Larry had set down was very narrow. It was barely wide enough for the ship, with only a very few feet of tolerance left over on either side. A few feet off in one direction and they would have gone tumbling down the mountain. A few feet in the other direction and they would have crashed into it. It seemed Larry really was good at his job, and NASA had done well in choosing him. Without his unquestionable skill in this difficult and delicate landing, they would have all been dead already....

A preliminary look at the vehicle seemed to indicate that the only real problem was its location. Every one of the four legs had a sound footing. Underneath the ship, however, was a big sharp jagged rock that, had it been much taller, would most likely have punctured it. There were only a couple of inches clearance between it and the bottom surface.... yet another stroke of luck. As he made his way around looking at every square foot of exterior surface area the best he could, he was pleasantly surprised at every turn. A couple of the landing feet had been bent and mangled due to the rocky landing surface, which must have been why the landing was so loud. But the good news was that there was no real structural damage. So, after inspecting everything as thoroughly as possible in a relatively short period of time, he decided to go back inside. He had been keeping his teammates apprised of the situation through his headset, but it would be good to have a face-to-face discussion... The news was better than he had expected when they first landed....

Joanne had been busy pulling up satellite images taken by the orbits of the many previous robotic missions, and she had a pretty good idea of where they were geographically.... Looking at the maps confirmed that it definitely could have been worse. At least they were on the right side of the mountains. Things weren't going to be easy, and maybe not even possible, but it seemed there was a good chance they could figure out a way to access their all-important base camp. It was probably less than thirty miles away and, for the most part, it was all downhill....

SIXTEEN

It was an interesting moment, and the significance wasn't lost. The light was so vibrant and energetic on one hand and, for lack of a better term, " lost souls" on the other. Strangely, I found myself curious about both; but, upon noticing the brilliance of the light, the first choice seemed obvious. The light was obviously the more positive of these two sides of the same coin, and I was instinctively drawn towards it. It wasn't a difficult decision and, with that thought, I realized I was already slowly being enveloped in it. The light was transcendent, permeating everything. The light literally **was** everything, and I realized the previous sensation of somehow being separate from it was simply a misconception, a simple lack of perspective if you will....

My understanding continuing to grow, I realized the light had always been and will always be. In the simplest of terms, the light was the very essence of God, and I was now a part of that light. There was an incredible sense of loving and being loved. And then, for the first time, I became aware of loved ones from my own life. Grandparents, aunts, uncles, friends, all made themselves known in the most joyous reunion

96

I could have ever imagined- and for more than the obvious reasons. First, it was of course good to simply be in their presence again..... but beyond that, any preconceived personality-based assumptions of who they were, good or bad, completely dissolved. And, for the first time, I knew them for the whole perfect beings they were. Even the sense that we'd ever been separated lost any real meaning. That, too, had in many ways been an illusion. We'd all always been, and with this knowledge came an incredible sense of peaceful calm and understanding, as if we were all breathing a huge collective sigh of relief from the imaginary stresses of the world.....

As I slowly settled into this new reality, I realized that I had the option of staying here forever; and there seemed to be no good reason to ever want to leave. This place, this existence, was paradise, and I immersed myself in it wholly for hours, days, weeks, even months.... Time of course had no real meaning anyway. This place, this feeling, was timeless. Maybe that's what eternity meant? And, with this realization, something even stranger happened......

Suddenly, I remembered that I'd made a decision to go into the light when there'd been another choice as well. It dawned on me that the ghosts in the field were still there, and I found myself curious again. It was very strange. Here I was in this state of perfect peaceful calm, and somehow, for some reason, I wanted to explore something else.... Maybe this meant something too?.... Maybe there was yet another, even higher state of consciousness of which I was not yet aware? In many ways, ever wanting to leave the position I was already in made no sense. But, nonetheless, I was once again being pulled to do something new. Maybe this was also the natural way of things? But, whatever the case, I realized I'd already made a decision- and, with that thought, there I was in the field again ......

Not that the specific geography was of any real consequence, but I had the distinct feeling of being somewhere in central Virginia- and it seemed to be fairly late in a beautiful sunny afternoon. The huge field of tall swaying grass was surrounded by a dense forest, and I slowly began to move through the grass, becoming the breeze that was making it move. Life was abundant and diverse in the field. Critters were buzzing, jumping, running, flying in any and every direction. There were butterflies, grasshoppers, bugs of all kinds, an occasional chirping bird, mice, rats, snakes, possums, rabbits, and even a skunk. It was beautiful and briefly reminded me of the previous experience in the Amazon..... Life, in all its forms, was never anything less than

97

miraculous….. Then I stopped…. For no apparent reason, I suddenly felt the need to just be perfectly still and observe…..

For a moment, time seemed to slip past very quickly… Before I knew it, it was dark and, with this new circumstance, a thick fog had fallen. The light of the full moon above was barely getting through, leaving an eerie glow and strange blue shadows across the landscape. I stayed still, simply looking around with an ever-increasing awareness…. I started to notice sounds. There were of course the countless sounds of the nature- crickets, owls, frogs, the occasional howling coyote….. but there were other sounds, too, sounds unlike any I'd ever heard before. They were very strange. They'd begin in a very low pitch and slowly rise. As the pitch would increase, so would the volume, until it reached a screeching peak. Then, still slowly, it would retreat and disappear again in much the same way it had arrived, as if something, or someone, was coming from a specific direction, and then leaving again in the opposite. But very oddly, in this context, spatial dimensions lost any distinct definition……

In truth, I knew what it was. It was the reason I'd come here in the first place. These were the sounds of soldiers from a long ago war, and I was slowly tuning into their presence here…. I pictured myself in my body again, and suddenly I was standing in the middle of a battleground…. Immediately upon realizing this, I was shocked to feel something grab my ankle, or perhaps more accurately, I felt **someone** grab my ankle. And, with this sudden awareness, I looked down into a horrible and pitiful site. A young man of no more than sixteen or seventeen years old was looking back up at me, and he was terrified….

My first reaction was worse than I might have expected of myself… Maybe I was briefly terrified too?… But this initial feeling only lasted a brief moment before I realized there was really nothing for me to fear. After all, I was free…However, according to his apparent circumstance, there was much for him to be afraid of. First of all, his injuries were numerous and had to be painful. He had a large cut on his forehead and abrasions on his face. He was covered in blood nearly head to toe, and intestines had spilled from his mid-section from what looked to be a large bayonet wound. I could tell he'd been doing his best to hold them in with his hands, but with little success. Both his legs had been badly broken, as if a large cannon on wheels had been rolled over them in the heat of battle. He had one good arm, but the other was twisted behind him with a jagged bloody bone sticking through his skin and shirt… Bluntly, he was a horrible mess and had to know he was on the verge of his own death…Very naturally, it scared him...

However, I knew something he didn't.... The truth was he'd been dead for a very long time, which was information I wasn't quite sure what to do with. Intuitively, I knew my best move in the moment was to simply be compassionate.... He continued to look up at me, desperately asking for help with tears and fear welling in his eyes. His voice was soft and weak, but his face spoke volumes.... Saying nothing, but looking back at him with the most caring calm I could muster, I sat down beside him. I did care- this kid obviously did need help. Not having any idea what it might mean, I knew immediately that I would sit with him for all the time needed....

Instinctively, I knew that, for the time being, it was best to continue saying nothing, to be present, attentive, and loving. I took his hand in mine and, for the first time since my own death, I actually took notice of the physical sensation. I realized I was reaching into some strange middle ground between two realities. Maybe in this moment, I myself was a ghost and, under exactly the right circumstances, actual living breathing people could detect my presence here? But it was only a passing thought, there was no one around anyway.... And besides, now that was far from the point.... That wasn't the reason I'd come....... I continued to patiently sit. My simply being there was visibly easing the boy's misery, and slowly the expressions on his face began to change. In time, he went from a place of desperate pain and pleading, to a more inquisitive frame of mind. Slowly, I could see he was growing more and more curious about me and what I was doing there.... He asked.....Who are you?.... How did you get here?.... I could see what was beginning to dawn on him, that I seemed misplaced..... Continuing to say nothing, I realized he was slowly beginning to find his own answers.... He asked another question... Are you an angel?..... He was obviously getting a little closer to the truth, and it made me think.... He'd made an interesting point....Was I an angel?.... Maybe I was what angels were?.... Maybe angels were simply compassionate souls like myself open to helping out where they saw a need.... Hmmm, it was interesting?... Maybe I really was an angel?.... But in the moment, I didn't quite know how to answer the question, so I didn't....

However, after what had been quite a long time, I finally decided to engage him with some questions of my own. In effect, I turned the tables. I asked him who he was and how he had gotten here. I wanted him to think about who he truly was, realizing he was far more likely to find the answers he was looking for by asking profound questions of himself... He looked puzzled, but slowly answered the first question...

My name is Paul...We're fighting a war here... the North has to win this war...We have to free the slaves and keep our beautiful country whole... I just sat and listened. I could tell his reality was, in truth, becoming more vague. He was obviously a person of strong moral conviction trying desperately to hold on to his all-important cause that had so long ago been resolved... Before now, he had no way of knowing the war was over....

I could see he was slowly losing his grip on this false reality, and it was making him very uncomfortable. He started to fidget and look around in quick jerky movements.... What's happening?.... What are you doing to me?... I stayed with him, continuing to watch and smile with all the compassion of the universe behind me.... I could sense something deeply profound was beginning to happen, and I was helping in the process.... Whatever was happening to him was obviously far from pleasant, but I somehow knew it was necessary, a necessary purging....

For a moment, it seemed the universe itself began to shake. In the field, there were loud bursts of thunder and bright flashes of lightning. The boy, Paul, started to violently shake and tremble. He tried to scream, but instead both low and high pitched grunts and groans came emanating from his mouth, from his entire body. I could see the full force of the violent pain that racked his body in the grotesque twisting and grimacing on his face.... It was excruciating!.... I could barely take it and was tempted to leave, but deep down I knew what was happening and that I couldn't abandon him. I knew he was in a desperate battle with himself. He was beating his earthly ego to death, and moving through this process was the only way he would ever be free..... And then it happened..... With a loud booming sound, his entire body exploded. For an instant, blood and guts and bone and brains went flying outward at the speed of sound,... but within a fraction of a second, all this gruesome debris turned to bright brilliant vibrant light..... In an instant, the energy had changed completely... A peaceful joyful calm fell over everything.... His ordeal was over...

The sun shone into the field through the treetops of a beautifully forested horizon. It was a glorious summer morning, and a thick setting of dew was glistening in the tall grass. Paul, young, healthy, and smiling, was standing next to me...... He looked at me, suddenly knowing everything.... I'd been dead a long time hadn't I?.... Yes, I'm afraid so, but that's over now.... You're finally free, more free than you've ever been.... I could see the overwhelming joy on his face as it consumed him. This first wonderful taste of full spiritual consciousness was completely overwhelming as he was being flushed with it... It took a moment for him to gain his composure..... I didn't mind. We literally had all the time in the world.... After a few minutes, as he finally came around, his first words were grateful ones.... Thank you for helping me.... You know, I'd been lying in that field hurting and bleeding for who knows how long, and occasionally I'd noticed others like yourself. You weren't the only one you know. Others would sometimes pass by as if completely oblivious to the horrible war happening all around them. They always looked completely out of place too. To be honest, I'd always just thought they were hallucinations, figments of my imagination, like I was delirious or something. I knew I was hurt badly and thought maybe I was losing my mind as well. But now, for the first time, I think I know who they were. I think I was getting glimpses of people on both sides, those like yourself who are now completely spirit, and on the other side, actual living beings.... I think I was caught somewhere in the miserable middle.... I was a ghost, wasn't I?.... The question was rhetorical ....

I'm curious, Paul, can you see now that you always had the choice, the choice to move on into this next realm that's so obviously better than where you were?.... Paul, continuing to smile and beam with total contentment, paused at the question.... Hmmm, it's interesting because, as I stand here now, it does seem very obvious; but, in the time I was dying there in that field, it wasn't so simple. Something intangible wanted me to hold on to my situation as it was. I now know it was my ego trying desperately to hold on to my identity as I knew it. I was important, fighting an important war. For whatever reason, I couldn't seem to let it go.... It was absolute misery, and I couldn't see past it... I know it seems easy now, I just think I was too close to it all.... It was as if my true self was banging on a huge door, trying desperately to get out. You simply showed me that the door wasn't attached to any walls. All I had to do was walk around the door.... Does that make sense?... It did make sense... Somehow I did understand what had happened to him.... He'd been as close as anyone will ever come to the religious descriptions of hell. In fact, if one were so inclined to say it that way, he was in hell.... I was glad I'd shown him the way out... And he was genuinely very grateful...

Pausing, we both stood in the beautiful rolling pasture absorbing everything around us. It truly was an amazing place to be. The natural beauty was fully engrossing, and it was fun seeing Paul come to terms with it all.... I could see how grateful he was, which made me feel even better.... I could also see that Paul wanted to stay a while... He was coming to terms with the fact that others were still there, like he had been, and he wanted to help......I could see he felt a strong sense of responsibility, but it was more than obligation. He cared about his peers. He couldn't leave them behind, and he probably wasn't coming with me. I, on the other hand, felt unexplainably compelled to go elsewhere. I looked at him and smiled. Without saying a word, we had a very joyful goodbye..... Then, as the whole thing had begun, I meshed with the gentle breeze that moved the tall glistening grass... It was time to move on....

SEVENTEEN

As the astronauts sat discussing their plans, the radio finally crackled to life with a voice from home. There was a twenty-minute delay from transmission to reception, which meant the people at NASA had had time to hear the news of the problems, have some discussion of their own, and send back an initial response. Over an hour had passed since they'd first touched down, and this was their first full-circle communication. Everyone involved had always known that, by the time Mars was achieved, the delay would be long, and potentially a little frustrating; but, under the current circumstances, this seemed ridiculous... Granted, they had no choice but to work with the situation as it was; but from the perspective of the crew members, it really served to punctuate how truly on their own they were.... The lack of communication to this point made for a very lonely feeling...

Copy Mars 1, we understand you have a problem.... It sounds like you had quite a landing... First of all, we're very happy to hear you're all still alive and, from what we understand so far, the ship is still fairly intact too. You're system analysis reports are just starting to come in, and so far everything looks pretty good.... Also, we're just starting to download the first satellite images, as we're sure you've been trying to do... If you don't know already, the news could be worse... From the best information we've been able to put together so far, it seems you're roughly only about nineteen nautical miles from the base camp...We know you're going to have to find a way to get there at some point, but first things first. Some decisions need to be made. We don't want you to rush into anything just yet.... By the way, we're all very sorry for your troubles. From where you're sitting, this must be a very difficult situation... However, I think you'll be happy to know you're about to have the support of the whole world behind you.... I can assure you that the millions of people who will soon be hearing of this will all be sending you their best thoughts.... And, for what it's worth, congratulations! This is a great day for all of humanity. With you brave souls as our ambassadors, we've finally landed on a planet other than our own... The speaker went silent...

Even with the huge delay, it was great to finally hear from home.... Maybe they weren't so alone after all?.... Everyone was noticeably more calm and confident after that first transmission. Psychologically, there was no sensation of the delay at all as their ground commander was speaking, which was understandably great for morale. They were of course all very professional and capable of working around their personal stresses to get a job done, but they were also human. Hearing some encouraging words from home was as good for them as it would have been for anyone....

For the first time since their less than optimal landing, Scott, Joanne, Larry, and Julie, all sat back in their seats and smiled.... Sitting around the table, they were finally able to laugh and make light of their situation for the first time.... Scott wisecracked, well I guess we could check into a hotel for the night.... Larry chimed in, Yea, I'll make a couple of calls and order us some pizza and beer.... It was a fun funny moment as they all relaxed a little bit more.... It was interesting. The situation was now very different than anyone had anticipated, but it was great to see everyone let go and move past it. It was an extremely clear and sane way to look at things. After all, it was too late to worry about the way things were "supposed" to be. They had to work with the way things were now. They had to deal with the situation as it was and not look back, and it seemed everyone was able to switch gears fairly quickly.... It was a great testimony to their personal strengths and professionalism...

Finally, they all sighed a little sigh and got back to work. It was good that the first desperate sense of urgency had subsided a little.... Larry had run all the diagnostic programs he could, and it seemed all the ship's systems were still in perfect working order…. Meanwhile, Joanne had been downloading every relevant satellite image in an effort to pinpoint their location. She had aerial views of the mountains and of the base camp itself. In fact, she was able to zoom in on the camp with incredible detail and clarity. It looked amazing, and they all eagerly anticipated arriving there- when the time came. From there, she zoomed back out to a range that might include where they were in the neighboring mountains. If she was right, they could start plotting a course; but, as of yet, they didn't have quite enough information. However, within less than hour, another satellite was due to pass over. If they could get an image of the actual ship, it would be easy enough to start putting the puzzle pieces together. But, in the meantime, it was all too tempting to start guessing where they were from the images they already had, and the speculation was lively and intense by all four. They pointed at and shuffled through the maps…. If we're here, then we can do that?… On the other hand, if we're there, we can do this?… In reality, it was all fairly pointless, but it at least gave them something to think about until the real information came in..…. It finally did…….

Suddenly there they were- as they zoomed in on the picture they'd been waiting for, they could see themselves comfortably nestled into the mountains in their shiny metallic spaceship. It was beautiful and pretty amazing to think about. They were looking at a picture of themselves on the surface of Mars taken from a couple of hundred miles up…. However, their amazement quickly turned to something else as they saw their position a little more closely.…..

They all stopped and looked at each other as they realized what they were looking at. Directly below them, in both directions, there was what appeared to be a large vertical cliff that must have been over a thousand feet tall…. There was long pause…. Looking at Scott, Julie said something first…. That's not good…. No, it's not, and they all chimed in with agreement…. Scott smiled- well at least there's no argument about that little fact…. Ok, so we've got another obstacle…. Let's not waste a bunch of time worrying about it and start thinking about possible options. We know we probably can't go straight down, so if we end up having to rule that out, traversing in one direction or the other is what we'll have to start thinking about. However, as of right now, I don't want to completely rule out going straight off what appears to be the edge. There's a possibility it's not as bad as it looks from these pictures, so let's not rule anything out just yet….We've got a couple hundred yards of all-purpose utility cable on a spool, remember? I'm going to put on one of the tether harnesses and work my way down to have a look...

Larry immediately spoke up and, in no uncertain terms, asked if he could go instead..... Please let me do it. I really want to do it.... You have no idea how badly I just want to finally get out of this glorified beer can..... Please, Scott, let me go... Scott, given his title of commander, was reluctant to let someone else take the risk. But, then again, they were a team. If Larry really wanted out that badly, he wouldn't deny him... Ok, you can go. Just be careful out there... And, with that, Larry started suiting up...

As the airlock opened to the outside world, Larry looked down at the rusted Martian soil. He'd had some time to think about what he was doing and took his first steps with a certain amount of reverence. He wanted to fully appreciate the moment. After all, he was only the second person ever in history to be walking on the surface of Mars. He didn't want to take it lightly...It was fun looking at his feet in the Martian dirt for the first time... Several yards from the ship he stopped, just to look around for a minute. Being high in the mountains, the view was spectacular. The vast landscape below seemed to go on forever. As they'd all noticed before, the distant horizon was many miles away, but standing outside with nothing obstructing his view, he was amazed at how truly compelling it was. He was instinctively drawn towards it. A natural need to explore was welling up inside him and, with that, he started taking some action....

After anchoring the cable to a leg of the spacecraft, he clipped himself into the belay device attached to his harness at mid chest. The original purpose of the harness was for spacewalks. If any exterior work was needed during the trip, this, along with the cable itself, would be a way for an astronaut to stay tethered. But it was always in the back of everyone's minds that these devices could potentially be used for other purposes as well. In fact, literally everything they had could be used creatively in a given situation. Everyone had been taught to think in terms of what equipment could do- and not necessarily about was it was specifically designed to do. Creative thinking was encouraged at every step. So, when Scott first suggested using this equipment to explore the cliff, it seemed like a given....

Working his way down was a little awkward, but he was making it. Between fumbling with the equipment through the bulk of his spacesuit and weaving through and over the large boulders, it wasn't exactly easy; but, about thirty minutes later, he'd made it to where he could go no further. Another few feet away was what appeared to be the ledge, so, being an intelligent person, he stopped for a minute to think about where he was. Looking at the horizon line just in front of him, the terrain seemed to drop off into the abyss exactly the way the disappointing pictures had shown. He looked at his equipment and thought about his next move... Taking every last inch of slack out of the cable, he leaned back giving it most of his weight. Then he took the last tentative step in the loose gravel that led to the edge. Finally, he could see over and down the reddish face, and at first glance it didn't look good. It was completely vertical over the initial lip. However, further down, maybe fifty feet or so, there was a flat sloping ledge about three feet wide. As he looked closer and followed the ledge upward, he could see that it led to a point level with where he was several hundred yards to his right. Looking the other way, the ledge continued downward for a long way, too, but the cliff curved and he couldn't see where it lead. Nevertheless, this seemed like a good sign. It seemed they might have a virtual sidewalk to lead them down the mountain. It looked steep in places, but with the cable and harnesses they had to belay each other, it could probably work. The only problem was, where did the trail end? He could see it went well over halfway down the enormous wall, but beyond the curve, he had no idea what it looked like.... He'd have to find out...

As he relayed the information back to his companions in the ship, everybody was excited at this possibly very good news..... Don't get too worked up; I'm not sure if it will work yet, and it will be awhile before I do.... I'll have to come back up, walk as far as I can in the direction I can't see, and then go back down. But bear with me... I do have a good feeling about this...

Nearly four hours later, he was finally back inside. The truth was he'd been having a great time on his little adventure and hadn't felt rushed to do anything. He was smiling through it all, just happy in the knowledge of where he was. And the fact that he was taking back good news didn't hurt either. As he peeled himself out of his suit, all were eager to hear every word of what he had to say. Granted, they'd been communicating with him all along, but there's nothing like talking face-to-face, and they were all as excited as he was with what he'd found- especially Julie and Joanne, who hadn't even been outside yet. The thought of venturing towards base camp was fantastic. As far as they were concerned, they should get started right away, and Scott and Larry basically felt the same way. Upon hearing that a workable way out of the mountains had been discovered, there didn't seem to be much reason for further delay. However, given that, they also realized it wasn't wise to rush into anything without thoroughly thinking it through.... They'd make the move soon enough, but there was a lot to consider first...

What would they take with them?... How long did they think it might take? These were important factors that needed to be seriously considered. The ship had been their home and life-support system for quite some time now. Leaving it to venture out into the deadly Martian atmosphere was nothing to be taken lightly. They would have to rely on the systems of the bulky spacesuits for the entire distance to the camp. Out in the middle somewhere would be a delicate place. They wanted to take everything they'd need to ensure their success but, at the same time, not so much as to needlessly slow them down. It would be an interesting balance. They definitely needed to take a couple of days worth of food and drinking water, but what else? Other than the climbing equipment, was that it? Going the entire distance in one long push would be the idea, but what if that wasn't possible? Should they try to bring some sort of shelter?....

Once they got to the camp, they would have everything they needed. So the only concern was crossing the gap. The camp itself was well supplied. In fact, compared to the way they'd been living for months now, it would seem like an enormous lap of luxury. They looked forward to it. The ten total enclosures meant twenty thousand square feet of living space that had not only been designed to be very functional but very comfortable as well. There were living plants for fresh fruits and vegetables, not to mention clean breathable air. There were big cushy air mattresses, furniture, electricity, and much more. But mostly there was just a lot more room to move around.....

There were many important things in the ship they would need to bring to camp eventually, but they could always come back later in the surface rover. They knew it could at least get them back to the base of the mountain. They would have to climb back up, but they could worry about that when the time came. Everything they'd be back for could safely wait.... It was mostly electronics that were either redundancies of what would already be there, or luxuries like the big monitor. There were other things, too, like extra bedding and other personal items. Among the most important were some of the experiments on board, not the least of which included the frozen embryos of agricultural (farm) animals. Any practical use of these microscopic grazers was a long way off, but everybody thought it was at least a good idea to have them available on the planet. And, for that matter, there were even human embryos- thirty genetically unrelated males and females. The thinking was that, even though these might never be used for anything, maybe we should at least have the potential of planting the human race on Mars a little more permanently?.... Or.... Maybe just the stem cells would come in handy? The truth was that this last little detail was almost an afterthought, but as long as we were going anyway, why not?

Roughly forty eight hours after Larry's initial assessment and after considerable consultation with each other and those back on earth, the crew finally decided they were ready to make a break for it..... As they started putting on their suits, they all smiled with the same thought.... Base camp is waiting....

EIGHTEEN

It had been extremely hot and humid for nearly a week, so it was easy to stay inside enjoying the comfort of her air conditioning. She'd spent several good long days on her couch writing and had loved every minute of it. Being so incredibly engrossed in the imaginary world of her stories was a fantastic place to be....

...Finishing that last chapter on Mars, she stood up and stretched, still wondering how her crew's long trip to base camp would go for them... She chuckled.... It seemed it might not be easy....

It was about 8:30 and just starting to get dark outside. After another long productive day, rewarding herself with an ice cold beer seemed like a reasonable thing to do and she went to the kitchen to get one... Popping the cap and watching the sweat instantly condense on the outside of the bottle was a nice little moment in and of itself as she decided to take it out on the deck. The heat hit her like a wall as she opened the sliding glass door- but, under the circumstances, it almost felt good. After all, she didn't have to stay out there. Given that, it felt nice walking to the railing where she set the beer down and almost instantly started sweating herself.... Damn it's hot!.... But it was a beautiful evening otherwise.

Roughly fifteen minutes later, after the beer was gone and she was drenched, the phone started ringing in the house. A nice little trip into the sauna world had been okay, but it was good having an excuse to go back inside .... Wow, air conditioning is definitely a good thing..... She picked up the phone.... Hey Janet, how's it going?.... It was Mark, and she was happy to hear his voice. They hadn't had a substantial conversation since she'd been to New York sometime earlier... I'm great, thanks, how are you doing?.... I'm good too..... I just thought I'd call to see how things were going. It's been a while..... Well I'm glad you did.... She took the phone back to the couch as they continued to talk.... How's the writing going?.... It's going great, thanks for asking. In fact, it's been so hot here lately, I've barely left the house. It's been a fantastic excuse to get some work done..... You're not going to want to hear this, but I've even gotten some interesting work done on the Mars story.... She laughed as she said it.... I just can't seem to let it go. I have some strange insatiable need to let it play itself out.... Realizing she was getting a little uncomfortable with the conversation as it was, she quickly added, I've been working on some other things too..... That was enough of that, and she changed the subject altogether by turning the conversation back on him entirely..... So anyway, what about you? How have you been?.... Oh I've been good as usual. You know me, I've rarely got much to complain about. I've taken on a couple of new writers who are showing some promise and, generally speaking, things couldn't be better. In fact, I was thinking of heading your way, but maybe I'll wait a few days to see if the heat breaks.... He smiled, knowing that was most likely a ridiculous thing to say. It was always hot in eastern Tennessee that time of year, but it sounded funny anyway, and maybe that was his point......You know, I haven't seen my house for a while, and it would be good to see all of you guys too.... Anyway, nothing is for sure. But don't be surprised if I come knocking at your door sometime soon; or, on second thought, maybe I'll just let myself in.... He laughed. He knew he could get away with that, but she probably wouldn't like it..... There was a pause in the conversation for a few seconds...... Well, maybe I won't be here. Did you ever think of that?... She laughed too.... Ok, so I probably will be... But the truth is, I actually have been thinking about taking another trip... I've spent so much time writing about my characters' adventures lately, it's starting to make me a little antsy to do something interesting myself.... Mark's ears instantly perked up. His thoughts went immediately to a new book but, almost uncharacteristically, he managed to hold it back to some degree, at least for the time being.... Really, well, what are you thinking? Do you know where you might go?.... I've had some thoughts but certainly nothing concrete yet. And besides, it's not like I'm planning to leave tomorrow.... I'm just thinking about it, that's all..... Mark had a lot on his mind, so he managed to leave it at that too.....

The conversation continued for a good hour, though, as two old friends caught up.... Janet thought about mentioning the conversation she'd had with Sara and Carey in the park a few days earlier- the one where they'd given her a hard time about Mark and her getting together, but she never got around to it. When the conversation finally ended, she hung up a little surprised at her reluctance.... Hmmm, that's strange. I'm usually not afraid to talk to Mark about anything, and he probably would have thought it was funny too. So why didn't I say anything?.... It was just a passing thought.... But she did look forward to seeing him again....

The truth was that the conversation with Sara and Carey about Mark had strangely been on the back of her mind ever since it had taken place. But more importantly, and more true to herself, were the thoughts a little more on the forefront- namely, wanderlust.... It had been nearly a year since she'd been out of the country, and it was suddenly starting to catch up with her psychologically. Exploring and experiencing new things had always been an important part of who she was, and it came to her attention that perhaps she'd been neglecting that side of herself lately. Not completely of course. In fact, she was often getting outside for the sake of doing something interesting, but this was different. She decided it might be time to start thinking about the bigger world again. What that meant exactly, she wasn't sure? After hanging up with Mark, she went over and sat down by the huge globe that had been sitting in a living-room corner for years. It was beautiful and, in this seated position, it was bigger than she was.

 Roughly a decade earlier, it had gotten her attention sitting in the dusty back room of a rural antique store, and she knew immediately she had to have it. It was nearly a hundred and fifty years old and, as far as anyone knew, there wasn't another one like it in existence. Of course a lot of the political boundaries had changed, but the geography itself was incredibly accurate. It was beautifully enameled and had generous amounts of bronze inlay and delicate texture. It spun on incredibly smooth bearings, tilted on its axis within a beautifully sculpted iron stand. It was a work of art, and she loved it- possibly her most prized possession.

As she gently turned it with her hand, she reclined even further to where her eye line was just below the equator.... Even with the local heat wave, the tropics sounded nice. Maybe she'd go back to northern Australia, or perhaps Malaysia? As the globe continued to slowly spin, her expression left the room entirely as she began to lose herself in these pleasant little daydreams. Eventually she reclined all the way down in the thick soft carpet and looked up at the bottom of the globe. Antarctica? She smiled at the thought of going back there again.... Maybe someday?... No doubt it was an interesting place, but something else seemed to be calling. She wasn't sure what, but something, and she closed her eyes amused at the thought of traveling again.....Within a few minutes, she had drifted off into a calm peaceful nap....

Slowly, ever so slowly, a gentle motion came to her attention, a peaceful up and down, back and forth. There was light, too. And with this realization, she opened her eyes to a beautiful blue sky with occasional white cotton-candy clouds scattered throughout. It was all very calming, very relaxing. She smiled and continued to lie there for a good long time before finally sitting up to have a first look around. When she did, it was interesting to discover where she in fact was. She found herself lying on a pile of straw atop a floating log raft in the middle of nowhere. There was no land in site, and the horizon was miles away in every direction....

As she stood up to further assess her odd situation, a strange compulsion to dive in slowly came over her. She walked to the edge and took a last unhurried look around before jumping head first into the warm clear welcoming water. It was spectacular, swimming and moving in the slow motion of the water's strange resistance. Soon realizing she could hold her breath for as long as she wanted, she continued swimming downward to a depth of nearly a hundred feet below the raft where she could see it floating and bobbing on the sea's twinkling surface.... The water was incredibly clear...

Looking down, there was nothing but an ever darkening shade of blue that eventually disappeared altogether into the blackness of the abyss.... She stayed still, hovering as she watched the occasional air bubbles escaping from her mouth gradually make their assent. Her long curly red hair hovered around her. She could see it in front of her as she

111

began to spin a lock slowly around an index finger. The entire experience was fascinating and calming- everything was very slow, very peaceful. Time seemed to lose all meaning, even her own thoughts were practically nonexistent. She was just there, and it was beautiful...... Then, still swimming very slowly and still gazing toward the surface, she began to sense something happening in the other direction and started to turn around again. Looking into the deep void below seemed suddenly strange, something very large was slowly moving toward her.... Suddenly, it jumped much closer.... It was the open mouth of a giant eel-like fish, the size of a house.... It was like entering a dark cave as it engulfed her.... The creature closed its mouth and there was total blackness....

Her whole body jolted back to the reality of the carpet beneath the planet. Instantly, her eyes were wide open and blinking for a few seconds as she realized where she was. It was a strange place to wake up at first, and it took a brief moment to recall why she was there in the first place. But, as she did, a huge smile came across her face....Wow, that was interesting.......With that, she sat up and stretched.... It had been a nice little nap, and the dream was even pleasant enough until that last little twist.... She laughed a little more as she wandered into the kitchen still stretching...What was up with that?... Never having been too big on dream analysis, she did briefly wonder what it might mean, if anything.... Maybe being trapped in the mouth of a giant fish somehow represented her subconscious feelings of being so closely tied to own her house over these last few days? Maybe she'd been feeling a little trapped without even realizing it?... But, whatever the case and whatever the reasons for thinking about travel again, she took it seriously. There was no good reason to start ignoring her instincts now, regardless of the initial catalyst. Sure, she may have been feeling a little pinned down by the heat, but it wasn't like she'd been wasting that time... But it was good to be thinking about the bigger world again .... The dream itself had even propagated some interesting thoughts....

After fixing a sandwich, putting on a little Bob Marley, and cracking another cold beer, she sat back down on the couch with her computer, not to write, but to do a little surfing. A little random research sounded like fun.... Well, maybe it was specific in a way, meaning she wasn't exactly shopping for shoes or handbags? It was travel related for sure, but what that might mean as far as an actual destination was concerned was left pretty wide open... She googled "beaches" to see what might come up. Not necessarily as a surprise, 1-10 of apparently some seventy-five million possibilities did. Obviously the options needed whittling down a little and it seemed like a good first step to simply click on one.... Not that it helped- it turned out that the first "Beaches" was referring to a chain of resorts with several destinations worldwide which were probably nice enough places, but not what she had in mind at all. The kind of traveling she liked to do was a little more adventurous than just relaxing on a beach. She liked to get in and blend with people, see what the culture of an area was like, find her own way around, that kind of thing. As far as she was concerned, this was far more exciting than lying around in a lounge chair somewhere having some underpaid native serve her fruity drinks under a big umbrella all day....

Narrowing the search a little, she typed in "Costa Rica." The range of results was once again very broad.... There was everything from sites about the government, the geography in general, the rainforest, rivers, just to cite a few. And of course there were sites about the beaches that must have been somewhere in the seventy-five million of the previous search. In fact, if she'd been even remotely serious about getting any real work done, it might have been a little frustrating; but she was feeling pretty mellow about the whole thing and let herself get sucked into reading some things most likely not even related to her purposes. There was a sad story about pollution in a local river and another about an unsolved murder. After a couple hours of this, she turned the computer off and clicked on the television.

There was a documentary about giant anacondas in the Amazon. She smiled. Of course it reminded her of her story, so she stopped to see what they had to say.... It was probably interesting, but in truth, it was hard to stay focused.... She had other things on her mind...

The dream... being adrift on the open sea was an intriguing thought, and she wondered about the possibilities of actually making it happen. Maybe a sailing trip was exactly what she was looking for. She'd been sailing quite a few times before- enough to know the basics, but not enough to have acquired any real expertise. But she knew she could probably take out a reasonably-sized, live-aboard sailboat for an afternoon outing and have a pretty good chance of making it back in unscathed. From different marinas around the world, she'd met people in her travels who'd been happy to take her out sailing for a while. Maybe it was for a day, a week, or even several weeks at a time, and she'd always enjoyed it. They'd all been great experiences; and out of a simple curiosity, she'd learned a lot about how it was done.... Sure, it had been a while since she'd actually been; but, if she could get someone to give her a refresher course, maybe she could handle a big boat on her own. In fact, she might even be willing to pay for a few lessons if it proved necessary… Ok, now I'm getting somewhere….

The open ocean- wow, what an exciting thought…. She pictured herself on a nice boat, maybe a fifty footer designed for touring and big crossings? She knew if she really wanted to, she could easily afford such a ship. It would be the lap of luxury living on such a boat by herself. It would have a nice well-equipped galley, making it easy to store and prepare whatever meals she'd want in the long distances between remote destinations. There would be comfortable furnishings: a big deluxe bed and ample deck space to lounge and watch the vast beautiful world go by…. Hmmm, very interesting, just pick a place to start and set sail just to see what might happen…. I could do that..…

Finally, at around 2:00am, bed started sounding good, and she went there with these sorts of thoughts still bouncing around in her head…. It was a good idea; but, strangely, it still seemed to be missing something? It wasn't quite unique enough. The big luxurious boat almost sounded too easy. Too many people had already done something similar, and for some strange reason, she was suddenly feeling the need to push herself in some odd new direction. The ocean sounded good. Being adrift on the open water sounded very appealing in fact, but there had to be a more interesting way to go about it. What that meant she didn't exactly know, but she did know the idea deserved more thought…

NINETEEN

Swimming sounded good… It was as hot as it had ever been. Even at 8:00am when she first climbed out of bed and wandered out on the deck, it was already sweltering. She thought about the day ahead and knew she didn't want to spend it inside again. Thoughts of travel and adventure had her at least wanting to get out of the house, so she called Carey to see what she and the kids were up to. They were all still out of school for the summer, of course, so they were always looking for something fun to do. Today seemed like a perfect day for her to help out along those lines, and she was right. Carey was more than happy to play along knowing the kids would be too. They even brought their dog Bongo. Being the big brown happy mutt that he was, he was always glad to get to go anywhere, but he was going to love this…

About fifty miles away, there was a place she'd taken them all before. It was a beautiful swimming hole on a stream called Blue Creek, the last five miles to which were on a steep rocky road where four-wheel drive was almost a necessity. Luckily that wasn't a problem….

Justin and Sally rode in the back with Bongo, and Carey and little Jessica rode up front. They opened the window between the cab and the topper so the older kids could get some air too, which worked fairly well. It definitely made it cooler back there than it might have been otherwise.

The last few bumpy miles took the longest, and some hour and a half after leaving, they arrived and parked under a big oak tree. The kids and the dog, banging and crashing and making a lot noise as they went, made their way out the back as quickly as they possibly could, all extremely excited to be there. Bongo was bouncing and barking and smiling, and the kids were basically doing the same, including the barking. It was fun playing with their dog like he was a kid too.

Janet and Carey got out with little Jessica, who was as eager as everyone else. Not that she was completely sure what they were doing, but she was excited anyway, simply because everybody else was. After gathering up all the necessities, sunscreen, lunch, water bottles, and whatever else, they all headed down the trail. They weren't quite there yet, but almost. It was about a half mile pleasant walk through the forest to get where they wanted to be. But the kids could hardly stand the wait and took off running with Bongo running circles around them, not that he wasn't easily sidetracked by the occasional squirrel.

Less than ten minutes later they were there, and it was a really nice place to be. The trail first landed them on an overhanging rock ledge about fifteen feet above a deep calm pool. To the left was looking upstream where about fifty feet away a 20ft waterfall fed the pool. The trail made a "T" and, down and around to the right, it led to a rocky little beach which the sun would hit most of the day. And that's where they headed first. They put down their towels and stripped down to

115

swim suits. Without much hesitation, Justin ran into the clear cool bluish water first with Sally and Bongo following close behind. Janet could relate and was just as compelled as the kids to go running in but, being the nice responsible aunt she was, she stopped for a minute to see if Carey needed any help dealing with Jessica. They both seemed fine and content taking their time putting on sunscreen and gave her the go ahead- which was all she needed.

A minute later she was surfacing in the middle after gracefully swimming there beneath the surface. It felt great! Pulling her hair back out of her eyes, there was no other place she wanted to be as Bongo the dog swam out to greet her..... Good dog! That's a good boy!... Then she sank back under and headed for the waterfall with open eyes. The water was clean, clear, beautiful, and felt so good. It was cool and refreshing, a perfect relief from the otherwise oppressive heat. As she looked around, she could see the rocky bottom and an occasional small fish swimming by... For an instant, yesterday's dream pleasantly came to mind... Ahead, she could see the turbulence of the falling water as she moved towards it. It formed a white bubbling screen through which she couldn't see, and she surfaced about twenty feet away in the shadow of the trees and mossy cliff. The sound of the water tirelessly making its way downstream was music to her ears, and she reminisced about her high school days when she and her friends had come up here to swim and drink beer and whatever else.... Good Times..... Today was good, too, and she looked back encouraging her niece and nephew to follow.

They were both good swimmers and easily made their way out to her. They laughed and splashed water at each other before moving on and under the waterfall. It was loud and heavy as it pushed them down toward the deep bottom that they never touched. No water slide or ride in any park anywhere could have compared to how much fun it was. It was just the right size to be exciting without being dangerous and, behind the waterfall, there was even a little cave to sit in completely shrouded by the curtain. They were having a fantastic time- and hadn't even jumped from above yet.

There was a perfect rocky ledge next to the waterfall where a person could dive right in with no fear of hitting anything but water. It was awesome, and they could jump from anywhere along the ledge that curved back to the trail. There was a perfect overhanging ledge all the way around and, except where the water sloped in from the beach, it was all deep, making it the ideal swimming hole. They all played and jumped and dove and swam while the dog chased them around for over an hour without even realizing the time was passing.

Meanwhile, Carey and Jessica played in the shallows by the beach and were thoroughly enjoying themselves as well. After a while, Janet swam over to her sister and volunteered to watch her smallest niece for a while if Carey wanted to play and jump and dive for a while- and she did. Of course she did. Carey was a fun person and wanted to play with her older kids, too. And Janet certainly didn't mind watching Jessica. She was a cutie for sure, and they had fun splashing and rolling around in the cool clean water…. A harmless little water snake about a foot long came swimming by, and Janet gently picked him up. As it wound its way around and through her fingers, Jessica was fascinated. She wanted to hold it herself…. Be gentle, don't hurt him…. The little snake wound himself around her little hand, and she squealed with delight before he quickly managed to escape and swim off in another direction…

After a while, Carey made her way back over as the kids continued to play. They were all having a great day as she and her sister relaxed and started to talk. They'd always had good conversations and enjoyed each other's company. Carey of course liked talking about her kids and occasionally about her relationship with her husband Steve whom Janet had always liked. He was a nice guy who loved his family and provided well for them as a computer programmer. Even Carey didn't fully understand the details of what that meant in his day-to-day life, but it didn't seem to matter, so Janet didn't know much about it either. Their marriage got a bit stale at times, as with any marriage, but they loved and respected each other enough to push through the tough times. All things considered, they were doing as well as anybody else and didn't have much to complain about. But when things weren't going completely smoothly, Carey was always glad to have her sister to talk to, and Janet was happy to listen. They had a close relationship that they both valued.

They'd been talking for quite a while before Janet finally mentioned she'd been thinking of taking another trip. And of course Carey was curious…. What are you thinking about doing?… I'm not sure exactly, but just last night it actually crossed my mind to go sailing. I even thought about the possibility of buying a nice boat; but I have to say, and I'm not even sure what I mean by this, that doesn't sound exactly right?…. This is going to sound strange, but for some reason, that doesn't seem like enough of a challenge, and I'm pretty sure something a little more interesting is calling me….Well if you're not sure what you're talking about, then I certainly don't know either, but I can tell you this much. I gave up a long time ago trying to figure out why you do some of the things you do, and that's one of the things I love most about you. You've never been afraid to do things that would sound absurd to most of the general population. The point being, I'm obviously not going to discount anything you might be thinking.... So, what is it?... I know you're thinking something.... Ok, you're right. I am thinking something. Although I don't have it completely defined in my head yet, I do have some interesting thoughts... She smiled at herself, realizing she was about to say it out loud for the first time.... Well, the thing is, I had this dream yesterday while I was napping in my carpet.... It was a fun little dream. Well, until the end that is, which I'll tell you about in second. I was floating on a log raft in the middle of nowhere, and it was so beautiful and peaceful. In the end, I went for a swim and got eaten by a large fish, but that's beside the point... She laughed again.... Don't get sidetracked on that last point. The real point is the raft. It was the simplest thing you can imagine, and there was something appealing about that fact. Did you ever read Kon Tiki, about those guys who set sail from South America on a big balsa wood raft intent on proving that the original Polynesians had migrated from there? Anyway, it was a great book and a true story. I just realized right now that the dream reminded me of it.... Sorry, I'm getting off track.... The thing is, I'm intrigued with the thought of making my own boat of sorts- although, like I said, I'm not sure what that means exactly..... Hmmm, so you're going to make a boat out of "something" and take off sailing from "somewhere" for who knows how long?.....Ok.... They laughed a little bit, both realizing how ridiculous it all sounded.... They both knew if anyone else was talking like this, nobody would take it seriously. But this was Janet. Who knew what she might be capable of?.... She'd done crazy sounding things before, although granted, this seemed to rank right up there... Ok, I know. It sounds bizarre right?... But you have to admit, the idea has potential. It sounds like a hell of an adventure, doesn't it?... I was even thinking I could somehow tie it into a political statement of some sort. In fact, even as I'm saying this, I've got images coming to mind. Think about this. Maybe I could build a craft out some sort of recyclable trash, like 2-liter bottles? Although that doesn't really doesn't sound substantial enough. Maybe I'd need a little tougher building material than that? What about oil barrels?.... At this point she was just thinking out loud, and Carey was enjoying being witness to this strange process.... I could get a bunch of old oil drums and weld them together into pontoons. I'm sure those things could take a beating, and it would be easy enough to have it mean something too.

Empty oil barrels could represent our dwindling need for crude oil due to increasing conservation efforts and increased usage of alternative energy sources. I mean if I were to go on a huge adventure like this, it would be nice to use it to bring attention to an important issue like this, right? The first thing I'd need to do is decide a departure site, then lease a big warehouse somewhere close to the water where I could actually build the thing. That alone would be fun....

Carey could see her sister was getting more and more excited as she talked and watched as the idea was gaining momentum. She knew once Janet got her mind set on something there was no stopping her. Her first instinct was to worry, but she quickly realized how pointless that would be. People had to live the lives they were born to live, and that certainly included her wonderfully crazy sister. To some degree, she even envied Janet's wildly adventurous spirit. But mostly the truth was that she got a lot of vicarious pleasure watching Janet do her thing, and in no way wished things were otherwise. Meanwhile, Janet continued voicing her thoughts, getting more and more worked up as she went. Eventually the rather one-way tangent ended with the statement, "I'm going to have to do some homework." .... With that, she stood up and smiled as she walked back into the water. She was lost in her own little world by then and dove back into the pool with nothing else on her mind...

Sometime later, after what had been an incredible day, the sun was gone. It was late afternoon, so it wasn't dark yet. But the shadows of the canyon had slowly taken over, and everyone finally started realizing it might be time to leave. The kids were having a great time, but it was all catching up with them and they were tired. Bongo was nowhere to be found at first. But when they collectively called for him, he came charging out of the woods having been who knows where, but he'd obviously been having a great day too. They picked up all their things, including of course their garbage from lunch, and headed back up the trail towards the truck... The kids were much slower going the other direction. Justin and Sally were both exhausted, and everybody knew they'd sleep well that night. In fact, using their towels as pillows, they both fell asleep in the back of the truck on the way home. Luckily it wasn't too terribly far because Carey also fell asleep with Jessica asleep on her lap, and all of this sleeping made Janet sleepy too.... But they made it back alright without having to pull over for a nap...

Pulling into the driveway, Carey asked Janet if she wanted to come in and have dinner with them, and she accepted. Neither of them wanted to make it a late night, but food sounded good to everyone as they all slowly dragged themselves inside where Steve was sitting at the kitchen table working at his computer. He greeted them warmly and asked about their day. They were tired, but all agreed it had been a fantastic day. The older kids both ran off and found separate showers in the house while the "grownups" worked on a meal. They made a few hamburger patties to throw on the patio grill and threw together a nice salad too. In the meantime they enjoyed a cold beer, including Steve, who seemed happy to have the company. He enjoyed hearing the details of where they'd been and wished he could have gone along too. Not that it was even remotely possibly given his job, but he was a fun guy who enjoyed having a good time when he got the chance.... Anyway, he was getting some vicarious pleasure of his own when Carey chimed in with the possibly big news....

...So, Janet's thinking about taking another trip. Ask her about it.... Uh, Ok, tell me about your big trip Janet..... They were both looking at Carey at this point- Steve curiously confused, and Janet possibly annoyed at the way she'd mentioned it so abruptly, which in a fun way was probably her intension.... Not exactly sure where to start, she simply said, "yes, I guess I am thinking about another trip." From there she decided to just go with it..... I've kind of been thinking about doing something for a little while now, but as of very recently, I think I'm really starting to narrow down what that might mean.... Steve listened intently as she went on to tell him about the evolution of these most recent thoughts and where they seemed to be leading. At first he just shook his head as he looked at her and smiled.... He laughed a little bit... You know you're crazy, right?.... He was just giving her a hard time.... The truth was that he loved Janet and felt lucky to have her in his life. He loved listening to the way she thought about the world, never questioning that anything was possible. He was glad she was in the lives of his kids too. They all loved their aunt, and he knew she set a great example of how to live life to the fullest, always being true to yourself....

Although, through all of this conversation, the kids had barely made an appearance long enough to grab their burgers and disappear into another room to watch TV, and Carey had long ago put little Jessica to bed too. This was an adult conversation, as it should have been. The things they were talking about were just a little too much information for curious kids. If and when this crazy "boat trip" did take place, they knew it would have to be put in pretty simple terms so the kids wouldn't worry.... But that would be later.

In the meantime, Steve and Carey were both very supportive as they made occasional comments and suggestions on an idea that took hours to discuss. In fact, it went on much longer than any of them would have first anticipated, and it was close to midnight before Janet finally left. They walked her out to the driveway as they said goodbye, and shortly thereafter she was pulling into her own driveway. Glad to finally be home, she took a quick shower before diving into her bed that felt so good.... As she lay there the few minutes before falling asleep, she thought about that fact... Would it be this comfortable on a raft out in the middle of nowhere?...

It could be...

TWENTY

A day or two later, Janet was spending a hot afternoon riding her bike around the city just for the fun of it. She had decided to simply embrace the heat. After all, heat and humidity were a reality, and she got tired of labeling it so negatively. She caked on a bunch of sunscreen and wore a big wide-brimmed sunhat and sunglasses. As a redhead, she was fairly fair skinned and needed to pay attention to the possibility of sun damage which can age a person faster than necessary. But skin cancer was the main concern... Nobody wants that.

She was basically just goofing off but also trying to accomplish a few things as long as she was out. She mailed a few letters at the post office and bought some stamps while she was there. A stopped clock had reminded her she needed batteries, which she got at a local drug store. A little later she stopped at a sporting goods store to have a look around and bought a cold soda from the cooler at the checkout, but nothing else. Then the big bookstore at the mall lured her in. She bought a sailing magazine and stuck it in her daypack before wandering into the mall itself for an hour or so. The air conditioning did feel good, so she stopped at the food court to get a bite to eat as she thumbed through her new magazine. There were some interesting articles and definitely some good photography. However, she was pretty sure there was nothing overly helpful for her purposes…. Maybe an ad for a solar powered GPS?

Eventually she found herself in the big public library, where the air-conditioning also felt good. A little research seemed appropriate, and what better place? It had a productive atmosphere. Everyone appeared to be accomplishing something, and a person couldn't help but want to join in. So sitting down at one of their computers, she went to Google first. Of course she could have done that at home, but… At least it was a place to start.

She typed in "unusual ocean crossings," curious to see what would happen. Figuring she probably wasn't the only crazy person in the world, she was still surprised to see how not alone she in fact was. It turned out people had done all sorts of insane-sounding things over the years. They had peddled across oceans in ridiculous looking human-powered contraptions. They had sailed across in all kinds of strange looking hand-crafted boats made from anything a person could possibly imagine, including trash. There was even a guy building a boat from popsicle sticks with the same intention, although he hadn't set sail yet….

Adventurers had kayaked, windsurfed, wind kited, rowed, and even swum across oceans…. It seemed it might be more difficult than she'd originally thought to stand out among this group. In fact, it would be almost impossible; and, at first glance, this was a little disappointing. No matter what she might do, there would be others out there who could claim that what they'd done was somehow more impressive- and they would probably be right….. So, to be discouraged by this fact would just boil down to having a bad attitude. Besides, it was more about the adventure itself than it was about trying to impress anybody…. On that thought, she smiled and kept searching…

"Global wind patterns" sounded relevant, and sure enough there was some interesting information to be found. The first thing that caught her attention was the trade winds headed west about twenty or thirty degrees both north and south of the equator. Around the equator itself wasn't good. Apparently that's where the "dull-drums" were, where there was no wind at all most of the time. But as the wheels started to spin, she realized that if she could set sail from the southern west coast, possibly even the Baja Peninsula, she could catch these habitual winds and be on her way. On her way to where didn't necessarily matter.

West would be good enough, and from there she would quite literally just flow with the breeze… Wow, what an awesome thought….

As her little daydream continued, she thought about the design of her "boat" and how exactly it might be propelled. Currently she was picturing the boat itself as a big square platform of sorts, with a big square sail on a mast that could easily be taken down if need be. It seemed like a given that the thing would be virtually impossible to steer and would simply go where the winds took it. But, on second thought, maybe there would be a way to drop some sort of rudimentary keel in the water, and it might even be easy enough to fashion a rudder of some kind too. Making a solid enough keel would be the tricky part. She knew the stresses on a keel were enormous relative to any other part of the boat, which meant she'd have to come up with an ingenious way to rig it. That alone sounded like fun. A good challenge was always entertaining. After all, that's what this whole trip was about. So trying to figure out a way to give it some sort of "steer-ability" would simply add another element. And besides, no matter what she did, the thing wouldn't exactly be agile. So it wasn't like any of this would take much away from the unpredictability of the trip. It would simply mean that if she tried aiming for say, Hawaii, she'd at least have a chance of hitting one of the islands somewhere. Having destinations to shoot for could add an intriguing dimension to what she already knew would be an interesting experiment….

After hashing through these thoughts at the library computer for a couple of hours, she decided to head for home. Her head was swimming by this point, so staring at a computer screen was no more productive than her own thoughts anyway. She could daydream from her bike just as easily. As she arrived back in her own neighborhood, she decided to stop in and see if Sara was home. She wasn't, but Janet shoved one of several newspapers through the slot in the front door after writing a message on it…. *Hi Sara, Give me a call when you get a chance*…. She knew Sara would know who it was… She must have been out of town. Janet hadn't heard from her in a few days, which wasn't necessarily unusual, but the newspapers seemed to give it away…

When she got back to her house, she had a couple messages of her own, the first of which was from a telemarketer- which she briefly wondered about the legality. It definitely felt like harassment, and the fact that it was a recording made it even worse…. She quickly caught herself, though, realizing she'd given these sleazy people too much thought already…The second message was from Mark. Apparently he'd been in town for a few hours and was wondering where she was. She called him back, and they talked only long enough to confirm that she'd meet him at his place in an hour. Dinner and a drink or two in good company sounded good to them both…

Mark was a decent cook, and he offered to make one of his simple specialties. They sat in the kitchen and talked as he worked, but he made them both one of his classic margaritas first. He was making quesadillas and wanted to stick with his south-of-the-border theme…. So how's the writing going?… Mark, never having been one to beat around the bush, got right to the heart of what he was thinking. He was forever a businessman and couldn't have helped it if he wanted to…. He'd practically forgotten that she'd mentioned traveling again, or he probably would've asked about that first. But, whatever the case, it slipped his mind…..Well, like I told you earlier, I've actually gotten quite a bit of work done lately. It's going well…. She tried to act annoyed with his immediate line of questioning, but knew him too well to hold it against him. It was just his nature. What she really wanted was to start telling him her thoughts of another trip, but realized she could increase the potential shock value by putting it off a little while longer. She asked him about the new writers he had mentioned, again taking the focus off of her by letting him talk about himself first. Not realizing what she was up to, he was more than happy to oblige. And besides, she really was curious about his life too. She did want to know about the new writers. If Mark was serious about taking them on at all, they must have been interesting, and they were. Apparently they were both fiction writers. One was a coroner in his real life who wrote thrillers from the perspective of medical examiners, sort in the line of the legal thrillers by John Grisham from the perspective of lawyers… The other was a science-fiction writer apparently doing well in exploring the possibilities of time travel. Mark was easily lost in talking about them both. He was passionate about what he did and excited at the idea of having some talented new clients. It was fun to listen to, too. As Janet paid close attention, she forgot all about her own issues, and before they both knew it, dinner was ready…

Of course it was delicious, and afterwards they adjourned to the living room where they kicked back in his big comfortable over-stuffed furniture. She took the big blue chair and he the couch. They were both over stuffed themselves and enjoying the feeling. In fact, neither of them even said anything for a good long time, and they may have even dozed off for a minute or two. But finally, after a while, Mark sat up and suggested a swim…

He had a great place. The lot was more than two full acres, and the
house itself was just over four-thousand square feet, over half of which
constituted the one big space that was the kitchen, dining-room, and
living-room combined. The architecture was unique. From the outside
it had a very modern appearance, using concrete block walls that took
full advantage of their passive solar energy qualities. Practically the
entire south facing wall was thick doubled-paned glass partially for the
same reason, but all the natural light was a motivating part of the
design too. All the pitches of the roof slanted in the same direction,
down from south to north to allow good runoff and maximum height
for the glass walls. The property was well landscaped, including the
lagoon-style swimming pool in the back, along with a couple of
commissioned kinetic steel sculptures; and the older trees that had been
there for decades topped the whole thing off nicely…

From the inside, the place had a surprisingly comfortable, almost
cozy feel for its size. It was warm and pleasant and far from the cold
sterile feeling sometimes associated with modern architecture. The
entire house was thickly carpeted, and the large master suite had a
beautifully ceramic-tiled hot tub in one of the corners, while the
bathroom itself had a large walk-in shower and double of everything
else you might want in a bathroom. The other two bedrooms had
generous proportions as well, also with their own private lavatories.
But it was the large common space that truly made the house special. It
had a large fire place that, between it and the large windows, almost
made the radiant floor heat unnecessary. The large circular stone
chimney was equally in both the living room and on the outside back
patio. It separated the glass wall and could be opened to see the one big
fire from both inside and out. Or, through the coldest months, it could
easily be closed off to separate the two sides.

The large tapering wall that divided the house was whimsically used
for climbing and covered with hundreds of molded stone climbing
holds. The wall itself was painted with a brightly colored graffiti style
mural that he had commissioned another local artist to do. It was
purposefully done in way that all the shoe and chalk scuff marks would
almost look like an intentional part of the design… On the relative
short wall, there was built-in water feature in the form of a koi pond. It
was about fifteen feet long and roughly four feet wide coming out from
the wall made to look like natural rock. The containing wall also looked
like natural granite, and there were a few places that made nice seats

along the way, with planters full of healthy plants in between. In the center, there was a rather abstract stainless steel sculpture. As it climbed toward the ceiling, it contained seven separate bowl-like containers through which water poured from one to another until the final drop into the pond itself. The shiny steel contrasted nicely with the dark stone, and the whole thing was lit from both below and above…. It was nice having the sound of running water in the house, and the four large colorful fish and one slider turtle all had names.

Some might say the place was a bit strange, but Mark certainly didn't care. It's not like he'd consulted a designer about any of it anyway. He'd just done what sounded good to him, including the commissioned art. All ideas were his, and he loved everything about it- regardless of what anybody else thought. Although, almost anyone he'd ever had over throughout the years had genuinely seemed to like what he'd done with the place… And that definitely included Janet…

…. Sure, a swim sounds great… She had a swimsuit in her truck and a few minutes later was diving into the beautifully refreshing pool. Mark was still in the house; but a few minutes later, after setting a couple of fresh drinks on the side, he was diving in too. A few patio lights were on, as well as a few well-placed lights under the water's surface. Lenny Kravits was playing through some quality outdoor speakers, and everything combined was making for an incredibly pleasant evening. The water felt good. The custom pool looked good, the music sounded good, and the drinks tasted good. And, on top of all that, they both knew they were in good company….

They swam and talked and joked and splashed water at each other… Finally, as she nonchalantly took a sip of her salt-rimmed margarita, Janet blurted out…. So, I'm pretty seriously thinking about building a raft to set sail off the west coast headed for who knows where? Doesn't that sound like fun?…. She looked at him and smiled, watching as it slowly sank in….. WHAT!… Say that again…. as he practically choked on his drink… She laughed as the statement took its intended effect…. Based on your reaction, I'm pretty sure you heard me correctly…... Yea, I only came up with the idea a few days ago. But, the more I think about it, the more excited I seem to get…. Mark, shocked the way he was supposed to be, wanted to know every detail of what she was thinking- including how the idea came to be in the first place. She told him about the crazy dream under the globe, how she'd already been discussing the idea with Carey and Steve…. She told him about building a platform on pontoons made from oil drums and about her day at the library deciding that she wanted to leave from the peninsula south of California. Once again, she was having a really fun one-sided conversation on the subject. So far, she could feel her adrenaline levels rise and her heart beating faster every time she talked about it, which, at least in her own mind, seemed like a good sign... Mark, on the other hand, was flabbergasted by the whole thing. He barely knew what to think and was having a hard time just catching up, maybe even catching his breath, but he did his best to play along. If this story had been coming from anybody else, he would have laughed it off and chalked it up to the random rambling of a person who'd had one-too-many margaritas..... but this was Janet. He knew he should probably take it seriously.... So, when do you think you might leave on this little adventure?... Oh, I don't know. Obviously there will be a lot of work to do first, but it's work I'd like to get started on....

Without missing too many beats, Mark was quick to see the marketing value of the idea. After all, even though he never could have seen this coming, he'd been waiting for months to hear what her next big adventure might be....

You know, your fans are going to love this.... In fact, as the thought sank in further, his big cheesy smile got even bigger.... This might be your best-selling book ever!... At this point, he was just trying to be funny by making this about him when it obviously wasn't. In other words, he understood the annoyed look Janet shot him and started laughing.... Oh come on, you know how I am. You know I can't help it. Surely you've thought about it yourself?... It had crossed her mind, but barely. She already had her hands full with the book she was currently trying to write, but she knew he had a point. If and when this "sailing" thing ever did take place, it was bound to make a great story. But... even so. She was still trying to be annoyed.... Shouldn't you be worried about my safety or something?... I mean I just told you I'm planning to set sail on the vast Pacific Ocean on a raft I'm going to make myself out of practically nothing, and the only thing you can think about is your wallet.... I can't believe Sara and Carey think we would make a good couple. They have no idea how insensitive you are...

Again, WHAT!... Who thinks we would make a good couple?... Janet started laughing again too as she realized what she'd just said... Yea, we were all walking in the park the other day. Just out of the blue, they both started giving me a hard time about it. They were going on and on about how much we get along and how much we have in common, how much we obviously care about each other, blah blah

blah… They were trying to make the argument that it was the natural next step…. Well you're just full of surprises tonight, aren't you?… What did you say to all of that?… What do you think I said? I told them we were just friends and have been for years. I told them neither of us thinks that way and that neither of us would want to risk our friendship by experimenting with something it's not…. Yea, of course that's what you said…. And from there, Janet and Mark both just stood there in what might have been an awkward pause if they weren't both a little buzzed from the tequila…. Instead, they spaced out a little; but, as Mark thought about it, and being the male he was, he couldn't help but suddenly notice how beautiful she was…. standing there in the pool, in her swimsuit, with her long red hair. She was in great shape and had a great body, and her occasional freckle was so cute…. Meanwhile, she'd gone back to thinking about her raft and had practically forgotten about it…. He thought about pursuing the issue a little further but could see she was no longer there, so he let it drop too, thinking it was probably for the best. She was probably right. To start fooling around now probably wasn't a good idea at all, and he continued trying to convince himself of this. He'd let his mind wander someplace he probably shouldn't have, and it was taking him a few minutes to move past it…

So I was thinking, I might take an important first step and go out to Baja fairly soon…. I was thinking I might fly out to Cabo San Lucas next week to start having a look around….. you know, scope the place out a little. I figure starting at the end of the peninsula and going from there might be the most fun way to go about it. And besides, I've never been there. I've heard it's a nice place. I've just never been myself. I thought it might be a good idea to go spend a few days, maybe even longer. It would be a good opportunity to really start visualizing what I'm talking about. I think it would make the whole thing a little more real to start figuring out an actual starting point, and do you know what? I just thought of this…. Why don't you come with me? It'll be fun, and how long has it been since you've taken a real vacation anyway? Come to think of it, as much as I've traveled, you and I have never been anywhere significant together. It really would be fun… So what do you think? Do you want to go?

Mark, still having a little difficulty getting over the last conversation, wasn't sure what to think. Did this trip thing have anything to do with the previous discussion? Based on her energy, he was pretty sure it didn't, and he quickly chastised himself for still not getting over it…... Ummm, well maybe? I guess I could think about it. I'm not like you, Janet. I have a little harder time with spontaneity, but I have to admit it does sound like a good time…. Good then, it's settled. You are coming with me to Mexico…. Uh, ok, I guess there isn't anyone who can't live without me for a few days…. Sure, why not?…. He smiled as he realized what he'd just committed to…. And do you know what, I'll even pay for everything. It'll be easy enough to write it all off as a business expense anyway…. Ok, I'll let you…. as she splashed water in his face again….

TWENTY-ONE

Going back to New York first wasn't a hard sell. Of course Mark needed to tie up a few loose ends before he could feel good about leaving and, not that it mattered, but the flight was probably cheaper out of the city anyway…

It was a nice drive that gave them a good long time to talk before the trip. They took Janet's truck just because she wanted to. Mark had originally flown to Knoxville but had a couple of different cars they could have taken if need be. He was happy that she volunteered, though, and he paid for the gas simply because he already said he would… She had more than enough money to live very comfortably but knew that Mark had more and didn't feel a bit bad about letting him spend some, especially when he volunteered…

Anyway, it was a good opportunity to finally start opening up about what she'd been writing. Before now, except for the Mars story, she'd only jokingly beat around the bush about it from the beginning of her new project- and for a couple of different reasons. The first of which was probably Mark's less-than-favorable reaction to that story. He'd made it perfectly clear from the beginning that he was less than thrilled with the idea, which understandably may have left her feeling a little gun shy. But there was more to it than that. The more likely cause of her less-than-open attitude was that it was just a natural part of her personality. In practical terms, she was a very private person. It wasn't personal- that's just the way it was, and the people who knew her best had simply learned to live with it and not take it personally. They knew she lived life largely inside her own head and even came across as spacey and aloof a lot of the time. But none of that meant she didn't care. She just seemed to relate differently than most....

....Do you remember when I was last in the city and you were telling me all about your resident ghost?... What was his name again, Billy?.... Anyway... The question was a lead-in to telling him about her own ghost story.... She told him how much fun she was having with it, how in many ways it seemed to be opening her own mind to the possibilities of an unseen spiritual reality...

Mark listened intently as she went into more and more detail about the things she was working on and even gained a little more respect for the Mars travelers. It seemed theirs might be an interesting tale after all as she described their crash landing and everything else they were dealing with. She went on to tell him about the story of the divorcing couple and even some of the stories that had yet to make it to print. John, the guy who'd been hit by a scorching meteor, and the guy who'd been cut in half by the train were both characters she planned to include at some point.... It was easy to let Janet monopolize the conversation for as long as she wanted. In fact, he almost felt privileged having the opportunity to listen to the way she thought. She was the most wonderfully odd person he'd ever known..... Taking this little trip with her would be fun...

The next morning's flight to LA passed quickly, and the second flight was a short one.... Standing at the carousel waiting for their bags, Mark was nervously proud of himself for even being there. He tended to be a bit of a workaholic, so taking this trip "spur of the moment" was kind of a big deal for him. Not that he didn't enjoy the occasional sort-of-adventure... but he was with Janet now and feeling a bit like an amateur because, comparatively, he was. He was definitely out of his element and doing his best not to let his nearly neurotic need to know every detail of his life ahead of time ruin their fun. He was a planner and was trying his hardest not to let Janet's plan to just kind of "wing it" drive him crazy right from the beginning. If he'd had it his way, they would've had a hotel room reserved with a shuttle there waiting for them. But, even though he was paying for it, he knew this was her trip and wanted to enjoy it as such. The truth was, in their current situation, he wished he were more like Janet. So he was trying to see this as an opportunity to learn even when deep down it was stressing him out a little. ...... Although, he did rent them a car without telling her...

... A Hummer? you got us a Hummer?.... She laughed.... You don't know the first thing about not being the stereotypically obnoxious American tourist do you?... What? So I wanted us to have a cool car. What's the big deal?... He really didn't get it- and didn't care. He was actually pretty happy with his decision. She understood and just let it go- besides, it was a very comfortable ride. And she opened the map as they left the airport parking lot...

....Ok, well, I guess there's no better place to start than the beginning. Obviously we're here to start exploring the Pacific side, and it looks like highway 19 does just that. Let's find it and start heading north.... It was midafternoon, and she smiled at the thought that they didn't have to be anywhere.... It looks like it heads right up the coast toward the town of Todos Santos, maybe fifty or so miles from here. Now all we have to do is find the road. That should be easy enough.... And theoretically it should have been, but it took well over an hour before they were finally headed in the right direction. Being lost right off the bat could have been a little frustrating without the right attitude.... Luckily, at this point neither of them really cared and thought it was funny....

It was a beautiful place to be. Mark even had a hard time keeping his eyes on the road and, on more than one occasion, Janet was tempted to reach over and grab the wheel.... I'm glad you're enjoying the scenery, but in case you haven't noticed, you need to drive too. In fact, do you want me to drive?.... No, I've got a better idea. How about neither of us drives, and we pull over and go for a swim... He was already taking a left onto a dirt road .... Suddenly, he'd decided to do something completely spontaneous, and it felt great. The huge truck bounced off the main road as their heads nearly hit the ceiling....

Plowing through the sand and off the road completely, they came to a stop less than a hundred feet from the breaking surf. Mark was smiling and laughing like an excited little kid. Janet was glad to be there, too, although in the moment she looked at him like he was crazy... Calm down. What's gotten into you?.... Nothing, what do you mean? Look at this place. We've got this beautiful beach all to ourselves. Don't you want to go for a swim?... She briefly wondered if he was trying to show off, but then quickly tried to take the thought back.... It truly was a great place to be and she should just be proud of him for appreciating it...

131

They looked around, taking in deep breaths of the clean salty ocean air. It was about eighty-five degrees with a slight onshore breeze. They quickly changed into swimwear before making their way to the water. It felt just the slightest bit cold at first touch; but it was beautiful, clean, and clear, and the initial slight chill didn't cause either of them to hesitate. They walked out into the surf and both dove in under the same small wave. Some sets were bigger than others, as was always the case, but none of the waves was over five feet tall. They were all friendly enough, and the soft sandy bottom tapered out gently… Nearly fifty yards out they could still touch bottom in the wave troughs, and it was the perfect place for a mellow ocean swim….

Getting tumbled in the ocean for a while was a relaxing almost Zen-like experience. At one point, a California sea lion even swam by and almost certainly acknowledged their presence… He seemed to be smiling and trying to teach them to bodysurf…. He'd look up at them and glide down a shimmering face…. Later, a school of dolphins swam by, too, including a few youngsters. At their closest, they were probably less than thirty feet away… It was fantastic being out there with all of them; and by the time they finally walked back out a couple of hours later, they were both completely refreshed and ready for whatever might be next….. And it was ok if that meant doing nothing for a while…. In fact, they just sat in the sand for a good long time without even saying much. It was nice just listening to the surf and watching the seagulls as the sun slowly got lower on the horizon…

Janet posed a question first…. What should we do next?… It seemed there was no rush to do anything, but they did need to make a decision at some point. For example, where were they going to stay? She had camping gear and had told Mark to at least bring a sleeping bag and pad. This was a nice place for sure; and judging from the sky, they probably wouldn't even need the tent. However, other questions quickly became relevant when they realized all they had was junk food from the plane because they'd neglected to stop at a grocery store. Even if they did decide to spend the night, they needed to get something to eat first. Both suddenly realized they were starving, so it didn't take long for them to get changed and be on their way again…

At the highway, they agreed to take a left and head for the next town. It shouldn't be far, and they could wait that long to eat. They saw the sun dip below the horizon just as they pulled into town where thankfully it was easy enough to find a nice little restaurant. An hour later, they were both completely full and realizing how tired they were. As far as their personal body clocks were concerned, it was three hours later than the clock on the wall was claiming. And sleeping somewhere, anywhere, was quickly becoming the biggest priority. The option of a shower and a comfortable bed made them both glad they'd left the beach. So, after asking the waiter for a recommendation, they drove a couple of blocks down the street to where he'd suggested, and it seemed he'd steered them right. The place was modest but clean and nice, and the family who owned and ran it was extremely accommodating. Their English was fair, and Janet's Spanish was about the same. Between the two languages, they were all able to communicate fairly well, which allowed the very pleasant conversation to go on much longer than it might have otherwise. It seemed they were making some new friends. And by the time they finally went to their room, they'd all made plans to have breakfast together in the morning- as that was basically part of the deal anyway...

The next day, after sleeping in a little, it was nice to casually meet up again with Jorge and Rita. They were probably in their early sixties and running the hotel and small restaurant with the help of both their son and daughter. Maria appeared to be in her late thirties and had a couple of small children. Pedro was apparently a couple of years older, and as a family they seemed close. It was nice getting to know a little about them over a meal and few cups of coffee. They were very open and happy to talk about themselves and their simple wholesome lives. They were happy in general and appreciated what they had.

After a while, Janet finally got around to telling them the real reason they were there. Before then, neither of them had answered the question anything but vaguely... As she went on to tell them of her plans to set sail from somewhere along their beautiful coast, they were surprisingly unflustered......even when she told them what she planned to set sail on. It was great! And she pretty much immediately felt completely comfortable telling them every detail of her thought process. They were very curious but never judgmental. Before today, they had absolutely no idea who she was and yet never doubted for a minute that she was totally serious. In fact, after hearing that one of the reasons she was there was to start looking for a good place to build her boat, Pedro chimed in with an idea of his own ...

... My brother-in-law is probably someone you should meet. He runs a metal fabrication shop and has a nice piece of property with several buildings on it. He might be able to help. But regardless, I'm sure he'd be very interested in talking to you about it... Janet's eyes opened wide.... REALLY! It would be great to meet him! When do you think that might be possible?... I don't know, but he's probably around right now if you'd want to take a short ride over there…. Of course she was very interested and suggested they take the Hummer…..

They didn't have to go far, and Pedro greatly enjoyed the ride in their vehicle. According to him, it was the nicest car he'd ever been in…. as they bounced down the dirt road to Pete's place. Pete was an American Vietnam veteran who'd moved several decades earlier to get away from the less-than-accommodating American public after returning from the war. He was a great guy who'd had to work hard to overcome the psychological damage he'd suffered. He was kind of quiet but had a big heart. His only real goal in life was to live in peace and be as good a person as he could be. He'd been married to Pedro's wife's sister for many years, although they'd never had any children….

When they pulled up, sure enough they found him in his shop, welding mask on his head and torch in hand… He smiled a shy little smile as he was introduced…. It's nice to meet you, Janet, Mark…. Pedro went on to explain why they were there. He talked about Janet's plan to set sail and how she was looking for a place to build her boat. Janet quickly interjected…. If this seems like something that might be good for us both, I'd be happy to pay you a fair price of course…. Pete continued smiling his charmingly humble smile…. Well, let's not get ahead of ourselves. I might be interested in helping out if I can, but you might want to have a look around a little first…. He pointed down toward the vast beautiful ocean less than a quarter mile away… My property goes clear to the beach; and, as you can see, I've got a couple of buildings down that way. However, I can tell you now that only one of them has enough electricity to run a welder, and it sounds like that's what you're looking for. But, on second thought, it would probably be the better of the two for your purposes anyway…. He was basically just thinking out loud… There's even a fairly comfortable room above the shop that has a bed in it if you'd want to live up there while you worked. It's nothin' special, but it might be alright. There's a bathroom downstairs in the shop with a sink and a toilet, but there's no shower. You could probably rig something up fairly easily though… Well , why don't we just go down there so you can see it for yourself if you're still interested…. Sure, definitely, let's do that… As they walked, Janet raised her brow and looked at Mark as if to say, Can you believe this?…. He could tell she was getting excited already. After all, they'd only been there less than twenty four hours, and even he could see they may have stumbled into the perfect setup already. And it dawned on him that, if this was indeed the perfect place, it must have been much more than simple coincidence. He suddenly realized he might very well be witnessing destiny and intension manifesting themselves right before his eyes. He understood that when a person got in line with what she was supposed to be doing with her life, the universe had a strange way of cooperating.....

As they arrived, Pete took the big padlock off the door before they could enter. It was a bit jammed due to the settling of the old building, so he gave it a kick. There were several big windows and a big overhead door that they unlocked and opened to let the breeze blow through. A few big wooden crates scattered the floor, and there was a big piece of what looked like old farm equipment. There were considerable dust and cobwebs. It looked like the building hadn't been used for much of anything in a long time. They walked up the central stairs to the attic room above. Sure enough there were a bed and several old dressers lined up against one of the walls, but that was it. The one big room was empty otherwise. Each floor was at least 1800 square feet....There was no question the place needed a thorough cleaning, but that wasn't a problem...

She thought about trying to underplay her enthusiasm before figuring, WHY? The place did seem perfect... more than big enough and very close to the ocean.... So Pete, I must tell you, I am very interested.... How much do you think you'd need in rent?... He scratched his head for a minute before naming what seemed like a ridiculously low price... Janet played it cool and didn't over react, mostly because she didn't want to insult his sensibility in the moment. But she was already thinking that if things worked out well, she'd give him a big bonus somewhere down the road.... Well, that sounds fair enough. Although, I should probably think about it a little bit first... I'll tell you what..... Mark and I are going to be around for another few days just having some fun... Can I give you a call sometime over the next week or two? I promise I'll let you know either way... Sure, that's fine. Take your time. As you can probably see, I'm in no big hurry.... He chuckled.

After dropping Pedro back off at the hotel and saying their goodbyes to the family, Mark announced an idea... While you obviously have a lot to think about, why don't we take our time and drive back up to Los Angeles?... We'll stay wherever we feel like along the way. We can play and swim on the beaches, and it'll give you some time to think about what you want to do... Sure, that sounds great...... although, she was pretty sure she already knew what to do...

The remainder of the trip was great, and they had a fantastic time

135

doing exactly what Mark had described. But, as you can imagine, Janet was elsewhere a considerable amount of that time, thinking about what the near future probably held… But that didn't mean she couldn't recognize a good "now" too. She enjoyed that Mark seemed to be having the time of his life. They swam and snorkeled and even did a little surfing. Janet was a decent surfer, and Mark was having a good time trying on the boards he'd rented. They slept on beaches and occasionally shared a hotel room, although they both felt a slight sexual tension when this occurred. It was purely plutonic, but the possibility of something else was always on the back of both their minds. Neither ever verbalized it, but it never seemed far beneath the surface either… They partied a little, drinking the occasional big margarita and even smoking a little reefer a local kid had been more than happy to sell them… In the end, the trip was at least as good as either of them had hoped it would be…

When Mark was finally back in New York and Janet in Tennessee, she called Pete to tell him the news. After spending a long day in the library confirming that his would indeed be a good place to set sail from, and after further discussing it with those closest to her, she planned to head his way fairly soon intent on paying at least as much as he'd asked for in rent. She sincerely thanked him for the opportunity and formally confirmed that she looked forward to seeing him again…. The conversation was short, but sweet…

TWENTY-TWO

Over the next several weeks, she settled into the idea of being committed to this thing. Obviously, there was a lot that needed to be done before she could actually leave. The way she saw it, it could potentially be a very long time before she'd be back again. At the very minimum, it would probably be nearly a year and could very easily be much longer than that. Maybe she'd come back for a few days before actually setting sail. But at that point, it would be more like a visit; and she wouldn't want to have to worry about anything else...

She contacted the property management company who'd taken care of her place before when she'd been away for long periods of time. The idea wasn't to rent her house out- she just needed someone to look after it.... They'd water the plants, take care of the yard, and even dust occasionally so everything would stay clean. She knew them personally and liked them. And, most importantly, she trusted them. In fact, they were the same people who took care of Mark's place when he wasn't around, which was most of the time.... They had the phone numbers of her parents and sister and even Sara; and if anyone they knew was visiting and needed a place to stay, they were welcome to use her place. It was a very generous offer, but she was too laid back to see it that way. If she was going to be gone anyway, of course her friends and family and any of their friends and family were welcome to use it... It seemed like a given...

A little more research revealed that the oil drums would be easy enough to acquire, and she ordered fifty of them to be shipped down from southern California. They'd be waiting at Pete's place when she got there. Not knowing exactly what else she would need, she had fifty sheets of ¾" plywood sent down on the same truck along with a couple hundred 2x4's. Obviously she was thinking pretty big, and a phone conversation with her new landlord revealed that he could easily order any steel or hardware she might need. It was fine with him that a big delivery was headed his way, and he was happy to let them put the huge pile of supplies in her building. He didn't ask for it, but she mailed a check for three months rent shortly after confirming that she did indeed want to take him up on his offer... They seemed comfortable with each other and seemed to be building a mutual trust already...

In the very beginning of this planning process, she'd thought about trying to tie her little adventure to a political statement of one kind or another. However, after admitting to herself that it was never really anything but an afterthought and never her true focus, it started feeling a little tacky to try to attach some secondary meaning to it. While she had always been opinionated, she'd never been much of an activist before and trying to start now just didn't seem to fit. Plus, media attention would be necessary for it to have any meaning; and perhaps the biggest reason she didn't follow through was because deep down she didn't want the attention. She'd get enough of that later when she wrote the story, but as the trip was actually happening, it seemed it might take too much away from the true solitary nature of the experience she'd originally envisioned. Bottom line: she didn't want that many people knowing what she was doing as she was doing it. With a little more introspection, she realized the real point of this trip was the trip itself, the sheer adventure of it all, and that was enough. The idea had enough merit on its own.... And besides, she could always donate some of the book's proceeds to a favorite charity later...

As all her ducks seemed to be falling in line, she made the decision to drive across the country rather than fly; but she gave herself plenty of time to relax and enjoy thinking about it first. She hung out with the kids and took them all swimming again. She took some bike rides and did a little rock climbing with Sara and enjoyed getting some feedback from her. As one of her best friends, Sara was of course very supportive. Although, like most people, it was all difficult for her to relate to personally..... adventure was great and all, but setting sail on some homemade raft for who knows how long? She knew it wasn't something she'd ever want to do, but she wished her friend luck- and deep down admired Janet's spirit. Whatever happened, she knew it would be interesting...

Eventually she threw Janet a big going-away party with everyone there- friends, family, neighbors, and of course Mark came down from New York for the big send-off. He and Sara were already making plans to visit Baja at least once during the construction. It would just be too good an opportunity to pass up. They'd both be curious to witness this bizarre process firsthand and planned to come down for the actual launch, too, along with anyone else who wanted to come...

Finally, sometime in late September, the time came. She hugged the few people who'd come to see her off early one cloudy morning and waved goodbye as she pulled out of the driveway. She stopped at a mini mart, filled her tank with gas and a big travel mug with coffee and headed west on I40.... Jumping onto the open road was a great feeling...

The plan was to take her time and campout along the way, meaning sleeping in her truck most nights. The first night was spent in a park overlooking the Mississippi River, and the subsequent days and nights played out in places like Moab, Utah, the Grand Canyon, and Las

Vegas before heading down to San Diego where she eventually crossed the border...

However, a little shopping seemed in order first. Who knew how difficult it might be to get supplies where she was going? It just made sense to fill a huge cart full of anything she could think of in a last-minute gigantic store. She loaded up with everything from non-perishable groceries and kitchen tools, like a hot plate, microwave, and mini fridge, to a dozen 20'x 30' tarps- not to mention any other odds and ends that happened to catch her eye. By the time she was finished, there were several cart loads that filled most of the back of her truck, and it felt good, like she was doing what needed to be done.... Then, after topping off her gas tank one last time, she passed through the huge border gate to finally start making her way down the peninsula...

It was nice being back where there were beaches, and before long she felt the need to stop. Of course, after the big shopping spree, there was no room to sleep in the truck; but the sand was soft and the weather was nice. Although, it was slightly cooler than expected which made her little campfire feel especially nice. There were a few random pieces of driftwood scattered around that burned well and, after making herself some dinner, she kicked back intent on losing herself in the flames as it slowly got dark....

Tongues of brightly colored energy crackled and danced and flickered their way into her subconscious in the most wonderfully mesmerizing way. The pleasantness of the moment was like a meditation of sorts as all the other thoughts of the day seemed to gracefully slip away.... Eventually, she lay all the way back and slowly drifted off to sleep looking up at the stars....

...It was very odd standing atop a huge building amidst the seemingly enormous surrounding city. The brilliantly beautiful skyline seemed to go on forever in every direction as she spun around in the middle of what must have been a very long night.... Maybe it's always dark here?... Slowly, she made her way to the perimeter wall where she could see all the way to the ground that appeared to be thousands of feet below. There were a few tiny cars moving slowly and silently on the streets, and the few tiny pedestrians were almost indistinguishable. They were so far away they seemed unrelatable in a way, like perhaps they weren't even real? It was all too quiet to be real. The people down there were in a separate dimension of reality, interesting only as visual images as opposed to actual human beings...

With a subtle and distant smile, she slowly and mechanically climbed up on the wall and stood there for a minute. She took deep deliberate breaths while the tips of her toes hung ever so slightly over the edge. As she looked down, her smile broadened with the realization of where she was. This was the edge, the edge of life itself..... She liked it and continued standing there silently for several long minutes before turning to the right to take a first small step. The top of the building was huge, and the wall that went around the entire edge suddenly seemed worth exploring. She placed her next step squarely at the center and began moving very deliberately heal-to-toe as if balancing on a beam. She held out her arms pretending the wall was much narrower than it actually was. She looked up at the beautiful starry sky and noticed the full moon that suddenly made sense of the pleasant subtle glowing of blue light. As she came to a corner, she made the first of the four right turns and continued her deliberately unhurried journey of the outer edge. Each step was slow and purposeful, and the views were incredible all around and in every direction. The air was crisp and cool and the occasional slight breeze never seemed to come from any particular direction...The building itself must be causing the air to eddy and swirl... A bright shooting star burned across the sky and disappeared over the horizon, followed quickly by another, but that was it. There were only two, which seemed odd... and she scanned the sky for several long minutes looking for more....

Eventually, after a strangely gratifying little walk, she found herself back where she'd started. She turned her body back toward the city and once again hung her toes just the tiniest bit over the edge. It was odd, just standing there contemplating where she was. It was beautiful and peaceful, and strangely, for the first time, she wondered what in the world she could possibly be doing there?... Briefly, ever so briefly, it dawned on her that she had to be dreaming.... Nothing about any of this is real...?

With that thought, a huge smile crossed her face that expressed just how fully she accepted this notion. She leaned forward, curious what this dream gravity might be like, and immediately it worked. Although, it seemed to take its effect less quickly than one might normally expect. Sure enough, she started to fall. But as she did, she very naturally seemed to have complete control of her body as it accelerated into the open space. With very little effort, she did a perfect back flip, arms fully extended out from her side and her body completely straight. It was amazing, and she decided to turn several more times before falling into a steady head-first dive. As she went faster and faster, the ground far below moved closer, and she began to feel the strong wind in her face. It felt good. So to feel it more fully, she flattened herself, exposing more surface to the force of the air. With that came the discovery that she could stop the motion entirely if she so chose. She could stand completely still, suspended above the city streets. The few cars and people, much closer now, continued on their way completely unaffected.... She slowly turned around and peered into the building that just moments earlier she'd been standing so contently on top of....

There was a big window with the curtains mostly drawn, but there was a gap of several inches. As she looked closer, something appeared to be happening on the other side. Finally, with her face mere inches from the glass, she realized this wasn't the inside of a typical city building at all. It was completely different, something completely unrelated. Very strangely, she seemed to be looking at herself, and yet it wasn't as simple as a reflection. As the image became clearer, she realized she was looking at herself as a child. In fact, it was she and her sister playing on the floor of their childhood home. They were very young and playing in the thick carpet with toys scattered all around. They were smiling and seemed to be enjoying themselves, although she couldn't tell exactly what they were doing or saying... As she continued to watch for a while, the girls slowly became aware of her presence there. They looked toward the window, slowly stood up and began moving towards her. Their smiles gradually morphed into looks of confused curiosity... Suddenly, in an instant, they jumped forward and were mere inches away. They were glaring directly at her from the other side of the glass....

BANG! There was a loud noise and a sudden and intense burning sensation on her face. Swiftly, and very unpleasantly, she was jolted back to the beach by some popping embers in the fire. Something hot had landed on her cheek, and she jumped to a seated position as she quickly slapped it away.... What the hell? That was weird.... After a brief moment of confusion, she rolled over and went back to sleep without giving it much further thought...

The following morning, the rising sun slowly made its way over the horizon. Its warm glowing rays struck her face again, although in a decidedly more pleasant way. As she groaned and stretched, she found the beach an amazing place to wake up on a beautiful new day. As she looked toward the water, a flock of seagulls seemed to slowly be waking up too.... Hmmm, maybe I'll help?... A few pieces of bread from a loaf in the truck seemed like a pleasant way to greet them and, sure enough, they were very happy to see her as they gathered around. Meandering barefoot in the surf, she was happy to see them too as they eagerly devoured every small bit of food she offered.... Hmmm, maybe I'm hungry too?...

The fire was barely still smoldering, but with a little coaxing it was easy enough to get it going again..... A couple of relaxing hours later, after some creative campfire breakfast and coffee, she eventually decided to pack up and start moving south again ....

As she got into the groove of driving, the previous night's dream inevitably came to mind. She'd had a few surprisingly vivid dreams lately, including this one, and she wondered if there might be some reason why? Last night's had been especially strange, not in an unpleasant way necessarily, but it was interesting enough to make her ponder any possible meaning... Maybe it was something about chasing lost youth? Maybe somewhere deep down that's what this entire trip was about. Or maybe, just maybe, its only meaning was that she was supposed to write about it? That was the only meaning that had any practical use anyway- and she started thinking about her book again...

It seemed it had been somewhat neglected lately and probably deserved some attention. Luckily her laptop was at the top of the list when she'd first started packing. Maybe once she got settled in at Pete's place, she'd take it down to the beach with a folding chair to start writing again?... Of course she would- in fact, that was a big part of the plan all along..... Although, her thinking about it had been somewhat scattered in recent days. One of the main reasons was that she knew she wanted to document everything about what she was thinking and doing with regard to the plan itself. There was no doubt in anyone's mind, including hers, that this "sailing trip" would be a fantastic story which people would eventually enjoy reading- and she planned to oblige. However, that didn't mean she wanted to in any way give up on her other project. Writing fiction had already led to some of the most fulfilling days of creativity she'd ever experienced. It certainly wasn't something she wanted to let go of now. She was still very dedicated to the idea, and it seemed much of her down time from working on the actual boat was already claimed....

TWENTY-THREE

The pain was intense, searing in fact. It was so violent he may even have lost consciousness for a brief second before realizing what had happened. He'd felt his bones crack under the pressure. They'd snapped and come through his skin nearly puncturing his life-sustaining spacesuit, and blood was now spilling in.... No question, the situation was very dire...

As they'd left the spacecraft to begin the long journey to base camp, their spirits had been high. It seemed the strange circumstances they'd been dealt weren't going to get the best of them after all. Not that the immediate task at hand was going to be easy, or even safe, and they were all well aware of this fact.... But this was ugly, way worse than any of them would have wanted to foresee. Suddenly, Scott, their commander, was hanging upside down suspended hundreds of feet above the vast Martian plains below, and he was hurt very badly.

They'd been doing well making their way carefully down the cliff on the ledge that Larry had discovered a few days earlier. They'd made it down several long cable-length pitches belaying each other one at a time as they went, and it hadn't even been terribly difficult. In fact, had they been doing the same thing back on earth, they probably wouldn't have even bothered with all the technical equipment and trouble. A large part of it wasn't much different than walking down a fairly steep sidewalk. However, given where they were and all that was at stake, they wanted to do everything possible as far as dotting all the i's and crossing all the t's. Whatever happened, they all wanted to know they'd done everything they could to make this as safe as possible, and there was no doubt in anyone's mind that the tedium was worth the effort. After all, they knew that their personal safety was about much more than any of them as individuals.... So when Scott first slipped, they were stunned.... and when they heard him cry out, they knew it was bad...

They'd been waiting for him to set up the next pitch when a fist-sized rock falling from above startled him, and he slipped and fell as he tried to fend it off with his hand. He was clipped in, and an anchor in the cliff-side had already been firmly established. So, at least in theory, he should have been completely safe. However, he had unwittingly been standing with his right foot in the center of a coiled pile of cable and he'd had to fall over thirty feet before it finally caught him around his calf. When it did, the jolt was horrendous. It had leveraged his leg against the point of impact intended for the harness attached at mid chest. As it happened, his leg snapped like a twig and he was still tangled in it like a twisted and mangled rag doll. He was basically tangled in his own shattered leg, and the immediate sensation of pain was beyond comprehension. In fact, in those first few minutes he couldn't even deal with it. It was completely overwhelming. He was screaming and cursing with tears streaming from his eyes. It felt like his face would explode, and it took several very long minutes before he could even attempt to get a hold of himself....

It was a horrible situation. He could feel the blood slowly flooding his suit as it seeped through his underclothes and into his boot. And, because of the way he'd landed, it was working its way up his leg towards his beltline as well. It was bad, so bad he knew he would soon bleed to death if he couldn't find a way to do something about it. And, as he very slowly gained a tiny slice of composure, he realized a tourniquet was the only immediate solution. In a sudden flash of insight, it became obvious there was no other way; and he knew as he was taking the piece of webbing out of his pack, it would mean losing his leg. But it didn't matter..... if he didn't do something soon, he would lose his life. It was a poignant moment as he used his flashlight as a handle to crank down the strap.... Slowly, ever so slowly, the pain started to ease as his leg started to die... Finally, at long last, he could start catching his breath...

What the hell was that?... She tossed her computer onto the bed, a little shocked at what she'd just written. She was in the attic above her shop at Pete's place and a little taken back by this gruesome turn in the story. Having been there for about a week, she was just starting to settle into her new life on the beach, and it felt good to finally start writing again. Although, this dark twist seemed a little strange.... Is this really the way I want to go with this thing, damaging poor Scoot so badly?.... It was basically irrelevant, given the way she knew she would eventually end it.... But maybe it would be fun to draw the story out a little longer, just to see how they would all deal with this strange new circumstance?..... However, that was enough of that for now. It was a little too intense, so she decided to step away and think about something else for a while....

There was plenty of electricity in the building, and she'd been writing by the light of a nice little ceramic lamp on the dresser next to the bed with the thick soft feather-stuffed mattress. The bed was obviously old and she liked its vintage charm... She had a couple of sleeping bags and blankets, and she'd luckily thought to buy sheets at that last stop store in San Diego... All in all, she'd made herself a very comfortable and peaceful place to sleep. She was close enough to the beach to hear the gentle rhythm of the surf, and the open windows letting in the cool ocean breeze kept the temperature pleasant enough....

Two big evenly spaced 10" X 10" support posts were the only things breaking the otherwise completely open space of the upstairs. And hanging from a nail in each were old kerosene lamps she had found lying around downstairs. She decided to light them both and turn off the electric light. As she was doing it, she wondered why she didn't just put another gas lamp on the dresser. Aesthetically, the flame was much nicer, and there were several more where these had come from- but for the time being, it was just a thought...

Several days earlier at a flea market down the road, a used unicycle caught her attention and she'd purchased it for a very few dollars. It was leaning against the wall next to a window as it caught her eye again.... The big open space of her bedroom had been its inspiration in the first place; and within the first afternoon, she could already take short bursts between the post and walls. She walked over and jumped on, holding on to one of the dressers to keep her balance at first. Concentrating, she took off as quickly as possible toward the center of the room... About half way to the first the post, she lost control and the thing shot out from under her toward the opposite wall as she landed on her backside laughing. She just sat there for a minute looking across the floor with a smile on her face. The flickering flames of the lanterns were casting pleasant shadows throughout the room, and she liked it exactly where she was... Life was never dull...

It was roughly 1:00am, although the time seemed irrelevant as she eventually grabbed one of the lanterns to head down the stairs. She walked past her newly developing construction project and paused for a few minutes to look around. Content she was off to a good start, she went out the door where a little walk on the beach seemed to be calling. Sure enough, the cool clear water felt great on her feet as she walked in the gently breaking surf thinking about everything that had led her to this point....

Looking out, the ocean was of course immense. From where she was standing, it seemed to go on forever and an excited chill ran down her spine at the thought of eventually setting sail...This is going to be an incredible adventure..... She sat down in a comfortable lawn chair that had been there for several days already. The sky above was crystal clear as she looked up at the millions of stars... Just as many thoughts seemed to be racing through her own mind, and she briefly wondered about the strange similarities between human consciousness and the universe as a whole. Both were mystifying in a very delicate and intrinsically beautiful way...

She thought about everything that needed to be done to get the boat ready, not that there was necessarily any rush. In fact, she knew she had all the time she wanted, which was a pleasant thought considering the construction plans were only beginning to take shape... Although granted, they weren't exactly your typical engineering drawings... A mental image was all she planned to work from, and that fact alone was entertaining....

... A little bag of weed she'd purchased from a local kid with impeccable sales skills was in her front pocket. Suddenly remembering it was still there was a pleasant little surprise. As she put out the lamp, she pulled it out to burn a pinch.... The slight burning sensation felt good in her lungs as she held the smoke in for a few long seconds before releasing it into a quickly disappearing cloud.... A moment later she did it again, and a few minutes after that it started taking its intended effect.... Her thoughts slowed down as she relaxed into the chair... The sky, the ocean, the sound of the waves, they were all very relaxing... As she realized she was smiling, she smiled even more...

High above, a plane was flying over, and she could hear the dull roar of its propellers... It must have been a big plane, probably hauling cargo of some kind. Maybe they were drug smugglers? Maybe they were smuggling some of the same weed she'd just been smoking? She laughed... If so, she almost felt bad about wishing them luck... She relaxed a little more, sinking further into the chair. Continuing to look up, she thought about what it might be like to be inside that plane at that moment. Suddenly, she saw it as simply being empty, just a big open space, like a warehouse of sorts? Maybe thoughts of her own building were somehow translating to the inside of the plane... And a very strange image began to take shape....

As she imagined herself looking down the middle of this big empty flying space, the image of a large transparent sphere appeared... Hmmm, that's interesting, what do we suppose this means?... What am I supposed to do with this thing?.... And then, just as suddenly, an entire scenario began to play itself out in her mind. It was very strange, almost brilliant in its own absurd and twisted way. She pictured herself inside this strange giant acrylic crystal-clear ball. It had a diameter of probably eight feet, and the walls were maybe six inches thick or more, so it was obviously very strong. She imagined it was completely full of water, and she was suspended inside it breathing calmly through a regulator. Two big interconnected SCUBA tanks were securely fastened to the bottom providing plenty of good clean breathable air that could easily last for a very long time under these conditions of virtually zero depth...

As this bizarre scenario continued to develop, the plane's position suddenly shifted. It was now somewhere far above the Atlantic Ocean a few hundred miles off the eastern tip of southern Florida and had left the Baja peninsula far behind. There was a slight sensation of the plane vibrating due to the huge roaring engines, although the sound was significantly deadened by the density of the water and the sphere itself. It was indeed a very strange place to be imagining herself, and yet as she placed herself there in her mind, the image and even the emotions of the experience were extremely vividly.... She was right there and starting to get a little nervous as she realized where this odd little story was heading...

....It was now mid-afternoon and, far below, a monstrous hurricane was slowly grinding its way west.... She named it Hurricane Chester... The wind speeds near the clearly defined eye wall were topping 200mph; and it seemed she was designing, solely in her in her own mind, one of the craziest most exciting human experiences anyone had ever heard of. In fact, as she continued to relish in these thoughts, it occurred to her that with enough financial recourses it might even actually be possible... Wow! How great would that be!... As the picture continued to develop to this end, she imagined a pump attached near the air tanks, and knew what it was for. When the time came, a pushed button would quickly flush most of the water out through a several-inch-diameter hole.... But that would be much later. First things first, and she could feel that the time to begin this little experiment was quickly approaching...

As the plane neared its ultimate destination above the storm, approximately three miles outside the eye wall in the direction the storm was moving, purposefully the absolute most intense location, she began to anticipate the actual moment of truth...

Closing her eyes, she felt every muscle in her body tense up as she sat in the lawn chair vividly imagining every detail. She gripped the chairs arms tightly and thought OK, Let's go!

Suddenly the doors in the floor opened and she was released into the clear blue sky. She was quickly accelerating into a beautiful sunny day but could clearly see the raging storm below and knew she would soon be absorbed by it.... It was awesome!... Once the plane disappeared, there was virtually no sensation of speed at all. There was the slight hint of the sound of the wind but, for the most part, all she could hear was the sound of her own breathing through the regulator, the constant inhaling and exhaling through the scuba valve.... Tshhhhhh... Chshhhhh ... Tshhhhh... Chshhhhh....

The massive storm was slowly rising and, within minutes of her departure, the clear sky above disappeared. A thick grey haze enveloped her, and at first that was the only difference between this and the moment before. However, this would also soon change. Moments after she was swallowed by the clouds, the turbulence began to show itself. Suddenly she was being jolted in one direction then another by blasts of air, and for a minute these sensations were relatively mild. But as the time quickly passed, they became more and more intense. Before long she was in the meat of it. She was in the grip of the monster that was Chester, and he was having his way with her....

As she came closer and closer to the surface of the seething Atlantic Ocean below, the power of the massive storm was truly impressive. It was like being inside a giant soccer ball that was being kicked up and down a field by a team of professionals.... However, and this was the best part, the density of the water within was cushioning the blows with great affect. She was being spun and tossed as if in the grip of a mighty ocean wave; but as long as she kept her calm and just kept breathing, she was fine- only occasionally even touching the sides. In fact, as she realized just how survivable this part of the experience actually was, she was able to truly appreciate everything about it. She was witnessing firsthand a huge category V hurricane from the inside, quite literally, and from a perspective no one had ever known.... She was quite literally a part of the storm itself, like one of the thousands of raindrops that were pummeling the outside of her bubble. In fact, contemplated differently, she indeed was a raindrop... It was absolutely amazing! She was experiencing the massive hurricane by becoming the hurricane, and again she pondered that such an experience might actually be possible under the right and willing financial circumstances..... And the "adventure" was far from over as she quickly remembered the ocean below was still rising.... For a brief few seconds before impact, she even saw it coming and instinctively tucked into a ball herself...

148

....The splash must have been enormous as she penetrated the surface... And although it was a definite jolt, it wasn't nearly as violent as it might have been. Water was a key part of the design to begin with and the density of the ball made the collision with the sea far more gentle than it might otherwise have been... It was so heavy and so dense that it passed through hundreds of feet of ocean in a thick cloud of bubbles before even slowing down. It took nearly half a minute for the ball to finally come to a stop as the bubbles slowly trailed off above....

Holy shit! That was incredible!... She was literally shaking! But the stillness of her surroundings slowly took over... There was nothing but a beautifully dark shade of blue all around. The surface was long gone. She wasn't even sure which direction it was? There was only a dead calm, peaceful, amazing, even surreal... As a whale slowly approached, it nearly took her breath away as she realized just how clear the water actually was. He appeared from hundreds of feet away, in time that stood still, before slowly disappearing in the opposite direction... Her heart nearly skipped a beat in awe of its graceful beauty.... Then, almost sadly remembering the plan was still far from complete, she pushed the big red button that would take her into the next phase....

The pump made a huge strange noise as it very quickly got to work doing the job it was designed to do. The water that had been so safely cushioning her experience to this point was quickly being evacuated. It was being flushed out and replaced with clean breathable compressed air, and the ball started to accelerate into an upward motion toward the surface. As it continued to go faster and faster, she felt herself being pressed toward the bottom in the last remaining water, a couple feet of which would purposefully remain for stability once the orb actually reached the top....With her arms behind her for support, she was quickly approaching the raging storm once again. And although the view was very distorted by the turbulent waves above, she could see it coming as everything got brighter and brighter. At the last moment before actually breaking through, she instinctively took a deep breath and held it. The incredible buoyancy was about to send her flying into the air like a rocket....

As crazy as everything had been to this point, it was about to get even crazier. The ball leapt out of the ocean a good ten feet. She, along with all the remaining water, was momentarily suspended in midair before quickly crashing back down into the chaos. With much less water inside, she could now truly hear the storm for the first time, and it was ferocious. The howling winds sounded like a jet engine, and the contrast between this and where she'd been just seconds earlier was profound. It had been so quiet, and now she almost feared for her hearing. The noise alone was a shock to the senses. It was terrifying!

She quickly found the handles, and the flat clear plate securing all the technical equipment made a firm stable place to sit in sloshing water. It was an exciting ride for sure! And as she realized she could indeed hold herself firmly in place, the initial feelings of panic dissolved into sheer exhilaration. Huge towering waves were rising and falling, surging and crashing. They were distorted and twisted due to the constant coating of rain and wave water running off the outside of the sphere. There was a clear view of nothing. Everything was obscure except, of course, the sense of raw power that was all too vivid. The amount of energy Chester was expressing was incomprehensible…. And then, suddenly, it stopped…

Almost instantly, it was quiet again, and this too had been a purposeful part of the plan. The ball was dropped so the eye of the storm would catch up to it, and sure enough, the blue sky opened up again. Huge flocks of sea birds flew overhead and bobbed around in the waves, safe in the only refuge there was. Dark clouds surrounded everything. The eye wall was very well defined and easy to see. Slowly, she moved toward the center. And, although the waves were still sizable, they had a far more mellow disposition. They were more rhythmic and peaceful. It was a beautiful place to be, but the other side would eventually regain control, and she would once again be engulfed in the chaos…

The roaring storm continued for hours upon hours. It was fun and extremely exciting, but by the time she was finally deposited on the sands of Miami Beach, she was completely exhausted. As the winds gradually calmed, the storm slowly moved on. And finally, at long last, she could open the hatch and climb out….. Sprawling out in the soaking wet sand was a fantastic and relieving moment…

Wow!…. Smiling in vivid appreciation of her own imagination, she stood up from the chair on the beach for the first time in over an hour….. That was fun! I'll definitely have to write about that at some point…. However, for the time being, sleep was finally starting to sound good as she made her way back toward her bed….. Hmmm, maybe when I sell a few more books, I'll build that thing myself someday and ride it into a real hurricane…. Could that really be possible…?

TWENTY FOUR

Sparks flew and smoke drifted upward as two pieces of metal slowly became one. They were glowing a bright orangish color of red, far too bright to look at without the dark protection of the welder's helmet strapped securely to her head. Leather gloves protected her hands, and dirty canvas overalls shielded the rest of her body from this seemingly very violent process. Temperatures of thousands of degrees were being generated and controlled with near pinpoint accuracy, and it was all so much fun she could hardly sit still enough to do the work. She felt like a mad scientist experimenting with the powers of the gods, and it was awesome... Flipping the mask up, she stepped back to look at what she'd been doing. Smiling almost to the point of laughter, she set the tools down and took off the gloves, proud of the way she'd been spending the day. This last bead of weld had completed a circle attaching two of the oil drums that were becoming part of one of the pontoons....

Three of the four had already been completed, and it seemed the project was well under way. Each was approximately forty feet long with the idea that they would be separated by roughly ten feet, making the entire boat about thirty feet wide. Thirty by forty seemed like reasonable measurements. In fact, as she able to start visualizing the final product, it seemed huge. That would mean approximately 1200 square feet of living space which, for only one person, seemed enormous- and she liked that fact. There would be more than enough room to bring anything her heart desired, and she wasn't even sure what that would mean yet, but it felt good....

Several more welds were needed to complete the last of the four pontoons. However, for now, just pondering the next step was entertaining enough as she stepped over and around the huge mess it was becoming. Her shop looked like a bomb had gone off; and Pete, who'd come down to visit fairly frequently, thought it was hilarious. Being a fairly meticulous neat-freak in his own shop, it gave him plenty of ammunition to give her a hard time as they were slowly becoming friends...

Pete was a fairly soft-spoken guy and very genuinely kind and generous, and she'd seen that in him immediately. When they'd first met a couple of months earlier on the exploratory trip with Mark, she'd had a good feeling about him, which was comforting. Because, while she had a lot of confidence in her ability to figure things out, her actual experience regarding a project like this was very limited; and she had hoped all along that Pete would be willing to give her a pointer here and there if need be. In truth, "limited" was a pretty generous description of her experience. Obviously she'd never in her life built anything even similar. Quite a few years earlier, she'd briefly dated an artist who fabricated steel for the purpose of building big strange sculptures. And being the naturally curious person she was, she had taken the opportunity to learn a little about the process herself. But her experience was minimal, at best. However, running a basic arc welder had seemed easy enough. Since she didn't own one, though, she was hoping Pete might have an extra one lying around that he'd be willing to throw it in as part of the deal. And she was right. He'd been a professional metal worker for decades and, without hesitation, he donated to the cause. There was an old red tombstone-shaped stick welder over in the corner of his shop that he knew would be more than sufficient for her purposes. There was nothing terribly technical about what she was trying accomplish, anyway, and this thing was very easy to operate. Plus he knew he wouldn't be needing it for anything anytime soon. He even gave her a brief lesson on how to use it, and she was off and running in no time.....

After a little break and a little light lunch, she put the helmet and gloves back on and got back to work for several more hours. By the time she finally decided to hang it up for the night, only one long circular weld remained. By midafternoon the following day, all of the pontoons were complete.

A tightly stretched carpenter's string had been handy in keeping all the barrels in a straight line as they were being attached; and as she rolled them around trying to position them, she was impressed at what a good job she'd done. The pontoons were not only as straight as a pool cue, but as the last remaining slag fell off the welds, they looked almost professional in her opinion.... Ok, well maybe not professional exactly, but the last ones were obviously much neater than the early ones, so she'd at least gotten better at it as she went, which made her feel proud. And she'd been very generous with the amount of material she was adding, so the welds were all extremely strong, probably even stronger than the barrels themselves. However, it quickly became apparent she needed to find a more practical way to move the huge things around.

It dawned on her that as nice and big as her shop was, the actual platform of the boat would have to be put together outside or there would be no way to ever get it out…. Hmmm, it seems I need wheels…. As she glanced around the property, she saw no immediate solution to the problem, so she decided to look for Pete who was always eager to help. He had a chain hoist and a few hand carts lying around; and before long, all four of the pontoons were outside and only about thirty yards from the ocean. Pete assured her that when the time came, they could figure out how to get the whole boat to the water from there. It wouldn't be easy necessarily, but they'd find a way.

He made her feel comfortable in completing the boat right where the biggest pieces now lay. She thanked him for his help once again, and once again he smiled like it was no big deal. He assured her that she was welcome to use anything she could find around the property that wasn't being used for anything else- and even if it were, they could probably still work something out. It was fairly obvious he was getting a lot of vicarious pleasure out of this whole thing himself- not to downplay his genuine generosity. He was a great guy. In fact, he invited her to join him and his wife Sarah for dinner that night, and they all had a pleasant evening eating and drinking and getting to know each other a little better. He and Sarah were both nice people…

The following day, a little walk in the tall weeds led to the discovery of a pile of concrete blocks at the side of one of the other buildings. She asked Pete if they were available before carting the first load down the hill. The blocks were a way to prop the pontoons up to level the whole thing out. They were a way to get the flat surface and the spacing necessary to start building the deck. Once everything was where she wanted it, 3" X 1" bars of rectangular tubular steel were tacked on with little spots of weld every two feet for the entire length of the boat and the entire length of each individual pontoon. Then she went back and forth across the boat making sure each one of these welds was bomb-proof solid. Meanwhile, basically at the same time, she was cutting shorter lengths of the same material and welding them evenly in place between the pontoons at the narrowest point, essentially half the depth of the horizontal barrels. Slowly, ever so slowly, the boat was becoming very rigid and gaining strength with every added piece….

Days and weeks passed, and she was very much enjoying this strange process….

A month or so in, Mark and Sara made the trip down as they had promised. They even managed to find a way for Carrie to join them, which basically meant Steve was talked into taking care of the kids while she was gone. Of course she'd wanted to come, and a willing family friend volunteered to help Steve. When the time came for Janet to actually set sail, the whole family planned to come down along with their parents and whoever else. But in the meantime, this little visit would be fun too.

The first night they went back to the restaurant where Pete's place had first been suggested. Pete and Sarah joined them and it was a fun little gathering. Jorge and Rita were a fun couple, and their kids Pedro (the one who'd introduced Pete and Janet) and Maria were also there. Maria's kids were with her and, although there was a bit of a language barrier, Carrie enjoyed discussing her own kids with her. Janet felt good that everyone seemed to get along so well. In a way, all of these people were beginning to feel like family....

At around 11:00, the little party was essentially over and she and her three visitors went back to the beach. They'd all brought sleeping bags and pads thinking it would be fun to stay with her in her building, like a sleepover. Plus it was just fun feeling like they were a part of this crazy project themselves for a few days.... So far, they were pretty impressed with how well the whole thing seemed to be going. The boat was far enough along that they could all begin to visualize what the finished product would look like, a big crazy very-livable sailing "thing," or whatever it was? That was about as well as anyone could have described it. "Whatever it was," it was most definitely taking on a character of its own. Although, while they were actually there, not much more would get done, and none of them felt bad about it. They swam and snorkeled and played on the big beautiful beach that they had all to themselves. They spent a day touring around Cabo, a short drive to the south where they drank margaritas and basically turned themselves loose like they were kids again.....

It was early November by then, so they were enjoying the nice weather. When they finally left, the climate was just one more thing they envied about Janet's crazy life. They'd had a fantastic time and looked forward to the future reunion when even more people would join them for the big sendoff. And the truth was, they probably didn't envy her at all. They admired her spirit, but actually setting sail on the "whatever it was" they'd now seen for themselves didn't sound the least bit appealing to any of them....

...OK, bye, good luck.... And they were off, leaving Janet once again to her beach, her boat, her strange happy life....

No date had been set yet, and there was certainly no hurry to do so, but sometime in mid March was starting to sound reasonable. If there had been a rush, which there was not, she could have easily been ready much sooner than that, but the process was fun. As the days passed, little details previously un-thought of would come to mind, and when that happened, she wrote them down. After all, there was more than enough room to bring anything she could think of.......

Solar Panels? This idea seemed to open a whole world of possibilities, and it was easy to get a little carried away at first. All kinds of things came to mind- TV's, stereos, microwaves, DVD players, refrigerators, even a big massaging chair sounded good. But, admitting that if she really did want all of these things, she might as well just book a trip on a big cruise ship. Maybe all this stuff was a little beside the point, and she eventually decided to tone it down. But that didn't mean it wouldn't be nice having the power. The panels themselves would of course stay. Their use would just be somewhat limited, and the details of what that meant exactly would be worked out as the construction continued....

As the weeks passed, the deck went on by bolting the 2x4's on top of the steel struts and then plywood on top of that. It was easy to see the boat was becoming extremely rigid and strong. Strong was good. It would mean having confidence in the big boat in high seas; and because of the probably very long duration of the trip, that seemed highly likely at one time or another. It seemed inevitable she would encounter big storms as the days, weeks, and months passed on the open ocean; and a big strong durable boat almost seemed imperative. Luckily it was seeming more and more all the time that that's exactly what she had. It was obviously becoming heavy, there was no doubt about that. That was easy enough to see by simply looking at it. It was reinforced practically to the point of overkill. Steel bars were added on here, there, and everywhere. Plus, each of the barrels was still its own individual compartment, meaning if one of them somehow got punctured, the ones around it would still maintain their own structural integrity. It seemed it would be extremely difficult to actually sink the thing....

That was a comforting thought considering the reality of the trip was hitting home harder and harder all the time.... The truth was she was starting to get a little pleasantly nervous as things progressed, but having a boat that she knew was solid seemed to help....

TWENTY-FIVE

She could see him from a long way off as he slowly bounced down the hill on the four-wheeler he sometimes used to get around the property, and there was something strange on the back rack. Whatever it was, it must have been fragile? He couldn't have been going more than two or three miles per hour and seemed to be taking forever. She kept working for a few minutes placing and tightening bolts but couldn't help looking up to see what he was doing. Finally her curiosity got the best of her, and she put the wrench down and started walking up the hill.

As she got closer, the large strange cargo finally revealed itself as a bird cage, and there seemed to be an actual living bird inside it…. No wonder he was going so slowly..… The bird was having a hard enough time hanging on to the swinging perch as it was… So, what have you got there Pete? Or maybe I should say, who have you got? As she took a closer look…Well he doesn't really have a name yet. I thought maybe you'd want to take care of that. My neighbor a few miles down the road breeds these guys, and it dawned on Sarah and me the other night that one might make a good a companion for you on your little sailing trip… He's yours, if you want him? If you don't, we'll understand and it certainly won't be a problem to take him back…… She went up to the cage and looked in again… Hi birdie…Hi birdie… He was beautiful but looking a little traumatized from the ride…. But beautiful is what he mostly was. In fact, he was magnificent. He was a young healthy African Grey Parrot…. A bird, really? It's a little cliché, don't ya think?… He got off the machine and blushed a little as he smiled…Well, maybe, but we just thought you might need a friend out there, that's all…

She was a little taken back by the whole thing and not quite sure how to react at first; but in seeing the very sweet and genuine intention, it was suddenly an emotional little moment for them both. She gave him a big hug and kissed him on the cheek…. Thank you, that's very nice of you guys, Pete… These birds can be really expensive in the states. I hope you got a good deal on him…Well, don't you worry about that. But the truth is, yes, we got a very good deal…. He continued to smile. He and Sarah were doing fine for themselves, and they had spent a little money. The cage alone wasn't cheap, but they were growing very fond of Janet and wanted to do something nice. A friend in the form of a beautiful bird seemed like a good idea and they went with it.... Do you mind bringing him down to the shop?.... That's where I was headed... Several minutes later they were there, and together they unloaded the bird who was still looking a little stressed. They put the big cage on a table in the corner of her shop... Do you think we'll be okay, Pete? I don't really know anything about taking care of a bird like this.... Ohhhh, I wouldn't worry too much. From what I understand, they're pretty low maintenance in a climate like this. Just talk to him and give him some attention. Other than that, just make sure he always has food and water.... There was a big sealed container of food in the bottom of the cage already.... That'll be enough to last you quite a while, and I'll make sure to get you plenty more before you leave.... Thank you very much, really, I mean it. That was a very sweet thing to do... She hugged him again before he took off back up the hill....

Hmmm, well, this is an interesting little twist... She jumped up and sat on the table next to her new acquaintance... So, you don't even have a name yet huh?... I guess we'll have to do something about that.... How about Earl? You look like an Earl, don't you?... It was the first thing that came to mind. For no apparent reason, Earl just popped into her head, and it strangely seemed to fit.... She sat there for a good long time talking to him in a calm friendly voice saying nothing but, "Hello, my name is Earl." Over and over again she repeated these five simple words, and slowly he started to calm down. At first he was pacing and flapping his wings, but slowly he mellowed a little and clung to the cage as close to her as he could get. She put her finger through the bars and stroked his feathers as they looked at each other inquisitively.... Hello, my name is Earl. Hello, my name is Earl.... He never actually said the words, but she was sure he looked as if he might...

The work outside was going well, but she decided she was finished for the day and went out to put away her few tools. It was starting to look like rain anyway, so that alone was enough of an excuse to quit. But the bird needed some more attention, and it wasn't like she could not think about him at this point anyway. In the brief time they'd spent together, she could already tell he was an interesting character. He was a living, breathing, thinking being- and probably very intelligent. A lot was going on behind those beautiful eyes, and she wanted to know more about him....

She pulled up a chair and put her feet up on the table as she leaned back. The light rain made a very pleasant sound on the sheet metal roof.... This will be a fine way to spend the remainder of the daylight...

They sat and looked at each other, and the only words she said to him were the same five… He strutted and squawked a little, but never actually said anything…. After a while, it almost seemed he was being stubborn. She knew he could say it if he wanted to…. Look how smart he is. He's sizing me up?…. And she liked that about him. Earl was a cool bird. She'd only had him for a few hours and was already appreciating this strange gift more than she would have originally thought. She'd appreciated the kind gesture from the beginning, but now she was slowly starting to appreciate Earl for Earl. He was fascinating, the way he moved, the way he looked knowingly back at her… Getting to know more about him would be fun… It had never really dawned on her before, but it might be nice having a friend on the boat. A little companionship probably really would be a good thing…

It was still raining as it slowly got dark, and it seemed like it might last for a while. She lit a couple of the lanterns in the shop and went upstairs to light a couple more. Earl's cage was big and awkward but not necessarily all that heavy…. She wondered if she should bring him upstairs with her? In the moment she definitely wanted to, but realized it might not be all that practical. Most of her time wasn't spent up there, and it wouldn't be easy to keep bringing him up and down. But she decided that on this his first night, he should be up there with her; and she nearly broke her back making that happen. She set him down, plopped herself up on her bed, and turned on her computer… Earl seemed content, and the sound of the soft rain was very relaxing…

It had been a few days since she'd written anything, so it seemed like a good idea to get back to it- although she really wasn't sure what she wanted to do. Earl, sitting right there looking at her, seemed like a good topic; so she spent an hour or so writing about her experience with him that day. He was already a fun little addition to her life, so that seemed like a no-brainer. It was basically just journaling that she'd perhaps find a way to use later when writing the story of the trip. It didn't seem to matter why she was writing about him, she just wanted to…. However, after a while she started seriously thinking about her book again. A lot had been left up in the air… Last she remembered, Scott was still hanging from a Martian cliff with a badly broken leg. At some point, she would need to deal with him…. On the other hand, there was still the story of the strange spirit world that needed some more attention as well…. However, on another other hand, she was obviously free to do anything she wanted, which of course left the field wide open… She could finally get around to writing the story of the train victim, or maybe John the film maker. Or what about that story of flying into a hurricane in a big clear ball?... Damn, wouldn't that be exciting?....But in the end, none of that seemed to overpower the pull of the stranded astronauts.... She decided to drop in and see what they were up to again...

As the tourniquet took its intended effect, communication on some level was able to resume. It took a while, but Scott was finally able to start thinking somewhat clearly again as he uttered his first meaningful words.... Do you guys think you can pull me back up?.... He'd managed to untangle himself and was now hanging from the harness at mid-chest the way he was supposed to be.... Sure, we want you back up here, too... How are you doing Scott? Are you alright?.... No, not exactly, but first things first..... A few minutes later they were pulling him over the edge...

As they were getting their first look at the situation for what it truly was, Larry, Julie, and Joann were all shocked at what they saw.... Holy Shit, Scott, not to dwell on the obvious, but damn, this is ugly.... The truth was it was way worse than any of them had anticipated.... You're lucky to be alive.... As Julie, their chief medical officer, looked at his badly damaged leg, she realized how lucky he was that the splintered bones hadn't punctured the suit. If that had happened, he would have been dead already... Scott spoke up... OK, I don't know if any of you have realized this yet, but our only immediate option is for you guys to figure out a way to get me back up to the ship. From there, Julie's going to have to properly amputate what's left of my leg... It was bleak, but they all immediately recognized he was right. Larry stepped up and took the lead.... I'll go up and get the backboard. We'll have to strap him down to get him out of here. Any objections?... No, ok, I'm on my way...

Because the safety of belaying went out the window with this new situation, travel was much quicker and he was back in less than hour. He'd moved as quickly as he could, and the equipment was easy enough to find. He had everything they needed; and without much hesitation, they all started strapping their patient down for the trip. Scott was basically having the worst day of his life and was still in a significant amount of pain; but under the circumstances, he was staying extremely strong and keeping his suffering to himself. He knew his teammates were doing their absolute best to make this as easy as possible on him. He figured the least he could do was keep quiet as they struggled to carry him back up the narrow shelf.

At first they considered going completely without vertical protection, the way Larry had gone to get the gear. But then, realizing it was fairly simple to run a long line bolted into the wall at both ends allowing them all to clip in, it only made sense to do so. It wasn't exactly "by the book" rigging, but it was better than nothing. Some two hours after they started, they were all back in the ship far sooner than any of them would have guessed....

It was nice to be out of their spacesuits again, although for Scott it wasn't quite that simple. They got him out of his helmet, and that alone was a relief; but they were going to have to carefully cut him out of the rest starting with the leg that was broken. Leaving the tourniquet securely in place, Julie started the process with a large and extremely sharp scalpel. She moved fairly quickly just to start getting a sense of what she was dealing with. This was no time for delicacy- everything below the strap was already a write-off anyway.... Damn, Scott, you really messed yourself up here didn't you? Maybe you shouldn't look at this?.... She knew immediately that was the wrong thing to say because he immediately sat up to see, and it wasn't pretty. His leg was basically sheared off at the knee, and the only thing keeping it intact were the shredded muscles and tendons. Below that, both bones were broken and splintered. They were as sharp as weapons coming out of his skin, which was disturbing by itself. Actually seeing it for the first time, it seemed he truly was fortunate they hadn't come through the pressurized suit. He really was lucky to be alive, including the fact that he easily could have bled to death too... She quickly injected some local anesthetic to deaden the remaining pain before helping him out of the rest of his suit.... Ok Scott, I'm very sorry about your leg; but there's no good reason to put this off and every reason in the world to get it over with.....We're prepping for surgery... He didn't put up a fight. He knew she was right and had already resigned himself to it... A few hours passed while he was out; and, for all practical purposes, the operation went very well. From Julie's perspective, it was a fairly simple procedure, albeit somewhat emotionally difficult. Her friend and teammate would certainly never get his leg back...

By now, they'd had several rounds of communication with ground control back on earth, and of course the concerns ran deep. However, there was some very strange and unexpected news. It seemed they may have had some problems of their own...

Everyone back home wanted to know every detail of what was happening, what their future plans were with regard to getting to camp, how they planned to do it, and most importantly, if Scott would be alright?... All of their questions were answered somewhat vaguely, but confidently.... Yes, in the long run Julie seems very confident he'll be fine, although not without some obvious new challenges. But he's a tough guy. With our help, we're sure he'll figure it out. And, although we're not sure exactly how, or when, we're confident we'll all eventually make it to camp too.... So what's going on back there?....

There were obviously concerns over a dilemma of some sort, but the earth bound part of this team was being extremely vague about their problems too... In fact, it was almost an accident that they'd revealed there even was a problem... When the information first started coming in about Scott's ordeal, a junior operator had been sitting at the controls and he'd immediately replied with the statement, "well, it seems we might have an even bigger problem." He wasn't even thinking about it, and that's as much as they knew. But it was now dawning on them that maybe they should know more. Now that their own situation had at least stabilized somewhat, they wanted to know more about what that meant; and, although the delay was obviously still very long, they were about to find out...

....Well, we can't confirm it 100% yet.... There was a long pause... There continued to be a long pause as the tension in the air rose... Damn, what the hell can it be?.... The truth is we can't believe it ourselves, but the more we analyze all the data, the more real it seems to become.... The astronauts were on the edge of their seats at this point, and Scott, who was just coming out of his surgical sleep, couldn't even tell if he was dreaming or not.... I don't know how we missed it.... There was another long pause and a long sigh.... Ok, here it is.... There's an asteroid the size of Iowa less than a week away.... Right now our best guess is it will hit somewhere in the Atlantic Ocean between Africa and South America... We're going to try to shoot some nuclear weapons at it, but the realistic truth is that we don't have nearly enough time to come up with a feasible plan. In fact, given the size of this thing, we probably couldn't have done anything about it even if we had seen it coming. It's a big, very heavy, very dense rock. The best we can assess, there's seems to be about a 97% chance it's going to hit somewhere.... It means the end of the earth as we know it. Even microscopic life will be lucky to survive....

Over the course of that week, communication was nearly constant. At first, there was a sense of reserved optimism as the hurried defensive plans were executed; but as the days passed, every attempt failed miserably. The reality became way too real, way too quickly...

All the crew members had conversations with friends and family and

161

everyone closest to them. It was very surreal and hard to tell if the full weight of the moment was truly sinking in. Probably not, how could it? This was way too big for the human mind to wrap itself around. It meant the end of everything….. But not quite. It seemed the human race and a few other select species had escaped by the skin of their teeth…. Somehow, life would go on…

…There was a racket in the cage…. My name is Earl! My name is Earl!…

TWENTY-SIX

That was fun… It seemed the story of the Mars travelers was finally complete. Well, not really of course. In fact, the truth was that their story was really only a beginning. But don't most if not all good stories end that way, an end that launches an even bigger future? And what could be bigger than this? The fate of life itself was now in their hands, and they'd better not drop the ball. Any recognizable aspects of their lives on earth were gone forever. If truly nothing survived, it could conceivably take another four billion years for life to evolve to such an advanced point again; and even if it did, the new paths it would have to take probably wouldn't even be recognizable. It could easily be as different as an alien civilization in some distant galaxy. However, even that would most likely never happen, because four billion years in the future the sun would be close to living out its own life span; and the earth would no longer exist in any recognizable form anyway. So it seemed life truly was the sole responsibility of the four crew members…. Think of the pressure?….

She kicked back on her bed, happy in accomplishing something. She'd been working on the story for several months at this point and felt good about finishing it, and she was pretty pleased with the way it had turned out. She thought about the characters and the lives she'd given them. They were interesting because of her. She'd invented four people completely from nothing and felt quite good about it. In her own mind at least, they'd become real- real enough to feel genuine emotions for. When Scott busted his leg up so badly, she genuinely felt bad for him, even though she was the one who'd done it. It was a very odd feeling; and even now, she was concerned about their future, as she hoped any future reader of their story would be. She thought about what lay ahead, both immediately and in the long term… How would Scott adjust to living without his leg?… At first they'd probably rig him some simple crutches; but as time progressed, they might even find a way to build him a prosthetic of sorts. She figured it wouldn't be long before they'd find a way to get to base camp and then thought about their lives beyond that too…. How would they ever go about living up to such an awesome responsibility?

Eventually they'd get settled into their lives on this foreign planet. They would work out a plan and a routine to get on with the business at hand. Procreation would obviously be a big part of that plan, and she hoped they'd all enjoy getting that started. She thought about the fact that she'd decided to make them two couples almost from the beginning, and how wrong Mark had been for giving her a hard time about it…. See, I knew I was right… Although, she did see his point and took the focus off of that aspect knowing it would be important later, no matter how long she decided to draw the story out…

…. As children slowly started becoming a factor, they would have to find a way to incubate the embryos too- not only to make more humans, but animals as well. Although, they would have to be very careful not to go too quickly. For a long time, their resources would be very limited, and it would be important not to get ahead of themselves. Viable square footage would be a primary factor. 20,000 square feet would be all they'd have for quite some time…. Hmmm, how would they ever add to that?…. She calculated that their first option would most likely be to go underground. They could dig caves and take in plants to provide oxygen, although they'd have to be rotated in and out to get sunlight in order to photosynthesize.

Beyond that, thinking into the even more distant future, she realized a large part of their day-to-day lives would involve nothing but hard work. They would have to take the seeds from every species of plant they had and start planting almost immediately. Eventually they would have to plant hundreds and even thousands of square miles. It would be the only way to terraform the planet. Eventually they would need a hospitable atmosphere if life were to continue long term and with any kind of quality. The plants would be the only way to ever provide enough oxygen, and they'd have to come up with ingenious ways to plant as much as possible every single day. It would all be incredibly difficult given the restrictiveness of the spacesuits, but the sense of duty would be extremely compelling. Their lives would be far from easy, but there would be no alternative. The work would have to be done no matter what, and that would continue to be the case for at least the first several generations. In fact, it would probably be the case for the first several centuries. The children, grandchildren, and great great great grandchildren of Scott, Joann, Larry, and Julie would have to carry on the work if Mars was truly to become our new home and place to evolve from... It seemed **we** would eventually be the true Martians....

She thought about the history in which her four crew members would eventually be recorded. In this new reality, this new existence, they would be the greatest heroes for millennia to come. Even people like Christopher Columbus and George Washington wouldn't begin to compare in importance. Their legacy would be unlike any other in human history.... She caught herself laughing as she realized she was giving herself credit for creating the greatest heroes in literary history.... But in truth, at least in concept, she was. The fate of life itself was in their hands, and if they actually pulled it off, who could deny it?... However, she also remembered she had left that up to the imagination of any potential reader, and she was fine with that too. In the end, she hoped they'd see them as being successful in this pursuit. She hoped they'd imagine life going on, evolving into new forms and frontiers, which it would obviously be forced to do, given such drastic changes in environmental conditions. Even the human race itself would have to evolve relatively quickly, and eventually today's humans would barely be recognizable. She thought about them very long term, how they would eventually move beyond Mars. She thought about the technology they would build on to go further out into the solar system and perhaps even beyond that. They may even decide to resettle Earth, and Earth and Mars could be sister planets used as base camps for further exploration....

This was all fun to think about, but she eventually snapped out of it..... After all, the writing of the story was over....

It was very late, and the light rain was still falling. Earl looked content in his cage as she asked him to say his name again, which he did, once, and that was enough. Sleep was finally sounding good. She remembered hearing somewhere that you should cover a bird's cage if you wanted him to do the same. A clean sheet would suffice, and before long the day was over for them both....

The following day it was still raining and looked like it might continue for a while. She slept in just because it felt good and she hadn't gone to bed until the wee hours of the morning anyway... Earl seemed glad to see her again as she removed his sheet. He looked at her and moved as close as he could get. She reached through the bars and stroked his feathers with her fingers. He bobbed his head and whistled and said the only words he knew.... Hello, my name is Earl. Hello, my name is Earl.... She sat and talked to him for a few minutes before going downstairs.

She'd made herself a simple kitchen, "kitchen" probably overstating what it actually was. But the little refrigerator, two-burner hotplate, and microwave she'd purchased in San Diego were definitely coming in handy, and the long workbench against the wall served nicely as a kitchen counter. Of course, a coffee maker was there too, and getting it going was a first priority. She then boiled some water, threw in some oatmeal, and added some raisins and brown sugar. Hot cereal on a rainy day seemed strangely appropriate.... Hmmm, what should I do today? I could go outside and work in the rain, or I could sit on my bed and write and listen to the rain... The latter sounded a lot more inviting, and it seemed a decision had already been made. Besides, hanging out with Earl would be fun.

Earl seemed happy with her choice as she sat down on the floor next to him. He walked back and forth on his perch, bobbing his head and strutting like he was showing off. She finished her breakfast, took another sip of coffee, and leaned back against the bed pulling her computer down to her lap. She liked being close to him. It felt like they were hanging out, and the continued sound of lightly falling rain was still a nice little bonus....

Not knowing exactly what she hoped to accomplish was strangely a nice feeling, too, so she started by writing the first things that came to mind with regard to the trip. It was basically a kind of "housekeeping," and although there was no real sense of direction about it, she had confidence it was productive. After all, this was how she'd worked on all her previous books and they'd turned out pretty well. It was a basic building of resources to work from, like journaling or list making. She documented from memory a fairly thorough list of the materials used to build her boat, and then went through a box of receipts under the bed to get a handle on how much it was costing. Not that there was any fear of going over budget, because essentially there was no budget. It just seemed like interesting information to be aware of, information she thought her readers would be curious about someday too. She detailed the construction to this point and her thought processes about how and why the boat was the way it was. She thought about everything she might bring and listed it- thinking it would later be fun comparing this list with what she actually brought....

Meanwhile, this had of course been taking hours, and she realized the entire day could easily be spent this way. However, she also realized it wasn't exactly imperative that it even got done- or perhaps more accurately, Earl was reminding her. As the day progressed, he made more and more noise, demanding attention. He squawked and whistled and occasionally shouted his name.... HELLO MY NAME IS EARL!..... When she finally put the computer down and leaned over, he seemed relieved. The fact that she'd been sitting right there yet not paying him any mind must have been extremely stressful; but as he got what he wanted, he quickly calmed down. She talked softly and gently stroked his feathers...

For the first time, she wondered about the possibility of taking him out of his cage.... Hmmm, other people take their birds out of their cages?..... She'd seen it. She remembered seeing people walking down city streets with their birds on their shoulders. How was that possible? She knew she wouldn't feel comfortable doing that yet, definitely not. But this was only her second day with him. Surely she would get more comfortable with the idea as time passed..... It must be a progression. A bird can't go straight from never being out of his cage to walking down a street happily clinging to its owner. There must be steps to take to get to that point?...

First, she dragged a couple sheets of plywood up from downstairs. The entrance to her room was basically just a big rectangular hole in the floor that needed to be covered so he couldn't get very far. Then she made sure all the windows were closed before sitting down next to him again.... He seemed a little confused when she opened the cage door and sat back against the bed. At first he didn't do much of anything. He just sat and looked at her, tilting his head back and forth.... Hello, my name is Earl... He said it very calmly.... Yes, I know what your name is. Why don't you come out and play?.... Several minutes later he hopped over to the bottom bar of the door. He was halfway out.... So what are you going to do now buddy? Look, you're free to do whatever you want...... She slowly held out an index finger, and, tentatively, he jumped on. As she stood up and moved out to the middle of the room, he looked a little nervous, but excited.... What do you think Earl?...

Suddenly he jumped up and flapped his wings, and a few seconds later he was on the floor. He jumped up again, obviously trying to fly, and this time made it nearly to the wall....What are you doing Earl? Calm down.... She walked over to him talking in a very sweet and calm voice, and he jumped back on her finger.... What was that all about?... He took off again, this time smashing into the window.... What the hell Earl, are you trying to get away or what?... The truth was he probably didn't know what he was doing. The relative freedom was a little overwhelming, and he didn't quite know what to do with it. Finally, she decided that was enough; and when his cage was offered again, he took it....

Hmmm, maybe I need to get a book?... It dawned on her that if she was going to take this bird ownership thing at all seriously, there was probably a lot she needed to learn....

The next time she was in town, she picked one up....

TWENTY-SEVEN

February 29th seemed like a good day to take it easy. After all, it was an extra day anyway so why not see it as such and take advantage. And besides, there just happened to be a nice smooth curling break coming in....

Paddle! Paddle! Paddle! It picked her up and suddenly she was gliding down the face. She was low, knees bent, as she eased her weight to her toes and took off in a big arcing right turn. She looked back as this big, perfect, beautiful wave was just beginning to collapse on itself. Further to the right, it was just standing up, and she was exactly where she needed to be for yet another ride of her life. She cut back towards it; and, for a brief moment, her momentum carried her upwards just before she bounced off the breaking lip and back down into the glassy smooth tube. Roughly thirty feet in front of her, a sea lion was gliding down the same wave on his belly. He seemed to be smiling at her, and they were both having the time of their lives. It was incredible! The wave itself was perfect, if only because in that moment it was the only thing that existed. That wave was all that mattered, and she felt connected, connected with her own spirit, with the spirit of the sea, with existence itself.... Everything was right with the world....

Months had passed since she'd first arrived, and everything seemed to be going according to plan. The boat looked good. It even looked fairly close to the way she'd originally envisioned it. It was a big strong rectangular platform, and not much more. In the center she had built an A-frame out of plywood and 2x4's to serve as her primary shelter. It was very basic but structurally sound with steel reinforcement that was bolted and welded directly into the frame- the idea being that if a giant wave swept over the deck it wouldn't be washed away. Tarps were all that would be used to cover the ends so that, if the wave crashed over the bow, it could simply blow them out without much resistance. If the wave came from either side, she hoped the shape itself would deflect the water up and over. She knew the raw power of moving water and knew it was best to work with it and let it have its way whenever possible.

15' long by 12' wide were the measurements which allowed for plenty of room to sleep or sit and lounge around, out of the sun or out of the rain. She bought Earl another big cage and bolted it down inside. His other one would be bolted down outside so he could have the luxury of both. Although, once they were on their way, he would probably spend a significant amount of time in neither.... Big wooden weather-proofed boxes for storage bins were also bolted down both inside and out for whatever she might decide to bring, and four of the leftover 55-gallon drums would be used for fresh water storage. Two-hundred-plus gallons and a way to collect more with a big tarp seemed like more than enough. They were bound together with metal straps, and a square hole was cut in the center toward the back where they were all placed standing up. The bottoms of the barrels would ride approximately at the water line, strapped in and suspended in a strong steel cage with about half the height above the deck. A one-inch plastic tube could be run to the bottom of an individual tank and a foot pump used to get as much water as she needed at any given time. To the one big mast at the front of the boat she could attach a big, black, thick, plastic bag for the purpose of a solar shower. A hot fresh-water shower would be a great little treat from time to time.... The trip would be rustic, but comfortable.... A thick bowl-shaped piece of steel that Pete had in a scrap pile served nicely as a barbeque/fire pit. She welded on a low strong stand and made a sturdy grill that could be placed at different heights. It was heavy; but, with a little effort, she could move it around and tie it back down with metal straps and a screw gun. For fuel, she actually planned to carry more than a full cord of blocked and split firewood, as well as several hundred pounds of charcoal. Having an open fire out on the open ocean would be nice....

By late morning she was pretty well exhausted.... Finally, she decided to ride a wave as far as she could back toward the shore. The surf on this particular morning had been truly spectacular- the best she'd seen since she'd been there, maybe even the best she'd ever seen? The ocean was glassy smooth as perfectly spaced sets of 8-to-10 footers casually rolled in off of the north point, making for a spectacular right break that seemed to go on forever. Before today, she'd basically considered herself an intermediate surfer at best. But the way these were shaped and the way they came in such a friendly manner made her feel like an expert. For weeks, she had occasionally enjoyed this break on smaller days, but this particular morning had been absolutely indescribable. She'd never been so excited and yet so comfortable on such big waves... The endorphin-induced smile on her face would easily last the rest of the day.... Not that there weren't other things to think about...

The scheduled launch date was less than three weeks away, and the boat wasn't even in the water yet- but soon would be. The following day she planned to have several hired locals help her. And when the time came, the sheer number of people made it go more smoothly than any of them might have expected. Including Pete and herself, there were fifteen. And, on top of that, they'd figured out a good common sense way to go about it. Rolling it of course seemed like the best option, and there were still plenty of leftover barrels... They started by jacking the whole thing up at each of the four corners and removing the blocks before lowering it onto a row of the barrels on either side. From there, they simply pushed it, taking out the barrels left behind and placing them back in front. It worked extremely well, and in less than half a day the thing was in the ocean. Although, they weren't quite finished yet. One of the men owned a motor boat and, with everyone on board, they towed it north about a half mile to a small protected cove. They pulled it ashore and tied it off again so it could be loaded with all the supplies. It would remain there until the big day itself, at which point she planned to hire the boat again to tow her far enough out that the wind could catch her sail and she could be on her way. She paid all her helpers a fair wage, and then tipped them well on top of that. Everyone was happy and probably feeling a little privileged for getting to ride on the boat on its short maiden voyage... Sure enough, it floated high in the water and seemed sound...

A couple of months earlier, she'd been home for two weeks over the holidays- and, of course, it was great seeing everyone. But it was also a great opportunity to make plans for whoever wanted to come down and celebrate the day she would set sail. Everyone thought it made sense to go down a week or so ahead of time and make vacation of it. After all, it would basically still be winter where they were all coming from. A tropical departure would have sounded good even if it weren't for Janet's big trip, but what an excuse to go... And, generously, she even volunteered to sponsor it, including airfare and everything else. However, it just so happened that all of this was being discussed at Mark's big New Year's Eve party, and everyone involved in the trip just happened to be there. So when the topic of money came up, he, being by far the richest person in the room, couldn't help but volunteer himself..... Merry Christmas Everybody!.... As a matter of fact, let's do it up in style. I'll rent us all a couple of nice big condos on the beach somewhere. It'll be awesome! How does ten days sound?.... Everyone was of course gratefully enthusiastic....

Now, on the day she put the boat in the water, their arrival was less than two weeks away, and things were getting exciting... Once all her helpers were gone, she stood and looked at it, and past it to the big blue ocean beyond.... Holy Shit, this thing is actually going to happen, isn't it?..... She smiled, staring into her own thoughts for another few minutes before getting back to work. Luckily, Pete had offered his four-wheeler and a little trailer to take things out to the launch site... She started with the solar panels. She took them along with a few tools and a plan to attach them to the outside of the shelter where they wouldn't be in the way. Bolting them on and sealing around the drilled holes was a good afternoon project. The following day, getting them wired into workable outlets and storage batteries was another good project, possibly even an impossible project without the much-needed help of the instruction manuals. It wasn't necessarily easy, but she was a smart girl and gradually figured it out. In fact, testing it to make sure everything worked was a fun and gratifying little moment in and of itself. She wouldn't need all that much electricity anyway, and it seemed there'd be more than enough....

The next day she hauled over the firewood that she'd enjoyed splitting with an ax a few weeks earlier. She made trips back and forth until it was all there in a nice big pile on the beach. Then she tossed it onto the boat. By the time it was all neatly stored away in the bins, the better part of another day was gone.

In the several days that followed most everything else she could think of was taken out, including the blocks of charcoal that were just about the dirtiest job she could ever remember doing. She and all her clothes were black from head to toe, but she was sure she'd be glad to have it- and besides, it was funny. She laughed at herself as she dove into the ocean to clean up...

At first the plan was to throw her mattress directly on the floor under the shelter. But she realized that it would probably be wet more often than not, and a solid raised bed of some kind was probably needed. Another full day was spent getting that figured out....

There was still a lot of shopping to be done. For all practical purposes, she hadn't even started provisioning the boat yet, so a day trip down to Cabo seemed like the most likely solution.... Fresh fish would be her primary diet, so a fishing supplies store was one of the first stops. She bought several rods and reels and hundreds of yards of high-test fishing line, plenty enough to never run out. She bought all the spinners and lures and hooks recommended by the professional who was helping her, and he got a big kick out of hearing what she was about to do. He was more than happy to help as she bought just about everything he deemed necessary. A couple of big tackle boxes and tools and sharp knives all made sense as he explained how and why she might need everything he was selling her. Of course she wasn't an idiot, but was happy to play along. After all, now didn't seem like the time to suddenly be cheap. She bought rod holders to bolt to the sides and a pedestal seat to bolt to the deck. She even bought a little inflatable dingy with oars and a pump, having never seriously considered a life raft before then... It might even be fun to row around the raft just for fun at times? I might even need to row ashore on some remote island somewhere?... And on that thought, she bought the big anchor and cable that might also be necessary given that scenario.... Finally, several thousand dollars later, she left happy about her purchases, but happy to be moving on too....

A big grocery store was next. Fish couldn't be the only thing she ate, and what about the days she caught nothing? Although it didn't seem likely, it could happen. Plus it seemed obvious that her body would need more than just protein. She would need fruits and vegetables, too; and the only real solution was canned. Not nearly as good as fresh, but it was obvious that wasn't an option .... What else?... Rice and pasta could both last virtually forever, and she loaded a bunch of it on top of the cans before going to the front to get another cart. Pulling things from the shelves was fun.... She got oatmeal, spices, and powdered and dried things to along with the dried fruits, like raisins, and prunes, and whatever else. Knowing she might get a sweet tooth, she threw in big bags of hard candy, plus several bags of popcorn that might be fun to pop on an open fire.... Do I need cooking utensils?.. No, I've got plenty already, probably too many....

So, finally, with her truck pretty well loaded, she headed for home. When she got there, she backed right into her shop through the big overhead door where it all made a sizeable pile that she figured she could sort through the following day... In the moment, she was too tired to deal with it....

Earl had had a long lonely day and was happy to see her again as she took him out of his cage. By now they were fairly well acquainted, and the book she'd gotten in town had given her the confidence to know how to handle him. And on the flip side, from his perspective, he seemed capable of handling her too. The truth was they were becoming close friends. He was learning an occasional new word or phrase. He could whistle several whistles and say things like "Hello Janet," Hello Pete," and "Boat Ride, Boat Ride." In fact, she decided to name the boat "Earl's Boat," and he could say that too. She even painted it in the middle of the deck in big black letters before applying the thick clear waterproofing.... So it seemed it truly was Earl's boat...

He'd learned to get his wings clipped, although she never clipped them to the point where he couldn't fly at all. If he somehow went crazy and got loose in the field, she wanted him capable of getting away from any potential predator, like one of the otherwise friendly cats that roamed around the property. He could always jump up and make short burst, but he was never likely to want to be far away from her anyway...

As his little door was opened, he immediately climbed up to her shoulder and started nibbling on her ear, making soft noises like he was trying to tell her a secret. It was obvious he liked her and missed her when she was away, and the feeling was mutual. She was happy to see him again, too....

TWENTY-EIGHT

This can't be happening! I've been telling you people for years now. I'm innocent! There's no way I could have killed those people!..... I'm trembling on the bed with my arms around my knees. I can feel the warm wet tears running down my cheeks.... It's just not in me. I'm not a murderer! PLEASE! PLEASE! You have to believe me! You can't go through with this. I'm begging you! Please! You have to see this isn't right! Can't you see how terrified I am! Please, you have to help me! You can't do this! It's not right! It's not fair! PLEASE HELP ME!

It's 11:38pm and I'm due to be executed at 12:01am. I'm still in my cell sitting with the prison chaplain, but I can hear them coming down the hall. They're coming to get me. I'm sweating, and I can feel the blood draining from my face. I'm literally shaking. I look at my pale white fingers and they're twitching with fear. I've been thinking about this moment for a very long time, but it's finally a reality. In twenty short minutes, they're going to flip the switch and I'm literally going to die. And, on top of that, the people I love the most have insisted on being in there with me in my final moment. I don't want them to see it. I understand the sentiment, but I'm not sure I have the mental capacity to go through it with even the slightest shred of dignity. I don't want the intense anguished fear I'm feeling to be the last thing they see in me. I'm losing it already and can't imagine it's going to get any better as the final minute approaches. I'm innocent, and the people who love me know I'm innocent. As scared as I am, I'm worried about them. They shouldn't have to witness this. They did nothing to deserve this horrifically personal miscarriage of justice. It will soon be over for me, but they'll have to live with these images for the rest of their lives...

The guards are getting closer. I can tell by the sounds of their footsteps and jingling guard ornaments they'll be coming into view in only a few short seconds- and for a brief moment, time seems to slow down... I look at the man sitting with me and, for the first time, see the total and complete empathy on his face. In these brief few seconds, I can see he's truly capable of placing himself in my shoes. I see the horror on his face and know he's lost his professional composer... He knows I truly believe I'm innocent and am about to die at the hands of the state anyway...What if she is innocent?... I can see the question in his eyes and it terrifies him. He knows he can't do anything about it anyway.... Her fate is sealed no matter what I say or do?.... I can tell he feels the full weight of his uselessness as the thought flashes through his mind... His eyes give a weak and scared apology... I look back at him pleading and crying, knowing it means nothing......

I'm completely terrified, and the sudden poignancy of the moment makes everything about what I'm experiencing extremely vivid. The drab grey paint on the cinderblock walls has the occasional chip. I can sense the density and weight of the steel bars that have been keeping me trapped. The dull shine of my stainless steel sink and toilet seem strange as even my own breathing seems to slow down...

My whole life is coming back to me in snapshots, and I see myself in the field with the bodies...Why did I pick up the knife?... So Stupid! So Stupid!... I was shocked and stunned. I didn't know any better.... I'd called the police immediately, but those idiots didn't know their asses from a hole in the ground.... I should have known if no other suspects surfaced, they'd have to focus on somebody; and as far as they knew, I was the only one with any immediate connection to the scene.... I was simply in the wrong place at the wrong time, and now, nine years later, I'm finally about to die for it... Those stupid bastards haven't even been looking for anyone else... I've been doomed for a very long time, and it's all been a complete living hell. I can't believe how long I've had to think about this moment.... Oh God, why me! Why is this happening to me! I can't take it anymore!... For the first time, it dawns on me that my suffering is about to end.... But it isn't over yet, and the worst is about to come...

The guards are at my door... I hear the key enter the lock and the clicking of every mechanism being turned... The door opens and it's obnoxiously loud, as if my brain is somehow hung over. They enter with stern looks... IT'S TIME... I tuck my head between my knees crying and whimpering. I'm so overcome with fear, I can barely speak. In a soft weak voice, I plead some more as my whole body trembles.... No, No, Please no?... I don't move. I just sit there shaking in a pool of my own cold sweat.... They stand there for a few long seconds before saying it again.... Come on, get up. IT'S TIME... I don't want to move. I'm not even sure I can... I sit there, compressed, every muscle in my body tight and tense.... Finally, these two huge men each grab an arm and lift me up in what seems like an effortless motion.... I can't take it. I'm completely losing it. My tears and pleading mean nothing to them. They're like inhumane robots doing the evil job they've been programmed to do... My legs slowly stretch out and I feel the cold floor on my feet... I hate that these evil men are touching me, so I attempt to walk on my own. But I feel weak and faint. I'm not sure what to do. The only thing I think of is to desperately scream at them... NO! NO!!!! YOU CAN'T DO THIS!!!.. I flail my now handcuffed hands wildly in the air and hit one of them in the face. His nose starts to bleed, and yet he remains essentially expressionless as they both take a zip strap and tie my wrists down to my waist so I can't do it again...

The walk seems long and the hallway seems to grow. I take small shuffling steps, as the shackles won't allow anything else. They're tight around my ankles and probably hurt, but the slight pain means nothing. The polished concrete floor is dark and cold and smooth as glass. The men still have a hold on me, but I'm doing my best to support my own weight. The chaplain is following.... He's saying something... What is he saying?... I think it's Latin. He's praying in a language I can't understand and it's making things increasingly much worse. His low gravelly voice is echoing through the hallway, and it's the creepiest thing I've ever imagined. I feel like the starring victim in some grotesque horror movie. I simply can't take it anymore and my legs collapse, but this does nothing to slow my forward motion. It feels like the devil himself is carrying me to my fate behind the big iron door that we're now approaching.... The door opens, and there are those there to greet us... They're wearing white lab coats and green rubber gloves, as if what they're about to do is somehow productive science, or even medicine.... I imagine Nazi's in German death camps dressed the same way as the guards begin strapping my limp trembling body to the nearly vertical death table. My arms are securely fastened away from my sides on protrusions making the bed resemble a crucifixion cross. The thick leather straps are tight, and they use several across my legs and body in a process that feels like a sacrificial ceremony. The only apparent sounds are the mechanisms themselves and the still praying preacher. All the participants are essentially expressionless as I continue to plead for my life…. They don't care. I'm completely on my own, suffering relentlessly in complete and total mental anguish… These people are mere tools, an extension of the government, and far from actual human beings. They've allowed themselves to become machines, incapable of human emotion… A woman in a lab coat approaches, and I see the large needle for the first time. She scrubs my forearm with alcohol, and it strikes me how ridiculous this is. Is she worried I might get an infection? What a horrible person she is! How can she sleep at night? I know I'm correct in my assessment of her as less than human… The needle stings. It's more painful than anticipated, and I feel my face wince… Then, unbelievably, she does it again. Apparently she's missed what she was looking for the first time… Did she get it right this time?… Apparently so- she's taping it down and seems satisfied that I'm ready…

I'm not ready. I'm far from ready…

In front of me there is a big wide window with a drawn curtain. Suddenly, the sound of a little electric motor starts to open it. Behind it, there's what appears to be the rising seats of a small dark theater- and, if this is the case, I'm on the stage with my parents and sister in the front row…Upon seeing this, I instantly burst into anguished tears as they do the same. It's a horrible moment, and whoever else is in the theater doesn't seem to matter… Apparently there are some reporters and government officials…. Everything about where I am, where they are, is wrong, and doesn't make sense on any level… All I can mutter though my deep panicked tears is… I…m…. sor…ry. I… lo..ve…. You….. My family members hold their faces in their hands, finding it difficult to even look at me…. I love them all so much, but I wish they couldn't see. I'm so glad they're here, close to me, but I wish they couldn't actually watch…Why is this happening?… Why? Why?…. A voice comes through a speaker in the wall, and I realize I'm now the only one in my little room of cruel and unusual punishment…. A brief statement is read stating that I've been legally sentenced to die at this time and on this date, and lastly… Do you have any final words?….

I can see from the clock on the wall its 12: 01, my minute of fate. A cold shiver runs through my entire body. I say over and over again all I can muster through my deep whaling tears…. I.. love… you, I… love…you, I…. love…you…. I repeatedly make eye contact with my three family members, the closest people in the world to me that I'm about to leave forever…

Something enters my body… I can feel it… It feels cold as it

176

spreads... The sensation lasts, and continues to last.... I'm not sure what to think? Shouldn't something else be happening?... And then it comes, phase 2.... The instant it hits my arm it burns, and this horrible feeling spreads quickly too... IT'S SEARING!... I can't believe how badly it hurts as I cry out, but it's worse. I'm not crying out. My body isn't working, and there's no way to tell anyone how intense the pain is. It feels like they've poured gasoline on me and thrown a match. For the first time, I actually want to die...What the hell is going on!... Why isn't it working?... If I could, I'd be flailing and screaming like a crazy person, but I can't move a muscle. I'm trapped in a state of physical suffering I'd never imagined possible, the kind from which even a few seconds could psychologically damage a person forever. I'm burning alive and nobody knows but me.... Mere seconds seem like days, and years are passing without relief.... Finally, after what seems like an eternity, my body no longer exists.... I'm free...

Sitting alone on her bed, she laughed out loud in the dark. According to the clock on the dresser it's 2:37am, and the only other light in the room is coming from her computer screen.... Wow, what a dark place to go, but damn that was fun... It was like sitting and watching a horror movie alone in the dark, which she occasionally liked to do when she was home. But, here at Pete's place, she didn't even own a television and considered that a good thing. She'd been writing for hours, which was way better than watching a movie anyway. In a fun and darkly twisted way, she'd been living the movie, the experience, and yet another cold chill ran down her spine at the thought... That'll be a fun little filler somewhere in the book, *THE DEATH WALK,* or something like that... A title could come later... Currently it was too late to think about it anymore, and she turned off her notebook and went to sleep... There was a lot to do the next day...

March 15th was a warm sunny day, and late in the afternoon everyone would be arriving at the airport in Cabo. She got up, took a shower, and made some breakfast with Earl sitting contently on her shoulder.... He coooed and whistled.... Hello Janet... My name is Earl. My name is Earl.... Yes, I know what your name is. You're a good boy.... It was very pleasant, but she was too excited to stick around... Her truck was calling, Cabo was calling. She knew there was plenty of time but wanted to leave anyway. Pacing around her shop would drive her crazy. There was just too much to think about and driving would at least feel productive. So, after putting Earl in his cage and saying goodbye, she eagerly left with a hot mug of coffee in hand...

The weather was calm and clear, and the beaches along the coast were beautiful.... They're going to love this.... They were going to love this. When they'd all flown out on the same flight together, it had been cold and windy with a slight hint of frozen rain in the air. In Los Angeles they'd never have time to leave the airport. So when they finally arrived in Cabo they'd be stepping out into the warm sunny tropics where there'd be nothing not to love.... She smiled at the thought....

A bunch of people were coming: her parents, Mark's parents, Carrie and Steve and all three kids. (They considered bringing Bongo the dog, but in the end decided against it) Sara was coming with an ambiguous new friend, a date that nobody seemed to know much about, although she seemed excited at the chance to introduce him.... A few other welcome people managed to tag along too- mutual relatives, neighbors, and friends of everyone. No doubt it would be a good fun group, nearly twenty in all... They were due to arrive at 4:00pm, leaving Janet a few hours to pick up party supplies for their first of many rowdy evenings, which was good. She needed something to do anyway...

They'd taken up nearly half the plane that arrived right on schedule, and they exited as if they owned it. In a fun and very lighthearted way, they'd lived up to their reputations as American tourists. It seemed everyone including the flight crew had appreciated their company, and they mutually thanked each other while Janet was introduced as "the person of the hour." Apparently her reputation had preceded her.... Then, nearly two chaotic hours after the plane landed, they all left the airport in four separate vehicles including her truck...

The first couple of nights were spent in a nice hotel in the city where there was plenty to see and do. It was great time, and Janet of course stayed with them to help show them around and simply enjoy spending the time. From there, they worked their way up the coast to the condos Mark had reserved. Very purposefully they were close to Pete's place, and they were incredibly nice. Apparently he'd spared no expense. All three were large sprawling residences with large surrounding patio decks, and they had them all for a full week with the option of adding a couple of days if they decided to stay longer. It was the perfect setup. They were on a big beautiful beach with a big fire pit, barbeques, a volleyball net, and ample beach toys including surf boards, boogie boards, volley balls, snorkels, fins, and whatever else. There was even a rock outcropping jutting out into the ocean with about a thirty foot cliff to dive into the clear blue water from ...

They all gathered there every evening after whatever people had divided off to do during the day, which could have been anything from shopping in town, to sailing, snorkeling, riding jet skis, or even parasailing..... At one time or another, they all went over to check out the raft, to see what the whole trip was really all about. Although, most of them didn't have much to say upon seeing it. For the most part, they were quite literally speechless as they began to visualize the stark realities of what Janet was about to do. But, nonetheless, it was a chance for Pete and Sarah to see and meet everyone. And they of course had an open invitation to visit everyone at the condos, which they took full advantage of. In fact, on one of the final nights they even came over with their kids and grandkids whom Janet knew well by then, and Mark had actually met before too on the big scouting trip several months earlier. It was a great party. Everyone got along well, including the kids. But the real point of the event was Janet's official bon-voyage party. The day after the next, if everything went according to plan, she was due to finally set sail....

It was a nerve racking thought, and she briefly wondered if the execution story of a few nights earlier was somehow related.... At the time, it seemed to come from nowhere, but maybe? She laughed.... After all, I've only got a short time to go myself... It does seem related?....

TWENTY-NINE

The plan was for everyone to spend the next day at Janet's place; and, of course, Pete and Sarah were more than happy to welcome everyone on their property...They truly were kind people, and gracious hosts...

By this point, all of the real work had been done. The raft had been

179

loaded with everything needed- everything, of course, being relative. Remembering that the trip was meant to be an exercise in minimalism, she had done her best not to get carried away as she packed. So this, her last full day before being towed out to sea, was mostly just a chance to check and recheck everything, to make sure it was all the way she wanted it…. It was. In many ways she'd been doing this for days already, but it felt natural nonetheless….

However, more importantly by far, it was a last day to spend with loved ones who, truth be told, had mixed feelings about condoning this with their presence. Very reasonably, they were worried about her… Is this really a smart thing to do?… It was genuine heartfelt concern, and not without sound reasoning. They'd all had a chance to get a close look at the "boat" she was about to leave on, and there wasn't a person among them who envied the idea… It seemed crazy, and people were taking this last chance to, as diplomatically as possible, express their feelings… She understood. She wasn't stupid. It wasn't like she was unaware that people might question such an odd decision. She fully understood that this was a strange thing to be doing and probably wasn't for everybody- or, for that matter, most people. But that's what excited her most about it… From the beginning, the fact that it wasn't a "normal" thing to do was one of the main reasons she was doing it; and, throughout the course of the day, she took the time to explain this to anyone who really needed to hear it. It was strange in a way. In most cases it seemed she was the one giving the pep talk, convincing people that everything would be alright. Deep down she could have used a little convincing herself, but this was her decision, and she understood the responsibilities that came with it. If people needed encouragement, she was more than happy to give it…

Her parents probably needed it the most. As supportive as they'd always been over the years about whatever crazy sounding plan she may have come up with, this was a big one to digest…. Sometime in the middle of the afternoon, they took her for a little walk on the beach to hash things out. Her mom started…. Janet, you know we both love you very much. We just want to make sure you've thought this thing through, that's all…. I know Mom….. She stopped and gave them both a big hug before moving on…. I love you guys too. You have no idea how much I've always appreciated you both. You've always been supportive above and beyond the call of duty throughout my entire life, and I appreciate that it couldn't have always been easy…. She laughed…. I know I've been living a strange life…. However, with regard to this trip, and I know this might sound silly simply because I

180

know you won't be able to help it at times, I don't want you to worry. I'll be fine. I've taken and will continue to take every precaution possible. Believe me, I fully intend to come back in one piece, very much alive and well... It was serious heart to heart talk; and, by the time it was over, they'd all shed a few tears, good tears that left them all feeling a little better... Maybe everything really would be alright?... She loved her parents and was probably as concerned for their feelings as they were about her safety...

As the day continued, she found opportunities to have close conversations with everyone she needed to... Talking with Sara was interesting.... Robert, the guy who'd come with her, was apparently becoming a very important person in her life... Sara was very excited and animated as she talked about him, which was a nice little relief in a way. It meant their talk wouldn't necessarily be centered around the trip for once.... He's an awesome guy and, strangely enough, I've actually talked to you about him before. Do you remember quite a while ago, it was mid summer, way before you even came up with this sailing idea? We were walking in the park with Carrie and the kids? Anyway, I'd just been to California, and I distinctly remember telling you that I'd met a nice guy flying a kite on the beach and ended up spending the day with him.... Well, the truth is, we've been in touch pretty much every day since and have even been getting together fairly frequently. I've gone back out there or he's flown to Knoxville, and we're certainly having a good time on this little trip. Thanks for having us...... You should thank Mark, but go on, I'm listening.... Janet could tell her friend was very excited, and she was happy for her... OK, come on, I feel like this is all building up to something?.... Yes, you're right, it is!.... She grabbed Janet tightly by the arm, practically frantic. Whatever it was, it was about to come bursting out of her.... You're the first person I'm telling, Janet. He proposed to me last night!!! Can you believe it!!! You better believe I said yes too, immediately! I love him! I love him! He's the most wonderful, fun, exciting, kind, funny person I've ever met. In fact, and this is the only downside if there is one just because we won't be neighbors anymore, I'm already making plans to move to California as soon as possible... Wow! Well, that is exciting. Congratulations! That's awesome, Sara!

Robert seemed like a nice guy, and she was genuinely happy for Sara just because Sara was so obviously very happy; but it would be strange not having her around when she got back. She was a great friend and a great neighbor. She'd miss that friendship, their spontaneous bike rides or walks in the park, or even just sitting around having a beer together on the deck. But if anyone understood that a person had to do what a person had to do, Janet did. After all, look at what she was about to abandon everybody to do, and people were doing their best to understand that… They eventually got around to talking about that too..

Sara was extremely supportive and had even backed her up on several occasions, telling other people not to worry. She had faith that, as an experienced adventurer already, she was completely capable of pulling this thing off. She was tough and could handle whatever might be thrown at her out there… More than once she was overheard saying,… If anyone one can handle this, it's Janet,… and Janet appreciated it, taking the time to say so if she heard it personally…. Their conversation lasted for well over an hour and eventually ended in a long and sincere hug. They congratulated each other on the future excitement in store for both of them, then rejoined the group…

How's everybody doin'?…. The conversation was kept pretty light around the kids, her nieces and nephew. It made no sense to let on to them that this trip might in anyway be dangerous. They were enjoying climbing and playing all over the raft as Janet explained what everything was for, and mostly just how much fun it would all be. That was the part she really wanted them to understand- that this was her choice and her idea and what an awesome thing it was to get to do… It was inspiring and even made them want to come with her, to which she replied with a smile… Maybe someday?

It was nice talking with Carrie and Steve- and eventually a few minutes alone with her sister.…. They were very close and shared a very heartfelt "I love you" and goodbye… As it was ending, Janet slipped her the news about Sara like it was a secret, because it basically still was, and sharing a secret always felt good between sisters. It was a nice little way to feel connected….

All in all, it was a nice last day, and they all shared a sunset meal by roasting hotdogs over a big open fire in the field. As it slowly got dark, they broke out the cold beer and passed a bottle of peach brandy to anyone who wanted it. The mood was exceptionally light, given what was due to happen late the following morning. Watching Janet slowly disappear over the horizon would be a heavy moment; but as the hours slowly ticked by, everyone seemed to be celebrating…. It was a calm clear night with a bright half moon overhead….

Sometime around 11:00, a few of them decided to go for a swim- Mark, Janet, Carrie, Steve, and few others. Some of the older folks even waded into the glassy smooth ocean to see what was happening. Mark's and Janet's parents had all been friends for a long time, and they were having fun with Pete and Sarah who were essentially of the same generation…. It was a warm night, and the water felt great as everyone was starting to get a little rowdy…

After a while, Mark and Janet managed to slip away basically unnoticed. They slowly wandered down the beach happy that nobody was following. All things considered, they were probably each other's best friends, and it was nice to finally get some time alone…. So, are you excited?…. Yes, I'm very excited. From where I'm standing, it feels like this thing has been a long time coming. It's pretty much all I've I been thinking about for months now… Granted, I'm a little nervous about it, but very excited……. You know, you should be nervous. I've seen your raft, and I can tell you I'd be very nervous. In fact, the truth is I wouldn't touch this thing with a ten-foot pole personally, and if you're in any way having second thoughts, it's not too late to back out. Nobody's making you do this you know?… Yea, I know you're right? I know I don't have to and, believe me, I understand where you're coming from- but I have no intention of turning back now. The fact that I'm nervous doesn't mean I'm not looking forward to it. That's part of the fun. That's why it's exciting. If I weren't nervous, I've have a hard time seeing the point…. Neither of them said anything for a few minutes…. Yea, I guess I understand, I guess you've always been this way, right?… I'm just worried about you, that's all; a lot of people are…. I don't mean to put a damper on your fun; but for some strange reason, I just have a really strange feeling about this- and it's not a good feeling. And you know me- hell, when you first told me, dollar signs were the first thing that popped into my mind. And even now, I have no question that what you're about to do will make a great story someday… I'm not sure what my point is? I just care about you, that's all, and I'm concerned…… It was strange, almost out of character for Mark to be so emotional, and he was getting emotional. Standing in the pale blue moonlight, she could see it on his face and was somewhat taken back…. Oh, Mark?… She put her arms around him and squeezed….. Don't worry, everything's going to be fine…. All kinds of thoughts raced through her mind as she continued to hold on tightly…. Was everybody as scared as Mark? Maybe this really is an insane thing to be doing? Maybe his concern means something, maybe it's a sign? He's never been this worried about me before, not that he ever let on anyway? Maybe I really should be worried? Am I being completely naive?…. A dark feeling suddenly passed through her body in a cold shiver. Mark even felt it and instinctively held her even tighter. They stood silently holding each other in one of the strangest moments they'd ever shared. They felt connected, close, realizing the potential weight of their mutual circumstance on this beautiful night on this beautiful beach. They loosened their grips and looked each other in the eye, each suddenly seeing the other in a light never truly recognized before…

Their kiss was long, sweet, and very tender. It was special, an intense moment for them both; and yet, somehow, they instinctively knew to leave it at that- a single solitary kiss to hold dear until they were someday together again…

The following morning she got up slightly before the sun. Everyone else was either camped in the field or still asleep on the huge upstairs floor of her bedroom…. As quietly as possible, she crept down the stairs and carried Earl, whom everyone had enjoyed getting to know, out to her raft and climbed aboard. Understandably, she was eager to go through things one last time. She'd taken inventory dozens of times already, but this was it, her last chance, and it simply felt right….

The action itself was mostly just ritual. She was trying, but actual concentration on the task was difficult. A million other thoughts raced through her mind as she went through the motions..… She thought about all the people who cared about her, how lucky she was to have them in her life. She thought about Sara and her new life in California. She thought about her family and friends in Knoxville, and it was obviously hard to forget about the previous night with Mark… It was very nice, and very special. Although, regrettably, it seemed to be casting a dark shadow on the day. It was great to have such wonderful people in her life, perhaps him especially. But it was all suddenly making her doubt herself in a way she never really had before…. Am I being selfish? Have I always been selfish?..… Sure I've lived a life mostly for myself, but that doesn't mean I've ever tried to do it in a way that hurt anybody?… But maybe taking all these crazy risks isn't fair to the people who love me? I mean, really, do I truly have any idea what I'm getting myself into here?… It was a brutal way to be spending the beginning of the day, questioning herself so harshly, but she just couldn't seem to help it. The thoughts were overwhelming….

Luckily, she was about to get some relief. Suddenly seeing her nephew running down the beach forced her to snap out of it. Tears were running down her cheeks, and she had to get her act together quickly. She certainly couldn't let him see her this way; and by the time he was jumping onto the deck, she was able to greet him with a warm and sincere smile….

Justin was probably the best thing that could have happened... He was so happy and excited and full of curious questions. She couldn't help but warm to his energetic spirit and, within a very few minutes, she'd pulled herself out of the funk. She'd been planning this thing for months and didn't see a way out at this point anyway.... They laughed and joked and played and had a great thirty or so minutes together before the others started making their way out... When they did, she was genuinely in good spirits again... She stood up to greet them... Isn't it a beautiful day!!

It was a beautiful day. It was calm and clear. By mid morning the temperature was in the high seventies. There was even a slight offshore breeze to help gently carry her out. It seemed the conditions were perfect, and she couldn't have asked for anything more.

At 11 o'clock, the towboat showed up right on schedule.... She'd told him sometime late in the morning and, remembering the big tip of the last time he'd helped, he'd done his best to follow instructions... So 11:00 it was, and as they all saw him coming, the emotional energy was extremely high...

People were eager to help in any way they could but were, for all practical purposes, in the way as she untied the raft and coiled the rope on the deck. Not that she minded, of course; it was funny, and the intent was clear. Everyone was laughing and smiling nervously...Well, "I guess this is it" was the shared sentiment as last hugs were given. Everyone wished her luck and told her how much they loved and cared about her. She told them all the same and how much she appreciated them all showing up... As crazy as it all was, she felt good as she finally climbed aboard and shouted toward her pilot.... OK, Let's do this!... She held her arm in the air and made a large circling motion... He understood and revved the engine... Slowly, the boat drug away from the shore and began to fully float on its own...Very slightly, it bobbed up and down and back and forth. On what was sure to be an incredible adventure, she felt the ocean's motion for the first time....

It was exciting!...

THIRTY

From roughly a half mile out she could still see them all waving on the beach, but they were fading fast. The boat stopped on her signal, and she handed the driver a couple of $100 bills before he motored away smiling and wishing her luck. And as he slowly faded away, it dawned on her that he was probably the last person she'd have any personal interaction with for what could be a very long time.... She smiled, noticing the ocean current that was obviously carrying her even further from shore...Well, Earl, I guess it's finally just the two of us...

Before putting up the sail of tarps, she jumped up and waved her arms hoping people could get one last glimpse of her before disappearing over the horizon. Even with her binoculars, they were barely visible by this time and would soon be gone for good... On that thought, she pulled up the makeshift sail and watched it billow full of the gentle breeze for the first time. It crackled and flapped, and she realized that the only sounds now were the natural noises of her trip-the wind, the ocean lapping at the sides of the floating platform, the occasional calling seabird. It was a beautiful day and the skies were clear as she sat down in a comfortable folding deck chair to soak it all up. It was an extremely peaceful, almost Zen-like moment. Any of the negative thoughts from earlier in the day were now the furthest thing from her mind. Even Earl seemed content and, several hours in, it already seemed the experience would be exactly what she'd envisioned all along, a peaceful solitary existence..... Any of the potential hardships that lie ahead didn't seem to matter as she was slowly rocked into a peaceful afternoon sleep...

Effortlessly running down the forest trail at a high rate of speed was exhilarating and felt completely natural. Suddenly she was on the trail near her house in Knoxville that she'd been on so many times before... It was beautiful, and she knew every turn like the back of her hand. In an all-out sprint, she was negotiating every twist with exacting precision, like a surefooted deer bouncing through and over the creek, up and down the hills. She was completely absorbed and continued to run and run and run like nothing else existed....

Eventually she left the forest and continued running westward through and out of her neighborhood into the vast rolling countryside beyond. Her heart was pounding from sheer exhilaration, and her entire body seemed to pulse with every beat. The strength and smoothness with which she moved was mesmerizing. She was like a machine and could feel her body working precisely from the inside out. Every cell, every organ, every muscle, was functioning with the most incredible perfection anyone had ever imagined...

As a large river approached, its sheer size took her back for only a brief second before she made the obvious decision to jump. Running as fast as a race car already, she knew she was capable of seemingly impossible things. The river was hundreds of yards across, but the other side seemed to be coming quickly even before she decisively leapt into the air. As she did, the grassy soil underfoot appeared to drift away in slow motion. Time itself seemed to briefly slow down as her body stretched like a rubber band into the open space between the two banks. Then, as the opposite side approached, she sprang back together as if compressed and slingshotted into an even higher rate of speed. Now, she was running effortlessly at a speed of hundreds of miles an hour. Hundreds of feet of earth passed beneath her with each powerful step that kicked up dust like a tornado. She was running west, west toward the coast, and even entire states were now passing quickly by. The grand river had been the Mississippi; and a little later, an even bigger leap would easily carry her over the entire Grand Canyon of the Colorado in a similar spring-loaded fashion. She was having the time of her life, not even bothering to wonder why any of this was happening. Finally, as the Pacific Ocean quickly approached, she leapt into the air one final time about a mile before she even arrived. It was as if she were flying without the power of flight. The sheer power of the jump itself was the only thing that carried her, and it was a joyous occasion. Thousands of feet up, she passed the border between land and sea before gradually descending again. As the ocean below slowly began to rise, there was a tiny speck on the surface; and she was headed right towards it with pinpoint accuracy.... A second later, she was pleasantly jolted back to the reality of her comfortable chair on the gently bobbing raft....

The little afternoon nap felt good. Roughly an hour had passed since she'd drifted off to sleep, and the sun was now noticeably lower on the horizon. Earl was looking calmly out to sea from his cage on the corner, and the sail continued to blow with the gentle breeze. As she stood up to look around, she realized that all signs of land were now completely gone. When she'd first sat down, the rolling hills were still in the distance, and for a brief moment she missed them... This was finally it- the life at sea she'd been imagining for months. It was a great feeling. But, in that brief second or two, the feeling of isolation really hit home. If she didn't know herself well already, this would be an incredible opportunity..... She looked back toward the east with a distant smile and resigned herself to this new life she'd very intentionally created for herself...

Suddenly, she jumped up into a jumping jack and did twenty as she loudly counted them off... 1, 2, 3,.... 18, 19, 20... Then she ran in place for several minutes before doing twenty more... It felt good to get her heart pumping.... OK, Earl, what should we do now? Do you want out of your cage, buddy?... She approached him with a tinge of reluctance. The thought of losing him to the open ocean was far from pleasant, but she knew she would let him out at some point, so she may as well get it out of the way... OK, buddy, just be good and don't try to fly away... He didn't. In fact, he immediately climbed up her arm to the perch of her shoulder a little nervous about the idea too.... It's ok, as long as we both agree never to try to get away from our little raft here, we'll be fine.... She'd already been letting his feathers grow a little longer than before, so he could fly a little better if need be. It only seemed right since there would be no place for him to go anyway. But if a sudden gust of wind caught him off guard, or a rogue wave happened to crash over the boat, she wanted him to be able to get away and back again... However, for the time being, he held on tightly with no obvious intention to go anywhere.... Hello, my name is Earl, my name is Earl.... Yes Earl, you're a good boy....

With the sun continuing to sink lower, she decided to build their first open fire in the big iron firepot. A glowing crackling fire would be a nice way to top off what was sure to be an incredible first sunset at sea. And sure enough, as it slowly played itself out, the sky morphed and twisted into bright glowing orange and pink bands heightened by the ever-darkening blue sky within. It was a truly spectacular thing to witness. The sheer beauty brought a tear to her eye as she sat on the edge of her raft watching, with her bare feet dangling in the water.... Once again, she was left feeling grateful for who she was, and the glowing crackling fire slowing becoming more powerful than the darkening sky was an amazing transition...

By now she hadn't eaten for many hours, not since that morning with her family just before shoving off. It hadn't even dawned on her; but as it suddenly did, she realized she was starving. She grabbed a folding chair, different from the one she'd been sleeping in earlier. For no other reason than choice of design, she had several and sat down by the fire in one that was significantly more upright to boil a pot of water. As she found the perfect sturdy spot in the coals, she went to one of the big wooden pantries to find some pasta. She needed something fast so now certainly wasn't the time to start experimenting with fishing. She could start figuring out how to catch fish tomorrow. So, somewhat boringly, pasta and canned marinara it was, and it was delicious…

Eating it straight out the pot, as she usually did when she was alone, she kicked back and watched the crackling flames with Earl still securely perched on her shoulder. Millions of stars shone brightly in the sky above as the partial moon was just beginning to rise over the distant horizon. It was a beautiful night, and the gentle breeze was warm and pleasant. Eventually, after she'd had more than enough to eat, she washed her dishes in the ocean by lying on her stomach with her face and arms hanging over the side. The water was warm and felt good as she noticed her splashing had begun to ignite tiny bits of phosphorescent plankton. It was beautiful, and suddenly the tiny piece of ocean directly in front of her began to resemble the starry sky above. She'd seen this before from different places around the world, but it was fun seeing it for the first time from her own little boat, her own little world. Strangely, it made her want to jump in. So, using the ankle leash she'd planned to swim with all along, she tethered herself to the raft and jumped completely naked into the deep black sparkling ocean. It felt incredible as she splashed and kicked, stirring up huge amounts of the tiny bright green glowing creatures….

Earl, who was now back in his cage, squawked and whistled like he was confused by the whole thing…. Why is Janet in the water? Has she gone crazy?… He may have even had a point, maybe she was a little crazy but, if so, only in the best sense of the word…. As a bird, he had enough sense to see the potential danger of being in water. He knew it was no place he'd want to be in the middle of the night, and he was obviously worried about her. But in reality she was most likely fine, and it wasn't like she wouldn't go swimming most days anyway. If some big scary creature wanted to eat her, it would have plenty of opportunity. It seemed extremely unlikely anyway, so she figured why start worrying about it now, and she was basically right. In an odd way, it was a very sane way to look at things, although decidedly difficult for your average "unadventurous" bird to relate to….

After playing and swimming for nearly an hour, she finally pulled herself back up on the raft, using the little metal ladder she'd welded to the back. She partially dried with a towel and then stood in the middle of the deck happy to let the breeze do the rest. Life was good, and she smiled and extended her arms happier than ever about where she was in the world… Then she got dressed and turned on the GPS to see exactly what that meant…

The glow from the screen lit up the little shelter nicely, and the information it showed was no big surprise. But she was curious nonetheless. She hadn't gotten far enough not to know roughly where she was anyway; and sure enough, it showed her roughly fifty miles off the coast of the peninsula. The thing was supposed to be accurate within a few feet, a few hundred feet for sure, and she trusted this notion. The illuminated screen and detailed information certainly made it seem like it knew what it was talking about. Sure it did, and she knew immediately this would be a fun way to track her progress. To this point, it said she'd been averaging 3.4 knots, which she figured was probably pretty good considering the less-than-hydrodynamically sound design of her craft. She was headed west, a little to the southwest, but mostly to the west, which again seemed like a good thing- not that it mattered really. At this point the ocean was welcome to carry her anywhere it wanted; but she did like the idea of eventually crossing it, maybe even by way of Hawaii? In fact, she decided in that moment that when the sun rose the next day she'd start putting a little effort into making that happen… And with that thought, she brought Earl to his cage inside and went to bed at sea for the first time…

The following morning, the dawn woke her before the actual sunrise. She yawned and stretched looking out the end of her little "A frame" toward the gently rolling ocean. Before even attempting to sit up, she took a few deep breaths in appreciation of this satisfying little moment in her life. Waking up from a good night's sleep adrift on the open ocean was incredibly peaceful. Her little raft was moving gently with the waves. She looked up at the slanted plywood ceiling above, noticing for the first time the innate beauty of the wood's grain. An eye-shaped knot almost seemed to be looking back at her, and it dawned on her that over time the boat itself would become like a dear friend. She and Earl and the raft would slowly become one. Even the ocean itself, the wind, the weather, the sea life, would all become like one strangely wonderful being …… Hmmm, she smiled in wonderment of what that thought even meant….

A workable electric coffee maker had of course been a priority when planning for all of this, and she'd found a good one in a marina's supply shop. It was bolted to the floor close to the bed, and the pot itself had a metal ring around its base that held it firmly to the magnetized hot plate that warmed it. From there, the entire system was sealed as to not allow any spillage even in the heaviest of seas. So, as usual, getting a hot pot going was the first step in getting the new day started, which she easily accomplished without even getting out of bed.... As she listened to it brew, she thought about how this first full day would play itself out...

Upon pouring her first hot cup, she got up and went outside with Earl on her shoulder. As she looked around, the diamond glow of the sun's first peek shown over the eastern horizon. Seagulls were flying all around and bobbing on the ocean's twinkling surface. Their calling sounds were as beautiful as a well-written song. And just then, only a hundred or so feet off the right stern, a big diving pelican hit the surface at a high rate of speed with a huge splashing sound. A few seconds later, he surfaced- obviously trying and succeeding in swallowing a struggling fish. He'd searched and found breakfast then continued to bob around with his seagull friends looking rather content with himself. With this as an example, Janet made herself some oatmeal and sprinkled in some cinnamon and raisins content with herself as well.... It was good to get a first bite to eat; but as she finished, she got right to work on what she'd been thinking about the night before- namely, trying to actually steer her raft for the first time...

During the months of construction, she'd welded narrow steel slots on both sides of the raft, each spanning twelve feet forward from the back end. The purpose of the slots was to drop a six-foot deep, heavily treated and sealed plywood keel into the water on both sides. As of this morning, they were both still safely stowed on the deck. But within a half an hour after the sunrise, they were both securely fastened and locked into place. Then, a slightly deeper wide rudder that had also been safely stowed was dropped and fastened to its swivel on the center of the stern. If she were to have any control at all over her direction, this would be how. However, she was well aware that this was still up for debate. Due to her relatively very slow speed, it simply might not work- and she'd be fine with that, too. But in the spirit of at least giving it an effort and a chance, this was it. She locked the rudder in place with the idea of heading slightly to the right of her current direction, namely due west rather than southwest. Within a day or so, she figured she'd know whether or not it was working... In the meantime, all she could do was relax and go on with her life as she waited to see....

THIRTY-ONE

The sails were made from the tarps she'd purchased in the San Diego big-box store months earlier. At the time she wasn't even sure why she was buying them. It was simply a mindless hunch really, but sure enough, she was right. In the end they turned out to be vital.

She had about a dozen to begin with, and they were huge. In fact they were the biggest they had available. At 20 X 30ft they were almost unmanageable, but she found a way to work with them. She started by sewing three of them together for triple the thickness with a sewing machine she found at the same flea market as the unicycle, which by the way was also on board. She'd placed them out flat one on top of another in the huge upstairs room of her building; then, systematically, she fed them into the machine, lining them up as perfectly as possible as she went back and forth dozens of times. She figured the more thoroughly they were sewn together, the stronger they'd be, and therefore less likely to blow apart as they were actually doing their job holding the wind and propelling the raft. She did this twice, making two huge sails and using roughly half the available tarps. Then, taking two more one on top of the other, she folded them in half, in affect making them four layers thick but only half the square footage, and sewed them together as well. The purpose, or at least the thought process, was that these sails could be more easily used on days when the wind was exceptionally strong. In theory, it was the same principal windsurfers used in having different sized sails. She took two more and made another one. All together now she had four useable sails and a backup for each of the two sizes. Additionally, she still had two of the huge tarps left over for whatever else might come in handy. So, at least as far as the tarps were concerned, it seemed all the bases were covered.

On that first day out, the day of the launching, the first sail she'd put up was one of the big ones. The winds were fairly light and, as she watched it billow full of air, it seemed like more than enough to get things moving. In fact she'd actually been fairly impressed watching it inflate for the first time. It was big and blue and was even quite beautiful. She wondered what she must look like from a distance- from, say, a hundred yards away. She laughed at the thought of herself out there on this big sailing swimming dock. She must look like some sort of strange refugee pirate, either running away from home or looking for treasure, or maybe a little of both. Whatever the case, she thought it

would be fun to get pictures of the thing from an outlying point of view
......

She actually did have a nice digital camera on board and enough
storage for literally thousands of high resolution pictures. Although
she'd never been much of a photographer before, she'd always taken a
few pictures along the way in her previous travels. It was just never
with much enthusiasm, almost as if it were beside the point. Granted,
she was always glad to have the few images later, but she was never
that serious about it. However, Mark was always somewhat frustrated
with the lack of physical imagery she returned with. So, taking the bull
by the horns, as they say, he'd given her this really nice, really
expensive camera as a Christmas gift a few months earlier in hopes that
she might actually get interested and bother to learn how to use it. She
saw it for what it was and knew where he was coming from, because
he'd said as much.... Janet, this next little adventure of yours is just
going to be too good for you to not come home with tons of good
pictures, damn it!....

It actually was a very generous gift, and she appreciated it. It came in
a nice big pelican box with multiple lenses, flash accessories, and even
a tripod in case she accidentally decided to go crazy with it. He'd
obviously spent a lot of money, probably several thousand dollars, and
his strategy had even worked to some degree. At some point she would
have felt guilty for not using it, so she actually had been. In fact, she
was even having some fun with it. She'd taken sunset pictures from her
beach, pictures of Earl, and tons more around Pete and Sarah's
property. She didn't know what she was doing necessarily; but by
experimenting and reading the owner's manual, she was starting to get
the hang of it... She'd pull up the pictures on her computer and delete
the many she didn't like. The few she did like were enough to keep her
coming back, and slowly she started to appreciate what this whole
"photography thing" was really all about. It was fun. It was creative,
and she finally started to see it for the art that it was...

On this, her second and first full day at sea, she was already
beginning to settle into the idea of this new lifestyle. After setting the
keels and rudder in a first attempt to set a course, she started thinking
about the layout of her new home at sea. She'd never been afraid to
alter and customize her equipment in order to make it more comfortable
or more functional, and there was still plenty of room to get creative
with this...

The first thing she noticed was the lack of shade on the deck. For most of the day there would be none except under her little shelter, and there had to be a way to improve the situation. As sensitive as she was to the sun anyway, she'd almost have to. Wearing her wide brimmed sunhat and sunscreen were practical only within limits. And although she always caked sunscreen on her arms and legs, they were already about as tan as they were ever going to get and in need of some refuge too.

One of the remaining tarps was the first thing that came to mind, and she took it out contemplating how to use it. It was way too big to use as a whole, so she started by folding it in half, and then folding it in half again before it finally started feeling manageable. None of it was easy due to the otherwise appreciated wind, but she figured it out and fastened one end to the top of the shelter with a screw gun and big wide washers to keep it from tearing. Then, since she was still north of the equator, she extended it to the north side of the raft to provide the most shade most of the time. Then she draped it over one of the big wooden storage boxes where once again screws and big washers served nicely to hold it down. It gave her enough room to lounge out in a chair while at the same time letting the wind blow through to keep the sail inflated. The plan seemed to work, and she kicked back for a while to test it. The shade felt good, and now there was considerably more of it.... Sure it was also shading half her solar panels, but the storage batteries were full, and it seemed there'd be more than enough electricity anyway....

Meanwhile, Earl was slowly getting more comfortable with his new surroundings. The doors on both of his cages were left open so he could come and go as he pleased. And although he was still spending a significant amount of time in one or the other, he was starting to cautiously venture out a little too. She watched him as she relaxed under her new shelter. From the doorway he clung tightly to the lower bar as he reached his head out to grab one of the vertical bars with his beak, all the while looking around as if wondering whether or not this was really a good idea....

She smiled and laughed at him.... C'mon Earl, you can do it.... You're a good boy. You can do it.... You can do it.... She smiled like a proud mom knowing the encouragement was helping. He jumped and flapped his wings a couple of times before hitting the deck that was too slick for a good grip. He scrambled and slid as he fought against the strong breeze. Then he jumped and flapped again, this time making it all the way to her lap where he immediately clung like she was the only thing between him and certain death... With a little sympathy, she laughed at him again...You're OK, good boy Earl. Look how brave you are. You're such a good boy!... He squawked and whistled like he was happy just to be alive.... My name is Earl! I'm a good boy! I'm a good boy!.... She continued to sit as he made it up to her shoulder and slowly started to calm down a little.... What should we do now buddy? It seems we've got plenty of time for anything we can think of?.... She chuckled at the ridiculous understatement..... What do you say we start learning to fish? That sounds like fun, don't ya think?....

There was plenty of fishing gear on board- several rods and reels and tons of various tackle spread between two fairly large tackle boxes. She found a couple of the rods and a bright shiny spinner for each, one golden and one silver, and then tied them to the end of the high-test line on each of the reels.... Casting was fun. She held on tightly and took several big steps before flinging the lure into the air as hard as she could off the back of the raft. The reel gave a high-pitched whine as the thing sped out toward the horizon, twice. After each cast, she locked off the line and stuck the rod in one of the several holders bolted to the back and sides. Sure enough, she was moving just fast enough to maintain a viable tension on the lines, meaning of course that the spinners would in fact spin.. Something was bound to be interested sooner or later.... However, from the onset, she figured patience would probably be a virtue...

Bang!.... Less than five minutes passed before one of the poles was jerked over with an instantly screaming reel.... Holy Shit, Earl! Can you believe this?...Very excited, she grabbed the pole with Earl still clinging tightly to her shoulder and whistling anxiously.... Then, just as she was starting to strap herself into the mounted fishing chair, the other one went off .... Holy Shit again, Earl! I had no idea we'd be so good at this!...What the hell do we do now!...

The only thing that made sense in the moment was to concentrate on the one she already had in her hands.... It seemed obvious there was no way to deal with two rods at the same time anyway. All she could do was deal with the one she had and hope the lines didn't get crossed. She got up from her seat and walked over to the side, doing her best to keep them separated. Whatever was on there felt huge. Just keeping her balance took all the concentration she could muster as she leaned against the force of the beast on the other end. It quickly became apparent she couldn't keep this up for long. Every muscle in her body was completely maxed out. So, thinking quickly, she plopped herself down on the deck behind one of the storage bins to get some leverage. With her feet firmly planted on the box, she could relax a little again as she leaned back with the pole anchored between her legs.... Damn,

Earl, what do think? This is pretty exciting, huh?....

Meanwhile the other rod continued to bob and jerk with the force of whatever was on the other end of its line.... She kept an eye on it as she slowly started gaining some ground. She'd lean back with a big pull and reel like crazy as she leaned forward again. It was an exhausting task; but as the minutes passed, whatever was out there slowly got closer. Roughly ten minutes in, the other line suddenly popped and went slack. It had obviously broken. There was no tension at all, not even that of the spinning lure.... Somewhere in the vast Pacific Ocean there would now be a fish with a lure hanging out of its mouth. She hoped it would find a way to work it loose and wishfully pictured the shiny object slowly drifting unobstructed into the abyss....

The broken line was a relief in a way. It meant she wouldn't have to deal with it and could more fully focus on the task at hand. She figured she had probably reeled in half the original distance when her worthy opponent suddenly revealed himself for the first time. He came flying out of the water, fighting like hell to free himself; but the hook stayed stubbornly locked deep in his jaw. As hard as he tried, it seemed his fate was sealed; and although he wasn't exactly tiny, the size of his fight made him seem deceptively bigger than he actually was. She had no idea what kind of fish he was, but he looked to be about two feet long and very plump, probably weighing somewhere between fifteen and twenty pounds..... Damn, Earl, if this guy's giving us this hard a time, just think if we'd hooked into something bigger.... Earl continued to squawk and pace and hang on as tightly as he could to her back and shoulders. No doubt, he knew something exciting was happening..... Slowly but surely the fish got closer...

Finally, after a long and respectable battle, she could see him clearly at the back of the raft as she struggled to scoop him out with the long handled net. Once on the deck he continued to flop and bounce with everything he had, still refusing to surrender. Wanting to quickly put an end to his suffering, she hastily went over with a big hunting knife and stepped on his tail long enough to stab him through the head. His body went into tiny vibrating convulsions as his nerves slowly shut down.... It was over.... Wooo Hoooo! Looks like we'll eat well tonight Earl!

At the back of the boat, she took off two very nice sides of fresh meat with a thin and very effective fillet knife. One side alone was way more than she could handle in one sitting, so she threw the other in a cooler with thoughts of using it for bait the following day. Then, realizing it was probably too early to start cooking even on this day, she threw the other in as well and slid it under the shelter knowing it would easily keep for a couple of hours...

It was mid afternoon by this time and turning into a hot day. As her nerves started to settle a little from all the excitement, she noticed for the first time how much she was sweating.... Hmmm, the water looks pretty damn good, don't ya think Earl?... It was beautiful. The dark bluish hue resembled pictures of the earth taken from space, and the gently rolling waves were peaceful with a gently calming rhythm. She knew from witnessing her swimming dinner how incredibly clear it was... I think I'm going to go for a dip...You can do what you want buddy, but I'll start by putting you back in your cage.... She put him in the one on the corner, and for the moment he seemed content to swing on his perch....

She barely made a splash as she slid gracefully into the sea. Her thin but strong leash was 50 feet long, and she swam straight down to see if she could make it to the end. She swam with incredible grace, waving her entire body with images of dolphins dancing in her head as she went. More easily than imagined, she was 50 feet deep in no time with plenty of air to spare. She looked back toward the surface... Instinctively, a deep calm seemed to well up inside her, like a meditation of sorts.... Immediately, these tranquil thoughts went back to the day she'd dreamt of this on the carpet beneath her beloved globe....

It was a moment laced with incredible irony... It was intense, vibrant, and yet incredibly peaceful. The bobbing raft on the twinkling surface was beautiful. Everything seemed right with the world. Suddenly, she knew she'd realized the dream that had started it all....

.... With the exception of being eaten by a giant fish, that is.....

THIRTY-TWO

A week later the GPS claimed she was just over four-hundred miles from where she'd started; and, perhaps even more interestingly, it also confirmed that her descent toward the south had indeed shallowed up a bit. This was good news. It meant that to some degree she actually was directing her own course, that the keels and rudder were doing their job. And, as she looked even more closely, it also meant there was still a very real chance she could indeed intersect with the Hawaiian Islands. The latitude from which she'd started was roughly parallel with Hawaii- Hawaii being just slightly further south. So starting off with a southwest trajectory, there was also the very real possibility of missing the islands to the south. However, with these most recent calculations, the rudder was adjusted again in hopes of driving even more to the right. For the best chance, she really needed to be running exactly parallel with her current latitude and couldn't afford to lose much more ground toward the equator....

None of this was in any way stressful. In the end it didn't really matter if she missed the islands entirely, although it would be a little disappointing. The thought of spending some time on a beautiful tropical island was very pleasant; but the real point of the trip was, to a large degree, surrendering to the will of the sea. With plenty of time for introspection, she realized the only way to truly know nature, and in effect herself, was to completely accept without judgment whatever was going to happen. Nevertheless, continuing to try to plot a course had genuine entertainment value. To this point, everything seemed to be going perfectly according to plan. Even the wind had been reliable, blowing at a steady eight to ten knots almost continuously from the day she pushed off....

However, at around noon on this the eighth day, the sky ahead began to darken for the first time. It seemed the minute she stopped to think about how reliable the wind had been, it ceased. It was very strange. As the sun gradually slipped behind the clouds, a dead calm fell over everything and the sail went limp for the first time.... Earl stepped out of his cage and flew to her shoulder... What do you think, buddy? It looks like we might get a little rain. That'll be something new.... Instinctively, she took the sail down thinking they were probably experiencing the calm before the storm, which was very wise. The wind could get unpredictable; and if a big gust came up, it could easily destroy the sail, possibly even the mast...

Just as she got it all stuffed into one of the bins, big drops of rain started to fall. Earl shook and shuttered his feathers before diving for cover under the shelter and settling onto the perch of his "indoor" cage. Janet, on the other hand, loved it. The warm rain felt good- and before long, it was literally pouring out of the beautifully dark grey sky. It rained and rained, and slowly the ocean flattened as the wind continued to stay very calm.... Screaming at the top of her lungs... WOOOO HOOOO!!!.... she stood in the middle looking toward the sky, spinning with her arms extended.... This is awesome!!... She grabbed the unicycle and rode circles both backward and forward around the deck... Then, suddenly realizing she should be taking advantage of the situation, she grabbed a five-gallon bucket and put it under the stream of water pouring from the sun-shelter tarp. The rain was falling in sheets, and soon the bucket was full. She poured the water into one of the storage containers; and before the rain eventually tapered off and quit sometime later, the better part of another one had filled as well. This one storm alone had completely restored her fresh water supply- and, almost accidentally, it seemed she'd discovered the perfect way to capture it....

It had been a truly spectacular event. As the rain subsided, the calm air remained along with a thin layer of misty fog. The ocean's surface was smooth as glass. Suddenly, it was so completely still that even the sound of her own breathing seemed loud... It was incredible. In that moment, the vibrant universe itself seemed strangely present in everything around her. The simple sound of water dripping off of the objects on the deck was mystifying. Each single solitary drop radiated a sense of awesome mystical power... Earl looked out, paused, and once again flew to her shoulder. Even he seemed peaceful, somehow powerfully calm...

A dolphin breached the surface some twenty feet off the back of the raft, followed by another, and then another. They were all swimming slowly toward her in a row, and one at a time they were surfacing again just before diving directly beneath her dangling feet.... They were beautiful, radiating an incredible sense of peace and tranquility... Their breaching breaths were rhythmic and resonant, yet unlabored, under the raft. She was deeply moved by their acceptance and company.... An unexpected tear ran down her cheek.... Can you believe this, Earl?... It was an absolutely incredible moment that she wished could last forever...

Without even thinking, she grabbed the camera and was able to focus just in time to see one of her new friends launch playfully out of the water into the most incredible photograph anyone could ever hope to capture…

An hour or so later the sun was back, and the steady, seemingly predictable, wind had also returned. She put the big sail up again, and slowly the gently rolling waves rose again as well. The deck slowly dried as the clouds and fog disappeared into the distance as if the storm had never happened… But it had happened, and she knew she would never forget it… For the rest of the day, she had a subtle distant smile. The strange rainy break in her day made her think, think about her life, her writing, everything that had transpired to get her to this day, this moment in time. She'd been living an amazing life and was taking some time to reflect on that fact. The storm sparked memories of similar experiences from other places around the world… She thought about some of the stories she'd told in previous books and felt rather inspired… Maybe I should pick up my computer and start writing again?…

Trying to find words to describe the strange little storm was fun; although, deep down, she knew it had been a very personal experience, somehow meant for her alone- but she had to at least give it a shot. So she did- and she did a very good job. She'd been writing for years, after all, and was very skilled with words. The few pages on the topic were descriptive and moving, and she was glad to have this new entry among her other random notes…. No doubt, there'd be plenty to work with when the time finally came to put the story together….

She kept thinking, thinking about her other book and where she was going with it. Ideas for wonderfully strange short little stories were adding up. If she was still serious about it, she would eventually need to do some catching up on that too? But, for the time being, she was content just to kick back letting her mind wander….

She wondered where some of her odd stories must have originated. Going to Mars had been fun, and she wondered how her crew was doing trying to save mankind from extinction and all…. She thought out the divorcing couple who had somehow made their way into her files and hoped they and their kids were doing well. The reality of their existence was also very entertaining, even if they were real only in her own mind… In fact, this alone was a very strange thought….

Hmmm, what did that mean exactly? There was certainly no doubt that thoughts were somehow a manifestation of energy. Through incredible new technologies and advances in brain science, we were learning more and more all the time what thoughts consist of in the physical world. They're synapses firing, little bursts of electrical energy happening in one area of the brain or another depending on what the particular thought is about.... So what implications did this really have?... Was something happening at the quantum level we didn't understand quite yet?... Could the simple act of thinking one thing or another somehow be physically manifested in some alternate dimension of reality? In fact, do these thoughts right now have meanings that resonate beyond my own head? Or maybe it's something else entirely. Maybe my thoughts are happening in a realm so much bigger than I understand that I barely exist myself as a part of it? Maybe my thoughts are "happening" to me rather than I creating them the way I "think" I am?- which, by reason of simple logic, might also be true of the inverse. Maybe the things I think of as being "real" are merely thoughts and nothing else. If there's any truth to either notion, what does that say about my thoughts regarding my own strange little book of short stories? Maybe the stories really were coming from somewhere beyond me? Wow, it's starting to feel like I'm going in circles here, but maybe I could really be on to something?

Take the guy run over by a train, the man who'd died with such grace and dignity with his family at his side. Maybe my thoughts on his strange plight somehow had meaning in my own life and weren't necessarily just for the odd benefit of some future unknown reader? Maybe I was meant to learn something simply by thinking the thoughts?... What exactly?.... Life is short, live it to the fullest?... Yes, but these were things I thought I already knew... Ok, but that doesn't mean I couldn't almost always use a little reinforcement...

Or what about John, the guy hit by the meteor?... Or even better, what about the Mars story I spent so much energy on? What were the implications of it? Was there somehow a collective consciousness among all of humanity trying to will itself into existence through my thoughts on the subject? Was I simply manifesting a collective will to explore, the same collective intension that probably really will carry us out into our solar system and beyond someday? Maybe by simply thinking and writing about it, I was in my own small way working toward making it happen? After all, there would almost have to be a breaking point, a point at which just enough people think it's possible and want to make it happen, that it finally does.... She smiled... If this is the case, I guess I'm happy to help....?

However, if there is any truth to any of this, then I'm really curious what it says about my little ghost story. Obviously I've wondered about it before, but all of this would seem to make it even more interesting.... Maybe in thinking about what it would mean to exist in spirit alone, I was somehow making it happen? Maybe in imaging what it was like to literally become a rock or even a large snake in the Amazon, I was somehow correct? By simply being willing to go there in my imagination, I was somehow becoming privy to the reality of such a possibility. Maybe in truly placing oneself in the situation, truly imaging it's actually happening, a person can know what it's like to become the presence of a rock, like a meditation of sorts, feeling the calm majesty of its being. Maybe before the inevitable physical death of us all, we can tap into this realm simply by being willing to put some effort into it...? In writing about it, maybe that's exactly what I was doing?.... Maybe I should do it again?... What had last happened? Oh, yes- Paul - Paul was, with my help, standing in the field feeling for the first time what pure joy felt like as I was slowly drifting away... Maybe I should go back there to see what I'll do next?... Apparently, it could be anything...?

THIRTY-THREE

I drifted slowly out of the grass and into the surrounding trees. The forest floor was spacious, even cavernous, due to the dense and lush canopy above. It was dark and shadowed, with pieces of broken and dead branches and whole fallen trunks of decaying trees. Green ivy-like vegetation crawled in long random lines through the whole of it, and the air was dense and moist, permeating everything with the fresh-scent of living biological processes....

I floated literally into the trees, briefly feeling what it was like to actually be the tree, before slowly emerging out the other side. They had powerful life energies, standing calmly confident in their ability to exist and interact with their surroundings, growing ever taller and ever stronger. I melded into the tiny growing end of a strand of ivy that was making its way up the side of one of these trees, becoming microscopic. In relative terms, the plant was growing extremely fast; and I could feel the individual living cells quickly dividing again and again as its DNA copied itself to quickly move upward toward the sky. Its cause seemed random, yet strangely and simultaneously purposeful... It was on a mission not only to survive, but to flourish and thrive....

Next to it, ants marched with a similar sense of purpose in a long single-file line. One directly behind another, each of their individual missions was deeply connected to the mission of the group as a whole. The group was an individual's entire reason for living, none of them even realizing they were in fact a separate entity. They were functioning as a "super organism," communicating with one another through a complex chemical language that they all instinctively understood. They were leaving traces of themselves behind that were instantly comprehensible to any of the rest, like bold signposts instructing every move. As I moved my own presence from one individual to the next, it was extremely difficult to even tell the difference. Their consciousness and purpose were so closely aligned that it didn't seem to matter which of the individual physical bodies I was experiencing. However, as an individual, my purpose seemed clear. I was focused solely on the task at hand without question. For the time being, marching in the line was all that mattered, and there was no room for anything else. The present moment of the march was all I needed; and when the next task came along, I was sure the same would be true of it. **Now** was giving me all of the life fulfillment I would ever need.... It was intense and insatiable, and I left the ants with a profound new respect and understanding of their strange and complex little societies...

Suddenly a large owl took flight from above, and I was instantly attracted to its movement. I floated slightly above before gradually merging with its flight where I could feel its large wingspan as if it were my own. The wings were long and wide, comfortably resting on the large pockets of air beneath. I maneuvered through the trees in virtual silence until several incredible seconds later finding perch on another large branch. From there, I scanned the forest floor for movement. I was calm and focused, rotating my head practically all the way around as I listened intently to everything around me. I became aware of the physical capabilities of my large round eyes. Incredibly, from nearly a hundred yards away, I could see the individual ants still purposefully marching along on the tree I'd been on just a moment earlier....

I stopped! Slightly stunned, I realized for a brief moment I was using the owl rather than simply observing its behavior. Intuitively, this interference felt wrong, and I left him with the greatest respect for what an amazing and beautiful creature he truly was. For several minutes I drifted through the forest on my own as if I were floating on his wings. It seemed this was good, too, if only because I felt good in my decision to leave him on his own.... Not long after, I decided to leave the forest altogether....

Above the trees, the sun was shining into a beautiful day, and I briefly looked back toward the field wondering how Paul might be doing?... He must be having a wonderfully strange day?... I pondered what a strange thought that was... In this realm, even concepts of night and day didn't have any real meaning. I realized that, at this same instant in time, I could just as easily be on the other side of the planet where it was in fact "night." I could do so instantaneously, and an even more interesting thought came to mind..... If I want to be on the other side of the earth, why not try passing directly through the earth?...Without hesitation, I dove literally straight into the ground....

At first it was dark and moist, teeming with microscopic life forms. I could feel the soil's fertility, its ability to nourish and nurture other forms of life. As I went deeper into the soil, it slowly became more and more dense with the increasing pressure of the earth on itself. Eventually the density increased to bedrock; and then even the tiniest of life forms slowly faded away as things gradually began to heat up. I was approaching the earth's mantle; and before I knew it, the solid earth was gone. Suddenly I'd slipped into the molten magma and it was light again. It was a bright glowing vibrant shade of orange, the color of lava spewing from a live volcano. Now, I was swimming through the source of this "life," and indeed it felt like the earth itself was very much alive. The natural processes of the interior planet made it feel like a living being; and perhaps in its own way, it was. It was definitely very vibrant and energetic. Huge amounts of energy were being expressed through heat and light and swirling motion... It was amazing and, as I continued to move on, it continued to get hotter. Going deeper into the mantel, I could feel the density continuing to increase until finally I passed through and into the spinning molten-iron core itself. I was inside the creator of the magnetic field that so effectively blanketed the planet from the harsh realities of solar radiation. In many ways, this turbulent core was the reason life had been so successful on our small blue world. And this source was extremely bright and extremely hot. It was incredible as I spun and flowed as a part of this energy... I found what I thought to be the exact center and joyously pondered the fact that the earth's surface was now thousands of miles away in every direction.

I stayed there for quite a long time. My being consisted of outrageously hot and turbulent molten iron, and it was absolutely and thoroughly mesmerizing. I was fully aware of myself as this substance as I spun and did back flips through it. I pictured my hand as my hand, only it wasn't my hand. It was the shape of my hand. In fact, my whole body was the shape of itself; but, wondrously, it was made of this liquid heat, this dense liquid energy.... It was truly incredible as I watched myself move. I stayed and played for hours until eventually making smooth swimming-like motions to continue my movement out toward the other side. With my arms at my side, I gracefully waved my body like a dolphin as I felt my speed increase.... I continued swimming back into the mantel and eventually into and through the crust where I finally emerged at the bottom of the Indian Ocean.

In vast contrast to where I'd just been, the water was very dark and very cold. However, there was once again life. Strange creatures of all shapes and sizes swam and pulsed and drifted, depending on their particular set of adaptive survival skills. Some even glowed strange shades of iridescent greens, purples, and pinks into the darkness. There were those who simply looked like fish, but others were so strange and unfamiliar they could have easily been aliens from a distant galaxy...They weren't, however, and it struck me how incredible it was that these too were earthlings...

I continued upward toward the surface and watched the distant light grow brighter. Once completely through, I emerged just as the sun was setting over the distant western horizon. It was beautiful, with deepening shades of oranges and pinks and yellows. Mild rolling waves rippled the surface as a pod of migrating whales passed beneath me.... What next?... And I once again pondered my endless options...

The strange alien-like creatures of the sea floor suddenly made me curious about the possibility of true aliens, aliens beyond the earth- and I drifted up and out of the atmosphere. I continued moving outward, passing briefly by the cratered surface of the moon and on to Mars where I sped only a few tens of feet above its surface at a speed of thousands of miles per hour. Suddenly the ground disappeared beneath me, and I descended into a long and deep canyon before deciding to stop and settle at its bottom. Although it was midday, most of the canyon floor was dark and eerily shadowed... Then, as the large opening of a cave grabbed my attention, I drifted inside...

Roughly a hundred feet past the entrance, I stopped and stood still. A dim light still shone on the reddish walls, and the floor was covered with soft evenly-textured sand. A long ago river had once delivered this beach-like surface, and I wondered about the possible life forms the water may have cultivated. Maybe there really had been life on Mars, Earth's closest neighbor, and I sank a few feet into the sand to see what I could sense. Sure enough, I knew instantly I was surrounded by microscopic fossils. It was very strange. As a little time passed, I realized I could somehow sense the ancestors of these life forms as well as the life that had divided from it. In a stunning lightning bolt-like flash, I realized there was still life on Mars. Its forms were very small, but they were there and all around me... It was incredible as the reality of what this meant slowly sank in, which was all I needed to start moving again...

I went further out into our solar system, deeper and deeper into space. I passed all the great gas giants, past the orbit of Pluto, and into the last distant asteroid belt where the furthest objects that still orbited our sun dwelled. From there, it looked no different than many other brightly lit stars, and Earth was nothing more than a dim blue speck. The perspective seemed to highlight how insignificant we were on the scale of the universe as a whole, or even just our own Milky Way Galaxy. But it was strange because, as small as we seemed to be, it struck me as truly amazing that we existed at all..... It meant something that we even were, and even now, as a purely spiritual being, I realized that I still had an innate connection to my home planet. Earth, for whatever intended reason, and I did feel as if it were intended, was where I sprang from; and now, from the outer most reaches of our sun's pull, I could tell this had a significance beyond my comprehension. It was a strange sensation- and with that thought, I stretched my being into the full circumference of this outermost ring, a distance of many trillions of miles. I could now see the distant sun from every angle along this disk-like plain. This immense solar system was home to my spirit, and the unimaginably huge universe beyond felt somehow welcoming- yet at the same time, very foreign.

I pulled myself together from around the distance of this immense circle and moved out and away from it with certain feelings of trepidation. The dark void was exciting and mysterious. The next closest sun was light years away, and it took all the confidence I could muster to move toward it, as if I were somehow afraid of getting lost. In this galaxy of billions of stars, how could I ever be sure of finding my own home star again?... And then it hit me.

There were many levels of spiritual awareness still beyond me, and I actually felt it viscerally for the first time. I'd had an inkling of it before when I'd first felt the unexplainable urge to leave "The Light," for example. The light had been very real simply because in that moment I'd wanted it to be, which of course didn't make it any less so. For the purposes of feeling so legitimately connected to loved ones, to spiritual oneness itself, the light served as the perfect medium; and I knew it would always be accessible. However, on an even bigger scale, the entirety of the universe was also that light, and it seemed that perhaps the light I'd experienced was only a very tiny fraction of the whole. Drifting away from our solar system suddenly made me feel this smallness, and I wondered how one might ever evolve into what I now understood to be these higher levels of consciousness. Could it ever be that one might be comfortable in the spiritual being of the entire universe or, perhaps even more accurately, everything that exists? Because from where I now was, I wasn't even comfortable suggesting that this was the only universe.... Wow!... As I continued to slowly move away, these new insights were really quite stunning....

As wonderfully frightening as it all was, I suddenly willed myself into the orbit of the next closest star. And, almost as expected, it also had several orbiting planets... As I calmed my senses, I slowly realized how beautiful they were too. Taking some time to notice each of them individually, I witnessed them slowly spinning on their axis, and watched days gradually turning to relative nights. It was incredible. I felt my awareness and understanding slightly growing already as I pondered the possibility of life in this foreign system. And then it dawned on me that I could already sense it even without descending to the surface of an individual planet. Two of the few were teeming with species of microbial life, but as far as I could tell, that was as much of a foothold as it had attained here. As miraculous as this was, it seemed nothing in this new solar system had evolved to think beyond its own instinct to survive. Spirit alone had propelled these physical beings into animation, and in the very truest sense, was the only thing that maintained it. Then I realized the universe itself was the only thing with such a capability anyway. Life in any form was the universe's innate will to experience itself as such. It could even be called god, although even this term seemed perilously inadequate given its nature to be twisted into a religious context. What I was witnessing, experiencing, even feeling, was all so far beyond any of these simple labels...

Tentatively, I moved out even further to the orbit of a star more than twice as far away, and it had an orbiting planet as well. It had one single solitary planet, and its solidarity alone had a perfect and unique natural beauty. With its amazing shades of blues and greens, it had vast oceans of water and vast expanses of forested land masses. It was spectacular, with a huge diversity of life in both its aquatic and terrestrial environments. Much like Earth, there were literally millions of species, and I decided to visit its surface. I floated down into the trees that were nothing like anything I'd ever seen before. Many looked more like gigantic house plants than what I've normally thought of as trees. There were huge winged insects with multiple eyes and a creature rolling along the ground like a ball that could direct its own course. I could feel the huge diversity in the microscopic life and understood its place at the bottom of this food chain. There were mammal-like creatures, and reptilian-like creatures, and I understood their place within this foreign ecosystem as well. Each was serving the planet's life as a whole; and in this sense, the planet as a whole was very much alive- which deepened my appreciation for the same fact about my own planet Earth...

With that thought, and as beautiful as this place was, I felt the sudden intangible need for more familiar territory again. I could sense there were more intelligent life forms and even advanced civilizations further out into the void, and part of me was curious to know more about what that meant. But, unexplainably, I felt a strong pull back toward my home planet. I knew I needed to go, needed to grow; and the familiarity of Earth was instinctively the best place for me to serve this purpose. There was a system in place much bigger than my current understanding, and I knew I was being pulled back for reasons that were beyond me. The tug itself was undeniable....

The distant sun was like a warm welcoming lighthouse. Relative to the great expanse of space behind me, I was well aware that'd I barely left. Nevertheless, from my own small perspective, it seemed I'd been away on the grandest adventure anyone had ever taken, and it was good to be returning home....

As I arrived, I took several big sweeping loops around the sun, basking in its warmth. It was nurturing. It felt like life itself, and it felt good- which again struck me as odd. As I slowly drifted back down into Earth's atmosphere, I wondered why the concept of physical life was so strangely compelling....

THIRTY-FOUR

Simply existing was slowly becoming like a pleasant meditation of sorts. Although she was putting a hash mark on the deck to represent every passing day, time was in many ways losing any relevant meaning...

Over three weeks had passed and well over a thousand miles. She could feel the gentle rhythm of the ocean slowly becoming a part of who she was, not that it was always a gentle rhythm. About a week earlier, she'd passed through an incredible storm that was a stark reminder of who was truly in charge. The wind raged and the turbulent seas grew to nearly twenty feet. It only lasted for a couple of hours, but it was extremely exciting in a way that approached terrifying. She had dealt with it well, though. She'd seen it coming from a long way off and was as ready as she ever could have been. The sail was put away, and even the mast itself was folded down and secured. Earl was put in his cage under the shelter and his door was latched shut. At first he'd seemed a little leery about this; but by the time the storm had passed, he almost seemed to understand why he'd been locked in. It was for his own good, and he didn't seem to have a problem with it.... The rain and lightning and thunder and the sheer sound of the raging wind were incredible as they were being tossed around in the chaos like toys...

However, the pigmy ship held together well, and it quickly became apparent why she'd spent so much time adding such robust steel reinforcement…. It all made sense; and when the storm finally did pass over, she was left feeling extremely confident in her ability to survive whatever the open ocean might have in store. Of course she didn't feel the need to dare anything. Her respect had also grown- acknowledging that her confidence in her own ability to survive was more like a confidence that the ocean was perhaps willing to allow her survival, simply because she had prepared. She'd always believed that Mother Nature seemed to respect those who took her seriously- and Janet did. In fact such a powerful storm left her feeling quite small in its presence….

Just after the storm, the raft had passed through a huge wandering patch of driftwood; and after a few hours of hard work, she'd managed to scoop out a huge pile of it… A brightly burning and crackling fire was inspiring and extremely pleasant throughout the night. On more than one occasion she'd seen the sun come up with absolutely no concept of the time until it did. Her body clock had adjusted to needing no regular schedule at all. Somehow, the gentle rocking of the ocean allowed her to sleep well day or night. And even if she went long periods of time without sleep, it seemed easy enough to simply catch up. When not sleeping, it seemed she was more keenly aware than she'd been in years. There was no lethargic middle ground, and it was fantastic. She either felt vibrantly alive or was sound asleep most of the time which, creatively, was very productive…The writing was going well. She'd thought out and written well the short story ideas that had been accumulating for a long time.

It felt good to finally get some of these characters into her files- like John, the poor guy struck down with a fiery meteor in the middle of the night….. Although, the way she had described it, dying in such a unique fashion was strangely a very positive experience for him…. In an odd way, the story had a substantially happy ending, much like the guy who was run over by the train. On the surface, it seemed his was a sad story too. It was certainly very emotional. In fact, tears ran down her face as she sat by the fire reliving it as she typed; but in understanding that everyone had to die someday, this was about as graceful a death as anyone could ever hope to have. Did that make it happy? She supposed a joyfully peaceful resignation to the naturally changing way of things was a more accurate description, a profound joy that could include grieving a momentary loss….

Continuing, she wrote several stories inspired by dreams, including the one which had at least partially inspired this entire trip. Although, in the written version, it went on somewhat further. The giant swallowing fish carried her to an amazing deep sea civilization and ended with a message about not being too quick to discount seemingly impossible things.... She wrote about the dream of walking on the ledge of the tall building, only to jump off into the most incredible and mystical flight. This, along with several others, was written in the first person; but here, she'd unexpectedly stopped mid way down only to discover herself and her sister in their childhood living room, which was of course quite intriguing. She had stopped and peered into a window, only to be looking at herself at a younger age. It was stunning, and she masterfully turned it into a story about the foolishness of chasing lost youth, making meaning of the fact that there was a time and place for everything, like the changing of seasons...

Flying stoned into a hurricane in a clear plastic ball was probably the most fun, simply because she knew it might actually be possible in the real world. With enough money and enough will to make it happen, someone might actually pull it off, possibly even she someday, and it was fun to think about..... It only made sense to smoke a little pot before writing the story, too- if only because smoking was at least partially responsible for inspiring the story from the beginning.....

However, the most thought provoking of all of these stories was by far her own personal ghost story. The freedom it allowed was innately profound. Anything seemed possible, and exploring these seemingly endless possibilities was, if nothing else, a good time... She thought about herself venturing out into the universe, knowing where the story was going..... It was deep and intriguing, and the subtext of the thoughts alone was somehow eerily powerful...

She seemed to instinctively know to eventually bring herself back home. After such a fantastic journey through the interior of her own beautiful planet, to moving out beyond the entire solar system, coming back to Earth was the only thing that made sense.... And she realized how odd this was. After all, she could have gone anywhere, done anything? She could have traveled in time through worm holes or into the outer reaches of the known universe, and it wasn't like she didn't have the imagination to write about such things. There were infinite opportunities to go in any direction she wanted; but in the end, she decided to make at least a theoretical point. It seemed reasonable that maybe death wasn't necessarily the end all and be all, and perhaps there was still more to learn even beyond it. If so, reincarnation seemed like a reasonable way for this to play itself out, and perhaps the teachers of eastern philosophies had been on to something all along. Maybe total spiritual awareness took many life times to achieve, no matter how outwardly together a person may have appeared to be…

The theory seemed viable, at least as viable as anything else. After all, it was difficult to find other natural processes that didn't take place in cycles. Even weather patterns were cyclical, both in short and seasonal terms, and on even grander scales that took millennia to fully understand the connection…. Even the evolution of life was cyclical, changing only through cycles of life and death. Salmon spawned and died, only after hatching and migrating many miles to return only once for this purpose, allowing the next generation to do the same. Other animals migrated annually with the seasons- whales swimming long ocean distances, and flocks of geese and ducks over land. They did this time and time again until their individual deaths when the next generation took the cycle over…. Fire through certain forest was a cleansing cycle, paving the way for a healthy, thriving, new generation of trees, and on a bigger scale yet, even periods of mass extinction seemed to serve a cyclical long-term purpose…. The large impact that caused the demise of the dinosaurs allowed new species to take root and thrive, only to move the evolutionary process forward. In fact, without the incident, humans may never have come to be…

Cycles of life and death seemed to have meaning on levels beyond just the simple understanding that in birth a physical life begins; and in death, it ceases. The span of that physical life must have meaning in many ways too, perhaps not the least of which was personal spiritual growth… and that's where she was eventually headed with her story…

As it continued into yet another chapter and another fun evening with Earl perched comfortably on her shoulder, she drifted down to the Earth's surface only to discover many years had passed…. Perhaps it was the distant travel that had caused this anomaly, or maybe it was simply that time lost all meaning and passed without recognition…? Her friends and family were gone, as they too had once again experienced the realm of pure spirit. She'd felt their presence, and they'd all recognized that everything was okay…. In fact, it was impossible to move on without reconciling that they all would at some point. It was set up so no one could incarnate again without those they'd always loved approving, knowing that they'd meet again someday, perhaps after yet another lifetime….?

From there, it was acceptable to choose to feel the physical world again, perhaps only briefly through the lifespan of a mayfly, or maybe from the comparatively long lifespan of a giant sea turtle. The only catch being that you had to commit to the life as a whole, from birth to death, and were only allowed to briefly experience a life as an uninterfering observer. If you chose to actually be that life, you had to make a commitment and there were no guarantees of what you were truly getting yourself into. It could be a short life. Due to the actions of someone else, you could be killed in the first hour; but whatever the case, if your chosen life turned out to be a long and healthy one, your essence would somehow come through. If you'd been an evil miserable person, most likely you'd quickly be returned to yet another miserable life, barely recognizing that those from your past life had quickly approved, knowing it was the only way you'd ever improve. On the other hand, decent beings were rewarded with choices, even the choice to never return at all if they felt they'd had enough to finally and comfortably mesh with the whole true light that everything already was. It was heaven, or nirvana, or any other label that seemed to fit... The catch was that it seemed a very rare thing for anyone to deem himself ultimately ready to claim this realm forever....

The pull to live again was strong... This too was the natural way of things, and so it was as she poignantly ended the story by being born again into the loving family of an agricultural community somewhere in the middle of rural France.... Very naturally, the story finally ended with a new beginning....

THIRTY-FIVE

Out of consideration for those who cared about her most, Janet had a satellite transmitter attached to the raft so it could be tracked by GPS. Only a select few were given the password so that news about what she was up to wouldn't get out to the media. Once the trip was complete, it would be fun letting her reading fans in on every detail by eventually releasing the book; but, until then, this was meant to be as personal an experience as possible.... Given all that, it was nice knowing that she and Earl weren't completely alone.... In fact, there was a "loophole" in this plan for a completely solitary experience. One day a month communication was allowed, and it was nice knowing this day was quickly approaching. It meant she would actually get to talk with the people most important in her life....

Midday meant early morning in the eastern United States, which is when she first made contact with her parents who were of course thrilled to hear her voice. Quickly thereafter, they even got to see her face. They'd given her a webcam as a last minute gift just for this reason, and everyone was happy to see how well it actually worked. She showed them around the raft and how comfortably she'd set things up for herself- the shelter, the big stack of firewood and firepot, how everything had its place in one of the bins, the ample shade under the pale blue tarp. Earl even had a few a words to say, "my name is Earl," that, and some random and laughable whistling...

They were probably most taken back by the panoramic view of nothing but rolling waves trailing off toward a distant horizon. They'd known from the satellite tracking how far she was from pretty much anywhere, but the view of what that meant from her perspective was a little overwhelming, so much so they both struggled to hold back tears... If Janet hadn't been so genuinely content about where she was and what she was doing, her mother probably wouldn't have been able to take it; but deep down they understood their daughter wasn't exactly typical.... Naturally they worried, but only in the best sense. They knew they wouldn't have wanted to try to stop her anyway....

A day, according to the roughly predetermined rules, meant twelve hours and they talked several times throughout it....

She of course talked to Carey and Steve and her nieces and nephew... The kids were excited to see where she was. Without a true understanding of what it would mean, they all wished they could be out there with her. It looked like fun; but if they'd deeply understood that hours, days, and weeks were passing with nowhere else to go, what they really wanted was to visit for a few hours and then go back to their comfortable neighborhood. What their Aunt Janet was doing definitely wasn't for kids. They'd go crazy. Nevertheless, everyone was happy they at least thought it looked great. It was far better than having them worried....

She had a nice conversation alone with her sister. They talked about everything sisters might, almost as if there was nothing at all strange about the difference in their locations. Carey told about her life, how she and Steve were doing, how the kids were all doing in school and whatnot. Trying to reciprocate by telling her what life was like on the open ocean was fun… It was all so hard to relate to. Carey was definitely interested, but there was no way in hell you'd ever catch her doing something similar. She was happy with her house, her family, her relatively peaceful and predictable domestic life….. Relatively speaking, her life was fairly "normal," and she liked it that way. Being adrift on a raft a thousand miles from nowhere didn't seem the least bit appealing, not that she didn't at least try to appreciate certain aspects of it. Some of the little details even sounded nice. Stories of the beautiful sunsets, experiences with friendly dolphins and breaching whales, seeing the occasional migrating sea turtle sounded nice, even inspiring. Almost sadly, on that level, she knew she couldn't truly relate. There was a part of her, probably of everyone, that wished she could have such incredible experiences with the natural world. It just seemed too much sacrifice was required in order to get them……

Sara was fine- great, in fact. Although the conversation didn't necessarily come easily. Even as they talked, she was in the middle of the big move to California. It was fun, but the moving guys were in her new house and asking a lot of questions. It was easy to see she was enjoying the chaos though; and somehow, through it all, they actually managed to talk for quite a while and were both happy for the opportunity…..

Mark had planned all along to take the day off. He'd been monitoring her progress probably more than anyone else. He had a big map on the wall with pushpins plotting her course. At times the pins were as little as a couple of hours apart in the real-time of her trip. As far as knowing exactly where she was, he was likely more obsessive about it than even she was. In fact, she didn't care nearly as much and was actually happier just letting things happen. The way she saw it, mariners of centuries past had lived without GPS. Granted it was a nice thing to have, but she definitely wasn't looking at it on a minute-to-minute basis, or even day to day necessarily. Mark, on the other hand, couldn't stop thinking about it.

First and foremost, he was genuinely concerned for her welfare; and secondarily, the whole thing was like a fun little game. Knowing her exact speed and whereabouts (within about a hundred feet) from thousands of miles away was intriguing, the technology entertaining.

He loved it. He had ratios and graphs and, based on information from other websites, he had information on her local wind, temperature, surface water temperature, and almost exactly how much rainfall she'd experienced…. When they first got in touch, he was so excited to relay all of this information he could hardly stand it….

But truthfully, it was partly his strange way of avoiding the emotional side of how much he missed and cared about her; but that showed through anyway, and she understood it in no uncertain terms….

Finally, after letting him ramble for a while, she stopped him to ask about how he was doing; and he was basically doing fine, as always. His new writers were doing well and he was constantly looking for more. She knew what his life was like, but always enjoyed hearing a few of the details from him directly. However, under the current circumstances, he uncharacteristically really didn't want to talk about himself…..

Janet, have you noticed anything odd about the route you seem to be on?….. What? What do you mean? No, not really, I guess- other than the obvious. My entire route would seem pretty odd, wouldn't you say?…. Yes I know, but something just seems a little strange to me, and you know I've been watching all of this very carefully…. OK, go on….. Well, it probably means nothing. I'm not even sure why it's gotten my attention; but, for a long time there, you seemed to be going along at a fairly steady pace- with the natural wind and current fluctuations of course. However, and again I'm not even sure why I noticed, but in the last week or so you seem to be slowing down a little. None of the other variables seemed to have changed, and yet on average, you're gradually slowing by several miles a day. It just seems a little strange, that's all….. Hmmm, well no, I guess I really hadn't noticed that, but if it'll make you feel better I'll look into it…… Oh, I'm not worried about it necessarily, and I'm not trying to worry you either. It's just something I noticed…. And with that, the subject was dropped as if it really did mean nothing….

They continued to talk though. In fact, they talked on and off through most of the day, and she enjoyed showing him what her life was like on this amazing trip. She'd settled nicely into her new lifestyle and enjoyed showing him how well she was doing, how truly content she was. And he was of course glad to hear the writing was going well too. They both, in their own subtle ways, expressed how much they missed each other, though…. Independently, they were both content in their lives, but they greatly appreciated how important they were to each other too… The kiss on the beach the night before she left was never mentioned, but it was never far from either of their thoughts...

At the end of the day, she was very happy to have talked to the people she loved; but it all left her feeling slightly melancholy too. It would be a while before she could do it again- and for a moment, she felt the full weight of how alone she was, how remote her true whereabouts.

Earl helped. He sat on her shoulder and cooed, almost sensing she needed him in the moment. Together they went over to the edge where she slowly sat down and dangled her feet in the water. It was a crystal-clear night and a steady gentle breeze filled the sail. Due to an obvious preoccupation with other things, a fire had never been lit. So, with no other light, it was easy to fully appreciate the night sky. A perfect half moon loomed directly overhead, and a million million twinkling stars shown in varying strengths beyond it. It was beautiful... The shimmering echo of it all on the water's surface created the strange illusion of the cosmos and earth almost as one incredible interlocking entity... It was mesmerizing, truly spectacular. She wished those she'd been talking with throughout the day could see it. Maybe they'd better understand why she was out there in the first place? Maybe they'd see how worthwhile it really was?...

She lay down on her stomach and looked down into the abyss as Earl walked on her back... You are such a good boy, Earl.... It felt good, like a massage.... I wonder how deep it is?... There were literally miles between her tiny bobbing raft and the sea floor far beneath. From her perspective, it could have been bottomless. She continued lying there, splashing her hands in the water, wondering what was down there?... There could be anything, things beyond imagining... In fact, she already knew there were strange and unexpected creatures. This wasn't the first time she'd found herself in such a position. Often in the middle of the day or night she'd take some time to do exactly what she was doing now, just gazing downward, letting her thoughts drift.

On bright sunlit days she'd seen huge schools of fish, solitary giant sea turtles who, seemingly in the middle of nowhere, had an obvious sense of purpose and direction. There'd been whales, dolphins, giant rays, and the occasional hunting shark. Any of these things could have been as far away as hundreds of feet below, but due to the perfect clarity of the mid-ocean water, they were still clearly visible.... It was all amazing... However, the strangest were the things she saw at night, when the light was shining through from the other direction...

On more than one occasion, things previously completely unknown to her mysteriously revealed themselves, things that glowed beautifully eerie shades of iridescent pinks, greens, yellows, and purples. They were deep, too, many many feet below and varied in size. Some seemed individually small but traveled in schools, at first almost appearing as one huge creature.... Others were bigger, appearing as large circular shapes. It was hard to tell how big they were simply because it was so difficult to judge distance, but she guessed some may have been as big as fifty feet across... What were they, these strange glowing creatures?...Whatever they were, they were fascinating and beautiful- and for whatever reason, not the slightest bit frightening. Maybe it was because they seemed so completely oblivious to her presence? Or maybe because it felt like such a strange and rare privilege to be witnessing them at all? Probably very few human eyes had ever even seen them, at least recently. Hundreds of years ago mariners, who traveled as silently and unobtrusively as she was, had probably seen them. She wondered if those on modern huge and noisy cargo ships ever saw them. If so, she'd certainly never heard of it... The ships were probably scaring them away?... But whatever they were, she figured they'd probably been there for millions of years. After all, modern deep-sea submarines were discovering new species of iridescent creatures all the time. Whatever she was seeing, while extremely unfamiliar to most people, may have been earthlings longer than even humans had been? And again she appreciated what an incredible privilege it was to spend time with them, if only from the relative distance of her surface-dwelling raft....

....However, there were other creatures that were somewhat more friendly, perhaps simply because they were capable of being. They were fellow mammals so more closely related. Perhaps, therefore, they could relate on some level?

A school of dolphins she'd encountered in the first week or so seemed to be traveling with her. She was pretty sure she recognized them even though others would come and go, too, and it could be a couple of days between visits. They had familiar markings and fins, but it was more than that. The more she encountered them, the more she seemed to recognize individual personalities. They were fun and funny and seemed to have their own subtle ways of interacting... At times they even seemed to be showing off. They'd jump out of the water doing big spinning flips, sometimes so close they'd even splash her, and it was awesome!... Not only was it great fun to get a visit, but they made her feel less alone as well- like someone was looking after her.

There was even a giant whale that seemed to appear periodically, as if he too was curious to see how she was doing. It seemed as though these intelligent beings of the sea knew she didn't belong but wanted her to feel welcome anyway.... It was nice, and she always appreciated their appearances. Sometimes she wished they'd never go away, but she knew that was too much to ask .... These were creatures with lives of their own to live.... Plus, the fact that they returned at all meant, in relative terms, that they were never too far away anyway.... When they did appear, she always smiled and gave a silent thank you.....
Sometimes it wasn't even silent.... THANK YOU!!

THIRTY-SIX

What was Mark talking about, slowing down?

She went to her computer to see what she could learn. The GPS wasn't just for her family and friends, after all. She did enjoy having it for her own purposes too. It was a very valuable tool; and even if it did take something away from the way the ancients used to do it, it was still worth having... Hey, the modern world wasn't all bad?

As she looked with intention to see if there was anything to it, it seemed there might actually be. Seeing the details of what each twenty-four-hour period held, she realized that maybe he'd been right?... Ok, but how was that relevant, if at all?... She took the time to find out by doing what he'd apparently already done. With the help of the same satellites that had made their conversation possible, she went to all the relevant websites to confirm what did appear to be true.

There had been varying wind speeds, temperatures, and rainfall throughout the trip so far. So the first thing she attempted to do was find a daily average for each, as if this might somehow be helpful. However, even as she was making these calculations, it dawned on her that perhaps a month at sea really wasn't long enough to get a real

219

sense of what the ocean's complicated cycles were actually doing. He was nevertheless correct, though, that over the last several days she had in fact been noticeably slowing down- and for no apparent reason that made any sense... Not that it was worrisome in any way, just interesting. And with that, she moved on to thinking about other things again....

It was still dark, so she thought about starting a fire but concluded that the night was easy enough to appreciate on its own. Earl was making himself comfortable perched on the top point of the shelter. He was pruning his feathers and seemed content with business of his own. She smiled at him, paced back and forth for several minutes, and finally lay down on a couple of blankets in the middle of the deck. The sky was absolutely brilliant. The mysterious haze of the Milky Way streaked across the sky like the trace of some strange all-powerful fairy who'd suddenly waved her enormous wand.

There were two visible satellites that appeared to be on colliding paths; and, after several long minutes, the first distant shooting star quickly burnt itself out in her right peripheral vision. Several minutes later another did the same more directly overhead; and as time passed, it became evident there would be a fairly regular rhythm of them. Silently, with each new showing, she made a wish regarding the health and wellbeing of herself and loved ones....

What were these things exactly? Were they falling space junk that humans had put up there over the years, the remains of dead or dying satellites? Were they the remnants of an old and decaying comet or maybe meteorites that had once been pieces of a neighboring planet, cast out and upward with the violent collision of some long-ago cosmic impact? As more and more appeared, it seemed all of these strange scenarios were probably true. She smiled.... The night sky was never less than completely fascinating....

It was a nice moment, noticing the cosmos and all the grand mystery it represented. Slowly, it dawned on her that thinking about the big celestial picture was, in a strange way, a form of introspection as well. One couldn't help but think about their own place in all of this grand and undeniably spectacular creation..... Why were we here? What did it all mean? It must all have meaning on some level, some form of purpose.... She thought about how we came to be, the academics of it all, so to speak. She'd gone to college, read lots of books, and basically had a pretty good handle on at least the broad concepts of our modern human understanding of reality....

Where did it all begin....? BANG! At one time, some 14 billion years ago, everything in the known universe was condensed into an unimaginably small and dense singularity. It was "time zero," an incredible concept that modern science had yet to push through to find another side. What had happened before this? Did time itself even exist? Nobody seemed to know..... However, since that first incredible catalyst, whatever it was, she knew we seemed to have a pretty good picture of what happened next, right up to the moment we stopped to think about it....

In that first fraction of a second of existence, the force of gravity itself was repulsive and pushed all known matter to an unbelievably large size in a process and theory known as inflation. From there, slowly, over millions that turned to billions of years, matter began to gather again, around itself. Eventually it formed stars and planets, then galaxies and clusters of galaxies. They spun and meshed and interacted while, as a whole, the galaxies were expanding into space, for the most part away from each other. Space itself was getting bigger, and seemed to still be....

Meanwhile, some 8 or 9 billion years later, our own sun and solar system were born, perhaps from the remains of a neighboring much larger star that had destroyed itself in the magnificent explosion of a super nova.... Afterwards, the sun coalesced and came to life while the earth and other planets formed in their own spinning, orbiting, and fiery molten states, some with orbiting masses of their own- moons...... For millions of years the planets grew, as more and more orbiting debris collided in a scorchingly loud and violent process. Slowly, the earth's water rose to its surface and the oceans were formed even as the atmosphere itself remained very toxic for a very long time. Then, a billion or so years later, some 3 to 4 billion years ago, single-celled life first appeared and began the slow process of producing the oxygen that would lead to our modern atmosphere...

Hundreds of millions and billions more years would pass before the life would begin to reproduce sexually, an individual taking half its genetic code from one parent and half from the other in a quantum leap. Finally, at long last, creative and adaptive evolution could truly take hold. From there, in relative terms, it took only a very short amount of time for all sorts of shapes and sizes of sea life to appear. Predators developed as life was now feeding on itself and constantly looking for interesting new ways to gain more resources. Now, as potential prey, life adapted more and more sophisticated defensive systems as well, and the diversity continued to compound and grow...

Meanwhile, on the landmasses, plants and insects had started taking root and were gaining a foothold; and soon the environments would meet as a particular fish was developing lungs. It was crawling out onto the banks and going for longer and longer distances without returning…. Reptiles and amphibians were born, and the reptiles would reign supreme for millions and millions of years, growing to enormous sizes, the biggest land creatures the world has ever seen….

However, toward the end of their rule, small rodents and mammals were also coming into being, scurrying around their enormous feet and hiding the best they could underground, or in any other nook or cranny they could find… Little did they know that this adaptation of hiding from their many predators would soon come in handy otherwise, too, when roughly sixty-five million years ago the giant impact that would be the demise of the dinosaurs hit in what is now the Caribbean sea. The subsequent cloud of debris would lead to the greatest extinction event since that time. The dinosaurs, along with most other land-dwelling animals, wouldn't survive it. If they weren't killed as a direct result of the impact itself, they starved to death as their resources slowly disappeared. The small mammals, however, not needing nearly as much to sustain themselves, hid from all the destruction and lived on roots and insects until the skies once again cleared. When they finally emerged, it seemed they had the run of the place; and they thrived, eventually diversifying into all the modern animals we see today-including ourselves. And this, of course, included Janet who was now lying on a raft somewhere in the middle of the Pacific Ocean thinking about it all…. It was fascinating, looking at the stars considering all of this, tracing herself back to the very known beginning.

Taking it yet a step further, she surmised that we were all naturally born of the universe itself, and perhaps the first feeble steps we humans were now taking to go back into space had always been inevitable….We were the universe itself, striving to understand itself through human consciousness. Perhaps now we were only in the earliest phases of our planet's ability to manifest life with a complete understanding of itself, a complete understanding of natural and perhaps even spiritual realities….? Maybe Janet herself was a manifestation of this striving. Maybe in some of her imagined and written stories, she was in some strange way reaching into the cosmic void through creative thought. Ironically, even now as she was lost in these amazing thoughts, she was in reality gaining a deeper understanding of who she actually was….

As the brightest of the stars remained, the first hint of light began to appear over the distant eastern horizon.... A new day was dawning.....

It was very comfortable, very peaceful. As time passed, the sun eventually peeked up and over as the last of other celestial lights slowly faded away... She sat up and looked around. Earl had found his way into one of his cages and was resting quietly, and there was certainly no need to rush into anything herself. But she eventually stood up with the intension of putting on a pot of coffee. It was a beautiful new day, and that fact alone seemed in need of attention...

Simply taking the time for a long and powerful vertical stretch felt good. Her eyes were closed as she let out a giant groaning yawn... But, upon opening them again, something in the distance immediately caught her eye. She walked to the edge, squinting to get a better grip on this new and interesting visual information.... Is that? Is that?.... No, it can't be?... Well, maybe it is?.... And she quickly scrambled to get the binoculars... Sure enough, way off in the distance, an island seemed to be peeking over the western horizon, and she appeared to be headed right towards it.... Wow! Holy Crap! It must Hawaii! I didn't think we were that close yet... She looked at the sail to see if anything needed to be done and made some slight adjustments to the rudder, feeling in the excitement of the moment she should be doing something. Then she went back to her computer to see what she could see....

Hmmm, that's strange. Nothing about this makes any sense?.... Not only was she apparently only about half way there but, according to her current trajectory, she would most likely miss the islands several hundred miles to the south once she finally did get that far..... What the hell's going on?... But even more strangely, when she went out with the binoculars to look again, it was gone... Not knowing what to think, she just stood there looking again and again..... Am I losing my mind or what? Maybe I'm just imaging things? Or maybe there really is an island, and a haze has fallen around it? Maybe I just can't see it anymore?... Whatever was happening, it would be hard to forget....

As time passed, she did what needed to be done, basically meaning getting on with the business of enjoying the day. She fed herself and spent some time reading a good book, all the while looking over her shoulder to see if the distant island ever reappeared... It didn't, and it was always slightly troubling... But she kept busy. She went for a swim and eventually, as she'd been doing fairly regularly anyway, even threw the dinghy in the water to take a tethered row around the raft... The dinghy's true purposes were to either row ashore somewhere or, if necessary, to be used as a lifeboat. But it was a fun thing to have otherwise, too, just to putts around and get a little exercise with the oars. With all the strength she could muster, she'd get out in front as if trying to pull the giant raft. It was always a great workout. But on this day, even though deep down she knew the effort was futile, it was almost as if she were trying to get to the island more quickly with these efforts…. She laughed at herself… It was stupid to think it might be helping even a little bit?

Finally, day once again turned to night without another sighting of land. It was disappointing, but she was beginning to realize just how long it had been since she'd had a good sleep. When the time came, her waiting bed caught her, and she wouldn't wake again until the following rising sun, some ten or so hours later….

As her eyes first opened, the island was instinctively her first thought. If there really had been an island and she really had been headed towards it, surely it would be clearly visible by now…… Nothing?…. Damn, I must have just been imagining things… That's the only explanation? Right?….

It was slightly overcast; but the clouds were high, and it was clear beneath them. The relative shade was nice, and it seemed a little cooler than the previous morning too….The wind had also diminished, leaving the large flailing sail gasping for breath…Well Earl, buddy, it doesn't seem like we're going to be making much progress today… He flapped his wings and took a lap around the raft. At this point she'd been letting his feathers grow, figuring there weren't many options for him to go anywhere anyway…. He seemed to appreciate it and was enjoying learning to truly fly. He'd always been able to make short flights by flapping as hard as could to get from point A to point B, but things were different now. He was finally learning to actually float on his wings, feeling and manipulating the pockets of air under them for the first time in his life… But still he didn't go far and was never more than a couple of hundred feet away in any particular direction. As he soared above the raft, he could see even better than she that there really was no place to go… Nevertheless, it was obvious experimenting with his new wings was fun for him… He was like a nervous teenager driving the family car for the first time. It was a little intimidating but extremely entertaining all the same…

As he was busy keeping himself amused, she wondered what to do herself. Knowing a swim was always a good option, she stripped naked and dove in where the water was warm, crystal clear, and refreshing as always… As she surfaced, Earl tried to come to her in the water and awkwardly landed on her head for a few brief seconds not knowing what else to do… She laughed at him and tried to be accommodating, although it was obvious this really wouldn't work. He whistled and hovered slightly overhead. He went back and forth between her and the raft several times before finally giving up on the idea of the two of them playing in the water together…Seeming somewhat frustrated, almost pouting, he went to his cage on the deck and settled onto his perch… I'm sorry, buddy, what do you want me to do?…… Oh well, he'll get over it…

….Just then, quite literally out of the blue, her dolphin friends appeared- like they wanted to play too. Suddenly, and as a very pleasant surprise, it seemed she was in for one of the most spectacular mornings to date… She had tried swimming with them before but always with a certain trepidation they must have sensed, because as soon as she'd lower herself into the water, they'd quickly disappear. However, now, on this particular day, they had come to her and had taken her so off guard that there wasn't time to even think about it. They swam and squeaked and occasionally, as she was treading water trying to catch her breath, one would lift his head out of the water and they'd literally be looking at each other, face to face, from mere inches apart. It was amazing! They were interacting with her in a very personal way, like they were trying as hard as they could to make her feel a part of their group, if only in that moment, and of course she did her best to play along. She'd dive beneath the surface and swim alongside stoking their sides. At one point, she even felt compelled to gently grab one by his dorsal fin, and he obliged by quickly pulling her through the water for as long as she could hold on. He was giving her the ride of her life and seemed happy to do it… All totaled, the experience probably only lasted for ten or so minutes, but they were spectacular and unforgettable….

As they slowly disappeared into the blue, she thanked them, knowing they somehow understood how extremely grateful she was……

THIRTY-SEVEN

Another month passed... Two months at sea at her current rate and she should have been to a longitude at least parallel with the Hawaiian Islands, if not past them. But strangely, she wasn't even close. Only about 1500 of the nearly 2300 miles had been covered, and it was a little unsettling. There was no good reason for what was happening. According to the GPS, her forward progress had practically come to a complete halt....

How could this be? The sail was completely full on most days, or at least as much as it had always been, and the records indicated this too. The winds were as steady as they'd always been, and she could see the slight wake the pontoons were making as they moved through the water. The raft itself was moving relative to the water it was riding in. So what in the world was going on? It was almost as if some extremely large undetectable current was moving against her, and there was nothing she could do about it.... The only realistic option was to wait and see if anything changed.....

As far as her actual survival was concerned, there didn't seem to be any real problem. In fact it seemed she could last indefinitely under the current circumstances. Fresh fish was easy enough to come by from day to day, and it rained often enough that fresh water wasn't an issue. Even rations like rice and pasta seemed to be holding up nicely. The canned fruit was getting a little scarce, but it wasn't like she couldn't live without it. And Earl still had plenty of birdseed. Plus, he was even starting to enjoy a little fish himself....

She talked to everyone back home again as this next month rolled around. By now they'd all noticed how strange it was that her forward progress had so drastically slowed, which made it all the more difficult to convince them not to worry..... Maybe she'd been successful- it was hard to tell exactly. Her mother was so close to the edge already it was hard to tell how sincere she was about standing strong. But, to her credit, she at least managed to put on a good face..... Don't worry, Janet, everything's going to be fine.... Janet wasn't worried. If anything, she was worried about her mother worrying. But as far as her actual circumstances were concerned, frustrated was probably a better word to describe how she was feeling....

Some fairly obvious questions were coming to mind.... How is this going to play itself out? How long will it be before I see land again?....

And that was another strange thing. Ever since that one morning when she thought she'd spotted an island, neither it nor any other had ever reappeared..... Perhaps it really had been a figment of her imagination....?

Night turned to day, and day back to night.... Another moon cycle had passed, and the second half moon since her departure was now beautifully overhead as a raging fire crackled in the firepot. It was hot! So to get a little distance, she positioned a comfortable lounge chair on a far corner where she sat relaxing and staring at it. From where she was, her small world was visible in its entirety.... Granted, the raft was feeling smaller and smaller as the days passed; but it was cozy, it was comfortable, and in the moment, it was even comforting. She had everything she needed and, all things considered, life was good... Just then Earl flew over and landed on her lap... She even had a friend.... Everything was fine, and she fell asleep right where she was, happy....

HOLY CRAP! Suddenly wide awake, she jumped to her feet... In the early dawn light, a big densely forested island towered over the horizon. It grabbed her attention immediately, like someone had kicked her chair. It was beautiful and couldn't have been more than a couple of miles away. With the binoculars, she could even see the surf breaking on its wide sandy beach. She looked more closely, checking to see if there were any signs of a population... There didn't appear to be. In fact, it looked completely vacant, like maybe no one had ever been there......

Damn, Earl, look how beautiful it is. How are we going to get over there?... Based on their current position and direction, they were going to drift right past it. So the first thing she did was take the sail down to give herself some time to think. Now they were at least relatively stationary.... Damn! Damn! How am I going to get over there?... Her thoughts were racing.... Can I safely anchor the raft and just leave it here?... What if it somehow got loose though?.... I'd be screwed..... She got out the cable anyway, just to see if it was even possible.... There were 300 feet of it and, even with the heavy anchor attached, it wouldn't reach the bottom.... That's not going to work..... But she cleated it off at depth anyway, thinking it might somehow help to keep the raft where it was for the time being. It would take time to get it back anyway, time she didn't want to take at the moment.... Maybe if I trying pulling the raft, I can move it just enough that the anchor will catch on something?...

In less than a minute the inflatable was in the water…. Her heart was pounding. The idea of setting foot on dry land was so exciting she could barely take it… A beautiful, possibly uncharted, island in the middle of the Pacific Ocean- how awesome is that!… She rowed and pulled as hard as she possibly could, and it was exhausting. In ten minute's time, she was completely spent and had to take a break. She had attacked the project like a wrestler attacking an opponent, and it soon became apparent she would need to pace herself…. A few minutes later she was at it again, more slowly though, trying to get a good strong rhythm that she could maintain for a while…

A half an hour later her arms were like noodles. And although it seemed like she'd made a little progress, it was minimal at best…. Damn! Damn! Damn! What am I going to do?… Somewhat defeated, she rowed back to the raft to think about it.…. Maybe if I pull the anchor back up it will be easier?…. So another hour and a lot more effort later, it was back on the deck. And she climbed back in the dinghy with a jug of drinking water and something to snack on, like she was preparing for the long haul….

Some two hours later again, it seemed maybe she'd made some headway. Just guessing, it appeared perhaps a third of the original distance had been covered and the island was getting bigger all the time. It was exciting, and the fact that the huge raft was moving at all was encouraging. The only problem was her arms were getting very tired, and she was questioning whether or not she could maintain the effort…

She stopped, took a big drink of water, and talked to Earl who seemed excited and a little confused himself… He'd been enjoying flying back and forth between the raft and the little dingy. Occasionally he'd venture out toward the island like he was curious, but he hadn't gotten up the nerve to go all the way over…. He sat on the side of dingy looking in that direction and took off again…. He flew and flew and flew… Go Earl! Go!… And he did. He kept going, nearly disappearing from sight; but sure enough, he was still in view as he landed gently and safely on the beach…. WOOO HOOO!!!! Good boy Earl!… He sat for a few minutes and took off again, headed back. A few minutes later he landed once again on her shoulder, this time with sand on his feet…. My name is Earl!…. My name is Earl!…. Yes it is, you're quite the little explorer, aren't you buddy?… His efforts were inspiring, and she picked up the oars again….

Some five hours later, the sandy bottom began to appear far below. The water was still over a hundred feet deep; but finally, at long last, there was visible land under the boat, and the beach itself was less than a hundred yards away. The mild surf was breaking out in front of her, and it was finally time to anchor the raft.... Some twenty minutes later, after making sure it was secure and loading a few things onto the dingy, she was riding one of the gentle little waves ashore....

Stepping onto dry land for the first time was intense.... She took a few minutes just to standup, take in a deep breath, and gaze around in appreciation...... Earl, who'd been flying around soaking it all up for himself, flew over and landed on her extended arm...Wow, buddy, can you believe this!.... It seemed they had this incredible tropical paradise all to themselves.... I don't know about you, Earl, but I think we should at least spend the night, maybe a few nights?... She laughed at herself for this "well,duh!" decision. There was certainly no good reason to leave anytime soon. She assumed that the island was remote and probably very small, and she was probably the only person on it. Perhaps she was the only person who'd ever been on it, but it would be fun looking around to see what she could see. If anyone else had been there, at least recently, there should be fairly obvious evidence of it somewhere...

But, in the meantime, there was work to be done. She started by finding some branches to prop up one of the tarps on the beach and threw in a couple of blankets and a sleeping bag. Then she strung another large tarp in the palm trees just beyond the beach for a little bigger and more substantial shelter if need be. They were simple things that felt like they needed doing, and none of it took very long... There was plenty of driftwood lying around that she could gather up later for firewood- but first things first......

She stretched and a paced a little, trying to get used to the idea of walking on a surface that wasn't moving for the first time in over sixty days.... It was a gorgeous warm afternoon, and the friendly little waves were calling her back into the ocean already.... A little body surfing seemed in order as she waded back in. She took a deep breath before diving under and swimming out as far as she could beneath the surface. When she tried to stand up again, she still could..... She ducked down toward the bottom as a breaking wave passed overhead. When she surfaced, the raft was visible anchored way off shore.....

It looked safe enough, but the fact that it was so far away was understandably a little unsettling... Her whole life was on that raft. What if it somehow got away? Granted, there were people who had her coordinates, but they had the coordinates of the raft itself, and nobody was expecting to hear from her for another month. It could drift a long way in a month's time. It was probably a good idea to at least bring the computer and GPS ashore, which would of course mean one of the solar panels too..... It can wait until tomorrow though. I'll even find a big rock to take out and use for a secondary anchor.... It'll all be fine for only one night.... For the moment, it all sounded like too much work anyway... And besides, getting tumbled in the gentle surf was just about the happiest place in the world to be... Why bother worrying?

THIRTY-EIGHT

A strong gust of wind hit the tarp just as small drops of rain started to fall. Until that moment, she'd been very comfortably sound asleep. It was the middle of the night, and although lying on the stationary sand should have taken some getting used to, she was so exhausted when the time came that she'd gone out like a light....

She sat up and rubbed her eyes wondering if she would have to do anything. Still somewhat dazed, she was hoping she could just lie back down and go back to sleep; but she waited. And within minutes the rain literally poured out of the sky as the onshore wind got even stronger. The sides of her makeshift tent were anchored with some fairly big rocks, and the taut ropes on each end added even more stability; but the flapping was still making a lot of noise.... Within several more minutes a virtual river was running through, and it quickly became apparent that simply going back to sleep would not be an option.... Shit!.... At first this was the only real concern, but then it hit her.... OH SHIT! The raft!!...

She got up and ran out into the torrential storm. At the surf's edge, the waves were now considerably bigger than the ones she'd been playing in only hours earlier.... DAMN! This isn't good.... For the first time, she realized that the raft being washed ashore was almost as big a problem as having it completely float away. If it got blown inside the surf's breaking line, which due to the increased size of waves was now much further out anyway, it would eventually get tossed up on the beach where there would be no way to ever push it back out.... Maybe leaving it anchored offshore by itself wasn't the smartest thing I ever did?...

DAMN! DAMN!.... Where's Earl?.... She hadn't seen him since before going to sleep and knew he was probably out there in one of his cages trying to get some sleep himself.... She called his name a few times as loudly as she could, knowing it was pointless. He would never hear over the sound of the rain and wind and big crashing waves.... He'll be OK, he's tough.... As she said this to herself, she realized she actually believed it and basically stopped worrying about him... The raft coming ashore was a much bigger concern, and she paced up and down the beach in the drenching rain waiting to see what would happen... It seemed that, whatever it was, it would happen soon.... A storm as strong as this couldn't last long?...

However, with the thick cloud cover, it was nearly pitch dark as the last of the fire's embers fizzled out. For all practical purposes, she couldn't see anything, and thinking of her precious raft out there with everything on it was nerve-racking.... And then she heard it, a loud awful crashing noise that couldn't have been far away.... Shit! That can't be good.... It had to be the raft spilling over the top of one of the breaking waves.... Damn, here it comes...... It was a sobering moment. A few minutes later she heard something loudly scrape the sand less than fifty feet from where she was standing..... Tentatively, she walked towards it, knowing the news couldn't be good... As each new wave pulsed ashore she heard it scraping again, slightly less noisily each time and knew it was getting lodged further and further onto the sand with each new surge...

Sure enough, a few minutes later she bumped it with her knee and climbed aboard. For a second, it was almost nice having it onshore with her. At least she knew where it was and that everything was still intact. Earl looked a little stressed but was safe and sound on the perch of his indoor cage... It was good to see him again, too, and nice to get out of he rain herself for a minute.... Well buddy, what do you think this means? It looks like we might be here for a while?... She immediately checked to see that the computer and GPS were still working, and they were... She expected they would be, but it was nice to have confirmation. It meant that her actual life wasn't in any real danger as

231

far as she could tell. At least there were people who knew where she was. If worse came to worse, she could be rescued..... .

The next morning, after spending the rest of the night on the raft, she awoke to find that the storm had subsided and it was once again a beautiful new day. The sun was shining, there wasn't a cloud in the sky, and the winds were practically nonexistent. Almost remarkably, her tarp shelter on the beach was still standing, and the one in the trees was also where she remembered.... Apparently she'd gotten pretty good at rigging over the years, and she took a minute to pat herself on the back.... However, the bad news was at least as bad as she'd suspected. As the storm slowly passed, it left the raft parked on the sand like a beached whale. The now much smaller waves licked at the ocean side of it, but the reality was that none of it was floating even a little bit.... Well, Earl, it looks like we don't have to worry about it floating away anymore.... She laughed..... I guess there's no point in worrying about anything right now. So why don't we do a little exploring?....

A half an hour later, after having a bite to eat and putting together a little day pack with some food and water bottles, she headed up through the palm trees at the far side of the beach. It was nice being in the shade of living healthy plants, and the scattered coconuts were a welcomed sight....We're definitely not going to starve to death, Earl.... Earl wasn't paying attention. He was completely beside himself as he fluttered around between the branches of the numerous plants and trees. As far as he was concerned they were in paradise, and he was very busy loving the fact...

The terrain sloped upward, so the further they went the higher they got. From the beach, she had determined that her goal was to make it to the visually central high point. From there she could get a sense of how big the island actually was. She could see if there was any more to it than there appeared to be.... Eventually the trees gave way to steeper more rocky ground, and the hiking slowly gave way to more of a scramble. After about an hour, she neared the top. The last little pitch was steeper than anything had been so far, meaning she had to pay careful attention to each new hand and foot hold. In the last couple of moves, she questioned how smart any of this even was; but she made it, and the views were spectacular from the summit of her little island..

The first thing she noticed was that the island was indeed as small as she'd suspected. It was maybe a rough mile in diameter at the absolute most. And second, she noticed another island of approximately the same size several more miles away in the exact opposite direction from where she'd just come.... A sister island?.... Cool.... However, other than that, there was nothing in view but the vast Pacific Ocean all around in every other direction, and it was absolutely awe-inspiringly gorgeous.... It only made sense to sit and appreciate it for a while. She was atop a beautiful island where there was still no proof anyone else had ever even been... In the moment, she felt privileged to be there....

The rest of the day was spent establishing a nice camp for herself. A nice pile of firewood was gathered, and all the tarps were utilized for a creative gathering of shelters in the trees. Meanwhile, she noticed a subtly changing tide making the water a little deeper around the raft. It was still fiercely lodged on the sand but, at the same time, this seemed somewhat encouraging. Maybe there would eventually be a way to pry it off the beach?... But for the time being, it only made sense to see that it was safely anchored, which she easily did.....

As evening rolled around, it was easy enough to see that the beach was facing almost exactly due south. Facing the ocean, the sun had risen directly to her left and was now setting directly to her right, visibly beautiful on both ends of its journey. It was her first full day on dry land in over two months, and it had been a great one. The little island felt welcoming, happy to serve as a refuge for as long as she might want....

The sky was perfectly clear as darkness took over. The stars and partial moon were shining brightly as the big fire crackled and popped on the beach.... Earl sat contently pruning his feathers on a partial tree in the random stack of firewood.... Not bad, hey buddy?.... She smiled and opened her computer, thinking it might be fun to chronicle some of what the last couple of days had brought them... But before getting started, she checked the GPS to see exactly where they were again....

...The news was strange, to say the least, and didn't even seem possible... According to her computer, the island itself seemed to be moving. From where it had claimed she was some eighteen hours earlier, she was now nearly a mile further east. It didn't make sense on any level... How could that be?... Something must be malfunctioning?... Although, the more she thought about it, it did seem to fit the pattern. It appeared she'd been slowing down for weeks now. It even seemed she'd come to a complete stop as far as forward progress was concerned. While the raft had never appeared to be slowing down in the water, meaning the winds that propelled it had always appeared to blow in at least a steady pattern, physically her position relative to these facts had been changing.... It was bizarre....There appeared to be some massive force moving a huge portion of the ocean's surface, so big as to be undetectable from her much smaller perspective.... This of course didn't make any sense either; but from where she sat, all of the evidence seemed to be pointing in that direction. And not only that, it was being confirmed by people thousands of miles away... In fact, Mark in New York was the first person to even notice it. It was alarming. And as it slowly sank in, it finally dawned on her to break the communication rule for the first time... Maybe, under these extremely unforeseeable circumstances, it made sense to throw the once-a-month rule out the window for the time being, at least with Mark? Maybe it didn't make sense to upset anybody else yet, but Mark could at least further confirm what she was currently seeing?... Plus it would just be good to hear his voice again...

.... I'm so glad you called. I'm a little worried about you.... He tried not to sound too alarming....Well, to be perfectly honest, I'm a little unnerved myself. Something very weird definitely seems to be happening. I just can't figure out what it is exactly, and the fact that you're seeing basically the same thing from where you are certainly doesn't make me feel any better. If it were just me, I could simply discount it as equipment malfunctioning- not that that would be a good thing either...she laughed nervously..... but at least my whole world wouldn't appear to be turning on its head... What the hell's going on Mark?....

Mark didn't know. He was at least as perplexed as she was. But just talking to him made her feel a little better, even if he was confirming how bizarre her situation really was. If all the evidence actually was pointing in the right direction, her world was turning and warping in ways that made no sense on any rational level... Entire islands weren't supposed to move.... At least not this quickly.... Sure, there were things like the slow movement of tectonic plates that made land masses move, but things like that happened in geologic time, time scales that were nearly impossible to relate to in a human lifespan. Sure, things occasionally happened catastrophically, but she hadn't been aware of any earthquakes or tidal waves that would suggest any major movements of that sort...?

They continued talking throughout the night and into the wee hours of the morning. Finally, after hours of keeping each other company, they hung up reassuring each other they'd be back in touch soon. Even as they talked, her situation had continued to get more and more

234

bizarre; and neither of them would ever be able to stop thinking about it. It seemed her position in the ocean, the position of her island itself, was moving even as they watched. Even more precisely, she seemed to be moving in a giant arc that was slowly changing from east to north in a radius that would have to add up to tens if not hundreds of miles.... If things continued the way they were, she would eventually be making a giant circle somewhere in the middle of the Pacific Ocean...

After their conversation, she lay down and tried to get some much needed sleep. It would be hours before it started getting light again, and it only made sense to try to rest. Although, it was more logical than practical. Of course her was mind was racing in search of reasonable explanations, and there were none... In fact, the only thing that even might have made sense was that both hers and other GPS systems worldwide were malfunctioning simultaneously and in the same way... How could that be?... And she continued to toss and turn knowing that didn't make any sense either...

As dawn approached, she may have managed to drift off for an hour so. She'd lost track of the time completely so it was hard to tell, but she had definitely fallen asleep for at least a little while because when she awoke the morning light was finally beginning to show itself. She was on the soft comfortable sand with a blanket and pillow next to a fire that was still smoldering. It was a pleasantly relaxing moment that she consciously tried to make last for as long as possible.... But finally, several minutes later, thoughts of her odd circumstances were simply too strong to contain and she sat up wondering how bizarre this next new day would prove to be.... As she stood up and stretched and looked around, it suddenly seemed VERY....

THIRTY-NINE

Looking westward up the wide beautiful beach, it was a beautiful morning. And that was all she would've noticed if it weren't for the barely visible island peeking around the corner. She blinked and rubbed her eyes wondering if the recent facts might simply be playing tricks on her imagination....Did another island just appear out of nowhere?... She squinted and looked closer to see if it indeed even was another island?.... Sure enough, that was the only thing it could have been, and it looked like only several miles separated it from her own... But that wasn't the strangest part. As she continued watching it closely, it actually appeared to be moving slightly to the south even as she was looking at it.... It was incredible! If she weren't seeing it with her own eyes, it would have been impossible to believe. And, based on its apparent distance, it had to be moving fairly quickly for the movement to even be perceived.... This is crazy!...

She stood wide-eyed wondering what to do next. For the first time, a feeling of panic began to well up inside her. For the first time, she felt a genuine sense of dread about what this all might mean. The truth was she had absolutely no idea what was happening, but it seemed obvious that huge uncontrollable forces were at play....

After several long minutes of dizzyingly frightful contemplation, she decided her best option was to simply try to get a better assessment of what the situation truly was by returning to the high point. Getting a better view was perhaps the only thing she had personal control over. Perhaps from there things would somehow look better, somehow make more sense....? She grabbed a water bottle and started moving quickly with Earl happily following along.

Earl obviously had absolutely no idea there were any potential problems and was more than happy to go for another little hike- and at first his all-consuming playfulness was almost contagious. For a brief moment, she admired the natural skill he'd cultivated to go along with it. He truly was her naturally flying friend. He dipped and rose at will with the gusting upwardly sloping winds, and she could sense his joy... She almost envied his childlike innocence before thoughts of why she was hiking in the first place intrusively pushed their way back in...

As she poked her head over the top, the island that had been there the day before, the one she fully expected to be the first thing she saw again, wasn't there... Her heart sank as her fear level immediately rose again...Within seconds, she realized the island she'd first seen this morning must have been the one that was missing…The one that had once been opposite was itself the mysterious moving island…The day before, it must have been moving already, and she simply hadn't noticed yet?…

As she turned back, it had moved noticeably further than even when she'd started this little venture and appeared to be on route in a large circle around her. It was now perhaps 30 degrees further along this path…. So it had to be moving fast and was probably gaining speed…

It was by far the strangest thing she'd ever seen. In all her travels, she'd never felt so completely out of control, so completely outside of her ability to make sense of the world… It was scary and difficult to know how to do deal with these feelings. She felt her face wince with the anxiety, and it was far from pleasant. She sat down and put her head between her knees. She'd always been an extraordinarily strong person and hadn't genuinely cried hard in years, but everything she was feeling, in this the strangest moment of her life, needed expressing- so she decided to let it out…

In an all-out sob, she gave into it fully and felt the full weight of her vulnerability… It was humbling and came over her in an unexpectedly strong way……. If she'd been standing in a swift stream trying desperately to hold herself in place, she would finally let it just sweep her away. She completely surrendered, and it was oddly satisfying simply to relax into it….

She surrendered to God and actually began to pray… Please God, I don't know what's happening here, but please don't let it be anything awful. Please let everything be alright… It was an honest expression of total and complete humility…. She'd never been a religious person but had never been afraid to express her own kind of faith either… Her relationship with a higher force had always been very personal and had always worked well for her. In the moment, she truly believed her prayers were waves of energy filtering out into the universe in a perceivable way… She knew prayers weren't always received in the way people hoped; but, nonetheless, it felt good to be putting it all out there in such a genuinely heartfelt way…. She cried and prayed, and cried and prayed some more…. Please God, let my family and friends know how much I love them…. She went on like this for quite some time…

When she was finally finished, she wasn't any less afraid necessarily. It was a draining, even exhausting, purging of her spirit, a complete and open surrender that in the end left her feeling perhaps a little more accepting of whatever might happen…. Perhaps at this point, that was the best she could hope for.....?

Earl, who'd noticed her turmoil, had done his best to help simply by sitting with her through the worst of it. His presence was appreciated; and when he finally took off again, he seemed content she was feeling better....

When she finally stood up, the "sister island" had moved even further and was now directly offshore from her original beach. It had come a full 180 degrees from where she had first seen it.... It was amazing!.... As she wiped the tears from her eyes, it was so ridiculous that she burst out in an absurd fit of laughter... She extended her arms and felt the strange chaotic breeze on her entire body as she let out a loud...WOOOOHOOOOO!!!!... She was tired of crying.... She decided that whatever was going to happen was going to happen anyway, and there was no point in fighting it....

However, the actual strangeness of the situation never stopped getting stranger. As she continued to look around, she eventually looked back to where the other island had once been... In the furthest distance, there actually appeared to be a depression in the ocean's surface. It was very subtle and barely discernible; but, nevertheless, as the surface reached the horizon, it appeared to be taking the form of a gently depressing bowl, as if a hole was beginning to form at the top of the ocean....

She stood and stared.... An hour passed, then two... In that time, she noticed not only the position of her orbiting island changing but her own position changing as well. It was changing relative not only to the other island but to the deepening distant depression. It seemed she too was beginning an orbit of sorts... She thought about the other island that was obviously speeding up in its own movement. It was now almost back to its original position.... Maybe the movement of her own island was mimicking the motion of its sister? Maybe they were mutually orbiting each other and were together orbiting something even larger on this two-dimensional plane of the earth's surface.... In fact, as the day continued to pass, it became more and more apparent that her motion relative to this growing central depression was indeed an arc, an arc that would logically and inevitably form a circle....

Deep down, she knew what this new evidence was suggesting. As frightening as the thought was, it seemed an incomprehensibly large whirlpool was forming in the middle of the Pacific Ocean- and she and her entire island were being pulled towards it. It was a horrible realization. But if this was indeed going to be her extremely strange fate, she made a decision right then and there to go out with dignity....

In a brilliant flash of insight, she realized that nobody lived forever and this might very well turn out to be the strangest way to go out any human being had ever experienced. If this was the case, she would do her absolute best to appreciate it for the glorious moment it might turn out to be....

The best views of whatever was going to happen would be from right where she was standing. But if these were her actual final days or even hours, she needed to be in touch with loved ones. There was work to be done, and she decisively started moving back down toward the camp....

Seeing her distant raft lodged on the sand, it occurred to her how silly it was that she'd worried about that fact.... At this point, any of her previous problems seemed so incredibly irrelevant and petty... In her hurried struggle back down the mountain, she began to think about this fact relative to the ordinary lives of most people in general... Even her raft being lodged on the sand was a very real problem compared to the problems people sometimes had a tendency to invent for themselves.... Racing back toward the beach was itself becoming a profound moment.... As her own life was beginning to flash before her eyes, she realized what an apt word "petty" could really be.... In the end, barely any of it mattered even a little bit. Petty arguments between friends and relatives that led to long term resentments over the smallest of issues, getting upset over a lawn mower that wouldn't start, or a flat tire at the side of the road- it was all such a stupid waste of time in the grand scheme of things....

Personally, she'd never had any significant problems with any of this; but there were times in her life she wasn't necessarily proud of, and for a minute she wished she could take them back.... But as she reached the sand, she realized nobody was completely immune to it. It was all part of what it meant to be human, and when communication was finally made, she wasn't going to waste any valuable time bringing up negative moments from the past... She knew if the situation really was going to play out the way she suspected, it would be hard enough on the people she loved without her being anything but positive...

Finally back on the raft, her first thought was to make this all happen in a single trip. She would take only the essentials to last for as long as it might take.... The batteries for her computer were completely charged, and that was the primary reason she'd come back down in the first place. But as she thought about it, she realized that if it were at all possible she should take one of the solar panels too- and from there the list grew quickly…. Maybe I need a small tarp, and a jacket, and a blanket, and a pillow, and of course some food and drinking water?… Before long, she had it all bundled in the tarp and was carrying it back up the hill like a heavy garbage bag draped over her shoulder…. The return to the top wasn't nearly as quick as the trip down had been, but a couple of very difficult hours later, she was once again there….

It took several minutes to catch her breath as she reassessed the situation. Sure enough, everything was continuing to change. It was late in the afternoon by this time, and the sun was sinking deeper into the western side of the sky. The depression was now directly to her west, too; and our own glowing hot star would soon appear to drop directly into it. Meanwhile, the other little island had also continued to move. It had moved more than 180 degrees since she'd last seen it, and things were indeed speeding up….

It was mesmerizing, frightening, and fascinating all at the same time. On the distant horizon in every other direction, other objects were beginning to appear, other distant islands that seemed to be caught in the same bizarre process…. The island that had appeared and disappeared weeks earlier must have already been caught up in it. She must have already been caught up in it, too, and simply had no way of knowing it yet…. In the language of black holes, she and the other island must have already crossed the "event horizon" - the point of no return……

Powerful forces were at work, and the black hole analogy was hitting too close to home… If she actually was being sucked into a massive whirlpool hundreds of miles in diameter, what would the final moments be like?… Her entire body shuttered as she turned on the computer to check the details…. According to it, she and her island were moving at a speed of nearly a hundred miles an hour…. How could this be?… The winds were slowly becoming stranger and stranger, but they weren't nearly that strong…. The surrounding atmosphere must be moving at roughly the same rate…..?

She called her parents first…. It was the middle of the night in Tennessee, and they weren't expecting to hear from her….. It's great to hear your voice, Janet, but what's going on?….. They were worried immediately….. Yea, I know, and I'm sorry to wake you, but I think I've got some pretty strange news you should be aware of…. As she tried to explain, she did her best to speak slowly and deliberately so they'd have the best chance of understanding what she obviously didn't understand herself….. A giant whirlpool, what? Are you sure?…. They were flustered but sensed the seriousness in her voice and knew something was terribly wrong. There was no way for them to truly process the strange and horrifying information they were receiving in these, the wee hours of their new day; but very gratefully, she knew they were doing their best.... As the conversation continued, they slowly caught on. Their daughter was calling because she feared for her life, and she was slowly trying to ease them into the possibility that this could very well be the last time they'd talk... It was of course a parent's worst nightmare..... The fact that they didn't understand the details of why yet didn't seem to matter. They could tell she was very serious and felt a very real threat.... She even took the camera and scanned the horizon to give them a glimpse of what she was trying to explain, but there was no way to get any true perspective from their living room. The images, other than those of Janet's face of course, were for all practical purposes, meaningless.... But eventually, even that would change...

They stayed in close contact throughout the day. Mark, Carey, and even Sara eventually joined in what became a large split-screen video conference. They all loved Janet in their own ways, and they all dropped everything they were doing to be with her on this, the strangest day any of them had ever known.... As it progressed, the hole in the ocean grew, and her speed relative to it continued to increase....

Mark, the first to have noticed any hint of any of this, remembered how worried he'd been the night before she set sail. Obviously he was right to have been afraid, but now certainly wasn't the time to bring it up. Instead he professed his love in the presence of everyone.... You are a very special woman, Janet. Ever since we shared that kiss on the beach on that very special night, I've never stopped thinking about you. In fact, in my own weird and probably awkward way, I was planning to propose to you the next time we were together.... As the events continued to play themselves out, it became more and more apparent that would never happen..... She told everyone how much she loved and cared about them, and even told Mark in the last moments that she would have said yes...

Some twenty hours after first making contact, the story finally reached its ultimate conclusion.

In a thundering torrent, the island finally reached the lip and made its first full rotation at the point where she could actually see her destiny. The opening itself was nearly five miles wide and appeared bottomless. According to the calculations, she and her island had reached a speed of nearly three hundred miles an hour. A chaotic wind whipped up and down and all around as Earl stayed firmly gripped to her shoulders and back. In the final hours, a large sucking sound had continued to grow louder and had reached a deafening pitch. An unbelievable roar made verbal communication nearly impossible, but the images she was capturing let everyone know that this was indeed the end. Everyone could now see the immense whirlpool and everything that surrounded it. Other islands had accumulated from who knew how far away and were lining up to meet their impending fate as well. Bits of wood and debris and boats of all shapes and sizes were forming long random lines that led to the ultimate hole…

She made two huge loops at the swirling edge. On the second, her entire island pitched to angle of more than 50 degrees and she could see straight down into the mysterious abyss… Full of adrenaline, soaked with fear and excitement, she shouted to everyone at the top her lungs…. Don't worry, I'll see you on the other side!!!… Then, with her arms clinging tightly to the gentle bird she'd come to love, she and their entire beautiful island took the final plunge….

It was over…

FORTY

Larry Parsons was no hero. He wasn't on his way to saving all of humanity on the surface of Mars. In fact, as he drooped there with his head hanging in the cold porcelain bowl, he was having an extremely hard time figuring out where he was; and his face seemed to weigh a thousand pounds as he struggled to see. Undoubtedly, it was a strange and confusing moment; but as the reality of the situation slowly began to reveal itself, there was no island being sucked into a cavernous void in the middle of the ocean. The void, if one could call it that, was the

242

town's sewer system, and the islands and various bits of debris were pieces of his own vomit swirling in the water of a flushing toilet..... Holy Shit, man, what the hell's going on....?

Scott Williams, Larry Parsons, Julie Bowman, and Joann Luzern were all good friends, but they certainly weren't astronauts. Larry and Julie had been a couple since their first year as undergraduates at the University of Montana some six years earlier. Scott and Larry had been good friends since high school in Bozeman, Montana. And he'd been with Joann for nearly a year at the University of Tennessee where three of the four of them were now graduate students, and she was a fully-tenured professor....

They were all a little peculiar and strangely adventurous in their own rights, which was at least part of the reason why they were such a tightly knitted group. Their odd individualities complemented one another, and they never ceased to amaze themselves at the amount of fun they could coax from each other. They were interesting people and not afraid to test limits in the name of a good time or some form of further enlightenment; and on this particular evening, perhaps that concept had been tested to its limits?

Joann, the only one with an actual career, was a professor of cultural anthropology and had recently been studying the religious practices of certain Central American Indian tribes. More specifically, and the catalysts of Larry's strange findings, she'd been doing research on the use of peyote as a central aspect of certain religious ceremonies. And through weeks of planning and prodding, she'd convinced her closest friends that perhaps they should all try it. Although, to be clear, the convincing wasn't the hard part. In fact, from the earliest mentions of it, they were all intrigued by the idea. The problem, if there was one, was in setting aside an appropriate amount of time; and it took nearly a month for all of their schedules to come together in a manner that provided it...

At the time they all agreed to participate in this strangely exciting experiment, the Fourth of July weekend was the nearest approaching holiday, and they all quickly arranged to set it aside for the cause. From there, the idea had continued to grow quickly. And collectively, they decided that perhaps they should make an entire literal trip of it as well. Since the practice was primarily a Mexican tradition, Mexico seemed like the logical place to go; and for no real reason other than none of them had ever been there before, they decided Cabo San Lucas sounded like a fun place to be. They all booked the same flight and neighboring beachfront hotel rooms as they sat drinking wine in Joann's apartment one evening discussing it. With great enthusiasm, they booked it all online knowing it would be the greatest adventure any of them had been on in a long time. They'd be going to a foreign exotic sounding place to eat peyote on a beautiful sandy beach. There was nothing not to like about any of it....

In the meantime, school was out, so that wasn't an issue so much as they all had jobs and various other projects that kept them busy- or at least should have been keeping them busy. As an English student working on an MA in creative writing, Larry should have been busy working on his thesis project. However, it seemed he was having some problems along these lines. There were motivation problems, concentration problems, and procrastination problems. He couldn't come up with an idea for a story, or the ideas he did have were quickly discounted. They were either too much trouble, or he didn't know enough about the subject, or he would simply convince himself that an idea was too stupid without giving it much of a chance. Whatever the case, it was always much easier to sleep-in or veg-out in front of the television for hours on end. He had a job as a bartender in a local pub that kept him busy some thirty or so hours a week, but that was primarily evenings and nights...

It was a popular place, so he made enough in tips to pay his fairly modest bills comfortably, and his student loans wouldn't be coming due for what seemed like a very long time. All things considered, it had been surprisingly easy to fall into a pattern of procrastination. But he wasn't completely inactive. It was fairly easy for friends to talk him into doing a little mountain biking or rock-climbing. In fact, he'd even recently gotten into kayaking and was starting to get the hang of some of the local whitewater. He and his buddies would go out, smoke a little pot, and do their best to appreciate the local geography and beauty.... But it was he who had the most time for such things; and if there wasn't someone to play with, again the TV had a tendency to take up way too much of his time... Getting out of town would be good for him, even if the main purpose of the trip was to experiment with hallucinogenic drugs...

When the magic holiday weekend finally arrived, the two couples packed their bags and all got on the same flight. There was a slight layover in Los Angeles before the short flight the rest of the way. It was

244

fun, and they were enjoying each other's company as usual. Although, the tension about what they were about do was slowly beginning to sink in. Simply out of curiosity, they'd all done a little homework on what the effects of peyote truly were, and it wasn't something to be taken lightly....

Roughly an hour after the initial ingestion, it was almost guaranteed that a person would briefly become very violently ill. The stomach would interpret it as a poison and react accordingly by doing its best to get rid of it. It wasn't necessarily going to be pleasant. However, once successfully past this short initial phase, it was supposed to be a spectacular ride that could last for many hours -and, in rare cases, even several days. Whatever the case, it seemed a mindset of true and positive commitment was needed going in. They'd all read that without a positive approach there was the very real potential for things to go seriously wrong. Without the right attitude, a "bad trip" was a also a very real possibility. What that meant exactly, there was no way to know, but the descriptions were far less than amiable. Instead of fun and amusingly thought-provoking hallucinations, it could go the other way and visions of dark and evil demons could dominate instead.... Good thoughts and good company were important, and they were all consciously pumping each other up for the moment of truth....

They finally arrived at their destination early in the afternoon and started preparing immediately. Joann had taken the risk upon herself and smuggled the drugs in, including a little marijuana to help ease them into it. It was crazy in a way. Smuggling even a little amount in or out of any country was nothing to be taken lightly. But she'd learned a good trick and had confidently gotten away with it. A carved hollow spot in a large bar of soap worked well, and she sealed soap all around it knowing the scent would throw off the dogs if there happened to be any....

It was entirely possible to simply eat the small buttons of cactus, but they decided to brew them up in a tea instead. It was a process that took awhile, so they had a little time to look around as it simmered, which was nice. They wandered out their sliding glass doors onto a beautiful wide beach with gently rolling waves brushing the shoreline. Each in swimwear and nothing but towels and cocktails in hand, they tested the water- doing their best not to let it ruin their drinks. It was an amazing place to be. It seemed they had chosen their location wisely as they laughed and played still very consciously aware of the importance of a positive vibe.... not that it was difficult....

By the time the tea finally cooled, not one of them was even the slightest bit hesitant. They poured four equal portions, toasted their friendship, and then eagerly downed every last drop of what was theirs.... Some forty-five or fifty minutes later, it noticeably hit Scott first. He started looking a little pale and quickly walked several hundred feet away where he fell to his hands and knees and lost his lunch... That was it....

As he slowly became aware of his surroundings, this was the last thing about that reality Larry could recall. Although, as he smiled a big cheesy red-faced smile, it occurred to him what an abstract concept reality even was, and it was amusing. There was vomit on his face and on both of his wet hands. As the toilet continued to flush, bits of it were still islands disappearing into a vast vortex in the Pacific Ocean, then they were just bits of vomit, and then back again. It seemed multiple realities were colliding on some funny and profound level. Reality itself was vague and mushy. Time was confusing and unimportant other than a remote curiosity. How much of it had passed? Was passing time even real? Did time actually "pass?" and that thought alone was hilarious.... What did it even mean?...

Eventually he stood up and wandered outside, completely unconcerned with the mess he'd made or become.... He noticed his friends wandering around in various fits of laugher and deep contemplation. There were intense thoughts of love for them, but actual interaction was so surreal and seemed to take so much concentration that it wasn't worth the effort. As he momentarily recalled the dose itself, it seemed that whatever this was, it was somehow meant to be a personal experience; and he staggered off toward the sound of the pulsing surf to appreciate it as such...

The waves licking at his feet felt good, and he eventually just sat down. New dimensions of reality were pulsing through him in much the same way the waves moved. There was a rhythm to it, and whole universes of reality were revealing themselves. Lifetimes were experienced in mere minutes of this reality.... Without even knowing it at the time, the experience on the toilet had been the first of these many waves... Apparently his life as an aspiring, yet somewhat lazy, writer had immediately blended in to this experience in a uniquely strange way....

Janet, as a writer herself who'd been spending way too much time in front of the television, was simply an alternate expression of himself. And from there, her reality had quickly mushroomed into the strange tangents of his own imagination under the influence of this potent new substance. Her world had blended into his in an undetectable way, and she wasn't even real. Her friends and relatives weren't real. Her characters weren't even real, even though he'd somehow become one of them... At times he had truly felt he was an astronaut on Mars with the awesome responsibility of preserving all mankind. And at other times, he'd simply been aware of himself as a figment of her imagination. Like John who'd been hit by a meteor or the guy who had been run over by a train, or even herself as a spirit roaming in its own reality without any restrictions, they were all imaginary characters invented in her mind, and even more strangely, in his.... All of these realities, characters, and personalities were swirled together in a fun, funny, and personally profound way...

As the night continued to pass, he re-experienced some of these realities in new lights, and many other strange worlds were also revealed and explored as he reveled in this strange and foreign state of being. It was a wild and revealing ride, informing him of himself and the limitless nature of possibility....

When it was all over, when he and his friends were long ago home again, perhaps he'd take all of this possibility to heart? Maybe he'd find a way to have it all make sense, a way to make it all worthwhile beyond just a fun and random little vacation. Perhaps he'd somehow take this incredibly mind-broadening experience home with him and put it to good use? Maybe, just maybe, he'd even find a writable story in it.....?

Perhaps, when it was all said and done, he wouldn't have to be such a lazy writer after all..... ?

THANK YOU FOR READING MY BOOK

HAVE AN AWESOME DAY!